Zena Shapter writes from a castle in a flying city hidden by a thunder-cloud. She's the winner of a dozen national writing competitions including a Ditmar Award, the Glen Miles Short Story Prize and the Australian Horror Writers' Association Award for Short Fiction. Her stories have appeared in collections such as the Hugo-nominated 'Sci Phi Journal', 'Midnight Echo' (as well as their 'best of' anthology), 'Award-Winning Australian Writing' (twice), and 'Antipodean SF'. Reviewer for Tangent Online Lillian Csernica has referred to her as a writer who "deserves your attention". In 2016 her co-authored science fiction novel 'Into Tordon' for 8-14 year olds was published by MidnightSun Publishing and distributed into school libraries by Scholastic under the pseudonym Z.F. Kingbolt. She's also the founder and leader of Sydney's award-winning Northern Beaches Writers' Group, with whom she's written several speculative adventure books for young readers to raise money for The Kids' Cancer Project.

When not writing, Zena is a writing mentor, editor, tutor, competition judge, book creator, and workshop presenter. She enjoys travelling, wine, movies, chocolate, frogs and connecting with fellow story nerds online. Find her via @zenashapter or zenashapter.com

T0118838

Praise for Towards White

'Zena Shapter's debut novel will hold you tight from start to finish. With characters as convoluted as the faultless plot, 'Towards White' expands the mind, and the mind's eye, as you track the journey of life, death, love and deception. Suspense that takes you to the brink, then pushes you over. The world building was perfection. Highly recommended!'

-Kim Falconer, author of 'The Blood in the Beginning', an Ava Sykes Novel.

'Zena Shapter's debut novel 'Towards White' is that rarest of books— an easy read that tackles hard subjects. Combining ominous vibes with science driven action, this slick technothriller will keep you turning the pages long past when you should have gone to bed. 'Towards White' shows the conflict and chaos of a meeting between the unstoppable force of scientific progress and the immovable object that is human nature—and what happens to those caught in the middle.'

- David McDonald, author of 'Guardians of the Galaxy: Castaways' and 'Captain America: Sub Rosa'

'Towards White' is a smart supernatural thriller, with a central mystery that is both heartbreaking and intriguing. Shapter blurs the line between technology and spirituality, all the while exploring a fascinating Icelandic setting through the eyes of a complex and driven female lead. It's a novel that delves deep into the nature of justice, religion and death, but at it's heart it's a story about family and the bonds that connect us all.'

- Joanne Anderton, award-winning author of 'Debris' and 'The Bone Chime Song and Other Stories'.

'Eerie and engrossing, 'Towards White' is an interrogation of the mystery of life wrapped in a Nordic sci-fi noir story about unravelling the mystery of a death. Set against a starkly beautiful landscape, the story is steeped in a deep sense of unease, alternating between white-knuckle action and a delibrate unfolding of the layers of truth.'

- Leife Shallcross, author of 'The Beast's Heart'

TOWARDS WHITE

BY ZENA SHAPTER

Towards White

All Rights Reserved

ISBN-13: 978-1-925496-53-6

Copyright ©2017 Zena Shapter

V1.0 US

Printed in Palatino Linotype, Gill Sans and Gill Sans MT.

IFWG Publishing International
Melbourne

www.ifwgpublishing.com

Acknowledgement

First and foremost, thank you to my readers—life is short and you've spent some of your time with me. That's both an honour and an encouragement. Thank you!

Big thanks of course go to everyone at IFWG Australia for publishing 'Towards White': Gerry Huntman, Rebecca Fraser, Steve McCracken and Elizabeth Lang—what an amazing team!

Thanks also to those who have read 'Towards White' and supported its development, specifically: Alex Adsett, Jo Butler, Roberta Ivers, Abigail Nathan and Cameron McClure—you rock! Thank you Bob Benton, Sara Galletly and Catherine Meek for answering my questions about entropy, diving and lawyers, respectively. Thank you also for helping at various stages of this novel's journey: Kim Falconer, Ian Irvine, Pip Harry, Fiona Howland-Rose, Susan Steggall, Tony McFadden, Mijmark, Anne Swan, Chris Lake, Malcolm Goff, Arthur Siannos, Tracey Jackson, Zoya Nojin, Madi Duncan, Kirsten Taylor, Andrew Mills, Rondel Freeman, Mike Blandamer, and Justine Joffe.

Finally, thank you to my children for their never-ending patience, and to my husband for his support. Bill, you've been there every step of the way since this story's inception back in Iceland in 2001, and I've appreciated every second you've ventured into this world with me. Thank you!

For those we've lost.

In 1917, Rudolf Otto, an eminent theologian, philosopher and scholar of comparative religion, identified a single element that all faiths share: the numinous experience. He said it was "like a hidden force of nature, like stored-up electricity, discharging itself upon any one who comes too near...in it we come upon something inherently wholly other, whose kind and character are incommensurable with our own, and before which we therefore recoil in a wonder that strikes us chill and numb."

Rudolf Otto, Oxford University Press, 1923, pp.10–28, 'Das Heilige' (1917), trans. John W Harvey

Prologue

I am suspended in warm water, ten metres beneath the brilliant turquoise surface of the Caribbean Sea, and I'm so glad I haven't eaten yet today. Lifting my arms above my head, I feel the stretch in my abdomen and watch the school of curious horse-eye jackfish circling me. They close in, their shimmering mass as solid as a revolving silver cylinder. Around them, lemon sunbeams rotate hypnotically through the quiet blue. This is how I want to always be. Amazed by life, not rushing through it.

Closing my eyes, I weave my fingers through silky ocean and let the strain of the last nine days melt away. Whoever thought lawyers living on Grand Cayman would be so uptight?

I listen to my breath escaping from my regulator and count my blessings. I am no longer one of them. I am something different now. That is at least a start.

Beyond the whooshing of my bubbles is the reassuring crackle of distant shrimp claws and fish crunching on coral. My body rocks in a gentle sway as I glide my fins to and fro under my body. Looking down, I peer into the impenetrable abyss beneath my fins.

"Plummets four miles into the heart of the Caribbean Sea," my dive guide said of the Cayman Trench. "Really these islands are the tips of underwater mountains, taller than any land mountain in the United States."

I survey the darkness. There is nothing but blue merging into navy; beyond that, black. The vast emptiness makes me feel like I'm falling. Of course I'm not. My instincts are just playing a trick on me. They don't know they're obsolete impulses. Inferior compulsions no rational person needs. But I do. I look up to see I'm still surrounded by glinting silver scales. The fish here are so beautiful. I glide closer, and closer, reaching out…until a piercing blast of white noise shoots through my earpiece.

What the hell?

"Becky?" My dive guide's voice detonates in my ear.

I flinch at the pain, scare the jackfish with my movement. They dart into an underwater canyon, their mustard yellow tails disappearing inside the North Wall in seconds.

"Becky, you need to ascend immediately."

I check my Seiko. There's fifteen minutes before the end of my dive, and so much of the North Wall still to see. Hulking lime and ochre corals cling to the craggy sides of the canyon where the jackfish darted. Blue tangs and butterfly fish weave through colourful submerged gardens. Where did those jackfish go? I glide closer to the Wall.

"Sorry, Becky. I know you said no interruptions for a whole hour, but there's an urgent phone call for you. They insist on talking to you, and only you, straight away."

I pause mid-stroke, rehearing words like 'urgent' and 'immediately'. Mark.

My brother Mark phones me every Saturday, or I phone him, irrespective of where we are in the world, but it's Tuesday already and he hasn't called me yet. This is the first time I haven't heard from him on a Saturday in over eighteen months. His phone's switched off and he's sent me no message. The phone call has to be him.

I turn towards the boat. My pulse quickens as I swim as fast as I can. Mark's been in Iceland these last few months, researching the country's new social philosophy, the *Heimspeki*, based on where the electrical energy in our brains goes when we die. His research is giving him the final bit of insight he needs to publish his thesis paper on world energy theories.

If it's not him calling, on the other hand, I'm going to be mad. I accept that one of the downsides to being in demand is the constant phone calls. And I accept that my Jersey report last year went viral. I even enjoy the industry fame that's come with it. What I don't appreciate is the fact that all I asked for was a single hour of peace. I don't get paid like a lawyer anymore, so needn't be as accessible, and the sooner my boss understands that the better.

The underside of the dive boat shadows the sea ahead, and I have a feeling I'm about to lose my temper. If my brother were the one calling, my guide would have said so. Instead he referred to 'they'.

I surface, stabilise my fins on the swim platform's ladder, then rip my mouthpiece from my lips. Taking a breath, I try to stay calm.

"Is it Mark, my brother?" I ask, struggling to keep irritation from my tone.

"They didn't give a name," he says, squinting hard against the water glare.

"It's not anyone from *Dictum*, or the British Law Commission, is it? Because they could have waited." I thrust my fins at him, ignore his out-stretched hand and use a rope to hoist myself free of the ocean. As I stand to face him, a heavy Cayman heat smothers saltwater from my skin. It doesn't help keep me cool. "Is it one of them?"

"No. But they said it was about your brother."

"*About* him?" I hurry out of my rebreather. *About* is another one of those words people use in emergencies.

"I think," my guide mutters, giving me a concerned expression, "it's someone from Iceland."

"You think?" My legs shake as I clamber into the cool grey shadows under the console's canopy.

Someone from Iceland is calling about my brother, and they need to speak with me immediately. It's urgent. Straight away. About...

Chapter 1

I sink down into my seat on the midnight Flybus and wish the Icelandic passengers would stop staring at me. I'm sure they don't mean to make me feel uncomfortable, that would be a negative thing to do. But the subtlety they're attempting simply isn't working. I've seen their multiple side-glances, gazes roaming the carpeted aisle only to pass over me. Too many people have pretended to look out my window — though at what I don't know. It's the early hours of the morning and there's nothing but black outside. Probably, they're just curious. They want to know if I'm one of them, and, if I'm not, to assure me that I should be. Still, I wish they'd stop. They're not the reason I'm here.

Please Mark, be okay.

I rest my forehead against the window's cold glass and clear a circle in the condensation as a shadowy white cabin flashes past. Mark travelled along this dark road recently; all visitors arriving in Iceland do. So for miles I watch for something more. Occasionally I cup a hand between my face and the glass. But it's no use. There's nothing more to see. The night is so dark it's like a black hole sucking at my body's warmth.

So with a shiver, I turn instead to re-check my seat pocket is clear of belongings. We're getting closer to Reykjavík. There's an artificial brightness that wasn't outside before and, as soon as the Flybus stops, I need to hit the ground running. My connection to Höfkállur leaves soon after this one arrives in Reykjavík, and I have to get up North tonight. Mark hasn't been in contact for days now. I'm sure he has his reasons, but I need to know them, otherwise the one Director Úlfar offered me yesterday morning on the dive boat will be all that's left. And it mustn't be. This mustn't be anything other than one big misunderstanding — a misunderstanding that's resulted in my flying hundreds of miles to see my brother, whom of course will be okay. He has to be okay. He's been urging me for months to visit him in Iceland, to experience the effects of the *Heimspeki* firsthand, as he's been doing. But I've been too busy.

I should have come earlier. I should have come when he first invited me. Now I have to face all these strange people alone. Why didn't Mark tell me how ridiculously serious the Icelanders have become about their new ideals?

I shift upright. A few heads bob up as I move, looking to see if they can offer me any assurances. I just want to check my smartphone. I log into every application and scan to see if Mark's sent me a text, a tweet, a post, a chat or an email and I haven't heard the ping alert for some reason.

There's nothing.

When I dial his number again, it goes straight to voicemail. Taking a deep breath, I grip onto the phone and will some message, any message, to appear on the phone's display. Of course none does. The screen fades with inactivity. Still I stare at it, until the Flybus takes a sharp right turn and swings through a well-lit set of tall iron gates.

We glide past a sign welcoming visitors to Reykjavík's Central Travel Depot then jerk to a stop beside a glass-walled tourist information centre. Stiff-limbed from travel, I ease myself down the Flybus's steps, glad to be moving again, albeit into a pre-dawn breeze so icy it bites at my face and shoulders. If this is Iceland's summer, maybe I'm glad I didn't join Mark earlier after all.

The driver points me towards the raised tarmac oval where I can wait for the Austurleid SBS to Höfkállur, then she passes me my suitcase and climbs back inside. By the time I reach the oval, the Flybus has disappeared down some distant street, taking all its rumbling resonance with it. Even so, it isn't until I sit on the oval's sheltered bench that I realise how deserted it is here. I know it's the middle of the night, still, shouldn't Reykjavík's Central Travel Depot have *some* travellers passing through other than me?

I look around. Five wooden shelters are spread throughout the depot offering passengers refuge, but no one is using them. Pools of pale yellow lamplight burn circles directly into the damp tarmac, yet no travellers huddle under them and no one hurries between them. Where is everyone? I scan the fluorescent brightness of the information centre and notice the top of someone's head bowed behind a reception desk. Given how cold it is out here, perhaps everyone's inside? I reach for my suitcase's handle to walk over.

"Rebecca Dales?" someone yells from the depot's gated entrance, their tone as crisp as the air.

I seek out a person or movement to accompany the voice but there's none. Maybe I misheard?

After waiting a moment I head along the oval towards the information centre, until a car door slams and a man in a long grey coat emerges through the shadows and strides in my direction. I search for a face but he's hunched into his collar against the night air. He also carries no luggage with him. Perhaps he's an official with a message about Mark? Perhaps Director Úlfar's realised he's made a mistake after all and really Mark *is* okay? I stop and wait.

As the man nears, I think of all the people who know I'm transiting through Reykjavík tonight. Mum and Dad. My boss. Director Úlfar. The guesthouse in Höfkállur where I'm staying tonight. They all have my phone number though, so why would any of them send someone to find me? Unless...maybe my phone isn't working?

I pull it out and activate its screen. There's nothing wrong with it, and now the man is stepping onto the oval, raising his face to greet me. It takes me a second, but when I recognise him I'm not sure how to react.

Director Úlfar Finnsson looks larger in person than he did over our video conferencing connection yesterday, when he called with the news about Mark. He's taller too, more sturdy. A roundness presses against his coat where his stomach sits. I don't know how he can bear it—doesn't he realise people can see?

"Velkominn, Miss Dales," he says, offering me a nervous half-smile before dropping his chin into the warmth of his upturned collar.

"Director Úlfar." I nod him a greeting.

"How are you? Do you need anything?" He glances around the depot, nods to himself as if in approval of something. "It can be a challenge, já, travelling alone?" He pulls a gloved hand from his coat pocket and smooths flat his bouncy brown hair while assessing my expression.

"Not at all, Director Úlfar." I smile. Travelling alone honestly doesn't bother me. "It's nice to have some peace and quiet. Why are you here?"

"I wanted to see that you are okay." He gestures at the shadows around the depot. "It is very late to be sitting alone in the dark."

"I'm fine thank you." Although, why does he care so much?

He shrugs, looks pleased with himself. "Still, when we spoke yesterday I said I would explain some things. There are twenty minutes before your transport to Höfkállur. So I was thinking, I will buy you a coffee, já, and we will chat a little?"

"Um, is now really the best time for chatting?"

"You said you are fine." He removes his gloves.

"That's not what I meant." I glance at my Seiko.

"Please, it will only take a few minutes." He gestures towards the information centre with firm presumption. "Shall we?"

I re-angle my suitcase and step off the oval. A cool hand closes around mine. Director Úlfar's touch is dainty yet sweaty.

"I will take it for you?" He means my suitcase.

"Thank you, but I've got it."

"Watch your step then."

I want to tell Director Úlfar to watch his own bloody step, but when I hear the echo of our footsteps across the depot, the emptiness of the sound silences me. Úlfar Finnsson is the director and press secretary of Iceland's information and intelligence bureau, or MUR. If he wanted to chat with me about something, check on me even, he wouldn't need to do it in person. So why is he here?

It had better not be because of what I said yesterday. I'm not in the right frame of mind to go through all that again. I just want to get to my brother.

Automatic doors whoosh open as we approach the information centre and we step inside through a heated wall of air. It smells of new carpet in here, fresh paint. A lanky blond receptionist stands to offer us a smile so broad it's almost inappropriate for the middle of the night.

"Director Úlfar!" he says, jogging over to greet us. "Gott kvöld!"

I can't help but smile back at him. He has that jolly kind of demeanour that's infectious.

Director Úlfar, also grinning, doesn't make a secret of looking him up and down. As they mutter in Icelandic, chuckling in a way that makes the whole exchange sound like flirting, I feel like I should leave them to it. When the receptionist swats the air before him and Úlfar flings a hand out to grasp at him, I go to move away.

I don't even manage a single step before the director places a hand on my shoulder. Still grinning, the receptionist mumbles something and Director Úlfar nods.

"Takk fyrir, Rut," Director Úlfar adds before ushering me toward a staircase. "This way, Miss Dales." His hand lingers on my shoulder as we walk, sending a shiver bristling down my spine.

I shake off his delicate fingers with a flick of my hair, only to notice we're passing a noticeboard of advertisements for government-sponsored *Heimspeki* seminars. Graphics of churches, mosques and synagogues indicate that the venues are all former places of worship. Of course they are.

Each notice is adorned with a *Heimspeki* symbol: electricity bolts zapping out of a circle supposed to represent the brain, a ring for the cyclic nature of energy. The largest notice is in English—a local litrúmtheology group invites passing theology-tourists to join next week's discussion topic: *Has the science behind the Heimspeki made God and religion obsolete?* I scan the guest speaker list, half expecting to see Mark's name on it. Then again, he's been so busy with his research in Höfkállur these last few months he's probably had little time for trips to Reykjavík, however pertinent the discussion to his doctoral studies.

At the foot of the staircase, a flat screen displays archived front pages from several Icelandic newspapers. As we walk towards it I check the English subtitles that report landmark headlines:

Crime Falls Wherever Heimspeki Rises.
Höfkállur Trials Sannlitró-Völva System.
Politicians and Lawyers Fear Positivity Tests.

I frown while trying to remember the reports. I know about Iceland's low crime rates. Who doesn't? The whole world's heard about the influence of the *Heimspeki* on Icelanders. But the other headlines haven't been reported online, I'm certain of it. Mark's not mentioned anything about them either, and Höfkállur is the town in northwest Iceland where he's been staying.

"So, Miss Dales," Director Úlfar says, waiting for me to lug my suitcase up the first step, "again, please accept my sincerest condolences for your loss. I cannot imagine how awful it must feel to have such terrible news. Really, I..." he shakes his head, "I have a brother and every time he goes overseas, I dread something like this happening to him. For you to receive a phone call like mine yesterday...please, if there's anything I can do to help, please let me know."

"I will."

"I'm absolutely serious. There is no worse news for a sister to receive. I am so sorry."

"Thank you."

"No, thank *you* for coming so quickly."

"You make it sound like I had a choice."

"And you were right to take my advice. You have saved your parents a very long plane flight, and much distress. It is also incredibly difficult for a parent to identify their own child, not that identification is really necessary in your brother's case. As I explained yesterday, the two of you look exactly alike—same blonde hair, same face, brown eyes—his jaw is wider perhaps. Did your parents have any questions after you told them the news? Anything I can help with?"

I swallow to stop my throat tightening. Until I've seen the body they say they have in Höfkállur, I can't let myself believe Mark might be dead. There has to be some mistake. Director Úlfar has only seen an image himself, and an image is hardly conclusive. At least, that's what I've told Mum and Dad. "Thank you, but what was it you wanted to chat about, Director Úlfar?"

"I, um," he clears his throat. "I have a proposal for you."

"About Mark?"

"Not exactly." He climbs a few steps before waiting for me again. "Miss Dales, there's another reason I hoped you would come, rather than your parents." He chuckles nervously. "I'm afraid I wasn't being entirely honest when I said yesterday I had no idea why you lived in London instead of Australia."

"You weren't?" Not that I remember him saying so. It must have been when I zoned out. The minute Director Úlfar said Mark had had an accident—that my brother had been hiking, alone, at the Jötunnsjökull Glacier and that his body was found at the Skepnasá River on Sunday—I couldn't think straight anymore. Director Úlfar kept talking, it all went in my ears, but then disappeared somewhere. Nothing about that conversation made any sense. It still doesn't. Mark doesn't even like hiking.

"Put it this way," Director Úlfar shrugs, taking off his coat and folding it neatly over his arm. "I know there can't be much work in Australia for someone like you."

"Someone like me?"

"A specialist in researching new court systems and procedures. Europe would be much better for that."

"Sounds like my LinkedIn profile has finally been good for something."

"No, no—I heard about you last year, when you wrote that editorial on Jersey's intranet usage: *Technology Versus Justice?* How was the Caribbean by the way? I understand you've been in the Cayman Islands finishing off some research. Was that for *Dictum* or for the British Law Commission?"

"Director Úlfar, it's late. Given the circumstances, why don't you just tell me your proposal?"

"Of course. Miss Dales, I believe you're in a position to help my country, if you're feeling...up to it." Waiting for me to ask the obvious, he raises a sculpted eyebrow so high on his forehead it actually creases his shiny taut skin.

"Help with what?"

"Our recent discoveries."

I meet his eyes as I continue to climb the stairs. "You want me to help with your discoveries when my brother may well be lying dead in a morgue?"

He squirms slightly but carries on. "I know how this must sound. Believe me, I've been in two minds as to whether to ask you at all. But your brother was an advocate for the *Heimspeki*, was he not?" he asks, well aware of the answer. "He did some work last month with Iceland Tourism. Don't you want to know what he was doing, finish what he started so to speak, get involved on his behalf? Not with the *Heimspeki* of course, but with the new legal technology we're developing alongside it. It is your speciality."

"Yeah, but here's the thing, Director Úlfar—I'm not here in a professional capacity. I'm here to see this...this body you seem to think is my brother, even though you haven't seen it yourself, then I'm going home. Perhaps I can return to report on your legal technology another time?"

"*Seem* to think? Ah, does this mean you've now heard from your brother?"

"No. Have you? Or have you physically seen this body in Höfkállur? Because you do know that striving to avoid negativity won't somehow prevent your countrymen from making mistakes, it doesn't make them immune from human error. And believe me, there's been some error."

Director Úlfar huffs in the same impatient way he did yesterday morning when I also resisted the news about Mark. But he just doesn't get it. Mark can't be dead. If he were, I would have sensed it. I would have felt some disturbance in my universe or something. Mark didn't even mention wanting to hike over any glacier. And if he did suddenly decide to go hiking, he would have rescheduled our weekly phone call first.

Also, Mark would never be so stupid as to hike over a glacier alone. Who did that?

Which is why I've every reason to believe he's alright, that this is simply a big mistake. He's probably just lost his phone or something. Besides, I'm acutely aware of the fact that hoping for a mistake is the only thing keeping me from breaking down right now. I need to function. I need to walk and talk. If believing Mark's okay gets me through that, so be it.

Anyway, Mark will be alright. I know he will.

Director Úlfar and I climb the rest of the stairwell in silence.

As we emerge into a multi-stationed computer room, he gestures towards a black leather sofa cornering a metallic table under the far window. "Take a seat," he says, turning to the coffee machine. "Espresso, no sugar, já?" Not waiting to see if he's right, he pushes the espresso button.

By the time I've lugged my suitcase up the final few steps and reached the sofa, he's already following me across the floorboards with two disposable cups.

"You know how I take my coffee too?"

He passes me my coffee, taps the side of his nose as we sit opposite each other. "Don't worry, I can't read people's minds, though I'd like to of course."

"Wouldn't we all?" I take a guilt-free sip. There's only one calorie in a cup of espresso. Since this is instant coffee, there could be up to four. So I add five to the mental count I keep each day, then savour another sip. Yesterday I ate well under my daily limit of 1,000 calories, so can relax a little today.

Noting the size of Director Úlfar's stomach again, I readjust my waistband until it sits directly on top of the bulge that rolls up my stomach and sides when I sit. Then I check my reflection in the darkened window opposite. As I'm straightening my back so my top skims over the right bits, I catch Director Úlfar watching me. "Imagine what you'd find out if you knew what other people were thinking," I say, grateful my secrets are safe.

"Well, we can only assume this is why your brother was in Höfkállur rather than Reykjavík." Director Úlfar runs a fingertip over his eyebrows but doesn't take his eyes off me. "To meet its people…and see the Sannlitró-Völva."

"The what?" I recognise that word from something Mark said recently. Every week he gives me an update on his progress with the *Heimspeki*. "Sannlitró-?"

"Precisely." Director Úlfar leans forward, squashing his thickened middle into a compact paunch and not caring—he neither readjusts his waistband nor moves an arm to hide it. "Now, I know you've only been in Ísland a few hours but you will have already noticed a difference in the people here, já?"

Not wanting to commit to an answer, I sip on my coffee.

"You met people on the plane, at the airport, on the Flybus?"

"I didn't meet anyone exactly."

"But you saw them. You saw their calm, perhaps a generosity of spirit? A trusting nature?"

A too-trusting nature is what I saw. When I was walking to the baggage carousel, Icelanders left their possessions outside restrooms rather than take them inside. I couldn't help but shake my head in disbelief. They gave me looks of pity in return, but were wrong if they thought I was judging out of ignorance. I've been following the development of Iceland's *Heimspeki* online because of Mark's theological thesis. I understand the theory behind why Icelanders do such things. I simply don't believe a social philosophy can overcome human nature. Only deterrence and fear can do that.

Unbidden, though, another scene flashes through my memory of the baggage claim hall. An old man's duffel bag slid onto the baggage carousel, caught on a corner of the shoot and ripped open. Its contents splayed over the conveyor belt's black folds. The distress on the old man's face slipped into relief as his fellow Icelanders pitched in to gather his belongings.

It's the way things should be, Mark's been saying a lot lately.

Director Úlfar moistens his lips before continuing. "Icelanders are this way because of the Sannlitró-Völva," he sounds proud, "our latest development in energy analysis."

That's right, I nod, remembering. Mark emailed me about this machine, this Sannlitró-Völva. He said that seeing it in action made him rethink his entire thesis. We were going to discuss his conclusions this weekend—he said he wanted my professional opinion about something.

"There's way more to the *Heimspeki* than I originally thought, Becky," Mark said the weekend before. "Energy. The numinous. It's both, together. I told you anything was possible!"

He made me promise to give him my full attention...this weekend.

Another reason why this all has to be some huge mistake.

"You see," Director Úlfar continues, "the Sannlitró-Völva changes you. Once you see your brain's electrical energy through it, once you see how closely your actions affect that energy and what your own individual life after death will be like, it makes you determined to do the right thing. Always."

"Always?"

He nods.

"So your asking me to report on your legal technology is the right thing?"

He places his coffee cup on the table then heaves himself backwards to retrieve his phone from his pocket.

"Miss Dales, Höfkállur is a very isolated town, much colder than here," he glances at the darkness outside the window. "So it would be wrong of me to let you go all that way north when you could be my guest here in Reykjavík. We have the same technology, yet more *Heimspeki* followers live here because *this* is where history is being made. Your brother would have wanted you to witness what you can while you're here, to see what made him so passionate about our theories. That is all I'm asking you to do—stay here. Then later, much later, when you're ready, publish whatever report you want in *Dictum*, if only to tell your readers about the systems we're proposing and give your brother's work a wider audience. *That* is the right thing to do in these circumstances. Who knows when you might be in Ísland again? You have your phone?"

He navigates through to a screen displaying his contact details, pauses to stare at them before handing the phone to me. I understand everything apart from the words under his name: *Miðju Upplýsingar Ráðuneyti*, not that it matters. I unlock my phone and tap his details into its memory. I have absolutely no intention of helping Director Úlfar with his legal technology—I still can't believe he's asking me, and he most certainly has zero idea what my brother would want me to do right now. Still, I want Director Úlfar's details. All of them. I pass the phone back.

"I'd also like to be a sounding board for you, Miss Dales," he says, re-crossing his ankles as if in a young lady's etiquette exam. "I cannot answer any questions about our machine's actual manufacture of course, but other than that," he taps my forearm with a sweaty finger and grins, "all you have to do is ask."

I knock back my coffee to detach his touch, and somehow manage to hold my temper.

"So," he slaps his thighs before scooping himself up from the sofa and grabbing his coat, "to which hotel? As my guest, the choice is yours. Your brother's body will be transported down from Höfkállur tomorrow before midday."

I clear my throat and pick my words carefully. "Thank you, Director Úlfar. But like I told you yesterday, I'm going straight to Höfkállur tonight." I hold his look until my determination seeps through. "I've come to Iceland to see where my brother spent the last four months. Perhaps I can help you in a professional capacity some other time?" I stand and roll my suitcase towards the stairwell.

"But," he hesitates, then scampers to catch up, "why go all that way when I can have your brother's body transported down here?"

"Because I'm not going to Höfkállur to see just any cadaver," I answer over my shoulder. "If my brother really is..." I can't say the word out loud, "then I'll want to know exactly what happened to him, and the only way I can do that is by going to Höfkállur." I start down the steps.

"At least wait until you've seen the body?"

"It's in Höfkállur, right?"

"But why put yourself through travelling all that way alone?" He follows me down the stairs. "Weren't you scared outside earlier?" His tone sounds...smug. "I have my car, I can drive you anywhere—the Hilton, Radisson—then you can wait in comfort until it...he, arrives."

"*Then* I can write your article?" I add a chuckle at the end of my question in case he's so insensitive he doesn't pick up on my sarcasm. When I glance back, I catch him smirking to himself. "Look, I don't care about your technology right now, about the *Heimspeki* or any history being made. I don't even care about travelling alone." His smirk fades. "I just want to get to Höfkállur, and find my brother." Regardless of whatever state he's in.

"How about," Director Úlfar's tone shifts, becomes more urgent, "I pay for your brother's repatriation to Sydney? Then will you stay in Reykjavík?"

He isn't getting it. "No, Director Úlfar. I need to see Höfkállur for myself. Surely you can understand that? Weren't you a lawyer too, before you joined the MUR?"

"I see someone else has been on LinkedIn."

"Which is why you'll understand my need to see where my brother's been living. I have to talk to people, and see this glacier where they say he went hiking." Instead of phoning me.

"You're not going to the glacier?"

This time, I can't stop a smile spreading over my lips. "You think I'd leave Iceland without seeing where my brother supposedly died?"

"You can't—it's much too dangerous. Come back upstairs," he grabs the sleeve of my jacket, "let me show you some hotels."

I wrench my sleeve free with such force I almost fall off the bottom step. "If it's that dangerous, I'll hire a guide."

"But," he pauses. I can almost hear his brain working. "At least return to Reykjavík before Friday? I will still pay for your brother's repatriation if you're back before then."

"Why Friday?"

"I can't tell you." He forces himself to add a qualification. "Yet."

His eyes flit between my face and something over my shoulder.

Turning, I see a hubbub of passenger activity around the oval. I check my watch. The Austurleid SBS is due to depart in minutes. I hurry towards the exit and, as I trigger the centre's automatic doors, the centre is flooded with the clamour of chattering passengers, accompanied by the purr of an expectant engine. "Where the hell have they all been waiting?"

"Oh, er, everyone must have...waited at home," Director Úlfar mumbles. "Leaving early inconveniences passengers, so *Heimspeki* drivers depart exactly on time. No need to wait in the cold."

Hearing us, Rut stands up behind the reception desk. He says something in Icelandic, shrugs and gestures at the passengers outside.

Director Úlfar bats him away, dismissive.

We walk across the depot in silence.

At the Austurleid, the bus driver raises his eyebrows at Director Úlfar. While I load my suitcase underneath the transport, they talk in hushed tones, glancing occasionally in my direction. If ever I had any doubt about travelling up to Höfkállur, alone or otherwise, I'm certain now. I flew to Iceland knowing Mark would never have gone hiking last Saturday instead of phoning me. Now, though, there's obviously something Director Úlfar doesn't want me to find, or know, or see in Höfkállur.

When I go to board the Austurleid he even blocks me, standing in front of the Austurleid's steps. "Tell me, Miss Dales, were you close to your brother?"

I notice the driver watching us. "Why else would I be here?"

"Then please, for his sake, do not go to Höfkállur."

"Give me one good reason why."

"If you stay in Reykjavík a few days, I will."

"I don't have a few days, Director Úlfar. I have to get to my brother, now."

He doesn't move so I push pass him.

Looking through the windows, I see him shove his hands into his pockets and exchange looks with the driver. Then the doors of the transport are being sucked into place and it's too late for me to change my mind. I'm on my way to Höfkállur, whether Director Úlfar likes it, or not.

As the transport pulls away from the oval, I get comfortable in the front row of seats and watch Director Úlfar through the windscreen. He must find something amusing, because he chuckles to himself then salutes the driver with a smirk.

Once we've left the depot, the driver glances over his shoulder and looks me up and down, as if assessing something.

We join the highway and head north. After the Austurleid has settled into a rhythm, he glances at me again; then regularly for miles.

It makes me uncomfortable.

But clearly he isn't the type of Icelander who cares about being subtle.

Chapter 2

The ground beneath me splits into fissures and I plummet through jagged shards of ice that slice my thighs and arms into shreds of gaping flesh. Something bites me. I scream and spin around in search of my attacker. With a smirk as wide as the moon, an icy quagmire is revelling in its feast, sinking and choking me under its suffocating wetness, feeding on my exposed wounds.

"Let's go!" it cackles, challenging me. "To the glacier!"

I thrash at it with limp punches from drowsy biceps, whack it with sluggish feet, and don't last long. In the end, I give up and the shivering finally wakes me.

Glancing around the Austurleid, I'm relieved to see no one's noticed me having my nightmare. The still-black night outside has cast a blanket of rest over the transport and everyone is occupied with the quiet, even the driver. His eyes are set on the black road ahead.

Shifting upright, I straighten my clothes and rub my eyes of sleep.

Why am I dreaming of drowning? Director Úlfar didn't say Mark was found *in* the Skepnasá River, did he?

I go over our conversation from yesterday morning but don't find anything in it other than my kernel of hope that there's been some mistake. I water my kernel of hope with the tears I can't cry until I get to Höfkállur, then plant in it the knowledge that if Mark really had died this weekend I would have sensed it. I haven't.

I check my phone again. Maybe Mark messaged me while I was asleep.

Nothing.

All that's changed is the time and the mounting taste of blood in my mouth. I've been gnawing the inside of my cheek. My jaw is tense too. I roll my jaw to release the pressure, then feel for grazes with my tongue. I trace the damage I've done to the inside of my mouth while searching for a distraction outside my window. It's still too dark to see anything. There are only rough shapes—the jagged outline of a mountain range in the distance; a flash of rubble beside the road. I always thought countries habitually tortured by seismic activity had rich fertile soil. But the lack of foliage along this highway makes Iceland seem barren and desolate.

"Babe, the landscapes over here are magical." Mark once told me. "They more than make up for the temperature. You gotta see them, Bex."

I rest my head against my window. The rhythmic bounce of the coach tempts my eyelids towards surrender again, so I push my cheeks up to meet them, taking the strain off the bruises pulling under my eyes. I need more rest, but anxiety has never been a kind lullaby for me. When I close my eyes, flashes of ice and roaring water torment me, twisting me back inside my nightmare. The air around me grows heavy with a fusty dampness, which fools me into thinking I must be drifting off to sleep, slipping back into that freezing water, until I recognise its source. Since moving to London, I've come to sense the atmospheric shift that comes with falling rain. Certain of seeing a delicate drizzle speckling the driver's windscreen, I open my eyes, and I'm right. His wipers are already swishing.

I watch them for a while, hoping their rhythm will put me under. Instead I notice a familiar glow lighting the ceiling: flat screens. Turning, I glance down the aisle to see the shadowed faces of still-awake passengers lit by the dim flickering of flat screens. It reminds me—Mark did some work recently with Iceland Tourism. Perhaps the documentary he helped film is in the Flybus's programming. I untuck my screen from my armrest and tap at its display.

A list of TV shows and promotional features appears onscreen. I squint to scan the list and one of the features catches my eye: *Iceland, The Truth About Life*. Is that the one? I reach into my bag for my reading glasses and activate my phone to take notes. It's habit. Whenever I speak to Mark, he's always got a whole new set of reasons prepared to convince me to follow the *Heimspeki*. These days, I like to have counterarguments ready.

As I swipe through my online notes application to find the right file, a blond presenter in a long-sleeved black t-shirt and jean breeches beams out from the display. My heart leaps at his resemblance to Mark. They have the same complexion, the same slim build and authoritative yet casual stance of fists on hips. It isn't Mark of course. An Australian shouldn't be the one to present Iceland's national treasure to the world, which is what Mark says the *Heimspeki* has become.

"The *Heimspeki*," the Icelander begins on cue, "people use the word to refer to scientific findings, philosophical and religious theory. But what does it really mean? For many people, Iceland's *Heimspeki* has come to represent the truth about life."

I roll my eyes as he talks about man's historic search for the meaning of life, how man has believed in a life after death for as long as there has been man.

"Karma, reincarnation, God's kingdom...electrical energy, souls, spirits," the presenter says, "they all follow the same idea—an unknown materialisation of *us* existing after death. When something is so believed across humanity for so long, surely there has to be some common universal truth behind it." He pauses to let the logic of his statement seep in, as Mark would do. "All we've been waiting for is a time when science would discover that truth...and that time is now."

The presenter sounds excited. Mark's done a great job of advising the producers on how to explain certain concepts, but I've heard it all before, and all it is is theory. Waiting for the presenter to finish his theoretical summary, I lean against my window to watch the Austurleid's headlights push yellow beams into the dark road ahead. I only half-listen until the presenter uses one of Mark's catchphrases.

"Think about it."

I sit up and force myself to pay attention. The film reel switches from orange-robed monks kneeling in communal prayer to lab technicians reading books on subatomic and quantum physics. Then the presenter jumps straight into the heart of Iceland's scientific breakthrough.

"Everything in the universe is cyclic." The presenter stands before a montage of life-cycle diagrams. "Everything has its place in the circle of life, everything becomes something else. There is no wastage. Nothing tangible ever disappears."

I know this part well. There are oxygen and water cycles, carbon and nitrogen cycles, as well as the energy cycle of course. The conservation of energy law is a fundamental law of physics. Everything always becomes something else.

"So where does the electrical energy in our brains go when we die?" The presenter taps his head, in the exact same way Mark does. The two of them have definitely been talking. "Think about it. Energy doesn't die. One form always becomes another form. Electrical energy is the most efficient of all energies too. It even outperforms hydrogen as a power source. So only a tiny portion would entropy as heat. Where does the rest go? It can't simply cease to exist. Just as our bodies go

23

to the worms, it *must* continue within the energy cycle and become another form of energy."

I chew on my penstick as the presenter explains the details. The reasoning in his summation sounds like it's been lifted straight from Mark's thesis, word-for-word.

"Until now we've had no choice but to believe in more mystical explanations for the gap in our knowledge," the presenter continues. "But no longer. The world is round, not flat. People can sometimes take a while to accept new facts as truth. But now that we have the *Heimspeki*, we have science's answer to the age-old question of life-after-death."

I stop chewing. Facts? Truth? Science's answer to life-after-death? This doesn't sound like Mark anymore. Iceland has no actual proof of life after death. No facts, no truth—only a new theory. Granted, it's an appealingly logical theory, grounded on some extraordinary discoveries. Nonetheless it is mere theory, and there are plenty of those in the world. I have my own. Mark has his. Neither of us claim our theories are facts though.

"And the ultimate result?" The presenter enthuses. "A perfect life, a perfect society..."

They're kidding!

I look away as the presenter concludes his presentation by welcoming both visitors and theology-tourists to Iceland. As far as I'm concerned, unsubstantiated theories are little more than hunches.

Once the flat screen zoops into a neat black silence, I shove its display into my armrest and fold away my reading glasses. If there's one thing I can't stand, it's people who think they know what's good for others, including me. Mark is the only exception. He knows me. You can't know a person after a twenty-minute appointment, no matter what your medical degree. You can't know why a person is the way they are after a brief summary of the facts, and you can't possibly know what 'perfection' means to them. A life lived. Then you know. Some random philosophers in Iceland have no idea about my life, just as I have no idea about theirs. What is perfect for one person simply isn't for another.

Expecting darkness to welcome me back, I look out my window to see a dull dawn of grey cloud breaking the night. Under its faint light, it seems like we're travelling along a highway lined with enormous rugged boulders. Are they noise barriers or roadside sculptures? Gigantic chunks of barbarous art maybe? They tower over the roof of the Austurleid, so it's hard to tell.

It isn't until the highway mounts the brow of a hill, and I see an endless plain of matt-black lava rocks stretching towards a horizon struggling to brighten, that I realise these boulders haven't been put here by man. We're travelling through a lava field.

Mark's told me about these lava fields, how expansive they are, sharp and black. Once, red-hot seas of magma bubbled across this volcanic landscape, plastering its soil with rocks fresh from the earth's core. Now winding roads cut through the cooled crust, curving around the hardest sections of basalt like white-icing messages on chocolate cake. Populated neither by animal nor human, invaded only by sporadic mosses and grasses, the remoteness of these never-ending extrusive igneous black rock fields used to remind Mark of Australia's outback, where dusty red forever-deserts are speckled only by wispy hummocks of long thin grass.

The vision resonates with me and I let it. Australia. I haven't been home to Sydney for a year and a half now. Not since Riley.

A heaviness descends on me at the thought of his name. *Riley*.

As the Austurleid speeds along, I gaze out trying not to remember. I'm here to find Mark, and whatever it is in Höfkállur that Director Úlfar doesn't want me to see or know.

Having long moments to myself like this is never a good idea though. These days, it's better if I have work to do. I suppose that's why I've been promoted so quickly over the last year and a half. Once I get involved in a project I don't stop. I don't because I can't. Mark phones to check on me on our Saturdays, more often if he can. The rest of the time I simply have to stay busy, lest I remember too much and shame drags me down into a pit of self-pity so deep I can't crawl out of it again.

If I let myself, everything reminds me of something to do with Riley and the mess he left me in eighteen months ago. Anyone would think he'd died, rather than find himself a new girlfriend. It's pathetic, really. And I hate thinking about it. That was the old me. This is the new me.

I straighten in my seat and focus again on the view. The drizzle abates and the enormity of each volcanic rock carves a dramatic form out of the black canvas of night. If I'm honest with myself, it truly is beautiful here. Magical enough, I suppose, to make some people wonder…to make me wonder.

Mark's says the wonder of life is what's led the Icelanders to find the peace they have. He says if I gave their ideas a chance, I could find peace too. Wondering and imagining, he says, is intrinsic to our nature and vital to our nirvana. Yet it's constantly downplayed by science.

25

Our imaginations aren't random, our instincts aren't the obsolete impulses I say they are, gut feelings aren't illogical nonsense, because all kinds of electrical energy can trigger our brains to think certain things at certain times. Why acknowledge the value of some, and not the others? We should—I should—trust every facet available to our senses. Or so he says.

"You analyse things too much," Mark's been telling me. "Not everything has to be deduced logically. What about things that *feel* right?" He thinks I should go with the flow more, stop listing potential boyfriends' attributes against incompatibilities, like some factual investigation. He's right about one thing: "You can't control people with notes or lists."

Still, I have good reason for the habit. Riley 'felt right', and look where that got me.

Images surface.

I push them back under, but also don't have the strength to resist them right now. I don't mind travelling alone. On a trip like this, though, it would have been better to have work to do. It's a shame really that I finished my report on time. Lots of things are a shame. It's a shame I even met Riley.

I wish I hadn't. I wish he'd never come up to me at Victoria's Christmas party, on the balcony, where he'd gone for a smoke. He said he couldn't believe I was a law student and leant in close to whisper: *but you're so beautiful.* He made me feel special, like one of those romantic heroines he played opposite in his local theatre each season—Juliet to his Romeo, Cleopatra to his Anthony, Isolde to his Tristan. A lawyer himself, working for one of the big Sydney law firms, Riley practiced amateur dramatics to 'keep him sane'. I didn't realise what he meant at the time. But I did go to watch him one night. He was so good—I couldn't understand why he didn't take up acting full time.

It rained on our first date, as it's raining outside the Austurleid now—though the drizzle in Sydney was warm. Running through the raindrops in the city, Riley said he refused to take an umbrella with him anywhere in summer, on principle—as ever the dramatic. Raising his face to the sky, he laughed and shook off the water, then gazed into my eyes and told me he could easily fall in love with someone who ran through the rain as I did. Our slippery palms squelched each time we readjusted our grip on each others' hands.

We stopped in a crowded restaurant in The Rocks, where the waiter wouldn't let me eat from the children's menu. Afterwards, we joined the late night Christmas shoppers in David Jones. When I went to find the restrooms, Riley got lost in the lingerie department but claimed he didn't like it without me. There were so many people, especially in the toy department. He spent half an hour looking at old-fashioned tin soldiers, while I got bored with Garfield. On our way home, we stuffed ourselves full of jellybeans and coloured fairy lights danced above our heads, glistening in the wet streets.

By autumn, we were spending every weekend together, bushwalking around Ku-ring-gai Chase National Park, past the fishermen at Bobbin Head, where it smelt as damp as this air is now, despite the Austurleid's air conditioning.

One Sunday, an old couple couldn't get their collie out of the mangroves. Having bolted from the boardwalk after a crab, their dog was covered in mud and couldn't be coaxed back out. Riley was amazing. He went in after her, couldn't keep a hold on her slippery wet leash, so grabbed her and carried her out. Covered in mud and dog hair, he dried off in the café where we warmed up with hot chocolate and I told him I could easily fall in love with someone who rescued animals as he did.

Remembering such good times, I feel myself smiling. There were such good times, and that's why I fell so hard afterwards. I close my eyes and drift into a haze of memories, one shifting into another as the Austurleid rocks me. The hum of its engine, steady and rhythmic, reminds me of the buses I used to catch when taking my finals at Sydney Law College. I couldn't wait to get to college and finish my exams— just as I can't wait to get to Höfkállur tonight—because after my exams Riley was taking time off work to help me celebrate. I was so excited.

What a summer that was too, my last month of freedom before starting work as a junior lawyer. I'd meet Riley at Manly Beach for fish and chips in The Corso. We'd throw Frisbees under the Norfolk Pines until the sun set, get drunk on schooners from Bacchus, before it became popular, and buy flavoured cider from the bottle-o to sip by the shore, snuggling close as the darkness grew cool. Of course that wasn't real life. It was holiday. Still, I don't know why Riley never thought back to that summer when tough times came.

Staring out at the passing lava plains, I remember too how we made plans for when I started work, for a trip to the Red Centre that winter, and to Fiji the next year. My law firm was close to Riley's, so we'd meet up at lunchtimes to browse through holiday brochures. If we both worked late, we'd have dinner together in the city and pick resorts. It was so good being with someone who understood the hours we kept, the clients, the conferences and the continual education. Riley even talked about moving in together and marriage. The gravity of marriage frightened me. Still I talked about saying yes. I was sleeping at his place so much as it was, practically living there already. Why not take a chance?

But that was all before the lawyers at my firm made my life hell. At first I just ignored their snubs and underhanded comments about my being a pushover. They could think what they liked. I was no pushover; I was good at my job. Smiling and being polite didn't make me weak, as they seemed to think. I negotiated with logic, not volume. My clients were happy. My boss was happy. It didn't matter what my colleagues thought.

After a while though, I still can't put a finger on when exactly, I found myself wishing time away as I longed for Friday, then dreading Mondays. I couldn't bear to be in the office anymore, so worked from home whenever I could. Even so, by Sunday morning, the dread would kick in.

There were no more smiles for my colleagues to scorn. I didn't have the energy for smiling anymore. I just wanted to be left alone. Going out at weekends distracted me, though I'd keep checking my watch—every hour was an hour closer to Monday morning and more put-downs. After a while, I doubt I was even the same person Riley first met.

I pull my knees up towards my chest, balancing my body weight against the safety bar in front of me on the Austurleid, and remember sitting cross-legged on Riley's sofa one Friday evening, almost a year after I'd started work. All I could do was stare at the plants on his balcony, just as all I can do now is stare at the lava plains ahead.

That Friday, Riley had come home in a bad mood too. The new girl in his accounts department must have been going to watch his plays for some months by that stage. I told him I needed to get out, go have a drink or two. Riley had a set of excuses ready. He didn't have enough money. He was still saving for Fiji. He was tired. He'd had a few drinks at lunchtime (probably with her), and wanted to crash out. He always had a good reason for not meeting up at lunchtimes anymore, and for not going out in the city at night. The new girl probably lived nearby.

My smile fades as I remember Riley slamming his way around the kitchen cupboards, looking for the popcorn I'd forgotten to buy. It was only popcorn but, to him, it was as if I'd lost his only copy of an original script.

"How could you have forgotten? I specifically texted you! Is there nothing in that brain of yours now but work?"

Honestly, there wasn't.

So I sat there and listened to him complain about the day he'd had, about the fucking shit crap of a day that had fucked all over him and left him smouldering in a hell he didn't deserve. All he'd been looking forward to was popcorn and a movie. Now he couldn't even have that, thanks to me.

He should have left his firm already, become a full-time actor. But me sitting there vacant, staring at plants, probably only reminded him of his own dread.

"You're not the only one with a stressful job, Becky," he muttered. "I'd love to leave Sydney, go home to Brisbane and get away from all this." He gestured around his apartment, finishing at me.

I resisted reminding him that it wasn't the stress of the job that bothered me. It was dealing with lawyers like him.

"Do you know what?" he said, coming into the lounge. "You're pathetic. Look at yourself, will you? Are you even there?" He pushed my forehead with a finger. "Pathetic." Words followed, like 'worthless', 'waste of space' and 'weak'. Words I heard at work too.

Of course he knew how those words would get to me. He used them on purpose; kept going until I cried. He only ever mellowed after tears fell. My despair made him feel better about himself, I suppose. Some people are too scared to make a career change until it's forced upon them. Riley was one such person. So was I.

"You're lucky to have me," he said once I was a snivelling mess, "do you know that?" He put an arm around me, tutting to himself. "Who else would put up with all your crap, eh?"

Later, I found out the new accounts girl was from Brisbane too. She'd acted in a local theatre there since she was sixteen. They had a lot in common.

Squeezing my eyes tight, I cradle my forehead and push from my mind the thought that I might have to face such memories alone from now on, that my Saturday phone calls with Mark might be over. If I do have a somewhat tougher skin these days, it's only because of my brother. I wish I could stop feeling bad about what happened with Riley, about what I did after I found out about his accounts girl, but I can't.

So I seek out my kernel of hope again and tell myself: this isn't the end. Mark will be fine. In the meantime, going over and over the past will do nothing for me. I've got to get on with life and stop dwelling on things so much. Today, of all days, I have to stop.

Determined, I take a deep breath, stare out at the lava plains, and listen to the Austurleid's engine until its gentle hum drowns out my thinking. Slowly the grey dawn eases into a rich sapphire sky, and I force myself to watch it lighten. It's beautiful, as is all of nature—if only for what it brings me. It lifts me, helps me to focus on what actually matters. And all that matters right now is that pale cerulean whitening the horizon, and getting over that horizon to find my brother. He's the one in trouble now.

An aroma carrying the warming of bread drifts to the front of the Austurleid, giving me another much-needed distraction. It makes my stomach growl and sends a euphoric ripple of hunger through me. Inhaling the homely scent, I enjoy both the smell of breakfast and the feel of my stomach flattening as I expand my lungs. This is my favourite time of day—hungry and slim with it. Easing into the stretch, I examine my reflection in the window. I shouldn't because I'm sitting down, so sure enough, there's the wobble around my middle that looks as solid as always, bulging against my clothes as if it wants everyone to admire the fold of fat it's become.

By the time a breakfast circulates of warm bread rolls with cold cuts of salami and cheese, pickled herring, dried fruits and coffee, I don't feel like eating anything, lest it bloats me even more. Then again, my head feels so light and spinny, I know what will happen if I get to Höfkállur without eating anything. I'll sway as I step down from the transport. I may even have to steady myself when I duck underneath to retrieve my suitcase. I'll grip my suitcase tight, though that won't improve my shaky walk as I roll it over to a seat where I can cradle my hunger some more. People will talk to me and I'll talk to them, but I won't remember anything because my mind will be chanting its hunger pangs too loud and too constant. My writing may even take on the loose scrawl I've seen on pages written after letting my stomach gnaw for too long. But I don't want any of that today.

Today it's all about Mark.

So I discard the bread and let myself pick at the rest. Cutting small pieces, I relish each morsel, sucking and savouring the flavours until it's time to swallow. This way the delight of eating lasts longer. Alternating between textures helps too—the rubbery thinness of salami followed by the crumble of cheese; the snap of dried banana, then the chewy tang of pickled herring...

After a bite of each I start over again, until I've added a hundred and fifty calories to my mental count. Then I stop. My stomach growls at me for more but I ignore it. I know I've eaten enough to start my day, and don't want to lose that feeling of tightness altogether.

I do anyway, then feel guilty. I should have stuck to a hundred calories.

Tutting, I bring unwanted attention to myself with a glance from the driver. When our eyes meet, I glare at him until he turns back to his driving. As he does so, he presses a key on his smartphone and pushes an earpiece into his ear. When whomever he's calling picks up, he talks in whispers. Then he hangs up and nothing happens.

Mountain ranges disappear with the hours, only to be replaced by new ones. Huge inky lava flows curl smoothly towards the coastline. The transport is so warm it's both stuffy and snug at the same time. Happy with the food in my stomach, my body tires again, my eyelids grow heavy. Having snatched only a few hours sleep since Director Úlfar called me yesterday, I wriggle until I'm comfortable in my seat and stare at the view to keep my mind from straying back to Riley, only to jump when my phone rings. Its caller ID says 'BLOCKED'.

Mark?

I bolt upright to answer.

"Miss Dales?" A man hisses down the earpiece.

"Yes? Rebecca Dales, speaking."

"You are going the wrong way." The man has an Icelandic accent. There's something about his voice too. His tone is staccato, like the jolted clatter of a Word2Word translator.

"I'm sorry, I didn't quite catch that," I say with a smile, in case my imagination is playing tricks on me again. "What did you say?"

"Get off at the next town and go back to Reykjavík."

I'm not imagining anything. "Who is this?"

"You've already been asked several times today, now I'm telling you. Stay away from Höfkállur."

"Who's speaking?"

"Tell the driver you're getting off. Go on, tap him on the shoulder and tell him now. I know you're close enough."

I shoot to my feet; search the Austurleid SBS for someone on a phone or speaking into a laptop.

"Nei, Miss Dales. I am not on the Austurleid. Nor should you be."

I scan the windows. There are no vehicles either side of the transport, nothing in front. I swagger towards the back.

"You're going the wrong way. Maybe I'm not making myself clear?" He inhales a deep rasping wheeze before continuing. "We don't want your kind in Höfkállur. Turn around, now. You don't want to cause your parents any more pain, do you?"

He hangs up as I spy a grey four-wheel drive roar around the back window and overtake the Austurleid with menacing acceleration.

Shaking with rage, I stumble back to my seat. My thumb finds the 'M' key on my phone and automatically depresses it to speed-dial Mark.

Please pick up, please pick up.

But his phone is still turned off. I sink into my seat and, keeping my eyes on the driver, dial the only other person who knows I'm on the Austurleid SBS to Höfkállur at that exact moment. Director Úlfar sounds sleepy when he answers. I try to imagine him wheezing, the sound has kind of stuck in my mind. Did he just call me?

"Director Úlfar, I have just been threatened."

"What? How?" He's good at sounding sincere. "When?"

I tell him what happened. The driver doesn't react, not to my tone or volume.

"Miss Dales," says Director Úlfar, "I have no idea how that man got your number—"

"I bet you don't."

"But let me assure you that you are in no immediate danger. If he wanted to harm you, he would have already. He's gone now, right?"

"I thought Iceland was full of happy people living in a perfect society?"

He sighs his reply. "It could be because you're a lawyer."

"Ex-lawyer. Why does that matter?" Guilt plucks at my attempt to sound innocent. "I've never represented anyone from Iceland." At least I don't think I have. "What's my ex-profession got to do with anything?" Apart from all the times I let my firm bleed clients of money, encouraging them to sue others when they had no possible chance of winning.

"It could have everything to do with it." Director Úlfar sounds almost as guilty as I feel. "The man never said *you* weren't welcome in Höfkállur. He said *your kind.* Miss Dales, as well as developing the Sannlitró-Völva, we've also been developing a new legal system in which to use that technology. The system involves the exclusion of lawyers, and Höfkállur is the first town to trial that system. So I expect some *Heimspeki* followers in Höfkállur don't want lawyers around right now. They believe lawyers are...not very good people."

So do I. "But I'm not in Iceland in a legal capacity—I'm here as a sister!"

"I know." Sympathy softens his voice. "But please understand,

with every new idea comes passion. Sometimes that passion can be…
misplaced."

"And this is why you didn't want me going to Höfkállur, because
you didn't want me seeing this—what did you call it—passion?"

"No." His tone cools. "I simply wanted to show you what we *have*
finished developing in Reykjavík, the technology we *are* ready to share
with the world. Our trials in Höfkállur are incomplete. Maybe you
should come back? I could send a car to meet you?"

"Just tell me how this even makes sense—there are people in
Höfkállur who know I'm on my way there, *and* what I used to do for a
living, yet until we spoke today I didn't even know about any trials?"

"Oh I'm sure you did know. You said you and your brother were
close."

"He never said anything about any new legal system." Although as
soon as I say it, I realise Mark probably has, even if in passing. Then
again, he's never had much interest in anything even remotely legal.
"Mark's PhD is in theology, not law. And there have been no official
announcements about any new legal system, not even a rumour of
any trials. If there had been, *Dictum* would have sent me to investigate
already."

"Still your brother, and people like him, know about Höfkállur. Are
you sure you didn't know?" There's a hint of pride in his voice now.
It grows when I don't answer. "I suppose it is possible, given there
are no lawyers in Höfkállur anymore. We did want to keep visitors to
a minimum for now. Maybe in your country it is different, but here
we do not like to announce developments until we have tested them
thoroughly."

I close my eyes to still the whirl of questions in my mind. As I rub
my forehead to concentrate, my stomach grumbles again. I should
have had more breakfast, not less. Finally, a question rises to the top.
"The man on the phone, he knew you'd asked me to stay in Reykjavík.
How did he know that?"

Director Úlfar stifles a laugh. "You think that man is somehow
linked to me?"

I let my silence answer him.

"Miss Dales, you are very worried—the phone call was intended to
scare you and it succeeded. But I will find the caller's number from the
phone company and trace him. I will also have one of my associates in
Höfkállur meet you from the Austurleid to make sure you are safe. Our
MUR representative in Höfkállur is J…oh, nei," he pauses to rethink,
"Ari, I will send Ari. He works at the Litrúm-Hús."

"The what?"

"It's what they call a courthouse now."

"Ah, yes." Mark mentioned that in an email too. Maybe I know more about these legal trials than I realise.

"Ari is *very* nice, you can trust him."

I don't like the emphasis he puts on the word 'very'. It implies something I can't put my finger on. "As long as he brings the police with him I will."

"Miss Dales, there are..." He makes an exasperated sound. "Please, forget about the phone call and let me deal with it. All you have to do is get your brother and come back to Reykjavík, before Friday if pos—"

I hang up before he says anything more about my returning to Reykjavík before Friday. My teeth clench just thinking about his persistence. How can any of this even be happening? Why aren't lawyers welcome in Höfkállur anymore? And if someone's so desperate for lawyers to stay away from the town, so desperate that they'd go to the trouble of finding my phone number and threatening me, what might they have done to Mark if they discovered his sister used to be one, and that he'd invited her to stay with him?

No, it's too far-fetched—why would anyone think to check who Mark's related to, especially given his unwavering support for the *Heimspeki*. My imagination's going into overdrive. Mark will be fine. He's fine.

Still, the thought makes my stomach contract into a knot so tight it's not a nice feeling anymore. I feel like vomiting.

Chapter 3

The Austurleid SBS finally swings into Höfkállur around mid-afternoon. The travel depot is off the highway, its bitumen yellowed by a strong summer light that strikes without interruption from any surrounding buildings or mountains. I sit up as we pass its car park, full of four-wheel drives that glint in the sunlight. As we glide to a stop, I search for the person Director Úlfar has sent to meet me, no doubt another of his watchful minions. There's a ticket office, and some bureaucrat in a high-necked white shirt and sash leans against it. Beside him is a placard bearing my name. That must be him, though he doesn't react to the Austurleid's arrival.

The transport's doors hiss open and our driver waddles down the steps to help passengers retrieve their luggage, watching me as he does so. I don't care about his surveillance anymore. All I care about is speaking to the police about the threat, then getting to Mark.

So, expecting the bureaucrat to make his way over to greet me, I follow some passengers outside and yank my suitcase from underneath the Austurleid. When I look up, I'm surprised to see him still relaxing against the wall. His eyes are closed, his head angled at the sun as if yearning to melt into some light warming breeze, hang off its gentle whispers. Director Úlfar must have told this guy about the threat and my reaction, about my brother and his...condition. So, shouldn't he be searching for me, anxious to locate and placate me?

Instead he's enjoying the weather?

He doesn't even look up at the clatter of my suitcase rattling over the bitumen towards him.

As I near the ticket office, however, and the sun infiltrates my own skin with its snug beams, I begin to understand. The air is warm yet crisp; the sun is welcoming yet invading. It reaches inside me and untwists my knots, warms my bones and relaxes my shoulders. I look up at my first unrestrained view of the sky in two days and fill my lungs with the forgiving freshness in the breeze, then release the air slowly. Like me, this guy has probably been inside all day, now he's taking a moment for himself, enjoying a break from work. I've been chewing the insides of my cheek so hard they're bleeding again. I'd like to rip the head off whoever threatened me on the Austurleid, possibly the driver and Director Úlfar too. Still, that's because Mark is my brother. To most other people, he's merely a name. He's paperwork and statistics, a task they have to complete before they go home or stand sunning themselves in a car park. I need to keep a lid on things. Take it step by step. Emotions can cloud clear thought.

I slow my pace to a stroll. This guy isn't going to understand why I need to know the things I do, he isn't going to understand that I'm tenacious on any usual day, let alone a day like this. The reason I used to be a good lawyer, the reason I'm good at my job now, is because when I decide to do something I do it well. I like to leave no stone unturned, then understand why those stones were put there in the first place and, if possible, who or what last touched those stones and for how long. Before I make a decision, I like to know details and reasons. And that's not only when I'm keeping my mind occupied with work. That's just me. I've come to accept it over the years, and I see it as a plus.

But this guy may see it differently, as my parents often do. He might see it as controlling, as Mum sometimes does. She thinks I take control away from people. Like with this trip to Iceland. Mum wanted to come, despite the distance, despite the reason. I told her it wasn't a good idea; that it would end up (hopefully) being an unnecessary trip, full of unnecessary angst. I was trying to help her, and Dad.

"Right, that's it then," she said to Dad when we spoke yesterday about Mark.

"What do you mean?" I asked, already knowing.

"There's no point discussing it any further—we both know it'll be your way or not at all."

Dad hadn't refuted her statement. They both think I'm stubborn. To me, it's simple persistence. That's how you get things done. Persistence leads to thoroughness, and a reputation for thoroughness gets me the best assignments. Mum thinks I'm too pushy. But for me pushiness is passion.

Then again, occasionally Mum is right. There's a fine line between pushiness and passion. Which is why, looking at this guy's face, I realise I'm going to have to tread softly in case I cross that line. Mum and Dad will never forgive me if I stuff this up by putting everyone I meet on the defensive, which could be easy in a place judgmental about lawyer types like me. Mum already believes Mark wouldn't be in Iceland if not for me. If I hadn't been so selfish that time, eighteen months ago, she reckons Mark would have finished his thesis already. In that, at least, Mum does have a point. So what if she has a point about the rest too?

Forcing a smile, I greet the guy with the placard as cordially as I can. "Halló. Ég heiti Rebecca Dales."

Hazel-brown eyes peer out from under low golden-white eyebrows. "Góðan dag." The man shoulders himself away from the wall, arches his back to crack some joint in his spine. "Talarðu íslensku? You speak Íslenska?"

"Not really. I keep trying, but everyone speaks such good English."

"It is true, we do. I am sorry." He bows his head, tousling his crop of bushy blond hair that needs a haircut. "I hope you will survive. My name is Ari Halldórsson, and I am Chief of Personnel at Höfkállur Litrúm-Hús. Please call me Ari. Director Úlfar instructs me to help you, in every way, while you are in Höfkállur. Which, I feel, will be a pleasure." He grins. "I have never met an Australian before. G'day!"

I tighten my grip on my suitcase handle to control my irritation. This isn't the time for joking, or flirting. "Thanks, but I'm not on holiday. Um…" standing my suitcase upright, I look around the depot, "…so, where are the police? Didn't Director Úlfar tell you I needed to talk to them straight away?"

The bureaucrat studies my face. "Are you sure you were supposed to get off here for that?"

I frown. "Of course."

"Because we have no police in Höfkállur. Director Úlfar explained this to you, já?"

"What do you mean? Are they on a training day or something?"

He scratches at the regrowth on his jaw while digesting my question. "Rebecca. Can I call you Rebecca?"

"Becky."

"Becky," he smiles the word like it's a luscious secret. "Director Úlfar told me your appointment with our coroner is very soon. Perhaps you would like to go there first, talk about the phone call with me as we go? Then you can decide who to speak with next. My car is over there." He jerks his head towards the car park, takes the handle of my suitcase but waits for me to make a decision before moving in any particular direction. "You want to see your brother first?"

I do. Mark is my priority. I can always speak to the police after I've seen whatever cadaver Director Úlfar wants me to see. Then, assuming the cadaver isn't Mark, the police can begin their official search for him at the same time as looking for the man on the phone. "Which car is yours?"

"The Eroder. The, er, purple one, there." He points to a huge mauve and silver four-wheel drive. "If you prefer to walk, the Litrúm-Hús is a little along the quay. I drove here in case I was late. But I forgot," he chuckles to himself, "transports are always on time now."

I survey the depot. There are no grey four-wheel drives in sight. Ari has no deep rasping wheeze like the man on the Austurleid. It wasn't the type of wheeze someone could control. Still, I'm not about to get into some stranger's car. "Um, if it's not far, we'll walk."

Ari gestures towards the exit where seagulls as big as albatrosses search the footpath for food. As we walk, he tries to orientate me with the town and its harbour, though nearing the depot's exit his words are drowned out by the passing of several tipper trucks heaving open trailers of fresh fish. The seagulls rocket into the air to reach the trailers, adding to the noise, so Ari gives up talking until the birds are further away. They squawk the loudest as they pilfer succulent silver morsels from the iced-up cargoes, not that the trailers stop. The birds follow after them too, hovering in the wisps of freezing vapour rising from their tops.

I shiver as we cross to the quayside and follow the harbour's dank shoreline towards the town centre. Ranges of lime green and taupe mountains throw their shadows over the mirror-flat waters of the harbour. Waist-high basalt boulders frame the docks and divide footpath from road, across from which wooden homes painted burgundy, olive and turquoise all face the view. Their corrugated-aluminium roofs stretch towards the ground, while balconets jut out from their upper floors. No wonder Mark stayed here as long as he did. It's beautiful.

"So," Ari begins once the squawking has died down and our pace settles. "Director Úlfar told you that we are a research town, já?"

"He said you were testing a legal system, based on the Sannli-tró-Völva." I remember Mark's explanation of the machine now. "Apparently you've developed some kind of lie-detector?"

Ari nods, yet frowns like he wants to disagree. "The Sannlitró-Völva is used for many things, detecting lies is only one. Its most important role is preventing crime, and it has been very successful to date, which is why," he breathes out his next sentence fast, as if anticipating a bad reaction, "we retired our police, permanently."

I stumble on a crack in the footpath. "You what?"

"I know," he grins, unmistakable pride in his voice. "It sounds crazy, right? But it is okay, because of the *Heimspeki*."

I stare at him, waiting for the punchline. None comes. "You're not joking? But how…how's that working for you, exactly?"

"Gott." His voice fills with wonder as he explains. "When you see the positivity, or negativity, of your electrical energy through the Sannlitró-Völva, something happens to you. You realise, wow, this is the type of energy I will become when I die. It makes you want to be very positive. Suddenly all our offenders asked to be examined. Lawyers had no work, so they left." He turns his palms up to indicate a lack of choice.

"No." I hear myself snap. "I meant, how could it be working for you at all when someone just threatened me?" My voice has a condescending tone to it. Keep a lid on things, I remind myself. "Last time I checked, threatening people is a crime."

Ari shakes his head as he speaks. "I know. It is a pity this has happened. Probably a lot of people are very passionate about the *Heimspeki* right now. Maybe, you are a lawyer, so Director Úlfar says…"

"Not a criminal lawyer though. I specialise in researching new court systems and their procedures…Oh, hold on," I realise the connection, "they think I'm going to condemn their new system because it puts lawyers out of work? I'd never do that. I'd never condemn a legal system for any reason other than it doesn't work, and to believe that I'd have to have a very good reason."

"Your brother just died here." Ari looks at me as if I'm being naïve. "Perhaps that is reason enough?"

"I don't even live here!" I glance over my shoulder to check the footpath behind me, and the road for grey four-wheel drives. It's empty. "If your crime rates are low without lawyers, or police, then good for you. What does it matter to me?"

Ari goes to say something but stops himself.

"What?"

"It is not about numbers, Becky. If this were your home, you would understand. When a community decides to trust each other it's like falling in love, with thousands of people."

"Ha! I didn't feel much love from the man who threatened me." I probably could have said that without the scoff.

"He will come forward. He will need to admit his mistake to neutralise his negativity."

"He'll need to do what?"

"That's how things work here now."

"So people simply...admit their mistakes, even if it's a crime?" Ari nods. "So when will this guy admit his? How long does it usually take?" Ari's shrug says it all. "So, you want me to just wait? I'm only here a few days." There must be something I can do. "How far away is the nearest town *with* police?"

"Two hours' drive. But they will not know where to start in Höfkállur. Straight ahead, please." He gestures across a boat ramp. "Do not worry, sometimes we have anonymous information, sometimes there is evidence first, but for a year now all of our offenders have come forward."

"This one won't."

"You will be surprised." He sounds both amused and proud.

"No, I won't. There must be something I can do!" I struggle to keep the urgency from my voice. "I can't just wait. When you say all your police have retired, what do you mean exactly? Is anyone keeping records or taking down information, maintaining files? Has anything like this happened before? Because if Director Úlfar sent you to pacify me rather than actually do something, you may as well go back to your car. I'll find someone else."

Ari stops walking and looks at me. "You are very..."

"What?"

He shakes his head, tuts. "I don't know." He starts walking again, then stops and glances across the harbour.

Fishing boats chug in and out of the harbour entrance, honking to each other as they bring in their catches to awaiting fish factories. He watches the boats for a moment. It looks like he's thinking. Even so, his silence infuriates me. I'm about to snap again when he clears his throat to speak.

"I could call my father," he says, standing my suitcase upright with a decisive thud. "He was Höfkállur's Police Commissioner, before. Now he's an einstaklingsráðgjafi, er, a counsellor for offenders. He knows a lot of people. He can ask around for you."

"Great. Let's call him."

"Now?"

"Right now."

He searches my face. "Are you alright, Becky? You seem in a hurry. Like you need to know everything very fast."

"I'm sorry." *Keep a lid on things.* "I'm not having the best day. It's... I'm...very upset about my brother. This is important, for me. Though of course I understand it might not be for other people."

Ari nods to himself. "I understand." He goes to say something more but pauses to make eye contact with me. His expression loosens then tenses to ensure nothing cheerful shows in it. "I know what it is like to lose someone."

"Really?" As soon as the sarcasm leaves my mouth, I regret adding it. He sounded sincere.

"Yes." He sighs quietly, glancing at the boats before looking at me again. "And I am here to help. I am trying to help. Okay?" He waits until I nod before leading me over to a sculpture just ahead. A gleaming circle of polished steel is topped by a full-size Viking ship skeleton, also crafted from steel. Its upper curves shine white and sometimes yellow in the sun, while lower sections and underneath reflect a dark foreboding grey. Ari mutters something about it being a tribute to the town's Viking ancestors, says there's an even bigger one in Reykjavík, then moves off to phone his father, indicating I should wait on a nearby bench and relax.

I cross my legs under the bench and lean on its armrest. But how can I possibly relax? Maybe coming here alone was a bad idea after all. It's too much responsibility. I'm clearly an uptight mess, and how can a mess help anyone?

As if in answer, a sea breeze wafts onto my face. It feels cool, smells salty and brings with it the sound of lapping waves. I gaze past the sculpture's silver arches to ripples bouncing across the harbour's briny surface. Closing my eyes, I tilt my face into the sun and listen to the water. Just as nature always lifts me, water brings me calm. Swimming above it, diving below it, gazing at it—I am a different person around water. There, I am not a mess. There, I am simply me—tenacious, careful me.

I wish I were there now.

I'm not, so all I can do is let this water soothe me. Emotions cloud clear thought and I'll think quicker if I'm calm.

So I inhale slowly; exhale slowly. The salty smell of the sea is the same the world over. Apart from Mark, it's my only constant. My inner sanctum. So I listen to the water's movement; ripples that rumble towards me and swash back, towards me and back. I feel my shoulders drop and my jaw loosen. I start feeling more chilled, until, when the breeze subsides, the water's movements grow suddenly louder.

Waves rumble so close it's as if water's swelling all around me. The tide surges as if to drench me; as if the Viking sculpture itself is a bursting fountain about to douse me in wetness. It feels like a waterfall is already plummeting onto my shoulders; that a burst thundercloud is already soaking me to the skin. I open my eyes. Of course I am still dry. Yet the thunder of surging water remains inside my head, filling my skull with gurgling rapids that gush against my eyes and course through my ears.

I pop my ears and crack my jaw. Still the imaginary flooding persists, roaring and swishing like the churning of high seas. I look around, blinking. My vision blurs until I see an image of my brother floating in darkness.

Mark?

A coolness cascades down my spine.

"Becky!" a voice calls.

My head heats like a migraine settling in for the day.

"Let's go, Becky. To the glacier!"

Mark's voice is so clear it sounds real. They're the same words from my dream earlier on the Austurleid. My mouth gapes open, ready to reply.

"The man who threatened you," Ari calls out, "you saw his car?"

"Huh?" Mark's image shatters into broken shards of ice, which melt quickly away. As the flooding in my head fades, I clear my throat. "Um, it was a grey four-wheel drive."

"Did you see the make or model?"

I cradle my head. "Sorry."

Ari speaks on his phone for another minute before snapping it shut and striding towards me. "My father says not to worry. Violent people do not warn their victims before acting."

"What a relief."

"He doesn't know any groups passionate enough about the *Heimspeki* to threaten you. Last year, there was a group who opposed it, the Skyggõur. But they all work for the government now, reviewing policy."

"Were they ever violent?"

"Only crazy. Science is science." He shrugs. "What is there to believe or not? My father is about to meet the family of an offender who once knew a Skyggõur." He leads me again towards the town centre. "While you are with the coroner, I will ask them if they know of any new groups."

"Thank you." I rub my chest as I walk. Everything feels tight. I'm not breathing properly. I push my shoulders back and inhale from my stomach. As I fill my lungs, I realise I haven't taken a decent breath since my imagination went into watery overload at the Viking sculpture.

Most probably it's simple tiredness affecting me, making me crave my sanctuary to the point of delirium.

It bothers me though. I've grown used to steadying myself in the shower, when the faintness that comes from skipping dinner the night before catches up to me. I've also become accustomed to holding on tight when climbing stairs in case my legs give way underneath me. Swooning and dizziness come hand-in-hand with my dietary lifestyle. I'm not worried about any of that though, because I'll stop calorie-counting as soon as I reach my ideal weight. Still, I've never had an actual hallucination before.

Ari leans forward and inspects my face. "Stop the worry," he whispers. "Höfkállur is safe. Look, we do not even lock things anymore."

He points to a bicycle resting unchained against a lamppost, then across the road to where a driver is getting out of an old car. She walks away without locking it. Up ahead a businessman leaves his briefcase on a bench to take his empty coffee cup to a recycling station further up the street. He pauses to greet a friend, and doesn't once check the bench behind him for his belongings. It reminds me that Mark often praised the coffee here, said some little shop by the harbour made the best coffee in the world. Well, apart from Australia of course.

"You see?" Ari says. "It is very safe. No one will hurt you, not here."

"What if you're wrong?" I ask, thinking about the phone call, about Director Úlfar and the driver. "What if someone discovered Mark had an ex-lawyer for a sister and threatened him? Or worse, what if someone was so passionate about the *Heimspeki* that they hurt him?" Though I can't imagine why, Mark was so wholeheartedly in support of the *Heimspeki*.

Still the suggestion silences Ari and we walk for a while without talking. Shops appear along the road. Hoardings advertise meal deals at McDonalds, Subway and KFC. The footpath fills out with people. Locals greet Ari as we pass and even teenagers make room for us with unassuming smiles. The town certainly has a relaxed vibe, much friendlier than London or Sydney. Yet I can't escape two simple facts.

Fact: someone from this town threatened me.

Fact: I'm on my way to see what's supposed to be my brother's dead body.

I check over my shoulder again. There's no harm in indulging the urge. If Höfkállur is as safe as Ari wants me to believe, all I should see as I look around is a population of content people going about their daily business. I'm so busy checking, however, that I don't notice Ari stop.

43

"We cross here." He steps toward the kerb opposite a T-junction. A coach is approaching but Ari goes to cross anyway. As soon as the coach driver sees Ari, he applies his brakes and brings the vehicle to a slow halt. Surprised, it takes me a moment to realise Ari's already on the road. I hurry to catch up, and don't see the four-wheel drive hurtling down the other side of the street until it's almost upon us.

I grab Ari's arm and dash for the opposite kerb. I hear brakes but keep going.

"It is okay, Becky," Ari says once we're on the footpath. "They saw us."

"But..." I go to show Ari the grey four-wheel drive. Only it isn't grey anymore. It's white and driven by a mum-of-two. "Oh. Sorry." *What's wrong with me?*

"No problem," Ari chuckles, shaking his head as if he's seen it a million times before. "The Litrúm-Hús is up here."

He mouths 'takk fyrir' to both drivers then guides me up a slight gradient towards a large white-rendered building set in square of mowed grass. Roads flank the building on every side.

"You see that road on the left? Your guesthouse, *The Himinn*, is down there. And this," he points at the building, "was our courthouse. Now it is our Litrúm-Hús. I work there." He points to the upper floor.

After eyeing its windows, my gaze quickly drops to lock on the building's main entrance. Thick concrete steps lead to a set of wooden doors framed by white columns. The sight makes me switch gears up a notch. That doorway is my portal between a world where Mark might still be alive, and a world where he isn't. The fate of my hopeful kernel lies over there. "And the coroner's office?" I ask Ari as we near.

"I will show you. Do you want me to come to the meeting with you?"

"Does he speak English?"

"He was an intern at Oxford."

"Then I'll be fine. Go find your father. I've got a lot of questions to ask."

Ari heaves my suitcase up the steps. "About your brother's accident?"

"About everything. If it is my brother's body, I'll want to know exactly where he was found, how he was found and by whom, every fact and figure your coroner can tell me."

"About how your brother was found *and* by whom?" Ari sounds surprised.

"That'll be in his records, right?"

"Já," Ari mumbles. "But you don't need to ask him that."

"Of course I do. If my brother died at one of your glaciers," which I hope, I truly hope he hasn't, "I'll need to look into every rock, every pebble, and every block of ice until I understand exactly how that was possible. So I'll need to know who found him, and I'll need to talk to them. Unless there's some kind of privacy issue?"

"Nei," Ari holds a door open for me. "It's impossible to be private around here. Everyone knows everything in Höfkállur."

"Good. So I'll be asking the coroner who found my brother."

"Then you may as well ask me."

"Why?" I step through the doorway. "Who found my brother?"

He clears his throat, then mumbles. "I did."

Chapter 4

I swing around to face Ari. "You found my brother?" My words echo into the cavernous foyer beyond the open door of the Litrúm-Hús with as much resonance as the idea echoes through my mind. Ari is real. He's standing here before me, breathing and talking. That makes his words real too. *Found.* He did not meet or rescue my brother. He found him, as one finds a coin on the ground, a pen between sofa cushions. Inanimate objects are found, lifeless ones you stumble across while doing other things. Found. Lifeless.

Ari nods once, coolly and simply, while motioning for me to step inside the building.

"Why the hell didn't you mention this before?"

"When?" He moves across the entrance.

"Er, as soon as I got off the Austurleid?"

"Instead of 'hello' perhaps?"

"No, but you're saying you were at this glacier, at the exact same time as my brother's allegedly fatal accident, yet you didn't think to mention that before now?" I follow him, intent on getting to the bottom of this, only to stop once I see what lies ahead.

Intricate stone white arches stretch above me, touching oak beams set in the foyer's ceiling. Beech-polished parquetry covers the floor. Then, spanning the width of the foyer, five shiny black cocoon-pods block our access to the rest of the Litrúm-Hús, their fronts embossed with large metallic *Heimspeki* symbols. I lower my voice. "What are those?"

"Security booths," Ari says, watching my expression.

"But," I pause, not understanding, "if you don't need police, if nothing in Höfkállur is even locked, why do you need security like this?"

"Director Úlfar believes that someone from overseas will try to steal the Sannlitró-Völva's technology. The booths record you, alert our MUR officer if they detect certain Litrúm Map results. Please, it will only take a few seconds."

I survey the security attendant as I step inside a pod. "Guns too?"

"Until our international patents are granted."

A thin plastic door slides behind me, sealing me inside the pod. A computer demands that I state my name and instructs me on how to use the fingerprint and retina scanners. A gentle hum indicates I'm being scanned, while a soft breeze and sucking sound tells me I'm being sniffed. Ten seconds later an exit door opens, giving me access to the rest of the building.

"You see, it is quick," Ari smiles as I emerge. "This way."

We enter a white-walled corridor opposite the pods and pass bright chambers equipped with state-of-the-art computers and simple pinewood furniture. I wait a few moments before bringing the subject of Mark back up, because I need to centre my thoughts. Why did Ari not mention finding Mark? Was he hoping I wouldn't ask too many questions? Like Director Úlfar, is there something he doesn't want me to know?

"Ari," I say, once my focus returns, "what were you doing at the glacier where you found my brother? Why were you even there?"

"I was hiking. I go to the Jötunnsjökull Glacier every weekend, if I can."

"Hiking?" I assess Ari's physique. The sleeves of his shirt are rolled up over tanned forearms thick with the strength of a rock climber. "And, um, what was he like when you found him? Injured, or...?"

"I'm sorry, he was already—"

"And, um..." I interrupt so I don't have to hear the 'd' word, "where did you find him, exactly? Beside the river, or in it?"

"In it, by a boulder."

"Actually in the river? He drowned?"

"Probably he fell in closer to the glacier and the river carried him down."

That would explain my nightmares. Director Úlfar must have mentioned drowning in the river after all. "Would you remember the exact boulder if you went there again?"

"Já." Ari frowns as if to say 'of course'. "I go there every weekend."

"After I've seen the coroner, I may need to see this river. Can you take me?"

"It is very dangerous."

"You seem to have survived."

"I have been going to the glacier since I was child."

"Then I'll be in good hands." He doesn't answer. "Look, I hope, I really hope I'm about to see some dead kid who looks like my brother but isn't. If, however," I swallow, "if I go in there and Mark is... dead," I close my eyes as if the action can counteract my having said it aloud, "I'll need to get to that glacier asap. I'll need to see what was so important about it my brother went there without telling me." And why I've now had a vision of him telling me to go there.

"Why should he tell you?"

I explain our weekly routine, though not the reason for it. "And he'd never have gone there alone."

"Maybe he went with someone?"

"Has anyone else been found?"

"Nei. But maybe they were injured also?" Ari shrugs. "Or maybe they will come forward in a few days with a good reason for not saying something already?"

"Like you had good reason for not telling me about finding my brother?"

"I was waiting for the right moment." His tone is indignant.

"Or maybe you were hoping I wouldn't ask?"

Ari stops in his tracks. "Becky, stop now, please." He looks insulted. "Maybe you don't trust many people, but you can trust me."

"I hope so, Ari. Though, to be fair, I don't really know you—no offence." I add. "Actually, it's funny," I chuckle without meaning it, "I'm yet to meet anyone in Iceland I *can* trust, which is surprising given, you know, everything your media is claiming right now."

"Becky." He waits until I look at him. There's exasperation in his eyes. "My family has hiked at the Skepnasá River for all I can remember. You said you wanted facts? There is one fact for you. Fact two: the river divides the Jötunnsjökull valley in two parts and there is no bridge between those parts, making the other side inaccessible. Still, some people like to see that other side, so they look for a safe place to cross the water. Of course they do not know the area like I do, and they are wrong, and they die.

"Fact three," he continues, "a few years ago a family complained after they lost some loved ones in the water, so our government made a rule. No one is to go within two metres of the Skepnasá River. Another fact. Your brother, I saw him because I was on the other side of the river. I only cross because I know what I'm doing and the hiking there is exceptional. I was reluctant to tell you about finding your brother," he clears his throat as if trying to compose himself, "until I had spoken to you for a while, because I was hiking somewhere I shouldn't have been. Four facts. Okay now?" He crosses his arms.

I look at Ari's tense expression, and the fists he's making under his arms, and realise he's nervous about getting into trouble. "Okay. I won't tell anyone." Unless I have to.

"Thank you." His shoulders relax.

"I'm sorry if I made you feel uncomfortable. I didn't mean to."

"I know you didn't." He tugs flat the glossy maize sash around his waist. "You are just very…" He pauses to find the right word, then doesn't finish the sentence. "Still, you are also a nice person. I can tell." He smiles.

"I'm glad you think so." Not that it's relevant.

"Of course. You wouldn't be here asking all these questions about your brother if you weren't."

We continue down the corridor. After a few paces, I have another question for him. "If the river is so dangerous, why don't they seal it off, put up barriers or something?"

"Fact five," he says, "the river is protected. It's a national park. All they can do is warn people."

"Oh, I imagine they can do a lot more than that if people are dying there." Just wait until I've finished with them.

"Then you must have a good imagination."

"Not r—" I stop myself and rephrase. "What imagination I have I can control."

"And control is important to you, já? I can tell that also." He holds a door open for an administrator as she emerges from an office, balancing a pile of documents on her laptop.

"Not so much control." Instinctively, my hand falls to my hips, as if to hide my secrets. "Though, as you saw when we were crossing the road outside, my imagination could benefit from some controlling. I prefer things I can rely on, don't you? Facts and figures, evidence, proof, details…"

"And what happens," he says, closing the administrator's door, "when two facts say different things?" We walk on.

"You mean when they contradict each other?" He nods. "There will always be one to tip the balance."

"You never trust your, er, this?" He points to his gut.

"No. Your gut relies on feelings, and feelings can change."

"Facts can change too."

"How?" I can't suppress the sarcasm in my voice.

"New facts can make you think differently about old ones. We feel things in our gut for a reason."

"You sound like my brother."

"I do?"

"He says our gut feelings, hunches and instincts result from our subconscious reasoning for us." I mimic Mark's voice, sensing an opportunity to loosen up our conversation. "Our subconscious generates perfectly logical analysis but reduces it, for speed, into inexplicable impulses."

"Then he was a very clever brother and you should trust your gut more." He nudges my arm with his, smiles again.

I wish it were that easy. Though Mark's always saying it is. "Look, are you going to take me to this glacier or not?" Despite myself, my instincts tell me to add a smile.

Ari looks at me, assesses my expression, then chuckles and mumbles something in Icelandic.

"What?"

"Nothing." He throws me a conciliatory grin. "You make me laugh. Though I am trying not to laugh of course. Okay, so...you are in a hurry to know everything. But only because you loved your brother. So I understand."

"That's refreshing to hear." Perhaps some people are capable of seeing what my parents can't after all. "I'm glad you understand my urgency."

"I also have instructions to help you, no limits, so I will clear my work for tomorrow. Do you hike?"

"I've been known to stagger over the odd hill in my time."

"Gott." He looks me up and down as if making his own assessment. "That will make it easier. Turn left. The coroner's office is right there." He passes me my suitcase and points at a door bearing a metal plaque labelled 'Doctor Emil'. "I will find my father and meet you, when you are ready, by the front entrance. And tomorrow we will go to the river." He goes to leave but turns back. There's a glint of playfulness in his eyes now. "Becky, you are still worried about the man who called you on the Austurleid?"

I nod, though Ari's expression makes me nervous. Riley used to adopt the same expression before telling me something unpleasant. And Riley turned out to be a self-centred cheat.

"So I wonder," Ari says, "why would you want to hike at a glacier with a complete stranger?"

"I can take care of myself."

"Ha!"

His laugh is loud and honest but I can't buy into it. I've been here before.

"I thought you might say that. But you are very small." He throws his shoulders back, moves closer until he towers above me, then slaps at his abdominals. "Hit me. Go on—I will not feel a thing."

"What?"

"Punch my stomach."

"No!"

"You can take care of yourself, huh? You are not so tough." His eyes linger on me as he reaches inside his coat pocket for his phone. He swipes through to his contact details then holds the phone out. "I think you will need my help more than you think."

He's probably right but I don't want to admit it. "Thanks, but I only need you to take me to the glacier."

"Take them, in case." He winks and stands over me until I tap his details into my phone. Then he knocks on Doctor Emil's door and moves back down the corridor.

"Já!" comes a gruff voice from behind the door.

My hand goes to the door handle, though my eyes alternate between Ari's details in my phone and his broad outline disappearing around a corner. He gives me a final wave without looking back.

"Já?" comes the voice again.

I depress the handle and inch my way inside a spacious office. A smile flickers under Doctor Emil's gruff blond beard as I enter, then he banishes it with an irritated mumble while shuffling papers around his antique pine desk. Once organised, he rises from behind his desk, his burly frame filling the room like a Viking at a tea party.

"Miss Dales," he says, moving towards an adjoining door, "your brother is through here. I assume you want to see him first? They usually do."

I take a deep breath and follow him through the door into a large room housing various computers and laptops. I pause in the doorway, but not because my world has come crashing down on me—I'm confused.

Sensing my hesitation, Doctor Emil turns to check on me. "Did you expect to see a body?"

Chapter 5

Doctor Emil stares at me as if the reason we're standing in a windowless room full of high-tech computers, and not a morgue, is obvious. But I don't understand.

"Where is he?" I shrug. "Where's this cadaver I'm supposed to be seeing?"

"We don't have refrigeration facilities here at the Litrúm-Hús. He's at the hospital." Doctor Emil heads towards a computer.

"Okay then, let's go."

"Most people prefer to wait until the *kistulagning*, er, funeral. Please, sit." He's already leaning over a keyboard, searching for a computer file. "I can show you here." Almost instantaneously, a photographic image appears onscreen. Doctor Emil straightens and waits for me to edge closer.

From where I'm standing, I can already see the face of someone sleeping, someone with short blond hair. It's not him. It can't be. As I near the screen though, the portal I dreaded only minutes before closes fast behind me. I am already in that other world.

Oh god.

It's him.

I sink into a chair. Mark is lying on a metallic trolley, his blond hair swept to one side, his mouth parted as if in thought. The full eyelashes he inherited from our mother are shut. My eyes drop to the floor. My hopes lie smashed there, a pulpy mess.

It can't be you. Please.

I take a long, slow breath and try clinging onto my hope. "I think I'd prefer to see him in the hospital." I mutter. It would be impossible to argue against flesh. You can do anything with images these days.

Doctor Emil checks his watch. "The morgue is closed now. You can see him in the morning, if you wish."

"I do."

"Can I recommend, though, that you complete the identification process here? The morgue is not a nice place to linger, and I can assure you this photograph is authentic."

"You've seen my brother?"

"I have seen him, yes."

I take another long breath. Tears well behind my eyes. I find the insides of my cheek and chew. If I let myself think Mark is dead, if I hear those words in my mind, I'll be blubbering within seconds. I know now he is. I also know ignoring that fact will enable me to stay in control. I blink back the drops and try to remember what questions to ask.

Nothing comes.

Instead, looking at my brother's motionless face, I only think of all the things he'll never do again. He'll never breathe again. He'll never eat again. I want to see him smile and laugh. But he never will.

Oh god.

I want this image to be manipulated. I want someone to be lying to me. But the likelihood of that is getting slimmer and slimmer. I am face-to-face with the town coroner. He trained at Oxford and speaks perfect English. He's seen this body, examined this body, the same body as the one on the screen in front of me: Mark. Dead. The morgue is closed. I can see him for myself in the morning.

"Miss Dales," Doctor Emil says, his tone softer, "is this your brother?"

"Yes." I croak, still scanning the image for some proof that it might not be. Anything, there must be something. I don't care what it is; just let there be a reason this isn't Mark.

I peer closer. His face seems out of proportion somehow. "Does the computer affect the image at all? Something isn't... Something's different." Something like me hoping against all odds.

"You thought he would look paler, já? Our software adds some colour. It makes them look...like they did before." He offers me an uncomfortable smile.

"Before? You saw my brother *before* he died?"

He died, oh god, he died. Don't think about it. Don't!

"Nei. Now, wait one minute please." He selects the computer's VoIP program to call someone. "I will tell Gunnar to prepare your brother's casket and paperwork for travel. You'll be leaving tomorrow, or Friday?" He looks to me for an answer.

"Oh, I'm not sure yet. After the weekend probably."

He glares at his screen, unmoving apart from a clenching in his jaw, then he switches programs and types a message instead. Written in Icelandic, I can't understand it. After clicking the 'send' button, he rises and motions towards his office. "Staying to see some of our beautiful countryside?" He avoids eye contact and doesn't sound particularly interested in my reply. "Not really the best time for it. Don't you think you should take your brother straight home to your parents?"

"I will," I say, thrown by his judgmental comments. "I have some loose ends to tie up first." Like how my brother died.

I glance at the ceiling, trying to focus my thoughts. On the flight over, I prepared a list of questions so I wouldn't forget anything once here. As I follow Doctor Emil into his office, I pull out my phone. Seeing those questions listed out will help me shift into lawyer mode. I'll have time to process everything else later. For now I need to gather facts. Given how unwelcome I am in Höfkállur, it's clear now that someone somewhere has been negligent of something to do with my brother — it's the only explanation for why it's relevant I'm a lawyer. Time to find out who's to blame, and for what.

"Actually, Doctor Emil, before I go, I'd like to ask you a few questions about my brother's, um, accident, if that's alright?" I swallow back my tears and close the computer room door behind me.

"Let me guess," Doctor Emil begins, shuffling round to his side of the desk. "You want to know why your brother's nose is swollen?"

"Right," I say, surprised he's anticipated my chief concern: Mark's face.

"Mark was found in the Skepnasá River, a glacial river full of boulders and rocks. It is our opinion that his nose hit a boulder."

I scan down my list of questions. "And how did he die, exactly? Did he fall onto a boulder *then* hit the water, or did he drown first?"

"There was sufficient water in his lungs to suggest he drowned."

"The injury to his nose then, to be clear, that occurred in the water?"

"The bruising suggests that, yes."

"I understand a number of people have died in the Skepnasá River? Did their bodies look similar to my brother's?"

Doctor Emil scratches his beard with a huge hairy hand. "Miss Dales, I have been in this business a long time, probably since before you were born. Usually when relatives question our findings it is because they don't believe them." He tilts his phone towards him, checks its display.

"It's not that." My instincts tell me to flash him a smile. "My parents will want to know how Mark fell in, exactly. I know a man of your position must be extremely busy, still I was hoping your expertise might throw some light on the issue. It would help them, and me."

"I didn't realise 'how he fell in' was an issue." Doctor Emil shifts in his seat. "He simply fell. That's what I understand."

I sit silent for a moment. Some people hate conversational silences, they jump in to fill the uncomfortable void with whatever's on their mind. On this occasion, it's a useful trap.

"Miss Dales," he leans forward to interconnect his fingers on the desk, "my staff are highly competent in their work. Our annual performance reviews are always outstanding. We have never had an autopsy report questioned."

"There's always a first time." I never mentioned any autopsy report. "Can I see Mark's autopsy report please?"

"It's in Icelandic."

"But you have Word2Word?"

Pursing his lips, Doctor Emil turns to his desktop computer. Moments later, he angles his screen towards me. Bright green comment boxes down the report's right-hand side contain its English translations.

This 26-year-old white male, Mark Dales, was found dead at the Skepnasá River. The main cause of death is asphyxia due to drowning. The manner of death is accident...

I scan past the photographs Ari must have taken of Mark's body washed up against a riverside boulder, and skim over the report's more complex terminology, understanding enough of the basics to get the gist. The toxicology tests show Mark's blood and urine contained no signs of alcohol, drugs, illnesses or infections. The anatomic summary is comprehensive too; so comprehensive in fact, the awful details of my brother's death start to become very real to me. Too real.

I stop reading, stare at the document instead and concentrate on not crying. I have more questions to ask but first have to pull myself together. That's never going to happen while I'm reading about Mark being cut open and weighed. I'll have to read the rest later. I clear my throat to say so, but before I can ask Doctor Emil to print the report, a gush of water surges through my head like a tidal wave. It heats my forehead like sunstroke and is identical in every way to the watery sounds I heard earlier beside the Viking sculpture, only this time there's little point in looking behind me. Only Doctor Emil and I are in the room.

A frosty shudder ripples down my spine. I look behind me anyway. There's no sink in the room, no pipes or water feature, nothing even containing water. Am I going into shock?

Finish reading, says a voice.

I look at Doctor Emil. He's staring at me as if awaiting an answer to a question.

"Sorry, did you say something?" I ask.

"Have you finished reading?"

"Um, no. Can you print it out for me?"

"You know," Doctor Emil says, folding his arms across his thick chest, "this is good for me. I forget what it's like to meet someone upset about their loss."

"The people you meet are usually happy?"

He pauses to study me, eyes twinkling over cheeks ruddy and weathered. He waggles a finger at me. "I think I know the real problem here, Miss Dales. You don't follow the *Heimspeki*, do you?"

"You're going to tell me I should, right?"

"Can you think of a good reason to not? What do you know about our discoveries?"

"Quite a lot actually."

"Humour me. How did the *Heimspeki* come about?"

It's so simple a question it's almost insulting. "How did the *Heimspeki* come about?" I repress the urge to answer with a list of my credentials. Doesn't he know what I do for a living, that I'm a professional like him? *Keep a lid on things*, I remind myself before answering. "It came about because your scientists wanted to know where the electrical energy in our brains went after we died. They conducted experiments and discovered that when our brains send messages into our bodies, and vice versa, excess ions diffuse out from our central nervous systems, then continue diffusing through our bodies until they reach the surface of our skin, where they are emitted into the atmosphere."

"Gott." He nods in approval, then leans to rest his head against a fist and relaxes into his chair a little, as if relieved to find himself conversing with an equal. "And would you say that we emit those ions randomly, like when we secrete water and salt in our sweat, or when our skin breathes out random oxygen and nitrogen atoms?"

"No." I say, feeling the urge to squirm under his gaze. "Water, salt, oxygen and nitrogen don't have electrical charges. Ions, on the other hand, have positive or negative charges that cause them to stay grouped once emitted."

"Which means the ions we emit retain whatever patterns they previously assumed in our brains, prior to being transmitted?"

"From what I've read, yes. Why?"

"Because," he turns to search on his computer for something, "if these ions carry such grouped patterns of consciousness with them when they leave our bodies on a daily basis—which I personally believe accounts for memory loss," he winks at me, "surely the entirety of our consciousness must leave our bodies when our brains' electrical energy also leaves us after we die?"

"I appreciate the logic of that—now *and* when it was first proffered by your scientific community, but—"

"But nothing." He clicks through some bookmarked pages on the Internet. "You remember the American neurologists who studied Buddhist monks a few years back, to determine the affects of meditation on the brain?"

The experiment sounds familiar but I can't recall the details. I shake my head.

He gestures towards his computer screen and leans back in his chair so I can see the webpage he's selected. It shows various coloured CT scans depicting cross-sections of the brain.

"Most people's minds are overwhelmed by thoughts and emotions they cannot control," he says, pointing to the scans. "On brain-scanning machines this appears as yellow, red and orange activity. It glows, like the embers of a fire. The more negative those thoughts and emotions, the harsher those colours burn. But," he points at the next set of CT scans, where the previous fiery colours have been replaced by large blue ovals, "when these particular monks were asked to meditate, the fire in their brains cooled into soft blue pearls of energy, which settled in those regions of the brain associated with positive thoughts and emotions. Such is the power of positivity. Now," he adds quickly, like he's afraid I'll interrupt, "did you know that the brains of those who have meditated regularly for years differ in shape from the rest of ours?"

"They mutate?"

"Nei. Their brains grow in the regions associated with positive thought and emotion, like a body-builder's muscles grow because they train. So," he smirks to add emphasis to his next statement, "if this is any indicator of how powerful positivity can be while we're alive, think how powerful it could be when no longer constrained by the shell of our physical bodies? Think how powerful your brother's energy is right now and how powerful you could make yours if you followed the *Heimspeki*."

If anyone's brain energy were to be powerful after death, it would be Mark's. "Still, we can never really know what happens after death, for sure, until we find a way to make that journey and come back. The *Heimspeki* is just another theory, unless you've conducted any near-death experiments?"

Doctor Emil's expression fades. Instead of answering he scratches at his beard.

He isn't denying it?

As he struggles to respond, an unpleasant thought occurs to me and I shift in my seat. Did they experiment on Mark?

The brain scans on Doctor Emil's computer glow on my skin as I lean towards him. "Have you conducted any NDEs, Doctor Emil?"

"I, wait…" He goes to the door, pulls it ajar, checks up and down the corridor, then closes it and shuffles back to his desk. "I wasn't supposed to tell anyone until our alliances were announced," he whispers as he sits. "Director Úlfar insists on keeping all negotiations confidential, for now. But," he runs a finger across the edge of his desk then taps it decisively, "you've asked me directly so I cannot lie—that would be a negative thing to do. So yes," he leans closer like I'm now his co-conspirator, "observing a death through the Sannlitró-Völva *is* now our highest priority."

I nod, but want specifics. "Are you saying, Doctor Emil, you're trying to observe one, or you've already observed one?"

"Neither."

I sit back. "But you *want* to kill someone and resuscitate them, so you can watch what happens to their electrical energy?"

"Kill someone? Nei," he chuckles, "we wouldn't have to kill someone. We're scientists, not butchers. No, no. We would simply wait for a car crash or heart attack."

"What, then rush a Sannlitró-Völva to their deathbed?"

"Nei! We are putting a Sannlitró-Völva in space!" He puts his finger on his mouth and makes a 'shhh' shape with his lips. "A Sannlitró-Völva on Earth wouldn't have the scope to observe where our posthumous energy goes, whether it merges with other energies in the atmosphere or leaves in a polar wind. We need one up there. And I'm on a special committee to ensure one gets there. My experience in post-mortem examinations of the—"

"Wait. Leave in a solar wind? You think our energies go into the sun?"

"Nei, not a *solar* wind!" He scowls at me like I'm an imbecile and turns to search on his computer again. Soon a rotating optic-light image of Earth beams out from the display. A column of fluorescent green light hovers above the North Pole, throbbing with an upward movement. "A *polar* wind." After gauging my blank expression, he explains further, no longer whispering. "A few years ago we needed to know more about solar winds. As you probably know, when there's a storm on the sun electrons and protons explode into space as solar flares. When those flares reach Earth, they collide with and energise the oxygen and nitrogen atoms in our atmosphere, causing them to glow."

I nod. "The Aurora Borealis and Aurora Australis."

"Já," he looks impressed again. "As you probably also know, solar winds can cause a lot of damage."

"More than people realise." I did a paper on them at school. Solar winds can travel at a thousand kilometres a second, carrying with them trillions of watts of electricity with currents of a million amps each. They distort the shape of Earth's magnetic field from a curve into a comet shape and, in extreme cases, can knock out satellites, electrical power plants, computers, radars, even corrode pipes.

"And because of the damage they can cause," Doctor Emil continues, "we decided we needed to know more about their interaction with Earth's magnetic field. So the United States launched a satellite into space, the Fast Auroral Snapshot, to capture the information we need to study the winds. But it also captured something else, something they didn't expect. They found a polar wind carrying particles out of Earth's atmosphere. *Out.*" Doctor Emil raises his eyebrows and waits for me to make my own logical connection.

"Doctor Emil," I say, after pausing to think, "are you suggesting our energies ultimately go into space?"

"We know there are auroras on Saturn, Uranus, Neptune, Jupiter and its moon, Ganymede. Perhaps we end up on one of those planets?"

For a moment I am silent. I haven't heard this theory before, not even from Mark. Though it does remind me of something else he used to say. "My brother always believed heaven and hell were in one place, the same place," I mutter.

"Did he explain why?"

"He said everything in the universe is cyclic, so our ultimate destination is bound to be the same. Our journey to hell is probably more unpleasant than our journey to heaven, but ultimately heaven and hell have to be in the same place."

As above, so below.

"I agree." Doctor Emil smiles, satisfied. "In this life, positives attract negatives, and vice versa. If this draw-of-opposites principle applies to our posthumous energy, irrespective of whether that energy is positive or negative or a balance of both, it will attract differently charged energies and keep attracting them until the final destination of all posthumous energy is in only one place. *Dominus Illuminatio Mea.* God is my light. We will know more when we study it further."

"From space."

"We could go a lot further scientifically," he lowers his voice again, "if we formed an alliance with another country, such as the UK, France, the States or Australia, to launch an adapted Sannlitró-Völva into space, like the FAST."

"Provided your adapted Sannlitró-Völva can detect our posthumous energy once it changes into its next form of course."

"Of course. What we are certain of is that death is most definitely not the end. Science will prove the rest, as it proved thunder and lightning, earthquakes and the auroras—all scientific equations, not mystical happenings. *Þú ert velkominn, gerðu svo vel.* Otherwise, where does the electrical energy in our brains go when we die?"

"I guess we'll see," I say, wondering what made us stray so far from the topic of Mark's death. I look out the window, down into the Litrúm-Hús car park, and try to place how we became so distracted. Why did we start talking about sending a Sannlitró-Völva into space? It feels like Doctor Emil is trying to sell the idea to me. The view doesn't give me any answers. Instead, in my peripheral vision, I see Doctor Emil turn to his computer, minimise his Internet browser, then close down Mark's autopsy report.

The report!

He hasn't printed it out for me.

"Well, thank you very much for your time, Doctor Emil." I stand, offering him my hand. "It was nice of you to spend so much time reassuring me. I hope you're right and that Mark is heading for a better place right now."

"I am certain he is," he replies, smiling and shaking my hand in a hurry. "Let me know when you're ready to fly home and I will have your brother ready for travel the next day. Unless you want to take his personal belongings separately, they will travel with his casket."

"What is there?"

"A backpack, briefcase, keys and wallet."

"No laptop, or phone?"

"Nei."

"I'll take his briefcase now please, leave the rest here."

"Ah, well, it's all at the hospital. So I will arrange for the briefcase to be delivered to your guesthouse." He moves around his desk and gestures at his office door.

"Tonight?"

"If I can arrange it," he opens the door open for me.

"Great. Thank you. I'm at *The Himinn*. Oh," I pretend to remember, "and don't forgot my copy of Mark's report. I'll take that with me now please."

Doctor Emil's expression drops. With a huff, he returns to his computer and pokes the relevant commands into his keyboard. What did he hope to achieve by talking to me about our brains' energy and the FAST? Surely he didn't expect me to forget about my brother's autopsy report? Even if I had forgotten, I would only have remembered later. Perhaps he hoped I was the type of person to give up at the first inconvenience? I'm not, but for him I suppose it was worth a try.

He goes to his printer, snatching out each page as they emerge.

"Takk fyrir." I thank him, holding out my hand.

He plonks himself back in his seat and staples the report together before thrusting it at me.

"What time did you say the morgue opens in the morning?"

"Nine a.m."

"Great. I'll be there then. Bless, Doctor Emil." I say, moving towards the door and curling the report under my arm. He doesn't return my farewell. Instead, as I leave the room, he picks up an earpiece and instructs his computer's VoIP. I'm tempted to leave the door ajar, loiter outside to see if he's going to speak in English. But as I try to rest the door against its frame, my phone bleeps, making me jump. The movement makes the door shut with a slam.

I look at my phone's display. There's no point rushing to read the message anymore—it won't be from Mark—but I do anyway. It's a new text message and the sender's number is one I don't recognise.

"If you are back in Reykjavik by Friday," the text reads, "I will not kill you. Be on the Austurleid tomorrow."

I read it until the words sink in.

When they do, I grip the phone as if my hold can erase the threat. Why is this happening to me? Dealing with Director Úlfar is enough. Dealing with my brother's death is more than enough. Having bus drivers watch me and threatening phone calls is plenty already. A death threat takes my day to a whole new level.

Frozen to the spot, staring at the demand, I don't know what to do. I hear a rustling of paper behind me. There's someone else in the corridor. I glance over my shoulder. There's a man a few metres away, standing beside a closed door, his face hidden behind a wodge of paper. Straight shoulder-length black hair shines atop a solid build. A light brown suit strains across his arms and thighs. He's as big as a bear. He also doesn't seem interested in me, so I angle my suitcase towards the hum of nearby voices and head towards human activity, and the main entrance where Ari will be waiting.

When Ari sees this text, he'll have to take action—it threatens my life!

I call him but the tone rings out and goes to voicemail. I leave a message, asking him to phone as soon as he can, unless I get to him first.

Streaks of light flash across me as I speed past open doorways. My suitcase clatters over the parquetry flooring but, as I follow the direction in which I came, I realise I've hurried too fast. Where am I?

I stop to look around and retrace my steps in my mind. I thought this was the right way. Now I'm not so sure. I try not to think about being lost in a strange place where I can't speak the language and where someone now wants to kill me, though both facts repeat through my mind like a nag. I've been complacent, striding around these corridors like I'm in the Royal Courts of Justice back in London. I'm not and at some point I need to acknowledge that.

There are many things I need to acknowledge, whether I'm ready to or not. Emotions cloud clear thought.

Chapter 6

People are laughing up ahead so, although it means turning down a corridor I don't recognise, I carry on until I find four Icelanders huddled around a smartphone. Beyond them the corridor is short, bending to the left. More voices echo from around the bend, and behind the group is the opening to a curved staircase leading down. The group consists of two middle-aged women and two younger men.

"Halló," I greet them. "Do you speak English?" They shake their heads, then wait while I access my phone's Word2Word application. As I select the right languages, the man in the light brown suit, the one from outside Doctor Emil's office, enters the corridor, his face still obscured by his reading material.

"Can you understand me now?" I ask the group, as the man walks past with a confident stride.

"Já," say the group.

Yes, my phone translates.

"I'm looking for the main entrance."

After my phone finishes its translation, a petite woman with spiky auburn hair smiles and points at the staircase behind me. A score of bangles jangle up and down her arms. "Down there," she and my phone say. "At the bottom, turn right, then use the second staircase on the left. It will take you straight there."

Her colleagues nod in agreement.

"Great. Takk, bless." I say, smiling and securing Mark's report under my arm. I pocket my phone, heave my suitcase into both arms, then duck down the stairs. It feels better, knowing where I'm going. Still I remain alert and watchful, assessing the embracing odour that wafts up as I spiral down the echoing stone steps and, as the group's voices grow more distant, the fact that it's very quiet down below. Perhaps I should have asked them to actually show me the way?

No, that would be an over-reaction. The security pods would sound an alarm should anyone try to enter the building with intent to cause harm. I'm safe here.

I'm also already at the bottom. I lower my suitcase and turn to see a corridor lined with what looks like the courthouse's old holding cells. Bleach has been used to overpower the pong of stale urine still sticking to the cells. Fresh manila paint attempts to disguise knobble-rusted pipes. But cells are still cells. Their walls have been exposed to so many years of caged testosterone that the corridor leading to them stinks of subjugation and silence.

I glance into each cell as I pass. They're occupied with empty single beds, toilets, sinks, and speckled brown and cream linoleum flooring. No one's down here. Clearly no one in Höfkállur needs locking up anymore.

When I reach the junction the woman described, I turn right as she said, down a corridor lined with staircases. I walk to the second staircase on my left, then pause at a clanking sound from the corridor above. Was I supposed to take the second staircase on the left after I turn right, or the second on the right after I turn left?

While I'm trying to remember, my phone rings. Ari?

No. I pull my phone from my pocket. Its caller-id says 'THE HIMINN'. It's the guesthouse where I'm staying tonight, and where Mark stayed these past few months. For some reason I answer with a whisper.

"Becky?" says a voice.

"A-hum." I mumble.

"This is Anna Naddoddur, from *The Himinn* Guesthouse." Her voice is sonorous with a Canadian accent. "Are you in Höfkállur yet? The Austurleid has arrived already I think. Shall I pick you up?"

Mark told me about his friend, Anna. From what he said in recent emails, he trusted her an awful lot. "Um, yes, okay. I'm at the Litrúm-Hús actually, just finished."

"Oh, I'm sorry. I would have come with you had I known. I can be there in ten minutes. You could wait for me out front?"

"Sure, as long as I can find my way there."

"Where are you now?"

"By the old holding cells, I think."

"Oh you're not far. Put your back to the cells and take a right. It's the second staircase on your left. At the top, turn right and follow the corridor. Once you pass the old law books, you'll see it."

"Okay, thanks." I must sound doubtful.

"Don't worry. My cousin works in the Litrúm-Hús, I know exactly where you are. You'll be at the front entrance in five minutes or less. Wait near the door and I'll see you there. Okay?"

I'm not okay of course—who would be in my position? But I want to get off the phone and start moving again. Down here my voice echoes in the emptiness and I don't like it. So I tell her I'm fine and try to sound chirpy. Then I hoist my suitcase again and scale the second staircase on the left. There's another clank from above but I keep going...until my phone rings a second time.

This time the caller is listed as someone called Ólaf Stefánson. I hesitate to answer in case it's another threat. But the man who texted me, and/or the one who threatened me on the Austurleid, wouldn't now suddenly reveal his identity. I put down my suitcase and answer quickly to silence the loud ringing.

"Halló?" I whisper.

"Rebecca Dales?" The caller has an Icelandic accent though thankfully doesn't sound like the man on the Austurleid. Then again, this one's not using a Word2Word translator.

"Yes?"

"This is Ólaf, Anna's cousin."

"Cousin?"

"Já. She spoke with you and thought you might be lost?" His voice has the resonant depth possessed by men of a certain maturity. It also sounds like he's walking somewhere in a hurry. "She said you knew I'd be calling."

"Um, no, I don't think she mentioned that." All she said was she had a cousin who worked here.

"Oh, I'm sorry. Do you know where you are now, my dear?"

"Anna said to take the second staircase on the left, after the junction from the cells."

"Can you see a number six at the top of that staircase?" His breathing is heavy.

I look up as another clank echoes towards me. There are no numbers anywhere. "Hold on." I take another a few steps. Closer to the top, I see both a number six and a door banging in the breeze from an open window. "Yes I see it. I go right at the top?"

"Já, correct. Gott. Anna sounded worried."

Obviously there's no fooling Anna. "I'm fine."

"Okay. But if you want, you have my number now, so call me if you need any help after speaking with Anna, okay?"

"Um, thanks." Though I'm not sure why I'd need to contact Anna's cousin again.

"Bless, Rebecca. Bless."

I hang up and store his number anyway. Mark wouldn't have invited me to Höfkállur if the whole town hated lawyers, some of its inhabitants must be indifferent. And Mark trusted Anna, and Anna obviously trusts her cousin Ólaf, so that's good enough for me. Thanks to Mark, I now have two friends; two people I can go to for help. I pick my suitcase back up and climb the remaining steps, towards the voices in the corridor above.

Wood panelling covers the walls until a series of glass walls and doors open up one side. A group of four men, a woman, and a boy stand in a stone alcove halfway down the corridor. Smiling as they slowly move away from each other, they look as if they're saying goodbye. I recognise the outline of one of the men. It's Ari, and he's turning right, striding towards the front entrance.

I'm about to call out when a smoked-glass door opens to my right. A bear of a man in a light brown suit with sleek shoulder-length black hair emerges. He walks with a confident stride. Holding no papers this time, texting on his phone instead, the side of his face shows weathered bronze Inuit skin, eyes that have spent a lifetime squinting into the distance, a high forehead and equally high cheekbones. With his spare hand, he strokes a thin black goatee. I didn't see his face before, but easily recognise the man who was outside Doctor Emil's office.

At the sound of the door clicking shut, the boy with Ari's group jerks his shaggy mop of hair aside to look behind him. When he sees the Inuit man, he narrows his eyes with unmistakable hostility.

The bear-man glances up from his phone to see the boy's reaction, then stops mid-stride to run his fingers through his hair and raise the middle finger of his free hand, sending the boy a message of his own. "Ari!" he calls out, not taking his eyes off the boy until he's passed him.

"Já, Jón?" Ari pauses long enough for 'Jón' to catch up. When he does Ari slaps him on the back in greeting and they walk towards the front entrance. After a few paces, a laugh bellows out between them.

I'm not sure what these exchanges tell me and, before I can decide, the rest of the group turns and heads for my staircase. I step out of their way, angle my suitcase on its rollers and head towards the entrance too. At least I try to—something is stopping me from moving. There's a grip on my arm. I look down to see a hand.

"Miss Dales?" pants a short man whose receding grey hair leads into a bald patch on the top of his head. Bulbous cheeks sit under metal glasses, much thinner than my reading glasses. His suit is grey yet so lacking in creases it has a silvery sheen. He releases his hold the instant I turn. "Sorry," he smiles briefly, catching his breath. "I'm Ólaf, Anna's cousin." His emphasis on the word 'cousin' indicates something I can't quite pinpoint. "I wanted to check you'd found your way alright. Anna would want me to check."

"Oh, yes. I, er…" I glance down the corridor after Ari and Jón.

"It is okay, my dear. I can see you're in a rush. I won't keep you." He holds up his palms. "You are alright now; you know where you're going?"

"Down there." I point.

"Want me to show you?"

"Um." I hesitate. Ólaf seems nice enough but I don't need his help right now. "It's fine," I say, listening closely to his breathing for a wheeze. "I'm fine."

He backs away. "Okay then. Have a nice day." He gives me a little bow before turning back towards the holding cells. "And say hello to my cousin for me. Tell her I checked on you, okay?" He waves and plods back down the stairs. Although his breathing is strained, it's also faultless.

So I turn down the busy corridor after Ari, past the displays of old law books and paraphernalia Anna mentioned, towards the scan pods. Ari leans against the curved black plastic of a pod, while Jón stands before him. They interrupt each other with jovial animation. Engrossed in conversation Ari doesn't notice me, but Jón does. He stares with tapered eyes that bore straight through me like the glare of an arctic hunter. Creases around his eyes deepen into furrows long familiar to his face, then relax when we make eye contact. He seems to allow himself the pleasure of a private smirk, then folds it into his beige lips and stares past me, as if I don't matter after all.

Ari looks up. "Becky," he says as I reach him. "Did things go well with Doctor Emil? I mean, I hope you are okay after meeting him."

"Did you get my phone message?"

"Um," he pulls out his phone. "Ah, I have a missed call. Sorry. It was on silent while I was in the Dómstóll. Is everything okay?"

"Not really."

He rolls his lips in sympathy, then gestures at his companion. "This is Officer Jón Ásmundsson, head of Höfkállur's MUR. He works with Director Úlfar."

Jón nods me a greeting, then reaches into his suit pocket and pulls out a smartphone. He clears his throat, giving Ari a look.

Ari's expression drops. "I am sorry, Becky, but I have bad news for you—I have found only dead ends." He says he's now spoken to the offender he thought could help, Sigmar Thorsteinson and his family, but they knew of no organised groups or activists passionate *for* the *Heimspeki*—only a friend, Haraldur-someone, who opposed the *Heimspeki* with the rest of the Skyggõur. Apparently Haraldur moved to Norway after the referenda. "I'm sorry," Ari shrugs.

I bite my lip as I contemplate when to tell Ari about the text threat. I'm itching to show him but my news won't change if I wait. Ari's news might change, however, once he knows mine.

So I listen while he explains that he's also spoken with Director Úlfar, who's traced the call I received on the Austurleid to an anonymous prepaid phone. It's been discarded, print-free, along the highway.

"My father will still make further enquiries," he adds, "but says you should simply ignore the call. Officer Jón is very good at his job also." He turns towards Jón. "He will ask around as well."

"Miss Dales," says Officer Jón, directing the speaker of his phone at me. His deep voice is proportionate to his height yet the staccato clipping of his translator makes it grate. "Director Úlfar has asked me to ensure you have everything you need to ensure the swift recovery of your brother's body. I also want to say how very sorry I am for your loss." He takes my hand. His clasp is warm and strong and he holds it silently. I look into his eyes. Now that they're looking straight into mine, they shine as if imploring me to engage with him, and in that moment he reminds me of Mark—open and honest; intelligent and sincere. "I met your brother a couple of times," he says. "He was a great kid. If there's anything I can do to make the process easier and quicker for you, please don't hesitate to ask." As his phone finishes its translation, he angles his eyes so I can perceive his sincerity, then releases my hand.

He met my brother. Who *was* a great kid.

I fix stray strands of hair behind an ear while debating what to make of Jón's words, and whether or not this is the right moment to tell Ari about the text.

"You look worried again," Ari says, reaching to pat my arm. "Jón, tell her she need not worry."

"I tell my mother this all the time," Jón chuckles, giving Ari a look. "It makes no difference. She worries about my brother, she worries about me, about the weather, getting old, money, politics...I tell her we're all fine, that the weather's fine, that all she need do is keep reading books, doing crossword puzzles and anything else to keep her mind alert, then old age will take care of her. Do you think she listens?" He scoffs. "Of course not. She worries too much. The same is true here. Ms Dales, I do not think there will be any problems with the man who threatened you," he tries to laugh it off, "because it was not an actual threat."

"It sounded like a threat to me," I say.

"No, no," he gives me a reassuring smile. It's not as wide with teeth as Ari's, but is full of warmth and concern. He's trying to reassure not contradict me. "Director Úlfar said the man only said your parents *might* be caused further pain. Did he threaten to actually harm you?"

I roll my eyes and look away, knowing what he's about to say.

"No, he did not," Jón continues. "This is good, you see, as it means the man who threatened you is very clever—because if we did have a police force, they wouldn't be able to act without a direct threat to your well-being, which this man has avoided. So he's obviously concerned about consequences, and if he's concerned about consequences he won't act impulsively. I have to say, I also agree with Ari's father. If the man had wanted to harm you he would have already. We are a happy town here. He probably wanted only to protect us from…disruption."

I turn to look him in the eye. "I have no intention of causing any disruption."

"Then I do not think you will hear from him again." His eyes shine once more with sincerity, reminding me again of Mark.

I don't know whether I find the look comforting or creepy this time, so angle my phone towards Ari, tap and scroll through to the text threat. "Ari, please tell Officer Jón what this says."

"If you are back in Reykjavik by Friday," Ari reads aloud, "I will not kill you. Be on the Austurleid tomorrow." He lets Jón's phone translate. "Ah. When did you get this?"

"As I was leaving Doctor Emil's office." I watch Jón's expression. "Actually, you were there, weren't you?"

After my phone completes its translation there's a pause as Jón hesitates to respond. Either he doesn't realise I'm referring to him, or he's excellent at pretending. "Me? Possibly. I have been checking today's Litrúm Maps. Ari wanted to be sure the Litrúm-Hús was safe for you. He's never asked me to do that before." He gives Ari a look I don't understand. "It took me a while to figure out what he meant."

"Why Friday?" Ari asks me, ignoring Jón. "Why does the text say Friday?"

"I was hoping you could tell me."

Ari shrugs, pursing his lips to indicate he doesn't know. "Have you spoken to Director Úlfar?"

"I haven't done anything yet."

"Gott. Show me the text again." He types the mobile number displayed into his phone.

"It will probably be another discarded, print-free pay-as-you-go."

"We will still check." He types a quick text of his own and sends it. "I will take you to your accommodation now, but I want you to stay inside tonight, until Director Úlfar and I have made more enquiries."

"Okay." I don't see any harm in agreeing. I can't imagine even wanting to go anywhere tonight, especially after the call I'll have to make to my parents. "But there's no need to take me. A friend of Mark's is picking me up. Sorry, I just arranged it."

"A friend? Who?"

"Anna?" Jón guesses.

I frown. "How did you...?"

"She and your brother were very close." His tone flattens and for the first time his expression tightens. He rubs his temples. "She has been upset. If she's outside, I will go and see her."

As Jón's phone translates, Ari notices him massaging his head. "Jón, you should go home. They're getting worse, aren't they?"

Jón scrunches his eyes shut. When he opens them again, they glisten. "It's okay," he says, jerking his head from side to side to crack his neck.

"Go home," Ari says again.

Jón smiles, though this time it's strained. "It's not a migraine yet."

"Ha!" Ari scoffs at him. "You work too hard to lie well, Jón."

"Fresh air will help. And I think you will need me here for the rest of today." Jón waves me a farewell and disappears inside a scan pod.

Ari stares into space for a moment, as if thinking about Jón's last comment. He nods to himself as if making a decision.

"I should go too," I prompt. Anna is waiting.

Ari nods again, this time to me, and indicates I should enter a scan pod. Once we've both emerged from the other side he seems to have control of his thoughts again. "Becky, if you receive any more texts or phone calls, call me immediately, okay? I will not have it on silent again."

"Thank you."

"Jón is right. This man will not hurt you. But why take the chance? So, if you decide you to go out tonight or tomorrow morning, call me."

"I have to stay in tonight for Mark's briefcase, but said I'd meet

Doctor Emil at the morgue tomorrow at nine."

"Director Úlfar has made it very clear that I am to look after you, so I will take you to the morgue. I will also call you as soon as I know more about the phone number."

We move across the foyer and emerge from the Litrúm-Hús to see a pink dusk draping over Höfkállur's distant mountains. Its colour isn't as deep and rich as the sunsets I enjoyed last week in the Cayman Islands—its beauty lies more in the delicacy with which it falls across the sky like a chiffon scarf. I remember Mark telling me the light faded early in Iceland. "What time are we going to the glacier tomorrow?" I ask Ari.

"You still want to go?"

"Of course." It's the only point on which my imaginary voices and lawyer brain both agree.

Ari looks at me as if I'm crazy, yet shakes his head and smiles to himself.

As we descend the Litrúm-Hús steps, he tells me what I need to bring and what to expect of Jötunnsjökull. Looking out for Anna I only half-listen. The road beneath me dips towards the pellucid waters of the harbour and there, at the kerb, stands a woman with the flowing white hair of an elfin queen, wearing a billowing floral dress topped with a jumper. Jón's large hands are on her petite shoulders. She's looking up at him, her head on an angle, a fading smile on her lips. Behind them is what I assume is Anna's car.

It takes me a second to realise, but when I do I momentarily lose my grip on my suitcase. Anna's car is a grey four-wheel drive.

"Let me take that," Ari says, reaching for my suitcase before I drop it altogether.

I let him. Of course there must be many other grey four-wheel drives in Höfkállur. The sight unnerves me, that's all.

Clearly unworried, Ari continues chatting as we descend the steps, and soon his innate calm soothes me like a snake charmer settling a cobra. I also fall back on my logic: Anna was Mark's close friend. I can trust her. Hers isn't the car I'm looking for.

The rumble of traffic draws my attention to the road behind her, full of black, white, and navy four-wheel drives. As if to prove a point, a grey four-wheel drive roars around the side of the Litrúm-Hús. I watch it pass behind Anna, then notice her face. Watching me over Jón's shoulder, her expression implores me to hurry, her eyes intent. For the past four months Mark has lived with this woman—she can tell me what he's been doing, where he's been going and why. I speed down the steps.

Jón leans in to mumble something to Anna before backing away to light up a cigarette. Anna watches him, then opens her passenger door and pushes a greeting into her rosy-cheeked face for me.

"Okay, so, rest tonight," Ari is saying as we descend the last few steps. "Tomorrow afternoon I will get you from *The Himinn*." He moves as if to kiss me on the cheek, settles for a handshake when he notices Jón staring. "Bless," he mutters, "for now."

"Bless, Ari."

Anna springs the boot for my suitcase but Jón's the one to heave it inside, clenching his cigarette between his lips so hard its filter disappears among the dark hair of his goatee. He watches me climb into Anna's car, offering me reassuring smiles whenever our eyes meet. I should consider him charming and considerate. Of course the middle finger he raised at that boy in the corridor earlier was anything but, so the contradiction bothers me.

He moves towards Anna, saying something in Icelandic that makes her turn and gaze up at him, hands on hips. He takes her face in his big hands, talking until she covers his hands with her own. After looking into each other's eyes Jón mumbles a final comment to her, which sounds distinctly like 'I love you', then kisses her.

Embarrassed to witness such intimacy Ari and I both look away. When I slam the passenger door shut, I remember Mark telling me that Anna had a boyfriend.

"He's a right knob, though," Mark said a few months ago, when I was asking him about Anna. "I can't put my finger on why, but he is."

Now I'm here I understand the quandary. Jón is still staring at Anna, his eyes intense, his face serious. It might be romantic if there weren't other people around, waiting for them to finish. They say a few more words to each other, then Anna walks around to the driver's seat, smiling to herself and biting her bottom lip like a teenage girl with a crush. I expect to see Jón watching her; instead he's shifted his gaze to me.

I cough in surprise, then realise the reflex has nothing to do with emotion—the inside of Anna's car stinks of stale cigarettes and the odour only worsens when she starts the engine and Jón leans in through her driver's window. He expels a lungful of smoke before kissing her goodbye.

As he taps the roof of the car twice, she bats away his smoke and flashes her topaz eyes reassuringly at me. But all the questions I have for her—about Mark and Jón, Mark's thesis and life here in Höfkállur— pale into insignificance when she pulls away from the kerb and Jón takes a breath in between puffs of his cigarette, inhaling with a familiar wheeze. I thought it would take longer to find the man who threatened me on the Austurleid, but I have no doubt—it's him.

Chapter 7

Before I can get my phone out to call Ari, Anna has turned down a wide street lined with large detached houses. I know this is the way to her guesthouse, *The Himinn*, because Ari pointed this street out to me earlier. Yet I am far from feeling good about the situation. Anna is clearly in a relationship with a maniac who wants to kill me. The reassuring looks she's been giving me, and the fact she is Mark's friend, make me want to believe she has nothing to do with Jón's threats. But logic argues otherwise.

So I find Ari's number in my phone while making a comment or two about the weather...until I realise the same could be true of Ari. He seems reliable enough. I should call and tell him my revelation. But he's also Jón's friend. Telling him might make matters worse. Really I don't know any of these people.

Anna asks after my journey to Höfkállur and I answer vaguely, thinking. What are my options? Right now, in Anna's car, I simply need to cut to it—ask her a question that will tell me, in under ten seconds, whether or not I can trust her.

"So, tell me more about the time you spent with my brother." I inflect my voice with sexual undertones. "You knew him quite well, I understand?"

She scowls, confused. "Um, no. I mean, yes, of course. But not that way. I have a boyfriend!" She glances at me a few times, then realises why I asked. Her expression softens. "No, Becky. Mark and I were not lovers. I know I look good for my age," she flicks shining white hair from her forehead to feign vanity, "but even my figure couldn't have enticed that boy."

I wait for her to spell it out.

"Besides our age difference, Mark was gay. He told me."

"He did?"

"He did."

I sigh in relief. Still coming to terms with his sexuality, Mark only disclosed his orientation to people who mattered to him. In one of his last messages, he mentioned having finally told Anna. Now I know the woman beside me is who she claims to be. She was Mark's friend. She could be mine.

"And Jón?" I clear my throat, try to sound neutral. "He's your—"

"Boyfriend," Anna mumbles. "Yes."

"And does he live at *The Himinn* too?"

"No." She glances in her rear vision mirror. "That wouldn't feel right."

"Does he stay over sometimes?"

"When he insists." A private smile flickers over her lips, which she bites again as if delighting in her memory of the last time he insisted.

"Tonight?" I ask a little too quickly. If he's staying there tonight, I'll need to find somewhere else to stay while I organise his arrest.

"I've asked him not to be."

"And what about last night, did he stay with you then?"

"Yes." She cocks her head, confused. "Why?"

"Um," I hesitate, tempted to blurt out the truth. I settle for a part of it. "I had a threatening phone call this morning on the Austurleid." I watch as her expression shifts to alarm. "And a death threat via text this afternoon."

"What?" She glances at me, her body stiffens. "From who? What did it say? Are you okay?" Her foot braces against the accelerator, making us speed up. She looks at me a little too long and we veer towards a parked car.

"Hey, watch out," I clutch my seat as she swerves to avoid it.

"Sorry. I'm not the best driver. I can't believe you had a death threat, an actual death threat."

"Didn't Jón tell you," I act surprised, "when you were waiting for me?"

"No, he was too busy trying to get me to change my mind about tonight. You must feel awful."

"I'm more confused than worried, I think. I don't understand how or why my being in Höfkállur is anyone's business."

"What's Höfkállur got to do with it?"

I tell her what the caller and the text said, about Director Úlfar and what he's been saying to me, and what Jón told me beside the scan pods. "The man on the phone this morning, he sounded a little like Jón actually." I resist saying 'a lot'. "Were you with him all morning?"

"Yes. But how do you know the man sounded anything like Jón? Didn't you say he used a Word2Word translator?"

"Jón also uses Word2Word, and the man had a very distinctive wheeze."

"A wheeze?" she chuckles.

"Yes, and so does Jón."

"Well," she glances in her rear vision mirror again, "it couldn't have been. He was far too busy this morning to make any calls, let alone drive up and down the highway, trust me!" She gives me a look that confirms her insinuation.

"Oh." So the deep rasping wheeze imprinted in my memory belongs to someone else? I was so sure… "He didn't pop out at all?"

"No. But," Anna muses, "that doesn't mean someone else from the Litrúm-Hús didn't call you. You said Ari met you from the Austurleid? How did he know you were even there?"

"Director Úlfar told him."

"Isn't that a little coincidental?" She pulls into the driveway of a large white house with a russet-red roof. Attached to its white picket fence is a sign bearing a maple leaf and black letters reading '*The Himinn*'. "Ari is the one who found Mark. Did he tell you that?"

"Yes, eventually." Although the coincidence of it hasn't occurred to me until now—that the man who found my brother is the same man sent to find me.

She lets me dwell on that for a moment, then points to Mark's report, resting on my lap. "What's that?"

"Mark's autopsy report." I flick through its pages as Anna turns off her engine. "Doctor Emil wasn't very happy about giving it to me."

"Why not?" She leans in to scan it as well. When I flick to the end, she cocks her head as if expecting to see an extra page.

"What?" I ask her.

"Hm?" She pulls her keys from the ignition.

I glance over the report's conclusion. Its translation seems complete. "Is something missing?"

"Oh, um, I was looking for the signature page."

I turn over the last page. There's nothing on the back. "Should it be signed?"

"I always thought they were. I've got one myself somewhere, if you want to compare." She pulls her door handle, checking her rear vision mirror before climbing out. At the boot, she glances up and down the street.

I follow her to the kerb and check the road too. There's no one there. "You seem nervous."

"Me?" She passes me my suitcase, then pretends to look over the sky while slamming the boot shut. Really she's still surveying the street. "I can't believe it's so late, that's all." Her tone is whimsical but loud. "Will you look at that sky now? My husband always used to say the light in Ísland could play tricks."

"Your husband?"

She laughs and beckons me inside, stepping ahead to hold the door open for me. We step inside a hallway decorated with embossed white wallpaper and a crimson floral carpet. There's a staircase at the end of the corridor. Anna pauses beside a photo hanging on the wall between two doorways, one leading into a dining room, the other into a kitchen. The photo is of a stocky, thick-necked bald man with full lips. In the photo he's brandishing a giant halibut aboard an open-sea Viksund. His blue jeans and tight marl jumper indicate a muscular body. A Canadian flag flies from the ship's mast.

"My husband, Pàll," she gazes at the man. "He was also my childhood sweetheart, if you can believe in love so young. I used to visit Höfkállur every summer with my family. They were from here originally."

"But you were born in…Canada?"

"Right." She nods. "We waited until I was twenty, then I moved here. That was, what, over thirty years ago?" With her next breath, her lungs quiver. A glossy sheen comes to her eyes. "He…he died a year and a half ago. It's his autopsy report I have upstairs."

"Oh, I'm so sorry." The words feel inadequate. She must have heard them a thousand times already, just as I'm destined to hear them.

"Takk," she thanks me before turning to climb the staircase.

As I follow, my mind does some maths. "So how long have you been with Jón?" I try to keep judgment out of my voice.

"Jón moved to Höfkállur a few months after Pàll died. He was a good friend to me, a shoulder to cry on, some comfort at night." She sighs as if forgiving herself. "His eyes, they sang to me like sirens. I tell you—a woman of my age, ah, it was flattering. Still, I should never have gone with him. If I could turn back time, I would."

I'm about to ask her why when we reach the top of the stairs and she pauses.

"There was nothing left for me, after Pàll died," she gestures around the guesthouse. "What was the point of anything? Breathing, eating? Jón, he gave me hope, something else to think about. You'll find out.

Having something else to think about can save your life." I understand that already, more than she knows.

She turns to her left. "This is my room. If you need anything, please knock—day or night."

Her door ajar, it's hard to miss the massive canvas above her bed. It's a photo of her standing with Jón, his arms wrapped tight around her. Behind them a verdant field rises towards a mossy cliff face with a wide but delicate waterfall. A rainbow is visible in the spray. Anna's head rests against Jón's shoulders, her eyes closed, a smile beaming with bliss. Jón stares straight at the camera. There's no smile on his lips, rather an intensity in his expression that speaks of possession.

"Beautiful, isn't it?" Anna says, catching me staring. "Pàll hates it, of course."

"Pàll? I thought you said you didn't meet Jón until after he..."

"I didn't." She laughs at my confusion. "Don't worry, I will explain later. You must be tired. This," she heads towards a door with a ceramic black number three on it, "was Mark's room." Taking a master keycard from her pocket, she swipes its door pad and reveals a large room with plush-pile cream carpet.

A king-sized wooden bed dominates the far wall, crammed with plump white pillows that appeal to my tired limbs. Beside the window are two pink leather armchairs that curl around a glass coffee table. I'm drawn to them, so walk over and place a hand on the back of a chair. This is where Mark would have worked on his thesis, where he would have emailed and phoned me, where he would have stayed up all night comparing and contrasting the world's energy theories, analysing his first hand experiences of all of them. He studied *feng shui*, Zen Buddhism, *chi* force and Taoism in Asia. He investigated the spiritual journeys of Navajo and Mandan Indians in America. But Iceland was where he planned to isolate the one element he said they all had in common.

"Energy. The numinous. It's both, together," he told me last weekend. He sounded so excited.

Anna taps a series of commands into the door pad and shows me how to swipe my keycard to preset it to this room if I want to lock it. "Most of my overseas guests prefer to lock their rooms. Habit. I'll go find Pàll's autopsy report. Coffee?"

"Sounds good."

"I'll meet you in the kitchen."

I throw some toiletries around the ensuite sink, hang up my skirts, then grab Mark's autopsy report and my phone. If Jón isn't the man who called or followed me, I'm safe enough here tonight, and my next priorities will be to get some sleep, so I can think straight tomorrow, and to ask Anna about Höfkállur. Anonymous and faceless, I have no real way of recognising the man who apparently wants me dead if I remain here after tomorrow. But Anna has known Höfkállur all her life—she might know someone or something.

A fresh coffee aroma greets me as I descend the stairs. Entering the grey and white kitchen, I see Anna swiping the barcode of an empty packet of ground Arabica beans across the sensor on her silver fridge. On the marble-topped kitchen island a steaming cafetière is brewing.

"Milk?" Anna asks. "Sugar?"

"Just milk please." Milk is twenty calories extra, but I need a boost. So I add twenty-five to my calorie count, then perch on a stool beside the island while Anna retrieves mugs and a sugar pot from her cupboards. Beside the cafetière is a plate of cookies that smell of cinnamon, as well as a typed document that looks similar to Mark's autopsy report, only without the translation comment boxes. I stare at its incomprehensible letters and wait for Anna to pour the coffee.

"Biscuit?" Anna nudges the plate towards me.

"No, thanks." My tummy grumbles in defiance but I ignore it. The hunger will pass once my coffee settles the gnawing. Giving into temptation this late in the day will only make me feel bad. Instead I imagine the warmth of cinnamon on my tongue and breathe in the spice to supplement my imagination. It doesn't satisfy my hunger, but it satisfies me.

"Is this Pàll's report?" I ask after stealing a sip of my coffee.

Anna slides her document across the island.

I turn to the last page. An inky blue signature is scrawled above a line, under which is the printed name 'Doctor Emil' and his title, 'Höfkállur Dánardómstjóri'. I check Mark's report. Of course there will be no signature, Doctor Emil printed out a fresh copy and didn't sign it before handing it over. There's also no signature strip. I look over the documents. Anna's autopsy report is on Doctor Emil's letterhead, mine isn't. "He must have printed on the wrong paper."

Anna shrugs. "Didn't you say he was reluctant to print it out at all?"

I frown. Even if Doctor Emil used the wrong paper, the signature strip should still have printed out with the rest of the document. I think back to my lawyer days. "Maybe it's still a draft?" Although it seems complete enough, and Doctor Emil didn't mention anything about it being a draft.

"Did Doctor Emil say he performed the autopsy himself?" Anna asks.

I try to remember. "I don't know. Why?"

"It's probably nothing."

"What?"

Anna jiggles her head like she's debating something. "Well, maybe he didn't perform the autopsy himself, and that's why he didn't sign it? He might have asked one of his juniors to do it."

"A junior?" A growl of nausea churns the coffee in my stomach. I stare at the two reports, willing them to tell me what else Doctor Emil might be hiding. Ideas rise but slip away before I can fully grasp them. I consider eating a biscuit, to give my brain the energy it must be craving to function properly, yet resist. The caffeine will kick in soon. I take another sip of coffee and focus on the reports.

Why was Doctor Emil so reluctant to give me Mark's report? Was it because it's still in draft, because some junior performed the autopsy and he didn't want to tell me, or because of something else? What other differences are there between the two deaths, Mark's and Pàll's. *Two?* Two reports? "Hold on. Anna, why was Pàll even given an autopsy? Didn't he die of natural causes?"

"No." Anna's eyes settle on the rim of her mug. "He was crossing the road. It was winter, very icy. A car tried to stop, there were marks on the road. It was the last unsolved hit and run in Höfkállur."

"Oh, I'm sorry to hear that. They never found the person who did it?"

"They, um," she struggles to finish her sentence, "they never looked. Never reviewed security camera footage. Never advertised for leads. The MUR said the driver would eventually come forward to clear their conscience."

"But no one did?"

She shakes her head, looks up at me. "That's how I met Jón. He was the town's new MUR officer." She looks away to dispel a memory. "He was going to help, but..."

"Never got around to it?"

"At first I thought it was because he didn't want to make waves." She looks back up. "He's an ambitious man and was new up here. Then I figured it was because he wanted more from me. But after, later...still nothing. He's got his reasons of course, he always does." Her expression lifts in realisation. "Becky, when you met Jón earlier at the Litrúm-Hús, what did he say about the man who called and threatened you?"

"I thought you said Jón was in bed with you this morning?"

"He was. But you said something that's got me thinking, something Jón said when you met him."

I summarise the conversation for her again.

"Disruption?" She lingers on the word. "Hmm, what kind of disruption could you cause, Becky, if you wanted to?"

"I don't know. Professionally, I suppose I could investigate the town's new legal systems and find fault in them, if I were so inclined."

"Which would be a problem for Director Úlfar, given he's deep in negotiations to sell the Sannlitró-Völva to the United States, Europe, Japan...Australia."

"He is? He never said."

"He hasn't announced it officially. Dating an MUR officer has its benefits, you know." She winks at me. "Still, you could have come here in six months' time and he'd still have been in negotiations with some of them, other countries too. So that's not it, at least not entirely. Let's think—what's brought you to Höfkállur today, specifically?"

I feel like she's leading me. I'm happy to let her if it gives me answers. "My brother's death."

"And what disruption could that cause?"

"Um, I don't know."

"I think you do." She leans forward and waits.

I purse my lips, reluctant to say what's been in the back of my mind since Director Úlfar called me yesterday. Anna's right, I could cause an element of disruption over Mark's death, if the doubts I've been having about his sudden hike alone were realised. I just don't want to admit that possibility yet.

I sip my coffee. How much longer can I ignore what's been bugging me since Director Úlfar—the director and press secretary of Iceland's information and intelligence bureau—phoned to tell me about my brother, since he met me from the Flybus in the middle of the night, since Doctor Emil tried so hard not to give me the autopsy report?

Anna raises her eyebrows.

I clear my throat and put my mug down. "In my experience, governments don't usually offer to pay for repatriation unless they're directly responsible for the death in question."

"Have they offered to fly Mark's body home then?"

"Twice. Anna, did Mark say anything to you about hiking at that glacier?"

"Nothing."

"He didn't mention anything about going, didn't talk to you about hiking in general, or leave a message for me?"

"No." She looks at me as if willing me to understand something. Clearly she thinks the circumstances of my brother's death are suspicious. As do I. As I've done for two days now. I can't bear to think exactly how suspicious those circumstances might be: criminal negligence, gross negligence, manslaughter...murder? But if the government's involved, I'll have little chance of discovering what—if they're somehow responsible, they won't want me finding out.

Step by step, I remind myself. "Did Mark even mention anyone who was thinking of going hiking?"

"He didn't really know anyone in Höfkállur well enough to go hiking with them. Why, what are you thinking?" She sips her coffee, doesn't take her eyes off me.

"I'm not sure."

"Not sure about what?"

"I've never been interested in conspiracy theories." I've had no need.

"But?"

"But," I say quickly, "they're claiming it was an accident yet Úlfar's still offering to pay and... Could Mark have gone to this glacier as part of some government experiment or expedition?"

She shrugs. "Anything's possible."

"That's what Mark used to say."

"I know."

"Okay." I make a decision. "At the very least, something's wrong with this." I point at the autopsy report. "Do you know where the hospital stores its...people?"

"You mean its morgue? Yes. Pàll stayed there. Why?"

I stand. "I'm going to see Mark, in the flesh."

Anna looks at the clock on the wall. "You don't mean now? There won't be anyone there."

"Exactly. I want to see my brother, all of him—not just the bits of him some government official is happy for me to see. And the morgue won't be locked, will it? Nothing in Höfkállur is locked."

"Why not simply ask for some privacy in the morning?"

"I can't wait until morning, Anna. Today is Wednesday." I think aloud. "Director Úlfar asked me to return to Reykjavík by Friday. The text threat demanded I be back on the Austurleid tomorrow. Doctor Emil wanted me gone as soon as possible. Something's happening in Höfkállur either tomorrow or Friday, something a lawyer like me shouldn't see. So if I'm not on the Austurleid tomorrow someone is going to come looking for me. I have to examine Mark now. If I wait, someone could tamper with his body, or lose him entirely." That could have been the very phone call Doctor Emil went to make when I left his office this afternoon. "All I need is a quick look. Take some photographs. It won't take long. I won't be able to sleep on this." Not anymore. "It has to be now. People are keeping things from me, Anna, and I need to find out what. Given what you've shown me here," I tap the reports, "my brother's body is clearly the best place to start."

"It...it's not a good idea, Becky." She pushes her empty mug to the centre of the island.

"Good and bad are just concepts, Anna." Although I've never fully believed that until now. "They're meaningless words people use to control others." Arguments Mark once used flow from my memory. "Religions use the words good and bad. Law uses the words right and wrong. Science uses positive and negative. They're all just words."

Anna shakes her head, speechless. A white curl falls over her face.

"Mark said you believe in the *Heimspeki*?"

"Passionately. But..."

"The *Heimspeki* says that, although staying positive can *include* being 'good' and doing the 'right' thing, it can also include committing a wrong *for a very good reason*. Like lying to a murderer who wants to find their next victim. Did Mark tell you about that?"

Anna's expression softens and she nods to confirm that, yes, he told her the conundrum that explained an aspect of his thesis: if a murderer were to demand you tell them the location of their next victim, you couldn't tell them the truth, you'd have to lie. But religion says that lying is bad and, if you were in a courtroom lying would also be wrong. Yet in this situation, lying could be neither bad nor wrong because otherwise your actions could lead to an innocent's death. Thus, according to the *Heimspeki*, lying would actually be a positive thing to do.

"I have good reason for going tonight," I tell Anna; I tell myself, "and Mark said such acts produce the same amounts of positivity and negativity, Yin and Yang, and there's nothing wrong with being equal, because then a single act of kindness can tip your equality towards being positive *in the majority*." Mark said a majority was all that mattered. "So, my going to the morgue is neither 'good' nor 'bad'." The more I say it, the more I'm convinced. "It's simply what I must do."

"No, Becky, you don't understand," Anna finally tells me. "You don't need to convince me going to the morgue tonight is, most probably, a positive thing to do. I don't even think your life is in that much danger—Director Úlfar couldn't have an Australian brother and sister die in the same town in the same week without attracting major international attention. It's just…I'm worried about Jón." Her expression fades into the beseeching look she gave me outside the Litrúm-Hús, only this time I'm close enough to realise my mistake. Her expression wasn't pleading with me before—it was fearful. It is fearful. She's both infatuated with her boyfriend, and afraid of him.

I catch the welling panic in her eyes as they flit across my face, searching for protection. A sour taste comes into my mouth. I've never really understood women who insist on staying with men who frighten them. Then again, I once stayed with someone who made me think of myself as worthless, and when he left me—knowing I believed life was nothing without him—I was frightened too. I shouldn't judge. Having met Jón, and seen how charming he can be one minute, how intense the next, I understand both his appeal and the terror of not knowing which way he could flip. "You don't need to come with me," I tell her, "all I need from you is directions."

"But," Anna lowers her voice, "Jón said you asked for Mark's briefcase to be delivered later."

"It still can be delivered. When it comes, tell them I'm asleep and take it for me."

She shakes her head. "Jón knows when I'm lying. He'll figure it out, and you said you didn't want *any* officials interrupting you at the morgue. He always follows up on his hunches."

"Wait, Jón's going to bring Mark's briefcase here himself?"

Anna nods. "That's why he was trying to get me to change my mind about staying here tonight, because he's coming here anyway." She pauses to think. "Yes, he definitely said he'd see me later."

"What time did he say?" I glance at the clock.

"He didn't. He usually texts when he's on his way."

"What time does he finish work?"

"About now. Though of course now he has to collect Mark's briefcase from the hospital, and he said he might eat dinner there. They have a really good canteen. He made some sarcastic remark about my not letting him eat here. Do you think you could be back before 8pm?"

"How far away is the hospital?"

"A ten minute walk."

"I should easily be able to get there and back within an hour, as long as I don't get lost."

"I've got a map, I'll show you. Once you're at the hospital, use the service entrance at the back. It's the quickest way to the morgue—it's down some stairs past the kitchen and laundry."

"Okay." I throw back the rest of my coffee.

She puts our mugs in the sink. "The morgue door's next to the service lift. Don't worry, the hospital is very small, you won't get lost. What about dinner?"

"Not hungry. I had a big lunch."

"Okay then, I'll go get that map."

"I'll get my jacket."

We both race up the stairs. At the top, Anna dashes one way, I dash the other.

"Becky," she calls from her room as I'm stuffing my arms into my jacket. "Would you come here a second?"

I fold Mark's autopsy report into my bag, grab a scarf to protect me from the cold night I know will be waiting for me, then hurry towards her voice. Poking my head around her bedroom door, I see she's standing by the window with the light off. "What's up?"

She points out the window.

I join her and follow her finger towards a black sedan parked opposite *The Himinn*. A lone figure sits behind its steering wheel. "I thought someone followed us from the Litrúm-Hús," she mutters.

"It's not a neighbour waiting for someone?"

"I don't recognise the car."

"And you know all the cars in Höfkállur?"

"He's been there so long the back windows have steamed up."

I suck a chunk of cheek flesh between my teeth and rock my molars back and forth over it. Why would someone have bothered to follow us here? I'm sure it's common knowledge I'm staying at *The Himinn*.

"It could be someone sent to watch over you." Anna steps back from the window and draws the curtains. "Maybe you should stay after all, go to the morgue in the morning?"

"I can't. I need to see Mark now. I have to go." Saying the words aloud reminds me of something.

Ari.

Ari said to call him if I changed my mind about going out. I step away from the window, find his number on my phone and dial. Mark wanted me to go with my instincts more, trust gut feelings. It's time to test his theory.

"Who are you calling?" Anna asks.

"Ari."

"I don't think that's a good idea."

But Ari's already answering. I apologise for calling. "There's some-one outside *The Himinn*, watching us."

"Where? Now? Are you okay?"

"I'm fine," I hear him rush into action: keys jangle and material rustles like he's pulling on a jacket, "we're watching him from Anna's room."

"Gott. Stay there, lock the door. I am on my way. Be there in ten minutes. You have a torch?"

"Anna will have one. Anna," I whisper, "do you have a torch?"

She goes to her bedside table, yanks open the bottom drawer.

"She's getting one," I tell Ari.

"Gott. Go to the window and point it into the road. Turn it on and off three times fast, three times slow, three times fast. A man will come. Do not let him in unless he knocks the same code on your door. His name is, um, wait, it's here somewhere."

I hear Ari drop something. "If we're signalling to a neighbour, Anna will know their name."

"It's not a neighbour," he says. "They're in a car on the road."

"In a black sedan?" I ask him.

"Já." It sounds as though he's trying to find something. "You see them?"

Anna goes to pass me her flashlight. I dismiss it with a shake of my hand. "Ari, do you have someone watching *The Himinn*?"

"Já. Point the torch…"

"Ari, the man in the black sedan, that's who I'm calling about. You sent someone to watch me?"

Silence. His fumbling stops.

Anna rolls her eyes.

"Ari?"

"Director Úlfar insisted," Ari mumbles down the phone. "He didn't want to take any chances with your safety."

"With my safety?"

"From any activists."

"Right, okay. You should have told me."

"I'm sorry, I didn't think…I have his name now if you want it. Gunnar Eyjólfsson."

"Gunnar Eyjólfsson?" I repeat, certain I recognise the name.

"Já, he was very keen to take the first shift. You see, people in Höfkállur care about you too."

Anna frowns, then flaps her hands as it comes to her. "Gunnar," she whispers, "he's Doctor Emil's assistant."

Of course he is. "I bet he was keen," I mutter.

"Pardon?" Ari says.

"Nothing. I'll see you tomorrow afternoon. I'm not going to the morgue in the morning now."

"Oh, okay. Gunnar is there if you need him, or if you want to go anywhere," Ari says before we hang up, "as am I."

I put my phone in my pocket, wind my scarf around my neck and zip up my jacket. "Map please." I hold my hand out to Anna.

"You're still going?" She passes it to me, open on the correct page.

"Absolutely. Unless you think Doctor Emil's assistant offered to take first watch out of the goodness of his heart?" I turn and jog back down the stairs.

"Wait!" Anna calls, catching up to me. "Use the back door. If you go through my neighbour's garden, then out the street behind, he won't see you. Here." She shows me where to go on her map.

"If Gunnar moves, call me." I tell her, moving into the kitchen. "Or if you hear from Jón."

I open Anna's back door and look out. Her white picket fence continues around from the front to border a long lawn. It's low enough for me to climb over but Anna comes to help anyway. Once I'm over she hurries back inside, gives me a nervous wave and closes the door.

The second she's gone, I realise I'm probably not making the wisest decision after all. It isn't theft to take information that already belongs to you. But if I'm this desperate to know whether something underhanded has happened to Mark's body, or if the government is somehow involved, how desperate might others be to ensure I don't find out?

I tiptoe past Anna's neighbouring house, bent low like a criminal even though there are no lights on inside. I reach the road parallel to Anna's and survey it up and down, peering into its shadows. There's no movement. The rest of my walk will be along main roads, so I hurry towards the sound of traffic, so fast that individual houses disappear in a blur.

Once on the main road, I glance over my shoulder every few paces to check for black sedans. There are none, though every time a vehicle zooms past I flinch. At the same time, the cacophony of their passing sounds so much like gushing water it serves only to remind me why I am doing this.

Mark.

I never thought the connection Mark and I had could get stronger. It did, though, after what happened with Riley. Every public holiday, we would synchronise activities. I got to know all his friends a little better; he got to know those I had left. We planned our New Years' Eve together. We read each other's research papers. We ate hangover breakfasts together. He knew Mum and Dad were a little unforgiving about my tenacity, so stuck up for me whenever the subject came up. I went to gay clubs with him and danced with abandon. We were there for each other, best friends. And I was supposed to find that best friend in Höfkállur. I was supposed to prove Director Úlfar wrong. Director Úlfar wasn't wrong, though I haven't had a moment yet to absorb that fact. Now I do, the thought weighs me down until my step thuds into the tarmac and I fade into a freezing cold daydream that splashes from boulder to boulder in some desolate river.

Mark is dead.

I am here alone, without him.

Busy traffic at junctions jars me into examining my immediate reality, but once safe on the footpath again my mind reels back to the wet coldness where I imagine Mark spending the last few moments of his life. I shiver. I've lost my only brother. Mum and Dad have lost their only son. Mark, my best friend, is gone.

"If you do not want to cause your parents further pain," the man on the Austurleid said, "turn around."

The chill of my daydream smashes into a wall of ice, making me gasp. As it ricochets backwards, I see my reflection mirrored. Slowly my clone fizzles into a likeness of Mark that thumps against the glass until I'm looking into my brother's brown eyes.

Am I walking into a cold grave of my own? I ask the reflection.

A wave crashes onto a pebble beach somewhere and I hear shells and stones clattering against each other as the swell retreats. It reminds me of the sounds I heard on the Austurleid, by the Viking sculpture and in Doctor Emil's office. I try to remember what the imaginary voices said. Only fragments come to me, *finish reading, let's go, to the glacier…* Why am I even hearing voices? Should I be going to the morgue in this state?

The ocean surges back up the sand.

Really? That sure?

A passing tipper truck sounds its horn as if trying to parp-parp me back to the highway. I'm climbing a small hill and beyond its brow, down its other side, is a building that can only be Höfkállur Hospital. Sat in a block of coarse yellow grass, the building's tall brown walls and vibrant jade roof resemble a tree, which would have been in keeping with its surroundings had it been set among the leafy stringybarks of

Kakadu. Here in a tree-less Iceland, set apart from the rest of the town, it stands out like an abstract Dali creation in the centre of a pale pastel Monet monotone. Just like Anna said it would.

I descend into its parking lot and hear a car reverse out of its spot, another car swing through the exit. Although it's not dark yet, headlights pan across me like a prison searchlight. A nightshift nurse walks into the emergency department at the right side of the building, where an ambulance sits waiting. I look away but the image triggers memories I'd rather not have right now.

I am back in Sydney, Mark is stopping in to check on me but he's too late. I see him crying, panicking, calling an ambulance then waiting, tears streaming. The vision fills me with something I cannot bear to feel.

Responsibility.

I shake the memory loose but it leaves me with a certainty that makes me straighten my back and walk with resolve. This isn't a bad idea, it's the best decision I've ever made. Mark would have done the same for me.

I pass the well-lit main entrance, step onto grass and head for the shadowy left side of the building. The service entrance is at the back. It's the quickest way to the morgue.

Chapter 8

As I approach the tall brown walls of Höfkállur Hospital, I take comfort in the fact that my confident stride will convince passers-by that I belong here this late. I don't want anyone thinking I'm lost or doing something negative. In fact, I don't want anyone noticing me at all. I glance behind me, notice the silent windows of the factory across the road from the hospital—all black with their reflection of coming night—and speed up.

Once at the side of the building, I check behind me once more. Looming beyond the factory, a rise of lemon and grey smudges suggest the now barely visible hills that sit on Höfkállur's outskirts. There are no black sedans or grey four-wheel drives in sight. So I pull my scarf high around my neck, stride around the corner and head for the back of the hospital. It's then that Anna texts me. The ping makes me jump.

Her text is easy to read on the glowing screen, yet its words confuse me. Only after I re-read her message do I realise she's communicating in code.

"Hope I didn't wake u," her text reads. "I've been looking out 4 Mark's watch, like u asked, but don't know where it is. Sorry. Perhaps it will turn up. Sometimes things do, when you least expect them!"

I glean two things from this. First, the black sedan 'watch'-ing *The Himinn* has left. Second, Anna believes someone is monitoring her phone. Why else would she be texting in code?

My heart pounds a little faster, heavier. There's only one reason Gunnar Eyjólfsson would leave *The Himinn*—he knows I'm not there anymore. I rush down the length of the building, ducking under every window and treading as softly as I can on the grass to evade detection—by Jón, Gunnar, or anyone. I have to get to Mark before anyone else does.

Concealed by the faintness of twilight, it isn't long before I'm sneaking around the back of the hospital to see a large dimly lit gap in the wall ahead. An access road disappears inside the gap, rising up a ramp. A grey roller door sits above it, making it look like a loading bay. A curtain of steam billows out from a nearby vent, sending a fishy aroma towards me. It sets off my hunger again. My body knows it hasn't eaten since breakfast on the Austurleid and it's not happy. Standing upright, now that there are no windows, I feel a familiar wooziness and reach for the wall as my sense of balance sways. I hate this light-headed feeling. Why can't my body be more efficient with the calories it gets? I rub my eyes to bring my brain into focus, and hear Icelandic voices chattering somewhere, pots clanging. The hospital kitchen must be nearby.

Eager to get inside, I feel my way towards the gap. Thankfully, the loading bay lights are turned off and only a thin light stretches out from the building. Stealth would be a lot harder under stark fluorescent lighting.

After deviating around a thin greenhouse sheltering soily sacks and shelves of plastic pots, I reconnect with the wall and approach the bay. Listening and looking out for people or sudden movements, I don't notice the wheelbarrow or the shears sticking out of it until I'm tripping over its wheel and my right thigh slices across its metal points. A spade clatters after me, clashing loud against the concrete as I trip to the ground.

Fuck!

I grip my thigh and clench my teeth and eyes tight against the sting of air invading my wound. The cut should only be slight, but its initial sharpness intensifies my wooziness and my head spins. I listen while I wait for it to settle. My collision hasn't disrupted the rhythm of pot-clanging and people-chatting. Still I wait another minute before sitting up, shaking clumps of soil and plant fragments from my aching palms, then seeking out my injury.

My thigh throbs. My hands are sore but not bleeding. Instead there's a long gash in my skirt, where lines of red weigh down the fabric. I wince as I peel back the skirt's petticoats to see a shallow gash bleeding steadily and skin bruising purple already. I've been lucky though, my thick skirt has borne the brunt of the damage.

I push the sides of the cut together and hold it firm with a pinch while rummaging in my bag for a Band Aid. I have one, but it's small. It won't cover the entire wound. So I use it to keep the sides of skin together then tie my scarf over the top.

More haste, less speed, I think to myself with annoyance.

Once finished, I stand and hobble towards the bay. There's still no one on the ramp so I step up into the shadows. Light spills from a double doorway up ahead. Through it, trays of crockery rattle, glasses clink, and food sizzles. I let my eyes grow accustomed to the light. I can see a long white corridor with orange wall guards. Periodic doorways. Signs hanging from the ceiling are all in Icelandic.

I creep towards what I assume is the kitchen door and peek through its hinges to see metal counters covered with food, stoves packed with bubbling pots and frantic white-uniformed cooks chopping and stirring. Heat from the cooking coats me, smothering any chill from my skin before passing and rising out the loading bay entrance. Everyone inside is busy with their work, apart from a man in a suit tasting something from a pot.

I take a breath then duck past, glancing inside on my way. Noticing the light brown colour of the man's suit, I remember Anna saying that Jón might eat at the hospital. Is that him?

Something squeaks to one side of the kitchen doorway so I hobble quickly away, but don't run—the sound of someone running would bring unwanted attention. Plus, my thigh is smarting with each hobble.

"It's down some stairs past the kitchen and laundry," Anna told me.

I pass a second doorway, closed and dark, then see two openings opposite one another—one corridor and one stairwell.

More squeaks. I check over my shoulder. A rectangular shadow appears in the kitchen doorway: a food trolley emerging into the corridor. I power ahead, reaching the stairwell as the food trolley's front wheels crash over the doorway's sill. The stairs are straight and short and I can see a basement corridor leading away from them.

I hurry down, holding onto the handrail like I do when I'm worried my starved muscles might give way. They shake as I descend into the darkness below, but I'm used to that.

A second set of wheels crashes into the corridor above and the trolley squeaks towards me. Individual food trays clatter on their runners. I hear voices too, deep and male. The door to the morgue is supposed to be near some service lift. Halfway down the corridor is a large silver glint. With one hand on the wall, I push towards it as a man's deep voice hums a familiar tune, hopefully indicating a complete disinterest in my presence. As it gets louder I near the door, reach it, slam into it and am relieved to find it moving with me.

Just as I'm steadying it from banging shut, his trolley crosses the stairwell, followed by footsteps that fit the allegro tempo of his hum—

the spring opening to Vivaldi's *Four Seasons*. His pace doesn't falter, though a sharp scraping noise screeches across the floor of the main corridor as he turns the trolley, scratching its caster wheels across the polished concrete.

I exhale in relief. I don't want anyone to find me here—not a member of the kitchen staff, not a receptionist, a hospital orderly, or someone 'watching over' me. All I want is to look at my brother in peace, alone, without having to convince anyone of my 'positive' reasons for hiding in the dark. I don't even know how I'd explain that if I had to.

Back in Sydney, when I was a lawyer, I often had to talk my way out of difficult situations. Clients overcharged by incompetent accounts clerks would need sincere apologies. Unethical lawyers on the 'other side' would need to be pressured into relinquishing confidential documents my secretary sent them by mistake. Power-hungry court officers would need flattery before giving me last-minute access to court documents forgotten by an inefficient assistant. My greatest asset in such situations was my innocence.

Tonight there's no one to blame for my sneaking around but me.

I search the darkness and notice tiny lights beaming steadily on the wall opposite me. Apart from them there's nothing but black. I blink and push my eyes to see more. Only a blind fuzz stares back. I stretch a hand out to my right and take a step sideways, keeping my back to the wall. A high-pitched hum buzzes around the room and there's a chemical pungency in the air that reminds me of…pickles.

Preservatives?

I take another step. My thigh slams into something, right on my cut. I muffle my cry by clenching my teeth. I need some light. I pull out my phone, turn on its display and shine its glow around the room.

Two long stainless steel counters run along the right-hand and far sides of the room—I collided with the edge of one. Hung over two sinks are retractable spotlights. There are no instruments anywhere, though plenty of cupboards and drawers under the counters. In the centre of the room is an empty mortuary slab and, on the wall opposite me, six mortuary cabinets.

Mark.

I grope my way towards the cabinets, keeping a hand on the wall to my left. After the doors, I expect to feel the room's internal window, but my hand makes contact with a smooth reflective surface. I shine my phone over the expanse. The reflective surface isn't glass—it's a wall-mounted x-ray film viewer.

And if there's no window…

Flashing my phone before me, I change direction and feel my way over to the spotlight furthest from the door. I switch it on, angle its beam against the back wall to send a ghostly glow around the room, then hurry back to the mortuary cabinets.

Each of the cabinet's six doors has a tiny light indicating occupation. Only the bottom two glow. I tug on the handles. Neither of them move. I give them a yank. The cabinet doesn't even quiver. Nothing in Höfkállur should be locked...

I search the cabinet's frame. At the top is a small panel with a keypad.

Fuck!

I take a step back to survey the cabinets and think. Leaning against the mortuary slab behind me, I realise there must be a host of sharp instruments somewhere. I examine the door seals. If I can find a sharp, thin instrument I might be able to pry open the cabinet doors.

I head for the cupboards and am mid-stride when the morgue doors swing open. I jump so hard my heart pinches inside my chest. A figure glides into the room.

"You won't be able to open them," a voice hisses.

I back away from the figure, fumbling in my bag for anything I might use as a weapon. All I find is a pen.

"They have an automatic locking system." The figure moves around the mortuary slab. "Looks like no one's thought to disable it. Habit." The figure reaches inside a pocket, retrieves their phone and shakes off the hood of a green and white jumper. I recognise her flowing white hair.

"Anna?" I press a hand against my breastbone to calm my heart. "What are you doing here?"

"Ólaf called, to see how you were. He's thoughtful like that. He told me about the mortuary cabinets, said you'd find out soon enough anyway. I'm supposed to call him when I get here; he's looking for the codes. We didn't want you hurting yourself."

"Hurting myself?"

"We figured you wouldn't let a simple lock panel defeat you, not once you were here. He said he'd rather hack into someone's computer than have you hacking through metal doors." She presses the call button on her phone.

"But," I don't get it, "isn't hacking into someone's computer a negative thing to do?"

"Not if it's for a good reason." She winks at me, holds up a finger. "Já, halló, Ólaf." She speaks a single Icelandic sentence before gesturing for me to go to the mortuary cabinets. "Zero, three, seven, nine. Hash. Then the number you want to open. Okay. Takk, Ólaf." She hangs up.

"That was brief," I say, typing the numbers into the keypad.

"I don't like using mobile phones."

"I noticed." Hearing a clunk, I tug at one of the doors with a glowing occupation light. It opens to reveal a pair of chilled feet. Wrinkled with age spots, I don't need to pull the inside tray out or check the toe tag. The feet are too old to be Mark's. I type the numbers into the keypad again and pull open the second door—the only other cabinet occupied. These feet are longer, younger. I don't have to check this toe tag either, but do anyway.

Mark Dales.

I give the tray a firm yank. Its rollers rattle. A small fluorescent tube flickers on inside the drawer, illuminating a cold body covered with a white sheet. I pull the sheet from my brother's sleeping face, down to his waist.

"Oh Mark."

Without any software to disguise the brutality of death, I see now how red and purple his nose is with bruising, the many cuts that slash his rubbery pale skin and, from the side, how deformed his jaw is from swelling.

Anna comes to stand beside me. "Oh love, I'm sorry. Ólaf said to take it easy."

But this was never going to be easy.

The more I stare at Mark's bashed body, the more details from his report come into focus—until I understand exactly how my brother died. I can even see it. A multitude of bruises cover his arms and torso: I see his body slamming against underwater boulders, him struggling against the current. Red patches show where his ribs fractured: I see him trapped under water, resisting the urge to breathe. A stained Y-incision touches his shoulders before flowing down his sternum like a red ribbon: someone has sawn through his chest to examine his waterlogged lungs. His body smells of raw chicken and ethanol, yet I still want to hold him close.

"Are you okay?" Anna asks.

I sense her moving away but can't pry my eyes from my brother. My focus is so intense the room behind me begins to rotate. I blink to refocus, feel myself drifting forward and back, like I'm on a dive, suspended by water and weightless above dark depths. Perhaps it's still yesterday and really I'm floating above the Cayman Trench, daydreaming while I dive. I look for the unfathomable abyss so deep beneath me that yesterday it made me feel as though I were falling.

"Plummets four miles into the heart of the Caribbean Sea," my dive guide's face looms large. "These islands are the tips of underwater mountains..."

I survey the darkness below my gliding fins. There's nothing but blue merging into black. The vast emptiness comes crashing down on me like a collapsing black hole.

"Just in time," Anna says.

Something taps against the insides of my knees as I fall backwards. Anna has dragged a chair behind me.

I crash into it.

"Take a minute." She pats my shoulder, though it also feels more like she's steadying herself. "It's a very," her voice trembles, "difficult thing to see."

I cradle my head on my knees.

Anna takes a step back and leans against the mortuary slab, taking long slow breaths herself. For a moment we're both silent. Then she moves close again. "What happened?" She's pointing at the blood on my skirt.

"I had a misunderstanding with a wheelbarrow. I'm fine." I sit upright, then instantly reel backwards.

"Concentrate on breathing." She opens and shuts drawers until she finds a first-aid kit. Minutes later, there's a line of Leukostrips across my gash and Anna's stuffing my scarf into her bag. The purple bruising on my leg has blackened and spread. It doesn't matter. My eyes wander back to my brother to examine individual wounds on his body. I ease Doctor Emil's report from my bag and squint at the anatomic summary in the dim light. I forgot to bring my reading glasses.

"Mark was long-sighted too. Want me to read it?" Anna suggests, pressing an adhesive dressing over the Leukostrips.

I hand over the report then stare at my brother's body.

"Lung pathology," Anna begins, clearing her throat. "The lining of the aorta was stained; lungs waterlogged with freshwater and heavy with oedema. The conclusion says such findings are consistent with asphyxia due to drowning." She pauses to check on me.

"Go on."

"Brain pathology. No gross or microscopic evidence of head trauma, intracranial injury, cerebral oedema, cervical cord injury, retinal haemorrhage, or mechanical asphyxia. Evidence was found of transient unconsciousness prior to death but it says that such findings are also consistent with asphyxia due to drowning. Trauma to torso.

Multiple abrasions and contusions on torso, multiple rib fractures and a fracture of the right scapula and clavicle. It also concludes that such injuries are consistent with river drowning among sunken boulders."

As far as I can tell from the front of Mark's body, the report is accurate. What about his back? I lean on the body tray and peer underneath.

"What are you doing?"

"I want to see if there are any injuries to his back."

Anna tucks the report under her arm and, after hesitating to touch him, places her hands on Mark's hip to roll him towards her. "Anything?"

"Not really." His back is crisscrossed with abrasions and contusions. "It's the same as his front."

"Okay," she lets Mark rest again and returns to the report, "so the final section is facial trauma. Nasal and jaw fractures, multiple abrasions and contusions on forehead, cheeks and chin, all sustained while submerged under the Skepnasá River by colliding with one or more large sunken boulders."

I tilt my head back and stare at the ceiling. Everything in the report is evident on his body. Yet there has to be more to this. I search his face for answers; reach forward to brush aside his hair. Mark was always very particular about his hair but rolling his body has disturbed a matted patch on the side of his head. I untangle it. Grainy black flakes fall as I ease the strands apart. They look like...dried blood?

"What's this?" I stand and part his hair to reveal a gaping flesh wound. "Correct me if I'm wrong, Anna, but isn't this head trauma?" I take Mark's autopsy report from her.

No gross or microscopic evidence of head trauma, it reads.

"Looks like head trauma to me," Anna says.

"Then I think we've found what we weren't supposed to find." I double-check the report. "If we're seeing a head trauma, why isn't it listed here?"

Chapter 9

Anna points to her watch as I go against her advice and call Doctor Emil from my phone. I have to speak to him, right away. This isn't something I can hold in. I have taken photographs; they're concrete proof. Time to find out who's to blame and for what.

The line rings then goes to his message bank.

"Doctor Emil," I mutter, unable to stop my voice shaking. "I am...livid. I am staring at my brother's head and looking at a head injury, a head injury not listed in your autopsy report. Why? You said your performance reviews are 'outstanding' every year, that you've never had an autopsy report questioned? Well, I don't know what the opposite of 'outstanding' is in your industry, but unless you look into this injury first thing tomorrow morning, I'll make sure your next performance reviews are the worst in the history of Icelandic pathology. I've taken photographs and they've already uploaded to my cloud, time-stamped, so you'd best get onto this fast. Why isn't this head injury in your report?"

I hang up and pace along the far wall of the morgue. No one should have to take photographs of their dead brother's unreported head wound. No one. My hands ball into fists, gripping my phone as if the squeezing will change things.

"We should go," Anna whispers, covering Mark with the sheet.

"No. Stop."

I rush to my brother and pull him into my arms. Pressing my cheek to his, I remember us as kids. Cheek-to-cheek we'd stumble around, one arm wrapped around the other's shoulders. Giggling, we'd stagger up to our parents chanting: 'together, together; we'll always be together'. I close my eyes to enjoy the memory. Dressing in similar colours, walking hand-in-hand, Mark and I always thought it hilarious when strangers mistook us for twins. With only eleven months between us in age the deception was easy enough, until our teenage growth spurts took Mark to a whole different height. Still we were special, we were best friends, we shared everything.

Until now.

Now it's my turn to be kept out in the cold.

As the comfort I so often felt from Mark's warm cheek materialises into the rubbery surface of his lifeless body, I realise how alone Mark must have felt back in Sydney, after I'd had enough of feeling worthless without Riley and, at home alone one night, did the single most selfish thing a sister could ever do to her brother.

And you kept your promise. You never told Mum and Dad.

If only I could wake Mark up from this nightmare, like he woke me up from mine. But where is his ambulance? Where are the paramedics that will revive him, as they revived his sister?

Sickening chalky sediment fills my mouth as I remember that night. The clean tang of hospital again infiltrates my nostrils, though this time it isn't a memory. I really am here. Anna really is retrieving the chair I sunk into moments ago and putting it back in place. This really is my brother's dead body.

Dead.

To her credit, Anna says nothing while I hold Mark. We should be rushing back to *The Himinn*. Whoever didn't want me to find this head injury is sure to be upset that I have.

Instead she waits for me to finish, to release my brother, place him back down on his bed, tuck him under his covers and let him sleep. Only then does she slide his tray into its drawer and close the door. It's time to go. I don't know how long we have until Jón's supposed to be dropping off Mark's briefcase, but it feels like it must be soon and neither Anna nor I want Jón inconvenienced by Anna's lack of presence at *The Himinn*.

So I move to switch off the spotlight and, once the room is dark again, turn on my phone's display to see by its light. The list of last dialled numbers catches my eye: Doctor Emil, Ari, Director Úlfar... "Sorry, Anna," I whisper, "one more quick call. I want to be here in case I need to check something quickly." I ignore Anna's terse expression and tap through to Director Úlfar's number. As I do, my phone's battery gives a fading bleep. "Oh, quick, give me your phone!" I look at Anna but she shakes her head and points to the wall-mounted POTS phone behind me. I grab its receiver and press zero for an outside line. Nothing happens. I hang up and press nine. A healthy tone hums down the line. I have time to tap Director Úlfar's number into the keypad, then my phone's display weakens to black.

He answers immediately.

"Director Úlfar, this is Rebecca Dales."

"Gott kvöld, Miss Dales," he says. "Thank you for calling. Are you okay?"

"Director Úlfar, my brother has a head injury. It's not mentioned in his autopsy report." I explain the details. "Is this why you didn't want me coming to Höfkállur?"

"What? No. I didn't want you travelling all that way only to have a negative experience, which I see," he sighs as he speaks, "is precisely what's happening—all because of a typo!"

"Your explanation for this is a typo?"

"I'm sorry, I don't mean to make light of your concerns. It's not good enough, it really isn't." He tuts. "I knew Doctor Emil had stopped performing every autopsy himself, he's involved in...other things. Still, I did think he checked all reports thoroughly, and I would have thought he'd check this one in particular. I will speak with him."

"I already have. He'll be looking into it first thing tomorrow morning."

"Gott. An oversight like this is not acceptable."

"Oversight?" I laugh. "Director Úlfar, Doctor Emil's oversight is not the issue here. Things simply aren't adding up. There's nothing at the glacier I shouldn't see, is there?"

"Like what?"

"No government presence or lack of care?"

"What are you talking about?"

"No *Heimspeki* experiments or studies?" I ask to gauge his reaction.

"At a glacier? No. None whatsoever," he states with confidence.

"So there's nothing you want to tell me before I go there tomorrow?"

"You're still going?"

"Of course. Do you have a problem with that, beyond my personal safety?"

"Miss Dales," cutlery chinks onto a plate in the background, "it's late, why don't you just tell me what's on your mind."

"Someone somewhere is responsible for my brother's death."

"So first there's an error and your brother isn't dead. Now he *is* dead but it's someone's fault. Miss Dales, you are grieving, searching for answers where there are none."

"Is that what you tell everyone who loses someone at that glacier? I understand quite a few people have died in the Skepnasá River. If so many people slip and fall, wouldn't it be negligent to *not* erect safety railings around the river, at the very least?" No reaction. Am I on to something? "The person threatening me is probably someone liable for doing exactly that, or not doing as the case may be, which is why they don't want an ex-lawyer hanging around—you'd be surprised how far even officials will go to avoid being sued for negligence."

Director Úlfar is silent for a moment. When he speaks again his tone is flat and firm. "Miss Dales, if our government were in any way responsible for your brother's death, we would happily pay your family. In this case, however, we do not believe we are responsible at all."

"Then why offer repatriation?"

"Purely diplomatic reasons, given your influence in the legal community. If, however, you have now looked into costs and realise you need to offset the expenses, you can..."

"What?" I am so insulted by his assumption my jaw tightens "I'm not calling you for any money! I want the truth, swiftly followed by change." I push the phone tight against my ear. "No one should have to go through this, no one!"

"I agree, no one should have to lose a loved one, but accidents happen. They are called accidents because they are not preventable."

"Of course they're preventable! Did I fly into the wrong country? Because I thought this was Iceland. There should be as many safety precautions at that river as in any first world country."

"There is adequate warning at Jötunnsjökull. Your brother knew not to go near the Skepnasá River, Miss Dales. It is not for tourists, they do not understand the danger."

"So put up safety railings! No one should have to take photos of their dead brother's head! It's negligence whether you *believe* it or not!"

A long breath blows down the phone: Director Úlfar losing patience with me. "If you have a photo of the injury, please send it to me. But I do not understand why this particular...injury means your brother's accident was preventable."

"Because if he ended up in the river because he slipped on a rock and hit his head, railings would have prevented his fall."

"He could have fallen in the river and hit his head after."

"He shouldn't have been close enough to the river to fall in the first place!"

Anna puts her finger to her lips. I'm shouting.

"And that, Becky, is why we warn people. If they ignore our warning, how can we stop them?"

"If you wanted to find a way," I lower my voice, "you would."

"I will hear any suggestions."

"I will have some for you tomorrow." After I've seen the glacier for myself.

"That is probably a good idea."

I slam the phone onto its wall fitting and flick off the spotlight, plunging the room into darkness. Forgetting the pain in my thigh, I storm towards the doors. Anna holds one open for me. There's some distant clanking and rattling in the kitchen but otherwise nothing. No Jón; no Gunnar. We scale the staircase, make it along the ground floor corridor, and burst into fresh air.

"Want any help?" Anna whispers, gesturing at my leg.

I shake my head and scurry away from the loading bay. My thigh pulses with each movement but there's too much adrenalin in my system for me to feel actual pain now. It's more a discomfort. The smell of food follows us as we round the corner of the building and head towards the parking lot. I'm surprised the smell doesn't fade as we near the road. For some reason I sniff my hands. They smell sweet, sickly sweet—like stale blood.

"Oh god," I realise—it's not food I can smell...

It's my brother.

I stop in my tracks to dry retch. Doubling over, disgust and guilt balls my stomach into a tight contraction that squeezes its meagre contents into my throat. The acidity makes my tonsils smart with the lingering taste of tart coffee. I straighten but can't stop thinking about Mark's smell on me. My stomach heaves again, not that there's anything in it to spew.

He's on me—on us—on our hands.

"We'll have showers when we get home," Anna whispers, reading my mind.

I wipe my mouth of saliva.

"Let's go." She helps me along the highway, glancing over her shoulder every few paces.

"Do you know where Gunnar went?" I ask her.

She shrugs and a quiet falls between us as we hurry. There's little to say after the evening we've had.

Even so, there's something I need to know. "Anna," I say, "why didn't you just call me with the code for the mortuary cabinets, why did you come down here? And what's with all the texting in code?"

"You never know who's listening to mobile phones and you said you didn't want company. Besides, I wanted to help you. I should have come in the first place. When Gunnar didn't return I was worried too. I couldn't wait around at home."

"But why? You don't know me, not really. We're not 'friends'."

After giving the question some thought, she smiles knowingly to herself. "You know, you should hear Jón in traffic," she looks me in the eye, "it's the one place he never bothers to control his temper."

So there it is. Not only does he have a temper but Anna's happy to admit it.

"He says he's proud of it," she continues, "thinks that most men don't believe aggression has a place in their modern lives anymore, so they allow that part of their brains to coma off into dormancy. He says they don't realise what will happen to them if they stop using their assertive cells. Their bodies will perceive those cells as nonessential and direct blood flow away from them. Then, when they need to act, they won't have the functionality to do so."

"He thinks," she goes on, "that natural selection has already begun to eradicate it from some men's brains, says it's entirely absent now from the brains of men who care more about moisturising and colour-coordinating than getting their hands dirty with 'real work'."

"Whatever that is!"

"I know! He says there are parts of his brain that understand aggression like a first language, that can fire instantaneous strength into his muscles if needed to defeat a threat—as if he's going to face lions or silverbacks walking down the street! However," she hangs on the word as if it's the single most important part of her sentence, "Mark." She stares down the street, lost in her thoughts.

"What about him?"

"Your brother was kind, Becky, gentle, caring, held doors open for me, brought in the shopping, cooked dinner sometimes—even though he was my guest. I haven't had that since Pàll. Aggression can be... useful sometimes. But Jón doesn't realise that men can be assertive and gentle at the same time."

"Jón is charming though."

"He is, yes, though sometimes I think that's a tactic too. Your brother, on the other hand, was a wonderfully evolved man. Brave and determined and thoughtful, all at the same time." She looks at my face. "You look so much like him." She reaches across as if to stroke my cheek with the back of her hand. Given we're walking, all she does is push some strands of hair over my shoulder. Still, the intimacy of her gesture takes me by surprise. It also makes me realise what happened between Mark and Anna. Mark touched Anna's life in that special way only he could. Of course he did. No one could live with Mark for as long as Anna did and not grow to love him on some level. "I miss him already," she murmurs, wiping at her eyes as we walk up the hill towards her house.

I feel a pang of jealousy seeing her tears. If grief is a gift, I haven't opened mine yet. How can I? I can't trust myself anymore, not after Sydney, not after Riley. Weakness can be like alcohol, sex, and drugs— addictive. When you're weak, other people often come to your rescue, solve your problems and make everything better. They don't expect you to do it all by yourself because you're having a hard time, and you don't expect it of yourself either. It's nice too, that they care so much.

In fact it's so nice that the next time you're feeling down, you don't hesitate to call for help. Then, before you know it, you're asking for help all the time, constantly relying on other people for your happiness.

It's a dangerous road.

Friends, family, lovers won't always have time for you. One day, when your boyfriend, the person you entrusted most with your happiness, leaves you to date the accounts girl at his firm, whom you always suspected he fancied even though he denied it, you'll be lost without anyone, with no memory of being able to solve things by yourself anymore.

Crying leads to weakness.

The second I let myself cry, that sadness will overwhelm me again, I know it. Last time I was lucky. I had Mark.

"He always did what he could for others," I mutter, my pace slowing with the hill climb.

"Tell me something Becky, do you sense Mark at all? Since he died, have you felt anything?" She studies my expression.

"Of course, I've been miserable." Not that I've immersed myself in that misery yet.

"I meant *felt* his presence, like he's still here?"

"I've always felt Mark's presence, whether he was down the street or the other side of the world."

"What about now?"

"What do you mean?" I try to remember if I've mentioned the gushing water, the voices, the visions. I don't think I have.

Anna notices my hesitation. "I knew it! You've sensed something, haven't you? Not only the sadness but an actual sensation. I knew I wouldn't be the only one! Pàll is here with me too, in the lights of the auroras, waiting for me to right the wrong done to him. So we are the same, you and I. What is it that you see or hear?"

I clear my throat to delay putting my experiences into words. Not only has Anna said something a little too crazy for my liking, but if I put my experiences into words they might sound crazy too. I'm in a foreign country, surrounded by strangers—I don't want to lose my mind. Then again, if I am going crazy, shouldn't I seek out all the help I can get?

Help starts with admission.

"Water," I purse my lips as I hear my own confession. "Swirling, rumbling, tumbling, that kind of thing."

"Pàll comes to me in the battlelights. Sometimes he shines through the windows at home. It's like being at the bottom of a bright mint sea."

I nod, appreciating the image. Although, if I'd had this conversation with Anna a few days ago I would never have believed her.

"Sometimes I go to a lookout," Anna continues, "about five kilometres east of here, on a hillside over the lava fields. But the best is Jötunnsjökull."

"Jötunnsjökull? You've been there?"

"Many times. Especially after Pàll died. I could talk to him there." She turns up a street. "You need a good off-road vehicle, you have to drive back in the dark or stay overnight, but it's worth it. The battlelights make the ice shine green, red, blue..."

"Sorry, the battlelights? You mean the auroras?"

She's about to say something when her phone bleeps. She fishes it out of her pocket, though her expression tells me she already knows who's texting. "It's Jón. He's on his way."

We speed up, changing pace from the stroll it's become into a run-walk. It helps that we're on our way down the hill.

"The battlelights?" I remind her a few paces later.

"Right, yes. They're where we all go when we die. The green lights are good, our positive energies. The reds and violets are negative, the evil." She starts speaking faster. "Before they leave for *himinn* or *helvíti*, heaven or hell, they battle for space in the sky. On some nights good wins, and the auroras are more green. Other nights evil wins, and they are more red. You didn't know we go into the auroras when we die?"

"Doctor Emil said it was possible," I grip my thigh where my cut throbs, "but they don't have any proof yet." And, based on my own experiences, they won't find any either.

"But," Anna says, breathless, "science only ever ends up proving what we sensed was true all along. Every culture on Earth believes in ghosts, in some shape or form. Did you know the Vikings used to believe the auroras were reflections from the shields of dead warriors on their way to Valhalla? Some Inuit, the Eskimo, believe the auroras are new souls coming to earth, dancing spirits. Different people round the world may talk about life and death in different ways, but there are so many similarities—the light in a child when it's born, luminous ghosts, the light shining off angels' wings, the white we walk towards when we die. It's all light."

"I can tell you and Mark have been talking alright," I say, struggling with my leg. Anna puts her arm around my waist to help. "Mark would argue people have centred their lives around their bodies' electrical energy for centuries, only they never knew that's what they were doing, not scientifically."

He used to say that, without science providing the correct terminology, people had simply believed their electrical energy to be a mystical force. When he first told me the different names mankind had given this mystical force over the centuries, I was astounded by the consistency of belief across the world. In Reiki they call it 'Ki', in Chinese 'Chi', in Sanskrit 'Prana', in Hawaiian 'Ti' or 'Ki', in Christianity 'Holy Spirit' or 'Holy Ghost', in Hebrew 'ruach', in Islam 'Created Spirit', in Rastafarianism 'Hola', in Greek 'pneuma'… Mark wanted his thesis to unite man's spiritual beliefs under the truth science was now in the process of revealing. I never had the courage to tell him that mankind and science might both be wrong.

"Sometimes," Anna continues, turning into the street behind *The Himinn*, "man searches for truth in the right spot. What was it Mark used to say about life after death? Anything is—"

"Anything is possible." It was his answer to everything.

"The auroras' electrified particles must carry our angels to heaven," she adds, "and bring our children to earth, because we sense it and because it makes sense. And what we sense is that our loved ones watch over us. Promise me you will not leave Ísland without seeing the auroras?"

"Okay. But Mark was wrong about the light." I want to swallow back my words but it's too late. I've said them and I have no idea why. "I mean he might be wrong, some people might not see any light when they die." I've kept this thought to myself for years—that lonely night years ago, I didn't see any light. Nothing reached for me in that dizzy half-dead world. Nothing called me towards anything. There were only muffled sounds, voices cutting through the haze, a vibration beneath me, the ceiling of the ambulance…then everything went blank. Plain nothingness. Empty void. Vacant…white.

Still, that didn't mean to say there couldn't be light for everybody else. I hope Anna glosses over my comment.

She's straight on it. "Mark told me about you. He said you never spoke about what it was like, when you were...unconscious."

Because I didn't want him knowing, it would only have upset him. I shrug. "I don't really remember it," I lie. I don't want to upset Anna either. People have a right to their beliefs, however misguided. "I didn't tell Mark about it because it was hard for him, that night. Why bring it up?" Besides, I moved on. I was never going to treat life with such disrespect again, no matter what. That was the only consequence Mark needed to know.

Anna's voice drops to a whisper as we approach the house bordering her garden. There are lights on downstairs now. "You're as damn practical as he said you were."

"He said that?"

"He said when you decided to switch professions and move to London, you quit your job, were packed and on a plane before he'd even had a chance to second-guess you. I think Mark wanted to be more like you."

"Stubborn?"

"Determined. Becky, I think you should go to the Litrúm-Hús tomorrow morning, see what Mark saw and take a look at the Sannlitró-Völva—not because it has anything to do with anyone's negligence, but because Mark would want you to know what he was doing here."

"You're the second person to suggest that."

"He'd want you to understand about the battlelights, about where he is now and the water. He's communicating with you, Becky, sending electrical pulses into your brain to tell you things. Ólaf was going to show him around before he died, but then Ólaf didn't get back from Akureyri in time. I'm sure he'd happily show you instead?"

I remember Mark describing his visits to Höfkállur's Litrúm-Hús in previous messages. "I thought Mark did take a look around the Litrúm-Hús?"

"He did," Anna climbs back over her fence, "but never with Ólaf, never behind the scenes."

Chapter 10

As I struggle over Anna's garden fence, she tells me more about Ólaf and Höfkállur's Litrúm-Hús, until a car engine slows to a stop outside *The Himinn*. Our conversation stops.

Anna's eyes widen. "Quick, that's Jón!" She helps me over the fence then jogs to her back door, waves at me to hurry.

I don't need any encouragement. Jón might not be the man who threatened me, it's likely no longer a secret I was at the morgue, but I still want to get upstairs before he arrives.

A car door slams as Anna shuts the back door behind me. I race upstairs though only manage to get halfway before the front door opens.

"Miss Dales?" Jón calls out.

I turn. "Halló, Officer Jón."

Showing me one of his charming smiles, he holds up a brown satchel and wiggles it in the air. We meet at the bottom of the staircase. "Okay?" he asks, handing it over.

"Yes. I mean, já. Takk."

Anna emerges from the kitchen, grinning and opening her arms to Jón. While they gush Icelandic greetings to each other, I creep back up the stairs. Despite everything she said earlier, she seems happy to see him.

Before I reach the top, Anna calls after me. "Becky! Jón says he's taken over watching the house from Gunnar. That's where Gunnar went, to collect Jón. Jón has dropped him home." She means it to reassure me. "He also says he's made a list of everything in Mark's backpack, in case you want to know exactly what's in there without having to go through it."

"Oh, okay. Thank you." I give Jón as much of a smile as I can.

Jón whispers something to Anna.

"Oh," she calls to me, "and he put Mark's wallet in there too, because he thought you might want to keep it safe. There's some money in it and photos." Jón whispers again. "As well as credit cards and driving license."

"Very thoughtful." I smile again.

As Anna translates, Jón's eyes glimmer with pride. "Gott," he says.

"Okay then," I say, glad Jón is clearly not tempersome this evening. "I'll see you in the morning."

"I'll phone you-know-who," Anna says, stepping towards the staircase to speak in a hushed tone, "and ask them to show you around the you-know-where tomorrow."

She means Ólaf and the Litrúm-Hús. But why is she avoiding use of the words in front of Jón? "Is there something in particular you want me to see there?"

"The machine, what it does, what it means. We'll speak in the morning." She glances at Jón.

I'm happy to take the hint. Jón is playing with Anna's hair, gazing at her as if she's a dazzling angel. There's no way she'll be able to resist that. Jón is here for the night. Clutching Mark's satchel to my chest, I turn and climb the stairs.

Gusts of night-chilled air shudder the outside of the windows as I open the bedroom door. I lock it behind me; search the pools of light cast by streetlamps for Gunnar's black sedan. It isn't opposite *The Himinn* anymore. It's parked in Anna's driveway and it's empty.

I draw the blinds and switch on the light. After finding my charger, I plug in my phone and, once I've washed my hands and face, turn it back on. Then I sink into one of the pink leather armchairs with my reading glasses and rest my neck on the back of the seat. My mind feels heavy and worn. My stomach feels flat and tight with emptiness, though it's aching in protest as it always does, and my thigh throbs to remind me it still needs care. I should have a shower but can't wait to look through Mark's things. I lift my leg onto the coffee table and hold his satchel close to my chest. Inside are his thesis notes. It's been a while since I've been this close to them.

The last time was at my parents' home in Sydney. Mum and Dad had gone to the movies. Mark was curled up on the sofa watching a *Star Trek* spin-off, some science book on his lap. I remember being at the dining table on the other side of the room, browsing the Internet for a fresh start—somewhere I could still use my legal qualifications, but where frustrated lawyers wouldn't exhaust and drag me down into a place where I couldn't cope when life threw me a curve ball.

I think some crewmember must have died on the television because Mark began probing me again about death. He wanted to know what I'd seen in the ambulance that time, when he'd watched me die. For three full minutes I was technically dead. He was sure I must have seen something, just as he was certain our brains' electrical energies amassed after we died, uniting our combined wisdoms, then existing as a kind of collective god before being re-born or recycled. I remember his certainty annoying me—no one would ever have all the answers.

He said something about not wanting all the answers, only one—he wanted to know if I'd seen anything to confirm his theory. He brought his thesis notes over to the table.

"People have to realise who God is, Bex. It's us. It always has been. If people understood that, if they based their beliefs on scientific fact rather than random myths dreamed up centuries ago, they'd stop waging war in God's name."

I remember saying something about science relying on as many assumptions as religion did myths. A strong belief in either was fanaticism.

What he said next stuck with me. "Good point." He paused, thinking something through. "And I suppose a scientific explanation doesn't mean you can't still wonder at why we're here, or have faith that there might be a higher purpose for our being…"

"Exactly."

"…or ask where all the atoms and energy and contemplations came from before they big-banged into our world. It doesn't mean we still can't value humanity's freedom to wonder and suppose. I do, I guess. Hmm. Good point. Thanks, Bex." Then he went back to the sofa and made some notes.

I sigh at the memory then open Mark's satchel. Maybe I'll find the notes he made that night. I pull out his wallet first, check its contents. Like Jón said there's some cash inside, Mark's various cards and some photos. I know I shouldn't look at the photos, they're bound to upset me, but curiosity has never been something I can control.

The first photo is of the two of us at my graduation from law school. The fact that it was taken by Riley would usually upset me yet, looking at Mark's face, I don't rush it away. Instead I stroke the glossy film. When my doorbell rang on the morning of my graduation, and I opened my door to a delivery man with a bouquet of flowers, I couldn't believe how lucky I was to have a boyfriend as considerate as Riley. Of course, when I opened and read the accompanying card,

I realised instead how lucky I was to have a brother as considerate as Mark.

The next two photos are of us with Mum and Dad, one taken on Mark's twenty-first birthday, and one on mine. We look so young, so powerful with the freedom of an uncharted life before us.

In the last photo, it's Mark and me standing on Manly Beach holding our PADI diving certificates. We were always good swimmers as kids but, after Riley, Mark suggested we learn scuba diving together. He was the one who got me into it. In a way he not only saved my life, he changed it too. Becoming an adventure diver helped to restore what confidence I'd lost, made me realise there's more to life than recovering from curve balls.

I tuck the photos inside my own wallet, stow Mark's wallet in my suitcase, then trawl through his research papers, searching for a reason, a hint, anything that might explain why he went hiking instead of phoning me that weekend. Instead, all I find are more memories.

There is the spreadsheet he showed me that night at Mum and Dad's house, listing all the references suggesting mankind has long known our brains' energies form or join into 'god' after death. Gurus in the Yogic tradition talk of connecting with a collective energy when they meditate, of God dwelling within us. "*The kingdom of God is within you*," said Jesus. "*Ye are gods*," is both a hermetic aphorism and a line from Psalms 82. Taoists believe that man can gain knowledge of the universe by first understanding himself, and vice versa. Christians, Muslims and Jews all over the world believe they physically connect with God when they die.

Next I find Mark's notes on the Sannlitró-Völva machine. Now I'm reading through his papers, I remember more about the machine from Mark's emails. I reach for my still-charging phone and jot down some of the details I've forgotten, ready for when I'm with Ólaf. While I'm at it, I write down some of the things people have told me today about the *Heimspeki* and the Litrúm-Hús. There's so much to take in, and I do want to understand what Mark was doing here.

Next, I recognise Mark's synopsis of man's relationship with electricity.

"People seriously overlook the intimacy of our relationship with electricity," he said that night in Sydney, munching on a double chocolate Tim Tam. "Despite the fact we have electricity running though our bodies, despite the fact we ourselves produce electricity."

Glancing over his summary, I'm still impressed by the depth of his analysis. When humans get an electric shock, they overcharge like any electrical appliance and their bodies short-circuit—whether that's momentarily as when touching wet electric sockets, or permanently as with electric chairs. Yet humans also need electricity to function. We use defibrillators to re-start hearts, and we define death as the absence of electricity from our brains. Acupuncture has been known for centuries for its ability to stimulate the flow of our bodies' electric currents, its use is endorsed by the World Health Organisation. Yet we still resist the importance of electricity in our lives.

Mark's arguments, on the other hand, are so thorough they make me feel I should isolate myself in some mountaintop temple and contemplate the exact electrical equilibrium I need to attain before I die.

Pulling out the last wodge of stapled paper from Mark's briefcase, I'm disappointed not to find a printout of his completed thesis among them. I've read some of it, mainly the beginning, but nothing he's written recently. There's only a printout of an email he sent to his university professor last week, attaching his thesis electronically and promising to append a new pedagogical postscript in a couple of weeks.

"That doesn't make sense," I mumble to myself.

If Mark already sent his thesis to his professor, why did he want to talk to me about its conclusions? I read the printout again, pausing on his reference to a pedagogical postscript. I look back through his notes.

There's one page headed 'proof' that I don't recognise. It describes how proof can exist without our seeing it, in the same way we can look at the ocean and only see blue, whereas really there's red and purple coral beneath its surface, rainbow fish glittering with colour, green and yellow seaweed, orange starfish, etc. The notes go on to say there are more things in the world than any single person can both see *and* know. Yet most individuals don't seek proof that all those things exist because they believe and rely on the other people who have seen them. In those things then, at least, they have faith.

Still, there's nothing in the notes about any pedagogical postscript.

There's another page too, with some random thoughts scrawled across it at different angles, as if Mark wrote them at different times. One note mentions Director Úlfar's Sannlitró-Völva machine, that it's a lot more than a lie-detection machine. The details make me think he must have seen it in action. Another note mentions me. It talks about *Heimspeki* followers being one hundred per cent committed to maintaining their positive energy, despite 'what Becky said the other week about human nature'. I have no idea what I said the other week about human nature but hope it will come to me. Then I see it, his first mention of any postscript.

'Of course,' he writes. 'I have to admit now there are those occasional few—the people who simply can't help themselves. That's why, in a way, my postscript will be more important than the thesis itself. Secularity doesn't matter. Energy. The numinous. It's both, together. I knew anything was possible! We need both. We need to be various.'

I recognise parts of that note from what Mark said to me last weekend, though don't understand what he means by his postscript being more important than his thesis. He's been working on his thesis for years, yet has only been in Iceland a few months. What could have changed his mind?

Making a mental note to ask Anna what she knows tomorrow, I shuffle and refile Mark's papers, fold away my reading glasses. My phone bleeps. At first I think it's letting me know it's finished charging, then I realise it's received a message. Expecting it to be from Doctor Emil, I'm surprised to see the image of a skinny young man wearing a crumbled white lab coat opposite the name 'Gunnar Eyjólfsson'. There's a voice message attached. Two voices greet me when I open it. The first is the quivering voice of a young man. The other is a Word2Word translator turning his sorrowful voice into English.

"Miss Dales, this is Gunnar Eyjólfsson, Doctor Emil's assistant. Doctor Emil got your message and contacted me about your brother's autopsy report. I am very sorry the report did not list your brother's head trauma. I did record it when examining your brother's body but I used a microphone to make my observations and obviously didn't type it up properly when I wrote the actual report. I have been very busy with other things this week. Of course that is no excuse. As you already know, your brother did indeed injure his head after he fell in the river. I have listened again to my observations and amended his autopsy report accordingly. Everything is included now. I attach a fresh copy.

"Doctor Emil is also very sorry for any confusion. He's had to leave Höfkállur this afternoon and will be away until next week, but when he returns he will take measures to ensure this never happens again. Since I am to blame for this mistake, the measures to be taken by me are very clear. I must take full responsibility. First I want to apologise to you. If you need to speak with Doctor Emil, please use the email address I will give you now, since he is accessing his account remotely: info@emilsveinsson.is. Thank you."

I open the attachment. Mark's report appears onscreen. Scrolling down to the anatomic summary, I see that Gunnar has inserted a description detailing Mark's head injury. The injury is now listed as being consistent with river drowning among sunken boulders.

Is it that simple? No listed head injury—then listed head injury?

Looking at Mark's updated autopsy report, it seems as if it is. If only I could apply the same magic to my brother: dead—not dead. I can't because Mark is some lifeless specimen this inexperienced junior cut open and weighed with blatant incompetency. The thought makes me want to scream. I close my eyes and try to clear my mind. I can't let myself think like that. I'm not sure what it means for my suspicions about Mark's death—he still wouldn't have gone hiking out there alone—but there's nothing more I can do tonight. I need to get some sleep.

I breathe slowly, counting to calm myself. My eyes drift to the digital clock on my phone. It reminds me it will be approaching dawn in Sydney. Mum and Dad will be waiting for reassurance that I've arrived. They'll want to talk too and I'll have to tell them I've seen Mark, that he really is dead. Can I tell them that?

Rehearsing the conversation in my head, I stare at my phone until my eyes settle on the changing seconds. Each one has to coax the next into sludging past. My eyelids feel heavy. I snatched only a few hours' sleep on the Austurleid. The muscles under my eyes have strained for far too long already...

I let my next blink relax into a moment's rest and press my palms into my closed eyelids. A few days ago Mark was sitting here, contemplating his afterlife theories. Was he happy here these last few months? Did he offset any negative energy in his brain before he died, like he told me to do back in Sydney? Or is he still out there somewhere, like Pàll, watching me retrace his last steps and waiting for me to bring balance to his posthumous disparity? Is he gushing water into my head to try and communicate, is that why my head heats when I hear voices? If so, what's he trying to say?

Or am I simply going mad?

Yes, maybe I'm mad, because I can't help but think there's something in Anna's theory about the gushing water I hear, about the voices in my head. I never heard voices in my head before now, so it has to be Mark. There's no other explanation.

I listen out for him but there's only the wind against the windows. It lulls me and I feel my head drop forward. My spine sinks into the armchair. I think I hear something outside my bedroom door, maybe closer. The distinct stench of cigarette smoke drifts into my nostrils. But I am already floating, diving through the air to land on fluffy clouds that wrap me in a white quilt, and rock me to sleep.

Chapter 11

A woman screams out in the dark. She has a Canadian accent.
"Anna, vakna!"

"Why does he still come Jón, why?"

"Ókei, Anna, ókei!"

"Nei, Jón. It's not okay."

The voices soften. I roll over and fall back to sleep.

Later, a slamming door wakes me. The enticing aroma of cooking bacon twists with the sharp tang of coffee. It wakens my senses and tells me the time for darkness and dreaming is over for another night. Remembering the voices, I place Anna's accent, recall hearing Jón's name, and am not surprised I've been dreaming of them.

With a rub I comfort my stomach's grumbles, then push myself up. With the movement comes a familiar wooziness, the top of my head feels like it's been sliced opened and my brain is floating off into the air. The rub does little to placate the clawing in my tummy, but I don't mind the sensation. Actually, I love it. It means my body isn't getting enough calories; so it can't be getting fatter, only thinner. At least something good came of losing Riley.

Eighteen months ago, after the paramedics revived me in that ambulance, the doctors told me I wouldn't be able to digest much for a while, apart from nutrition shakes and soup. I would have to wait until my stomach was stronger. My stomach got stronger, but by then I'd grown used to feeling flat and empty. Emptiness shouldn't make a person feel powerful. For me, it did. Running a hand over my growling emptiness, it still does.

I swing my legs over the side of the bed and think about burning off some extra calories by doing sit-ups or jogging on the spot. But something isn't right. The wooziness is still there of course, as is the throb in my thigh, but a dull flu-like ache pounds behind my eyes and stiffness pulls at my neck and limbs. I feel as though I've slept upright. I crack my neck, stretch my back. The stiffness persists. This isn't something I usually experience in the morning.

Another door slams, a car door this time. A car door outside. I look at the window, expecting it to be right in front of me. It isn't. I'm not in the pink armchair anymore. I'm in…bed?

Still groggy, my memory is slow to come. The last thing I remember is closing my eyes in the armchair. I look at my arms, at my fully clothed body. Did I somehow drag myself over to the bed, or did someone carry me? I spin around, check the room. No one's here. The door is shut. Did I lock it? Yes, I remember.

Mark's papers? They're still in a tidy pile on the coffee table, along with my phone and glasses.

The chugga-rip burst of an engine roars outside the window. I race over to see the black sedan moving away from the kerb. Jón is driving. After watching him disappear towards the Litrúm-Hús, I turn, almost missing the white hatchback that pulls up, driven by the short balding man I met yesterday: Ólaf.

He exits his vehicle and stands beside it, watching the road. His face is expressionless, only his rounded cheeks judder as his mouth twitches. He threads a hand around the back of his crisp white collar to rub at his neck, rolls his head from side to side, then readjusts his metal glasses and moves towards the guesthouse, buttoning his navy blue suit as he walks.

I need to get ready.

I stumble into the shower, lean a hip against the tiled wall to steady myself, and wash the rest of Mark's smell from my sleep-puffed skin. As the shower's warm water sluices over me, stinging my thigh wound like acid, the pungency of one odour is replaced with another. Yesterday, I'm sure Anna assured me I wouldn't be able to smell the unique aroma of Iceland's mineral-rich bore water once I was actually in the shower. Or was that Mark? Either way, even my coconut-scented shampoo offers no relief from the water's eggy stench. I smile as I remember Mark telling me a similar story about his first few days in Iceland. I'd forgotten that until now.

My smile fades. How could I forget?

As I stuff myself into clothes, I realise this is going to happen all the time now. I'm going to spend the rest of my life losing my brother each time I forget a memory. The thought is so overpowering I don't pay much attention to what I'm doing and, when I look in the mirror, I'm wearing jean pantaloons and a lace-necked jumper over several sensible layers. Nothing matches, but I don't care.

I grab my bag and jacket, then hobble downstairs, gripping the handrail tight in one hand, texting my parents with the other. I keep my update ambiguous. I can't bear to tell them the truth, not yet. I need to arm myself with more information first.

The kitchen is empty but on the island is a plate of cold cuts and bread, a hot serving dish of bacon and poached salmon, and a steaming black cafetière. Beside it is a handwritten note: *help yourself.*

Plate in hand, I pick at the salmon, restrain myself with the bacon and avoid the bread. I should cut my mouthfuls into smaller pieces to savour the experience of eating, but today I don't have time. I wish I had my nutrition shakes with me. It's amazing how long a bit of powder and water can stave off hunger. The pre-calculated calorie intake of a nutrition shake makes my mental count easier to keep too. I have a stash of them in my kitchen ready for mornings such as these, mornings when I don't have time to cut and weigh fruit or vegetables for breakfast. I wish I'd brought some.

Instead, the numbers of my daily calorie count race upwards as I eat in silence, straining to hear some movement in the house. In my head I estimate the weight of each mouthful. To sate the guilt I feel as I enjoy each bite, I tell myself that today I need to eat, given what lies ahead. I'm not going to be sat at a computer all day, burning only enough calories to power breath and brain. Today, I have discoveries to make, some of them by scouring a glacier.

Still, I wish I'd done some sit-ups.

I turn to check myself in the reflection of Anna's silver fridge. Its surface is not reflective enough, but there's a framed poster on the wall beside it that is. I try to see the roll of fat that clings to my stomach no matter what I do. Layered under my skin, festering into ugly wobbling pockets of excess skin, it looks like it's behaving today—staying under the waistband that cuts straight across it, pulling it in. If I were naked, the wobble would be hard to miss. The doctor I saw last month is most definitely wrong. I've seen the actresses in magazines with anorexia and I look nothing like them. Their bones jut right through their skin, all over their body. Whereas my tummy bulges, my arms flap, and I can't even bear to look at my hips. There must be some other reason why I've stopped having periods lately.

A floorboard or door creaks upstairs. I stop eating to listen. At another creak, I rush to retrieve my phone from my bag and switch on its Word2Word, ready to speak to Anna's cousin. I can't remember whether Ólaf used a Word2Word translator when we spoke yesterday.

As I insert my earpiece, they move downstairs talking in Icelandic. "Are you sure you want to involve her?"

My phone picks up on their conversation though it's loud in my ear. I hurry to turn it down—I can't tell whether Ólaf is irritated or if it's the volume. As the decibels dwindle, Anna replies.

"I have no choice, Ólaf. You know I don't."

Curious, I move to the kitchen doorway to greet them, readjusting my waistband to reduce the impact of the bloated flabby feeling. Ólaf is following Anna's svelte figure down the staircase, his eyes fixed on her long white curls as they bounce across her shoulders. His admiration is easy to understand. Her hair gleams like an iced-over lake in winter sunlight.

Anna turns to say more, notices me waiting. "Goðan dag, Becky!" She smiles as she speaks. *Good morning*, my translator says in my ear. "This is my cousin, Ólaf."

"Gaman að kynnast þér. Good to meet you again, Becky." Ólaf says switching to spoken English as immaculate as his tailoring. So he wasn't using Word2Word yesterday. He holds out his hand as he approaches. His large cheeks are flushed red, his breathing as heavy as his descent down the stairs is ungainly. I'm surprised his hand isn't hot and sweaty.

"*Again?*" Anna asks.

"Yes," I say, "we bumped into each other yesterday at the Litrúm-Hús. Sorry, I forgot to mention it. Ólaf was very helpful." I move forward to shake his hand. "Hello again."

"And please,' he says, bringing my hand to his lips, "I did not have the chance to say yesterday, but I am very sorry for your loss. All loss is unkind. It can hurt in ways you cannot even understand yourself."

"Thank you." I retrieve my hand discreetly so as not to offend him. "Have you lost someone recently too?"

His mouth twitches. "I remember the feeling."

Anna peers into the kitchen and at my empty plate. "Are you ready to go?"

I turn to collect my things.

"And don't mind, Ólaf. The only thing my cousin's lost recently is his memory."

"I told you, Anna," says Ólaf, running a hand over his bald patch. "I was too busy last month to help. I have apologised."

Anna reaches to hold her cousin's arm and switches back to Icelandic. My earpiece translates. "Don't apologise. I'm lucky to have you helping at all."

Ólaf looks at her hand on his arm, then glances back up to see Anna's eyes stray to Pàll's hallway photograph. "He wouldn't want you to be like this, my dear, and you know it," he says, also in Icelandic. Anna doesn't see, but he rolls his lips into a tight purse when his comment does little to shift her gaze.

"Everyone has their own path to walk in life," she replies. "I've chosen mine. You know why."

"Beauty doesn't make you untouchable, Anna." He moves his arm away from her. "A woman's deceit can hurt a man," he says, with emphasis on his verbs, "make him feel stupid, make him want to lose control."

Anna chuckles. "Jón would never lose control. He's too in touch with his...his maleness. He'd consider himself weak." She turns to kiss Ólaf on the cheek, then switches back to English and moves down the hallway. "So, you know what to show Becky at the Litrúm-Hús?"

"Yes," he mumbles in English, almost sadly.

Anna opens the front door, whispers to me as I pass her. "Becky, are you sure about going with Ari this afternoon?"

Ólaf walks on but I pause to reassure her. "Ari knows that place better than anyone. He says you haven't breathed until you've breathed the air up by the glaciers." I remember his saying so as we descended the Litrúm-Hús steps yesterday. He told me the breeze at Jötunnsjökull can sometimes be eerily still, like the ice has sucked up all the life around it. Then at other times it can whistle across the lake so ferociously it whips the water into a frenzy. He told me it cleanses you of all the frustrations of life, which tells me that Ari's going to the glacier is as cathartic for him as diving is for me. "He loves it up there, Anna. He found Mark because he was hiking, no other reason. He met me from the Austurleid because Director Úlfar told him to, that's all. I'll be fine. I need to see where Mark died. Gunnar's already apologised for missing the head trauma from Mark's report—"

"He has?" Anna mutters, her eyes drifting to the wall behind me.

"—but there's still more to this, I'm certain of it. When I see the glacier, I'll know more. Did, um, Jón stay here last night?"

"Yes," she murmurs, still staring at the wall, "he said he had a migraine, wanted a neck rub, then conveniently fell asleep on my bed. Your light was on in the middle of the night."

"I fell asleep in an armchair."

"I know. I checked on you, helped you into bed."

"But, I locked the door."

"I have a master key." Anna taps a pocket then gestures towards

Ólaf waiting in his car. "You'd better go. We can talk more tonight, after you've seen everything you need to see."

I move towards Ólaf though stop on the path when I remember my dream. "Anna, did you call out in the middle of the night? I think I heard you."

Anna glances at me then looks away again. "Oh, sorry. Yes, that was me."

"It's okay, I thought I was dreaming. What happened?"

"Pàll came." She looks up at me. "I don't like him visiting when Jón's there. It's like he's spying on me. I close the curtains, hide under the sheets, still he shines through." She sings the words in frustration, then seems to chide herself for it. "I shouldn't complain; I used to love it. I used to leave the windows open and beg him to come. Now, it's not always an ideal time. I can't blame him for being confused, I suppose. I wish I could help him understand."

I rub her arm. "I'm sure he does, Anna."

"He doesn't; he's angry. He will in time, of course, he'll have to. It just makes it hard for now. I wish you could see him. I wanted to wake you up, show you, but you were so tired."

"I'm sure I'll see him another time." Strangely it feels nice to admit the madness out loud. At least Anna and I can go mad together. Mad with grief.

"You'll see him soon. And then you'll see how beautiful he is. Pale neon greens tickling the dresser, dancing on the headboard. It...it's amazing."

"Did Jón see it?"

"No, as soon as Jón wakes up, Pàll always fades fast. Probably for the best."

"Probably."

Anna sighs in strained amusement and moves down the path towards Ólaf's car. I hesitate, sure there was something else I had to ask. I can't put my finger on it before I hear the purr of an approaching car. As we reach Ólaf, Anna and I peer up the street. It's a black sedan. I exchange glances with Anna.

"It's not Jón," she mumbles, ushering me into Ólaf's passenger seat. "Ólaf, take care of her?"

He nods and starts the engine.

Through Ólaf's rear vision mirror, I watch the black sedan follow us towards the Litrúm-Hús. I can't see who's driving.

"So, my dear," Ólaf readjusts his glasses and squints at the car behind us, "what have you done to deserve such special attention?"

I tell him about the threat.

"And Anna," he says after some thought, "I suppose she's already linked it to her conspiracy theories?"

The phrase puts me on edge. Has Anna told him what we talked about last night, what I said to Director Úlfar? Or does he mean to refer to Pàll? "Her husband's hit and run?"

He glances at my expression as we turn out of Anna's street. "Sorry I...I assumed she told you."

"Told me what?"

"Pàll was only the beginning. Anna thinks the entire Litrúm-Hús is corrupt."

"She does?" She didn't tell me that.

He chuckles. "The examinations, the Sannlitró-Völva, everything. She even believes Mark was murdered!"

"Murdered? As in purposely killed? Are you sure?"

"Something about a head injury?"

"Yes. We didn't talk murder though. She thinks someone actually hurt my brother *specifically*."

"Which is ridiculous, I know—who'd ever want to hurt someone as lovely as your brother? It's her grief talking."

"And she definitely used that word: murder?"

"Oh, I can't remember what she said exactly, something along the lines of Mark not having any reason to go hiking. As if a tourist needs a good reason to be a tourist," he chuckles, "or do tourist things. Our country is very beautiful, why wouldn't he want to explore it? Probably wanted to take some pictures to show his little sister, eh my dear? I wish Anna would stop reading into things so much. We should all stop worrying, get what we can from this life, enjoy it while it lasts. If there is another life, we can always make the best of that when we get there. Life is so precious, don't you think? We should value every second of life, every cell in our bodies, every synapse in our brain." His mouth twitches as he pulls it into a smile. "Try not to get caught up in her silliness. Don't be like me." He pauses. "Don't wait until it's too late."

"Too late for what?"

"To *not* get involved, caught up in things that won't lead anywhere." He readjusts his glasses by wrinkling his nose. "I have no choice but to help her. I'm the only family she has left in Höfkállur, and she's my only family too. My wife left me, you see." He mumbles, trying to sound casual. It has the opposite effect. "Took my son to live with her and her fancy man in Norway."

"I'm sorry."

"It's okay. My son flies to Reykjavík once a month. It's not enough of course, but what can I do? I am to move on with things. If only Anna could also. I thought it'd be easier if I showed her the Litrúm-Hús, proved there was nothing to worry about. Still she can't let Pàll rest. I think she's a little…unhinged."

He buzzes down his window. The sound of traffic roars through it like water bursting through a dam.

See things not there, a voice whispers. My cheeks flush with heat like I'm sitting too close to a fire.

Mark again.

See things not there.

It reminds me of his notes, the ones I was reading last night under the page titled 'proof', where it talked about people believing in things 'not there' for them as long as they were visible to others. It also reminds me of the pedagogical postscript he was supposed to be writing.

Ah, that's right! I was supposed to ask Anna if she knew anything about it.

I glance at Ólaf. His portly cheeks are moving as if he's just spoken. "Um, sorry, Ólaf, did you say something?"

"I said, she sees things that aren't there. It can be *very* frustrating." He lets his emphasis take its full effect, then follows with a revelation. "Maybe you could talk to her? She's asked me to show you around so must trust you. You could convince her to stay out of trouble?"

"What kind of trouble?"

He dips his chin and speaks like he's choosing his words carefully. "If she keeps snooping around the Litrúm-Hús, or getting other people to do it for her," he glances sideways at me, "she'll upset someone sooner or later."

"Why, who else does she have snooping around?"

He frowns. "Mark, of course."

I let the idea settle. Why would Mark have been snooping around the Litrúm-Hús? Surely only for his study, and he wouldn't have been 'snooping'. "What was he doing?"

"I don't know the full extent of things. I was away working with the Sannlitró-Völva last month."

"You're its technician?" I remember Anna telling me last night as we climbed her fence. Ólaf used to be a technical consultant and computer programmer before he worked at the Litrúm-Hús. He consulted on some contracts in England and Europe before helping develop the scan pods. Now he works exclusively with the Sannlitró-Völva.

"Já. So I go away a lot," he explains. "But, as you know, Anna refuses to leave messages on phones and simply will not trust VoiP. So she didn't tell me much about Mark. I...I didn't even meet him until he came to the Litrúm-Hús last week."

"What was he doing when you saw him?"

"I was hoping you'd be able to tell me that. But," he pauses, "if Anna didn't tell you what Mark was up to, why are you going to the Litrúm-Hús?"

"She wants me to understand more about the *Heimspeki* and life-after-death, because of Pàll." And because of what I'm hearing and seeing myself. "She didn't mention anything about any corruption."

Ólaf's frown deepens. "Well, all I know is what I saw: your brother was taking photos in an examination. I thought he was trying to steal the technology." He tuts as if the consequences of that would be more than a little negativity. "When we spoke he was lovely of course, and I knew who he was straight away because of his accent—Anna had told me about the Australian staying with her. Still, photographs are not allowed. I didn't report him of course, I knew it would get Anna into trouble, and that's the last thing I want."

"Thank you." I pause to take in everything he's said. "Did my brother say anything about going to the glacier?"

"Probably. Maybe that's why the idea doesn't sound strange to me." He pauses as we pull into the Litrúm-Hús car park. "Actually, yes, now that I think of it, I'm sure he said something about going with some girl. To impress her?"

"A girl? What girl?"

"I don't know." He shrugs and rolls his lips as if rethinking. "Maybe it wasn't a girl. Either way he...he was very interested in Jötunnsjökull, I remember now, and Anna's idea about the auroras. He was an inquisitive person, right?"

A memory of Mark and me on holiday with Mum and Dad flashes into my mind, him racing ahead to be the first around the next cold, dark corridor of Manly's old Quarantine Station complex. He always liked being first. "More inquisitive than me, if that's possible. But... Anna said Mark didn't have any other friends in Höfkállur?"

"Maybe he'd just met whoever it was and they didn't want Anna going with them?" He shrugs. "Maybe he thought Anna would get in the way of, well, you know?"

I doubt it. "I...okay."

"Please Becky, you're young, you have so much to do yet in life, don't be like Anna. Grief goes deep. It eats away at you and leaves nothing behind. Pàll died. It's sad. It was also an accident—no one did it on purpose. Don't get swept up in another person's grief when you still have your own to process." He parks the car and mutters. "Anna was the only one to benefit from Pàll's passing."

"Anna?" I frown. "How?"

"Oh nothing, forget I said it." He opens his door and moves towards the Litrúm-Hús steps, shaking his head as if berating himself.

I follow, clutching my thigh to catch up with him. "Go on, how did she benefit?" I try to keep the pain out of my voice. It's impossible—I need my thigh muscles to haul me up the steps. "Ólaf?" I wince. "I need to know everything my brother was doing here these past few months, including why he was helping Anna."

Ólaf glances at my thigh and slows his pace. "Anna said you hurt your leg. Are you okay?"

"I'm fine. Why was Mark helping Anna?"

"You already know, Becky, but you're not seeing it. Anna never grieved the way most people do. After Pàll died she called every official in Iceland, was obsessive about searching for information on the Internet. Now she talks about dancing spirits and angels' wings. She only dates Jón to find out if he's somehow protecting the identity of the driver who killed Pàll." He shakes his head in disappointment. "Her guilt is driving her crazy. Pàll and her were struggling for money, his life insurance helped *a lot*. Did you know they argued that night? Pàll was supposedly walking off his temper when 'the car' hit him."

"Oh."

"Like I said, grief can eat away at you, so can guilt. I expect Mark was trying to do the same as me—prove there was nothing wrong with the Litrúm-Hús so she can get on with her life. It's possible, yes?"

"Anything is possible."

"Sometimes Anna says she wants to die too," he continues, lowering his voice as we near the top of the steps. "Says life's only worth living if you have love and when Pàll died all her love left with him. She says Pàll and her believed they'd be together 'until the end', whatever that means. You can't feel that strongly about one person, then sleep with another—certainly not someone you've only known a few months! She's not well. She believes the things she does with all her heart, but they're simply not real. They're only real to her. Grief does that to people."

"It does," I mumble, rubbing at my ears. I'm beginning to see his point. "Maybe she needs professional help?" Maybe I do too?

"Of course she does. But I'm her best friend, her only family—if I suggest it she'll feel betrayed. And I couldn't bear to see that beautiful face of hers upset with me. Why did she ever let that man near her, Becky?" He means Jón. "Why are women so blind to the faults of such men, and equally blind to what other men can offer—men they've known a lot longer than a few months?"

"I wish I knew, Ólaf, I really do."

"Please help her. She liked your brother. She likes you. There's every chance she'll listen. She shouldn't be with Jón. He's not the man for her."

"I think I understand, Ólaf." He's in love with her. "I'll do what I can." Not that he has much of a chance at winning Anna's heart in that way, I don't think.

"Thank you." He gazes at me as if I'm his only hope, mouth twitching as he tries to smile. "After you," he says when we reach the top step, gesturing towards a scan pod. He must pass through his pod quicker, though, because when I emerge from the other side he's already speaking with a security guard. As they talk, Ólaf rubs his bald patch and tuts under his breath.

I can't understand what they're saying, but am certain I hear the name Úlfar Finnsson.

"We have to be quick," Ólaf says as I approach. "Jón isn't working today, he's called in sick."

"Anna said he had a migraine last night."

"A migraine?" he grunts. "Well, thanks to him I'm in charge of the Litrúm Map Monitoring staff today, which is not good."

"Why?"

"I'm the Sannlitró-Völva's senior technician, my dear, so it falls to me if Jón's not here."

"I meant, why isn't it good?"

"Because now I won't have much time to show you the Sannlitró-Völva after this morning's examination, not if I have to make sure everything's in order before Director Úlfar arrives." He starts walking.

"Úlfar's coming here, to Höfkállur?"

"Lunchtime." He dips his chin.

"Why?"

"I don't know. He usually comes when he's doing a review, but he did his quarterly review of the Litrúm-Hús last month. He'd better not be doing a review. If Jón's sick, I will end up showing him around. Ugh, it's going to be a busy day, Becky, and I do not like surprises."

"Neither do I, Ólaf," I mutter, wondering why Director Úlfar hasn't told me he's coming here. "Neither do I."

Chapter 12

Litrúm Dómstóll number nine is unlike any courtroom I've ever seen. Its asparagus carpets, bare pastel cream walls, and simple pinewood furniture differ starkly from London's Royal Courts of Justice, where solid oak panelling and paintings of robed judges adorn every wall. As the Dómstóll's administrators and the offender to be examined arrive, I notice that smartphones and portable netboards are still the norm, as I'd expect. Still, watching the administrators remote-access their microcomputers and organise their netboards makes me wonder what interest Mark could possibly have had in coming here. He's never been interested in anything even remotely legal before.

In front of my bench Ólaf sits at a portable workstation housing the Sannlitró-Völva, its metallic sides embossed with *Heimspeki* symbols. He angles it at the offender, a lanky man with thinning hair sat between us and the administrators' top table, then taps a series of commands into its controls. After he's recorded this examination, he's going to tell me how the machine works.

"I can't tell you how it's manufactured," he said on our way to the Dómstólls, "but I do need to prove to you there's nothing at the Litrúm-Hús Anna need worry about. Then maybe you can talk to her."

He makes one final onscreen tap before leaning back and folding his arms to wait for the machine to boot up. He bounces his head as it charges, his mouth moving silently to count the seconds it takes.

I find myself counting too, watching for some movement in the machine's liquid plasma screen, or in the four condensed coils of copper wire holding it. The magnetic power of those coils is reflected in the thick steel rods that connect them to a small electric generator housed in a glass box at the base of the machine. My eyes flick between the generator and the screen's swirling mass of oil and water. The oil glints a random array of metallic rainbow colours as it glides over and through the water.

When my counting reaches ten, a sound crackles inside the generator and something whirls. Gradually the crackling grows louder and there's a flash. At least I think there's a flash. My eyes glaze over as I hold them open.

Then... Zap! My bones jump inside my skin—a slim bolt of electricity rings out and kisses the generator's glass box before recoiling back like a scorpion's tail. The generator's transparent cage quivers, there's a buzzing noise, then another thicker bolt zigzags out like a whip against the glass. And again.

Soon a successive repetition of electric bolts finds a steady pace and the machine's shaking and crackling dies down to drum a low hum into the corners of the Dómstóll. The inside of the box looks like a hundred spindly electric tentacles wafting in an ocean's current. It's so beautiful I gaze at it too long and miss seeing the swirling oil and water in the screen condense to form the outline of the offender sitting behind it. A watery background now shines in ordered light pastels while a cohesive oil silhouette of the offender's torso glimmers with layered stripes of metallic colour. It's incredible.

While some colours are sucked back, others push forward, revealing the offender's every thought and feeling to the entire room. It's beautiful yet somehow terrifying. This machine can access the biological complexities of the human mind and reveal them in vibrant spectrums of colour.

I put on my reading glasses and scan over the colour guide Ólaf has given me. He said that long-term emotions—deep-reaching emotions such as love, resentment, bitterness, guilt *and* grief—all affect the positive or negative charge of a person's ions so fundamentally they determine the base colour of their energy. Whereas short-term superficial emotions—like comedy-inspired laughter, road rage or pre-speech nerves—merely change a person's outer hue or tone.

The prominent colour at the base of an offenders' energy will therefore always be navy blue: the colour for guilt. It won't change until that offender addresses their guilt through months of counselling, redemption, or closure.

"If they're happy for a moment," Ólaf told me, "their navy base colour will develop an outer rim of canary yellow, but will stay navy at its base. If they lie, their energy will have an outer rim of electric blue, but will still be navy at its base. The colour guide is only a draft," he added. "So if you see a colour during the examination that's not on it, use your common sense."

Looking at the colour guide, I see what he means. On the guide, anger and hate are crimsons while love is pastel pink and lust is deep pink. Jealously is electric green while power is royal purple. It all makes sense. For centuries, humans have drawn golden halos around holy people—on the list, truth and altruism are gold. Historically, we associated black with evil; good with white—on the list black is an absence of conscience; most shades of white indicate ethical contentment. Wisdom is deep brown. Curiosity is light brown. Greed and revenge are deep orange. Sad people often describe their mood as blue or grey—on the list, sadness is blue-grey.

"Our bodies cannot help but reflect what we feel," Ólaf explained. "People plod when sad, jump around when happy. When they're nervous they feel sick, when they're afraid they quiver. Some elderly even die from heartbreak and loneliness. Our cells and organs are acutely tuned into our subconscious, and by subconscious I mean mental activity not directly perceived by our consciousness. Memories, feelings and thoughts can all influence our behaviour without our realising it."

"You've said all that before, haven't you?"

"Once or twice. People use the term 'subconscious' in so many different contexts I like to be clear. The link between our subconscious and our bodies is extremely close, it's no wonder our ions are directly affected by what we think and feel."

I try to memorise the colour guide while I wait.

Without looking up from his laptop, an administrator eventually addresses Ólaf. "Is the machine ready?"

I smile to myself. Höfkállur may have stopped using judges, but their administrators still have the same sense of self-importance.

"Ég er tilbúinn," Ólaf tells them, pushing his glasses up his nose. *Ready*.

I flick my phone's Word2Word to 'record'. Mark's postscript might have been about the machine, so I may want to revisit whatever's about to happen. As the soft Icelandic tones lullabying my ears switch to the computerised staccato of my translator's voice, the offender is asked a series of administrative questions.

"Magnús, we usually ask offenders to lie at the beginning of their examination," says the administrator, "so the Sannlitró-Völva can register the resulting increase in negative energy. Please lie to the following question. What is your name?"

Magnús shuffles in his seat before saying something about being called Stefán. The water and oil onscreen refracts until his image consists of electric blue swirls of oil floating in a sea of navy blue water. "Thank you. And now, your real name?" Before Magnús can reply, the oil in his onscreen image glimmers into gold, turning the water cream apart from a navy blue base. An administrative question follows and the Sannlitró-Völva remains gold, cream, and blue, as it does with the next question, and the next.

I sense my mouth gaping open and close it. Mark and Ari were right. This machine is not a mere lie-detector—it's reading this man's mind before he speaks!

Seeing little point in lying, Magnús admits the tax evasion he committed, claims it was a careless mistake and apologises.

Ólaf turns to me and whispers. "Shame he didn't admit that when he was asked the first time."

"Didn't he realise he'd get found out?"

"Not everyone outside Höfkállur is a *Heimspeki* follower," Ólaf reminds me. "There are still plenty of sceptics who think they can get away with things. We bring them here to be examined, see for themselves."

"Ari said you often get anonymous information or evidence?"

"Right. But if we get that first, no one can trust the offender anymore. Like this one today, he should have come forward immediately. Examining him was the only way to convert him. It helps rehabilitate them too."

After conferring with each other, those on the top table ask the offender, Magnús, to repay his tax imbalance and spend a weekend gardening at the Reformation Cooperative. Ólaf whispers the Reformation Cooperative is an industrial-sized, geothermal communal greenhouse that replaced Höfkállur Prison. He stops talking to stand in respect when the administrators swish out of the top doors.

I press my lips together to rehydrate them. Once the top doors have clicked shut and the offender has been led out, Ólaf rocks back on his chair.

"You see?" he says, a smug smile pushing his cheeks into round mounds.

I lower my phone and fold away my glasses. "I certainly see why you might expect someone to steal the technology. It's...spectacular. The membrane, it has some kind of oily surface?"

Ólaf leaps up with childish enthusiasm, pushes back his glasses before pointing at various aspects of the machine. "It's an *olía* and *vatn* coated plasma membrane. Oil because of the nitrogen. Water because of the oxygen."

"And copper to generate a magnetic field?"

He jerks his head back, impressed. "That's right, well done. The magnetic field splits the coloured light emitted by the offender into its individual components. You've heard of the Zeeman effect?"

I shake my head. My scientific knowledge only goes so far.

"Well, you probably don't need to know that much detail, and it's so hard to explain—much easier to actually see it."

I tilt my head around the machine. "Can you show me then?"

"Nei!" Ólaf laughs. "Not you, my dear! You can't see it."

"Why not? Is it confidential?"

"You cannot see it unless you were born in a home insulated with lava brick, which I assume you weren't, given you're Australian."

"I don't follow." Though I definitely want to. Mark's postscript could have been about this.

Ólaf sits back down. "I see there's another thing Anna hasn't told you. For years, Höfkállur used lava brick to insulate its homes. Lava brick is full of iron and iron is very magnetic—so magnetic it affects the foetus while inside the womb."

"Affects them? How?"

"Humans are sixty percent water, so magnetic fields penetrate our bodies very easily—we offer no resistance to it, and tissues exposed to a magnetic field for long periods of time retain enhanced magnetic signals. So, after years of exposure during development, some babies absorbed magnetism through the rear sections of their occipital lobes, back here." He turns on an angle and moves his collar away from the thinning grey hair at the nape of his neck. At the base of his skull protrudes a crenation of flesh. "It made our eyes develop extra-sensitive cone cells, the receptor cells in our eyes, and left us with magnetic signals we can use to see…well, more than most."

I run a hand over the back of my neck. There is a small lump there too, at the base of my skull. Still it's nothing compared to the size of Ólaf's.

"We call it the litagjöf. The ability to see others' electrical energy is supposed to be a gift." He harrumphs like he considers it no such thing.

I'm not sure what to think. People often claim they can do things like this. It never turns out to be true. "You, um, don't think it's a gift?"

"Maybe when I was younger but…" He closes his eyes to dismiss the thought. "Nei. Doesn't matter. We have the Sannlitró-Völva now, so everyone can see their own energy."

"No, no, please go on. You were saying, when you were younger… Why isn't it a gift?"

"Ah, I made a mistake, that's all, my dear." His tone turning sour, he starts packing away the Sannlitró-Völva, then continues. "I told my friends I saw rainbows around them and they laughed at me. Halfviti." *Morons*, my phone translates. Ólaf tightens his lips in bitterness. "My parents thought I had delusions, that I was deformed."

I watch his eyes, checking to see if he's having a delusion about me right now. "Is that what it feels like, a delusion?"

"More like one of those magic-eye illusion puzzles. You have to refocus your eyes to see." He notices my expression. "Don't worry, my dear, you'd know if I were watching your energy. Here, I'll show you." He closes his eyes and bows his head. "If I don't concentrate, I can only see yellow and white, like the dust in sunbeams. But if I empty my mind and think about the muscles around my pupils, and if you stay perfectly still…"

His eyelids flutter open to reveal eyes so unfocussed he isn't so much as looking at me as through me.

"Now all around you, I see…yes, the atoms close to you are light blue-grey, typical for someone in mourning. But I think…yes, further out, you are light brown and pink…Do you have a boyfriend?"

"Me? No." Although that was another thing Mark wanted me to do—start dating again. "It's the last thing on my mind right now."

"Are you sure?"

"Ólaf, I saw my brother last night, in a morgue."

"Isn't Ari taking you to Jötunnsjökull this afternoon?"

I check my watch. "Soon, in fact."

"Good news for Ari. Me too. You will keep him busy enough." He pulls down his glasses. "*Eigi leyna augu ef ann kona manni.* Eyes cannot hide a woman's love for a man."

My eyebrows rise so high it widens my eyes. "Ólaf, I have no interest in Ari whatsoever."

"Ah, but everyone likes Ari. He has too much energy sometimes, physically—reminds me how little I have left. Still everyone likes him, including me. He's like my second son."

I look away, embarrassed, then remember the guide. "Light brown and pink, couldn't it also mean I'm curious about someone I love, like Mark?"

Ólaf shakes his head. His eyes refocus. "The tests sometimes used to say I made mistakes, but I am never wrong face-to-face." He notices my watch. "Oh, is that really the time?" He stretches over the machine's controls to depress a large burgundy button on the generator's side.

"Couldn't they think of a more original colour for the off-switch?" I ask, helping him wind up the electrical cords.

"I know. But people look for red in an emergency, and if the generator's glass broke while the machine was on, the damage that would be done—well, it's worth a bit of unoriginality!"

With the image of electric feelers whipping against the machine's glass still blazing in my mind, I couldn't agree more. "Surely the glass is shatterproof?"

"As are the glass walls behind us. It shouldn't stop us from being cautious. After all, it's why they invented this thing," he says, piling the electrical cords on top of the Sannlitró-Völva's trolley, "they thought using the litagjöf hurt us."

"Does it?"

"I get a slight headache. Though not enough to take the day off work, like some!" He means Jón. "Maybe it was worse for others? They probably did enough tests to know."

"And I suppose that's why the government based its research centre here?" I realise.

He shrugs. "It is where we all live."

Where we all live.

I can't tell if the words repeat in my head because they're significant or because a voice is putting them there. Either way, I decide to check. "Ólaf, have you seen anyone living in Höfkállur whose energy might suggest they're an activist or feeling guilty for threatening someone?"

He pulls a cover over the trolley, shakes his head. "Sorry."

"What about Gunnar, Doctor Emil's assistant? Have you ever checked his energy?"

"Who?"

"You don't know him?"

He shakes his head again.

"What about Jón? You must have checked him."

"Of course, he's with my cousin. Why?"

"Does he hold a grudge against...lawyers perhaps?"

He pauses to think. "Nei. And I don't think he drove past your Austurleid yesterday, if that's what you're thinking. He was here all day at an examination. Started early too."

"Oh, okay." So Jón's alibi checks out. "Thanks."

"If you like," Ólaf whispers conspiratorially, "I'll check him next time I see him. How about that?" He moves towards the exit.

"Sounds good."

"Come on I'll take you to the front entrance. I have to go that way to get to the Litrúm Maps anyway." As we leave the Dómstóll, he swipes a yellow keycard through the door pad to lock it. "Caution," he says, gesturing at the lock. "Until the patents are passed."

I try to think what else I can ask Ólaf about the Sannlitró-Völva, about Mark or his research, but the pounding of footsteps down the corridor stops me from thinking at all. It's Ari, and his face is filled with panic.

Chapter 13

"**G**ott. You are here." Ari puts his hands on his hips and heaves a sigh of relief when he sees me outside the Litrúm Dómstólls. "They said you left *The Himinn* with a man, went inside the Litrúm-Hús but didn't come out."

"Who's 'they'?" I ask. "Gunnar?"

"Nei, MUR officers from Akureyri, Director Úlfar sent them to help. It is okay though, you are with Ólaf."

"Anna thought I should know more about his litagjöf."

"You agreed to call me if you wanted to leave *The Himinn*."

"Sorry, I forgot." Like he forgot to tell me that someone was watching *The Himinn*. "I'm ready for Jötunnsjökull when you are."

"I'd go now," Ólaf tells Ari, leading us both away from the Dómstólls, "before Director Úlfar arrives."

"He's coming here?" Ari sounds as surprised as Ólaf. "Excuse us a minute, Becky," he says in English. "It will be easier for me in íslensku." He switches into Icelandic but my earpiece is still networked to Word2Word. "What happened with Sigmar?"

"Sigmar left for the Cooperative last night," Ólaf answers, also in Icelandic. "Are you caring too much again?"

"His father contacted me this morning, insisted the results are incorrect."

"Ha! They always say that when it doesn't go their way. What did you tell him?"

Ari grins. "I told him there's no possibility of that because not-guilty examinations are only performed by senior technicians and Ólaf Stefánson is the best senior technician our Litrúm-Hús has ever seen."

"Very funny. Did you also tell them I'm the *only* senior technician the Litrúm-Hús has ever seen. I think it's time I retired."

Ari laughs as we turn down a corridor. "You can't fool me, old man.

I saw that email of yours to Reykjavík, suggesting they send you some extra cases so that, what was it, their families were spared humiliation in the Capital? You love this job!"

"Are you spying on me?"

"Comes with the territory of promotion. That's why accounts give me those extra digits."

"Seriously Ari, you need to get a new hobby. Why don't you find yourself a nice girl, settle down." Ólaf eyes me up and down. "Some kids would keep you off my back."

Ari clears his throat, embarrassed. "Sorry Becky," he returns to English. "Some, er, work things."

"Speaking of which," Ólaf adds, still in Icelandic, "did you sort out those security guards—they have to get changed before, not after clocking on if they're to cover their shifts properly?"

"Jón did. I figured he'd know how to talk to them."

"Jón?"

"Of course. He was a security guard in Reykjavík for ten years, remember?"

Ólaf raises his eyebrows to say 'fair enough'.

As we reach the display cabinets I passed yesterday, Ólaf and Ari pause. As well as old law books, the displays contain even older scanning computers, microfiche machines and a freestanding franking machine. Behind them, rows of compactus shelving stretch into the building housing dusty old leather-bound volumes. Off to one side is a staircase.

"Well, Becky," Ólaf holds out his hand, "it was a pleasure meeting you again."

"Thank you for showing me around." I go to shake hands but he turns it around and gives it a light kiss.

"You're welcome. And if you need to know anything more, call me. I'd rather you have my facts than other people's fictions, if you know what I mean?"

"I do."

Ari invites me to ascend the staircase with him. "I must tell my assistant I'm leaving. Bless, Ólaf."

Ólaf waves then walks back towards the front entrance.

Ari bounds up the stairs and beckons for me to follow. As soon as we reach the open plan work area at the top of the stairs, he calls out. An assistant with black rinsed hair and dark wrinkled skin peers over her desk partition. When she notices me she folds her arms. "Are you going already?" she says. My phone translates.

"Shut down my computer for me?"

"Only if you give me a twirl."

"I wouldn't want to give you a heart attack, Jóhanna."

She ruffles her hair and pretends to sit back down. Really she hovers midway to watch Ari head back down the staircase.

I follow and realise he isn't wearing a suit today. He's in lace-up climbing boots, khaki pants, an army green jumper and a brown Elizabethan-replica leather jacket. Stubble extenuates his jawline. I suppose, under any other circumstances, if I'd met him at another time, he'd look good.

I remember my conversation with Mark a few weeks ago, in which he'd urged me to start dating again. He practically guaranteed I'd find love soon.

"One enchanted evening," he said, "it'll be like in the old black and white movies, with fireworks going off all around you. And he'll be the faithful type this time."

I take a deep breath. Mark always did have a stronger belief in the future than me. There couldn't be a worse time to meet someone than this.

As soon as we enter the car park I notice Ari's four-wheel drive. It's parked close to the steps, glinting beautiful silvers and mauves in the morning sun. I circle the vehicle. The tops of its wheels reach past my waist. Its door handles are at shoulder-height.

"What do you think of my big baby?" Ari's voice is as proud as his grin. "You cannot buy Eroders in Europe yet."

"It certainly is big."

"Naturally," Ari says, swinging the passenger door wide for me. "It's the only way to travel to Jötunnsjökull."

"How did Mark get up there, do you think?" I haul myself into the car, making sure my waistband sits over the top of my stomach as I sit. "Ólaf said he might have gone with a girl. Do you know any local girls with a car like yours?"

Ari laughs. "I do not know any Höfkállur girls who would even go there."

"It sounds like you have first-hand experience with that."

"I do." He tosses his daypack onto the back seat before leaping into the driver's seat and clacking on the headlights.

I smile as I realise I have the same brand of daypack back home, in a different colour.

"What's with the headlights?" I ask, easing up the hem of my pantaloons to check my thigh's adhesive dressing. It feels heavier than before. My cut must have bled a little. I check its seal. Nothing's leaked through. "Why turn them on when it's daylight?"

"Car lights must stay on all day in Iceland," Ari says. "The weather changes too quick."

We wait for the car's automatic headrest and seatbelt adjusters to determine our body height and girth, then Ari eases onto the road. Within minutes we're cruising out of Höfkállur. I gaze out the windows and again search a road my brother recently travelled. Apparently.

Ari accelerates to match the speed limit, then describes his plans for the afternoon ahead. His enthusiasm keeps the corners of his mouth in a constant state of elevation, he sounds like me before a dive. I can't help but mirror his excitement, and I too find a smile on my lips.

By the time the landscape is dominated by fields of thick black lava rock, I've heard so much about the Jötunnsjökull glacier I can picture the valley through which its rivers cut. It sounds like a lush warm Swiss valley, with white mountain peaks hovering above it. Then again, knowing Iceland's landscapes differ so distinctly from anything I've seen before, I put my assumptions aside. The unadulterated zeal with which Ari speaks about the land is infectious and, like a drug, I find his fervour addictive and impossible to resist. If he pauses too long I find myself prompting him for more. He loves this place and clearly wants anyone seeing it to love it too. To that, I offer little resistance. Faced with such austere beauty, what would be the point?

After an hour we turn east, away from the coast. Manmade rock-pillars appear amid the volcanic deluge.

"Farmers made them, a long time ago," Ari explains, "to help them home in fog. You can see each pillar from the one before, if you are on a horse."

"You wouldn't want to be short-sighted, would you?"

"In the most remote areas we have emergency huts. They have food, water, blankets and geothermic generators. You sign the guest book, write what you use, and someone restocks them regularly. If you need one they are easy to see, being bright orange."

It's good to know. Still, if Ari has been going to Jötunnsjökull since he was a kid, I doubt I'll need one. The thought comes to me so naturally I consider saying it aloud. But Ari's already smiling at me, and I realise I didn't just think the words, they've already left my mouth. Embarrassed, I concentrate on the view.

Soon the road veers northeast and the rock pillars disappear. Boulders as big as tanks make the land seem wild and untouched. Smaller rocks, lodged in the crevices and gullies between these monsters, make the ground appear so uneven I don't believe anyone could navigate it successfully, even on horseback. Ari tells me this is why farmers prefer to stay close to the coast. But I think it's also because these plains are bleak and desolate, black and dangerous as far as the eye can see.

"Of course it is not like this all the way," Ari adds. "You will see. It gets better."

I already know he's right.

"Are you hungry?" he asks.

"Um." I shrug, unsure how to answer. Hunger and I exist together on an entirely different level than most people.

"I am," he smiles. "Look in my bag." Inside are two baguettes. "Do you prefer chicken or tuna? I like both."

"So do I." Though I pass him the one that smells like tuna. Tuna sandwiches usually have more calories than chicken because of the mayonnaise. "Thanks. I wouldn't have thought to bring food." I truly wouldn't.

He smiles and we munch in silence for a while. Still digesting my breakfast I really don't want these extra calories. I also don't want to be rude.

Instead I take tiny bites and watch for when he's not looking. Then I pull bits of bread off and stuff them inside the wrappings. The fact that the chicken is delicious only makes me feel guiltier. If I can avoid the bread, I'll at least save on consuming empty calories. Still, looking at how much baguette I've already eaten, I need to calculate how much one of these things costs, calorie-wise. It's been such a long time since I've let myself eat anything like this. I'm pretty sure the bread alone would be four hundred calories. A slice of bread with butter is a hundred calories and there's far more bread in this.

I lift up a corner and examine the chicken. Chicken breast is a hundred and seventy calories for 100g if it's roasted, which this chicken is, but how much chicken is here? I look over the length of the baguette and decide to add a hundred calories to my count for good measure. If I were to eat the whole thing, it would surely add at least five hundred calories to my daily total. Most adults eat around two thousand calories a day, but I'm trying to lose weight so keep my count to less than a thousand. Six hundred if I can. Still, I wish I hadn't eaten breakfast. I should have known Ari would want to eat. I should have waited to eat with him instead. Now the bread I can't avoid will bloat me, making my tummy swell even more than it did after breakfast.

I pretend to get more comfortable in my seat, but really readjust my waistband to make sure it's pulling in the swelling. After this, I'm definitely not eating again until tomorrow.

"Wow, this is filling," I say, pushing against the bloating. "I'm stuffed." Aching too. My body always does this when I eat a lot of food back-to-back. It's straining to have a period, I can feel it twisting and pulling at me from the inside, and the consumption of vast quantities of food never helps. I guess a full stomach presses on all the wrong places. Once I've got my shape back, though, I'll concentrate on finding out what's really wrong with me. Most likely, my body's simply being slow to adapt to its new energy levels. I used to eat a lot more than I do now and it probably doesn't realise it has more than enough energy to menstruate. The doctor I saw last month is most definitely wrong about that.

"If you keep going the way you are," he told me, making me look in a mirror and turn so a shoulder blade bone pinched at the inside of my skin, "you'll make yourself infertile. Do you want children one day?"

What nonsense. It was just the way I was standing. He never saw the layer of fat around my stomach; he only saw what he wanted to see. There are plenty of other reasons I might not have had a period in so long—stress or hormone levels? I should have insisted he took blood for testing, rather than rely on his height and weight chart. Those charts are averages after all.

I scrunch up the rest of my baguette inside its wrapper and search for somewhere to put it.

"There is okay," Ari points to the empty drink holders under the dashboard. "I'll throw it out later."

"Thanks so much, it was yummy." It truly was.

I hold my hand out for his wrappings too, so he doesn't have to take his eyes off the road. When he passes them, our hands touch. The brevity of the contact disappoints me and, again, I wish I'd come to Iceland when Mark first asked me.

I don't realise until I've done it, but I sigh.

"What's up?" Ari glances at me. "Thinking about your brother?"

"I should have come to visit when he first asked me."

"How long ago was that?"

"Four months."

"*Four* months." He sounds impressed. "Why was he here so long?"

"Studying. Writing his thesis."

"What was he studying?"

I hesitate, unsure how much Ari will understand. His English is better than most Londoners, but Mark used a lot of long words to describe his thesis. "He was studying the world's approach to the post-mortem survival of the human conscience—culturally, religiously, and scientifically. In other words, what everyone in the world thinks about life after death."

"Oh, okay. Go on."

"Before he came here, he travelled all over the world looking for the one thing everyone could agree on, no matter what their belief. He," I swallow to keep my voice steady, "he wanted his thesis to make the world a better place."

"Did he find something?"

I nod. "The numinous experience."

"The what?"

"The numinous experience." I clear my throat and change my tone to mimic the university lecturer Mark often pretended to be, the one he always wanted to become. "From the Latin numen, numinous refers to the power or presence of a divinity, god, or spirit. The word was popularised by the imminent German theologian Rudolf Otto, in his influential book *Das Heilige*, translated into English in 1923 as *The Idea of the Holy*."

"You know a lot about your brother's thesis."

"What can I say?" I shrug. "I loved my brother. He was a pioneer in his field. I read everything he wrote. Want to know more?"

"It is a long drive."

I resume my lecturer's voice. "Rudolf Otto said there are two essential elements to experiencing a numinous encounter. The first, *mysterium tremendum*, is the sensation of being invoked with fear and trembling."

"So...being afraid?"

"Correct. The second, *mysterium fascinas*, is the sensation of being attracted, fascinated and compelled. Awe, I suppose. Or, um... admiration. Anyway," I slip back into my normal voice, "the result of a numinous experience is that a person is left with the distinct feeling they've been united with a hallowed other—be it a deity, transcendent, supernatural, sacred, or holy."

"You fear and admire, and you feel connected with something. Okay, got it."

"Good. Travelling everywhere made Mark realise that numinous experiences can more or less be encountered anywhere—of course in churches, temples, synagogues and other places of worship; but also while watching the sunset from a beautiful beach, listening to Debussy, cradling a newborn child, witnessing an aurora dance over a cooled lava plain…" I gesture out the window, thinking of Anna.

"Ah, now I understand. This numinous, it is like…wonder?"

"Yes. But of course humanity has never been able to simply enjoy its experiences, we've needed explanation or reason for them too. Which is why many religious figures over time—prophets, saviours, wise men—have come up with theories to best explain the numinous experience."

"Of course."

"It was okay for a while because, according to Mark's thesis, that probably helped countless communities—" I want to say homogenise, "—er, find peace, and evolve into countries, nations…multi-nations even. The only problem Mark found with it is fanaticism."

"Fanaticism? What is that?"

"It's what you and Director Úlfar were both saying yesterday, about people being too passionate about their newfound beliefs."

"Ah, okay. Go on."

"Well, the problem with fanaticism is that theories can be proved wrong."

"Unless it is from science."

"Yes and no. Science doesn't know everything. Yes, with every explanation science offers we grow to understand our place in the world with greater ease. But, what about the numinous experience? Can science actually explain something so spiritual? Mark," I swallow, my throat sticking with all this talk of him, "thought it could, to begin with, which is why he came here."

"To study how our science explains the numinous experience?"

I nod. "The numinous experience is very important for mankind. Mark said he put a whole section in his thesis about its influence over the centuries." I remember him telling me. "Life is hard and most people don't like to think of existence as years of hardship followed by infinite nothingness—they need to know there'll be some reward for being nice to each other, rather than protecting only themselves. And the numinous experience *must* come from somewhere. So, for most people, it feels right to connect the two together."

"And now science can connect them."

"Well, when Mark first came here, he wanted to use his thesis to persuade people to understand the numinous experience in scientific terms. He hoped for the ultimate demise of organised religion as we know it. In that he claimed to be a secular humanist."

"A what?"

I chuckle. "Sorry. Let's just say Mark believed—wrongly or rightly,

I don't know myself—that most of our remaining wars seem to be incited by religious differences, or at least between people claiming so, and he wanted to do something about that. He figured if people based their beliefs on scientific fact it would pacify fanaticism and the world would be a better place. But then...after he came here, I think he changed his mind."

Secularity doesn't matter, he said in his notes last night.

"He was writing a new, separate postscript to his thesis," I continue, "about something he'd realised was more important than the thesis itself. A couple of weeks ago, I'm sure he said something about mankind needing its spirituality more, about needing a sense of wonderment. I think he even started agreeing with me about human nature."

"What about it?"

"That it cannot be tamed." Yes, that's what Mark was referring to in his notes. Now that I'm talking about it, I recall having a whole discussion with him about it on the phone. "Or overcome."

"You really think so?"

"Absolutely!"

Ari shifts in his seat. "What about Höfkállur? What about how safe it is, how good everyone is to each other?"

"Er, apart from the threats I've been receiving."

"That is one person."

"Are you sure? We don't know anything yet."

Ari doesn't reply.

I don't know what else to say either. I'd love to believe people can change after learning a new theory. But I can't.

So a silence falls between us. It's not an awkward one though, more of a repose than a discomfort.

In it, I wish more than ever I knew exactly what Mark had decided about science's ability to explain the numinous experience. What was he so excited to tell me? What was in his postscript?

Energy. The numinous. It's both, together. He said in his thesis notes, and on the phone last weekend. *We need both. We need to be various.*

I remember, too, a discussion we had a few weeks ago, about human nature and spirituality. Bits come to me, so I attempt an imagined conversation to remember more.

"Without spirituality, science has no boundaries." Mark says in my memory; so he now also says in my imagination. "Nature may very well turn out to be a simple sequence of scientific equations and explanations. But, without the idea that there's more to life than the

147

material, and without organised groups supporting that idea, science would have no limits."

"I thought you were all for science. Why give it limits?" I ask him.

"To protect nature."

"Why protect nature?"

"To protect ourselves. Nature has spent thousands of years perfecting mankind—physically and psychologically. We can hunt on land, create flight in the sky, dive under the sea..." I remember his dive comment in particular, "...navigate the solar system. Because of nature we now have a wide enough range of attributes to face any danger as a species. If we were all the same, we would not survive as successfully as we do."

"And what's that got to do with the numinous experience?"

In my imagined conversation, he doesn't answer.

I wait but nothing more comes and my attention is drawn to a bridge on the road ahead. We cross a small river and a mountain range appears on the horizon. As we trundle towards it, the angular harshness of the plains is tamed by a soft green prettiness. The lava boulders shrink in size and a moist glaze hangs in the air. Moss clumps cover the rocks, more and more until occasional riots of green become so seditious in their rampage whole rocks disappear beneath the insurrection of colour. The emerging emerald mounds, so triumphant amid the dark plain, remind me of the swathes of spiky lime spinifex that spot the blackened bushwalks of home.

Home. I think of bushwalking with Mark, chatting as we ramble. Still nothing more comes of our conversation about spirituality.

"Water comes down from the glacier," Ari explains, noticing my gaze.

"All the way down here?" I ask, cheerfully enough.

"Já."

"It's beautiful."

Closer to the mountain range on the horizon, stalks of hard rubbery grasses appear, hugging the moss beds and sticking upright between the verdant rocks, whipping through the wind whistling between them.

We drive towards the mountains and I try to stop myself from flinching when the wind becomes ferocious, shaking the Eroder. Instead I hide my unease by commenting on how flat the land is, how tiny the black pebbles are, and how pretty the bedless brooks are trickling over them, soaking each pebble until their surfaces glisten. Ari beams as if pleased I see the land the way he does.

Slowly we cross this wet plain to arrive at a gap in the mountainside, where the road narrows before opening up into a valley. There I behold the source of each glistening rivulet. Each tiny stream is born of a river, each river is born of a bigger river, and each bigger river is in turn born from the torrent before me, the same torrent whose fast churning once sliced through the mountainside.

"The Skepnasá?" I guess as the watery monster sprints along the left side of the opening, forcing small branches, silt, and ice along its course at a tremendous pace.

"The Skepnasá." Ari sweeps a hand wide in welcome. "Most people stay on this side of the Skepnasá and hike in the valley. But I found Mark on the other side. If you want to see where I found him, exactly where I found him, we will have to cross the river. There is no bridge."

I look past the raging waters to scan the far side of the valley. A slim strip of land sits between the river and a sheer cliff face. "Okay."

"Are you sure? Remember, people can die trying to cross the Skepnasá. See that sign?" A huge aluminium 'welcome' sign dominates the roadside ahead. There is no other opening into the valley. "When you pass that sign, you agree to do what the government says and keep two metres between you and the river, always."

"And there's no other government presence here? No research facility or survey area?"

"It's a national park. Protected."

I study the sign. Its safety guidelines are printed in English as well as Icelandic. "So that's all the warning there is?"

"Remember what you were saying before about the power of human nature, how it cannot be tamed. This," he points, "is also nature. You cannot signpost a thunderstorm. You cannot flag a tsunami. Everyone knows an active volcano is dangerous, especially in Iceland. This river has its own mind. If you want the government to be responsible for your safety, do what they ask and stay away from the river."

"Director Úlfar was right then, about not being liable." This sign is one big official exclusion clause. "It's a wonder people do it," I say, fumbling in my bag for my phone. "It's a wonder Mark did. He wasn't adverse to taking risks, but never like this." Never with nature.

"People should not base-jump tall buildings," Ari reminds me. "They do, even though it kills. This is the same. So if you and I cross today, you cannot tell anyone. If you do, I will lose my job. You still want to cross?"

"Yes." I snap a photograph of the sign. Mum and Dad will want to see it. I turn to look Ari in the eye. "I need to get over there, see it for myself."

"You are sure?" Ari tries one last time. "It is okay for me to risk my life. I do not want to be responsible for yours."

"You've crossed this river since you were a kid, right? And none of your family ever died trying?"

"The people who die are tourists. The glacier melts at different speeds in different places, depending on the sun and season. The best place to cross changes from one minute to the next. You have to know the river to cross it."

"Sounds like you know it well enough for me. Let's go."

"Okay, tough-girl." He winds down the window for a better view. "We'll drive some more. It will be easier to cross closer to the lake."

"Who's tough-girl?"

"You are." He grins, though not for long. As he accelerates, his attention cements into a firm concentration that blocks out everything apart from the river and where best to cross it.

I'm glad because, despite everything I just said, looking at the frenetic water, at the beast of a river they call the Skepnasá, I also don't feel like smiling anymore.

Chapter 14

Jagged grey pebbles invade the road as we drive into Jötunnsjökull's valley, slowing our progress to a bumpy crawl. Wind still shakes the Eroder, although once deeper into the valley the air warms and, as we're freed from the shade cast by the valley's initial peaks, the temperature soars.

Ahead of us are two mountain ridges. The ridge on our right stops short of the riverbank, allowing plenty of room for the road. But the ridge along the opposite bank protrudes into the water. I can't see beyond it.

Before we reach either ridge, the temperature becomes so stifling I have to take off every layer down to my lilac corset. My eyes are fixed on the view while Ari scans the surface ahead for sharp rocks—yet I sense him glimpse at me undress. In the past I've happily stripped down to my bikini, without hesitation, in front of dive guides I've only just met. That's when I'm itching to get in the water. Ari's attention makes me self-conscious.

"Nothing to see here," I tell him, regretting going anywhere near that baguette. My stomach must be bloated to twice its usual size. I won't let myself do that again.

"Only because you see it every day."

"I…" I want to berate him further but the landscape is changing so fast it distracts me. Although the wheels of the Eroder are still scrambling over damp pebbles, grass stalks now sprout among them. Soon the stalks become clumps and the clumps multiply until, as we trundle around the corner of the roadside ridge, the valley opens up into a bushy meadow.

Dirty brown mountains with mossy olive bottoms surround this part of the valley, protecting it from the harsh winds and trapping in the heat. The road disappears under a blanket of grass where well-worn tyre tracks guide us. At the farthest end of the meadow are short stubby trees, their dwarfed yet full canopies furnished with leaves of emerald and jade. The thick smell of barbeque smoke pours through my open window and I spy a collection of wooden huts and tents hiding amid bushes, their roofs peek around the rich green foliage like children playing hide-and-seek.

"The best is to come," Ari says. "Keep your eyes ahead."

"Are you always this excited when you bring girls to Jötunnsjökull?"

"I've not yet managed to persuade one to come with me," he says, scanning the ground ahead rather than make eye contact.

"Oh." I feel sorry for him. "And the first time you do, it...it's like this."

"Yeah." He laughs.

I laugh too, relieved he can see the funny side.

"Keep your eyes ahead now," he says. "Or you will miss it."

I wiggle in my seat and stare out the windscreen.

As we get closer to the riverside ridge, a white edge appears behind it. Shining like a bright white torch across the valley, the Jötunnsjökull glacier looms into view. Wedged between the valley's two largest mountains, its top is covered in brilliant snow while its sun-sparkling ice face glistens. Its layers dim the further they stretch towards the valley floor, where a dark lake laps at its base. Huge silt-covered blocks of dark ice bob in its waters. Blocks floating too close to the river—roaring away from the lake's far left—are immediately sucked into it.

"Mum loved this glacier," Ari murmurs, gazing at my expression. "She would sit outside our tent, and every time she turned a page in her book, she'd look up at it with the same expression you have now. She died when I was fourteen. Dad has not been here since. I come every weekend, if I can."

So that's what he meant when he said he knew about loss.

"See those blocks?" he continues. "They make the Skepnasá strong, more strong in summer when there is more melting." To our left, the Skepnasá River snakes hungrily around the side of the valley, its tempestuous banks more rugged and ravenous closer to the glacier. The ridge behind it alternates between jutting into the water and holding back, forming occasional banks of glistening grey pebbles.

"And over there, is where I found Mark."

I follow his eyes to a slim triangle of taupe land trapped between the glacier, the lake and the ridge that protrudes into the river. There doesn't seem to be anything over there apart from an expanse of darker pebbles edged with silt. A few boulders line the lake and the river, but I can't see anything that would make Ari risk his job to hike over there. Anna's concerns about Ari flit into my head.

"So, um," I try to sound casual, "what's so special about hiking over there? I thought you said it was exceptional?"

"It is." Ari studies my face. "Why," he smirks innocently, "don't you trust me?"

"Can you really trust anyone?"

"This is the lawyer in you." He turns his attention back to scanning the river as we crawl alongside it.

"What do you mean?"

"Lawyers do not commit easy. You ask if they like spaghetti or pizza and they tell you they like both. They are afraid someone will remember if they choose and in the future will use it against them. They like to be ambiguous."

"I'm not a lawyer anymore."

He glances back at me. "Are you sure?"

"I'm not. I'm really not."

"It is okay, Becky. I don't mind. Habit is hard to change." He peers ahead. "Ah, a little further."

"But I'm happy to choose between pizza and spaghetti. I only became a lawyer because I hated..." It's difficult for me to put into words. It's lots of things.

"Because you hated...?" Ari asks.

"I..." I'm not even sure how to start explaining. I always thought it began when I was a little girl wearing my first pair of reading glasses to school—pink frames with rainbow hearts. I loved them. My 'friends' hid them under fresh grass clippings in the playground, giggled as I covered myself in fine green stems trying to find them. The boy wouldn't let me play kiss-chase anymore and called me 'four eyes'. I wished the teachers would notice and make it stop. They didn't. When someone dared the tallest boy in class to kiss me, he was standing near the fishpond, his back to the water. Instead of offering him my cheek, I pushed him in. Of course the teachers punished me.

Emotions cloud clear thought.

Still the satisfaction of standing up for myself resonated with me, enough to influence my career path. Until, that is, I graduated from law school and discovered most lawyers were unhappy. In hindsight, I guess most of them were like Riley—they lacked the confidence to pursue their real dreams, so either suffered their career choice in silence, or took their frustrations out on junior lawyers.

For me it was worse than being back at school. The senior lawyers made me feel bad about myself long before Riley even thought about cheating on me. In fact, that's probably why he did. When I met him I was an eager law student, a nice smiley girl intent on protecting the underdog. Within months of starting work I was an underdog myself. My insatiable drive made me popular among clients. But my supposed colleagues just bullied me.

"Because you hated…?" Ari asks again, turning the Eroder to face the water.

"Look, I actually hated being a lawyer—I wish I'd never become one. I'm no good at confrontation…"

Ari scoffs, smirking at the same time to let me know he means it as a tease.

"I'm not! Not compared to the rest of them. My firm was full of uptight egos, all trying to prove something. It was horrible. I still hate dealing with lawyers. At least now they don't work in my building and I don't have to see them every day." And I still get to stand up to unfairness and injustice—only now it's through my articles and research. In them, I can thrive. "I have more control now."

"Exactly."

I've just proven his point. He's probably right too. Staying in control means not needing to trust anyone, which means never again having to face the possibility of being let down. It's my preferred discomfort.

Grinning at his win, Ari stops the car directly opposite one of the wider banks of pebbles and jumps out. The meadow graduates into a few metres of shingle before disappearing under rushing water, swirling so fast it roars like a lion warning off a rival. I climb down and hobble to the river's edge.

"Gott," Ari mutters to himself, inspecting the riverbed.

I can't see anything good about it.

He dashes back to the car, presses something on the dashboard's plasma touch-screen.

"Erode okay," states a computerised voice.

Something clunks under the car. Ari leans down and unhooks what looks like a winch cable from under the front grill. A teethed snow anchor with a curved shaft hangs from its end. After measuring out a length of cable, he climbs onto a large flat-topped boulder jutting into the water, swings the anchor fast in a circle, then lobs it across the river. It lands with precision on the opposite bank, lodging in the sediment as water pulls at its wire.

"Get in!" Ari says.

Chapter 15

I strain to hear the sound of spurting water through cracked glass. After a while I realise there is only the fizz of the Skepnasá's speed-bubbles against the Eroder's outsides. I expect Ari to leap into action, urge the Eroder up the riverbank before we're flooded. Neither happens. Ari's hand, which cradled my head when I buried it in his shoulder, is simply stroking my hair. He murmurs something in Icelandic. Why isn't he panicking?

I turn to assess the rear passenger window. A large fracture quivers in the glass like a squashed spider's last spasms. The pressure of the water pulsating against it could splinter the glass at any second, submerging us under freezing liquid. Ari's eyes are fixed on the window as if willing it to hold.

This isn't happening, this isn't happening. It's a dream. Wake up!

My breath quivers like the glass. It isn't a dream. "Will it hold?" I ask Ari.

He shifts his feet and begins to accelerate. "It will hold. The Clear Defence coating on the glass will keep it together. I am sorry this happened today. It has been a long time." He shakes his head, confused. "There were no ice blocks near the river, I checked."

"Could one have floated closer after we submerged?"

Still shaking his head, he eases the Eroder up the riverbank. Daylight appears along the top of the windscreen. I loosen my grip on the seat. The front windows break free from the water, leaving the boot submerged.

A few metres more and sunbeams sparkle through the cracked window. I ease my lower back into the curve of my seat.

"What about on the way back?" I ask. "Doesn't glass shrink when it's cold?"

"I have a repair kit. I will fix it before we leave."

Ari turns off the Eroder's special features, waits for the winch to rehook its anchor, then buzzes down his dripping window to stick his elbow into the fresh clean air. He leans forward as we rumble over pebbled ground, looks up at the sky and smiles to himself, though at what, I can't imagine. We almost died.

Still, his calm certainty in the river probably saved our lives. "Thank you," I say, "for staying so calm."

"You're welcome. But that was not calm. That was me listening to my gut." He turns his smiles to me. "Instinct."

I roll my eyes. He's trying to make a point, though I'm not sure what about exactly. He saved us because he stayed in control. Doesn't that prove my point?

Ahead of us, a steep mountainside is split by narrow ravines. Ari stops the Eroder at the opening to one of them and parks behind a boulder.

I gaze up at the ravine's impenetrable heights and realise our river crossing has been a waste of time and risk. I can't hike over anything like that. My hand goes to the adhesive dressing on my thigh. It's no heavier with blood than before, but that's probably because I've been sitting down. "Ari, there's no way I'll make it over that. I've hurt my leg."

"Over?" Ari chuckles. "Nei, I did not say we would go 'over'."

"Yes you did."

"Nei, I said 'through'. Bring your jacket. It will be cold inside." He grabs his pack and jumps out the Eroder. "Don't worry, it is perfectly safe."

"That's what you said about the river."

"I know. I'm sorry." He helps me down.

I don't need his help, or at least I wouldn't if it weren't for my leg, but offering help seems to be a part of who Ari is and I don't want to insult him. It's not his fault the ice bullet hit us. So I take his help until I'm steady on my feet.

Ari shoulders his pack and slams the door behind me. "Let's go."

Let's go, an echo whispers behind me.

I spin around, hear the river rumbling fast in the background. There's no telling whether the echo was the river and my imagination, or Mark sending me another watery message. I listen for another sign but hear nothing. I feel my forehead. It's warm, but not unusually so.

Still, it's enough to push a moment of doubt into my mind. What am I doing here, about to explore some isolated ravine with a relative stranger? I must indeed be some form of crazy.

Then again, I'm here because Mark was here—I've seen the photographs to prove he was—so he may have passed through this very ravine, one way or another, mere days ago.

I hobble after Ari.

After rambling over a short expanse of silty pebbles, we enter the ravine's towering folds of velvet-green. A multitude of thin waterfalls trickle down its sides, over and around the clear stream bubbling down its centre. As the ravine narrows, it curls like the wavy slithering of a snake and feels as sly. At its far end, a moss-covered cliff face bars our way with a defiant stance, both proud of its impassable heights and daring us to saunter close. I stop and look to Ari for direction.

Silently, he takes my hand and leads me on. The floor is uneven, covered with moistened pebbles that make walking with a gash in my thigh, without hiking boots, difficult. Ari helps, the pressure of his fingers wrapped under my palm determining where I tread, the steadiness of his grasp allowing me to either lean or hold as needed. After a while I find myself following without hesitation, though not because of the firmness of his grip. Of its own accord, my hand begins to respond to his touch in a way I haven't felt for a long time. My senses switch to high alert, their first priority: not letting go.

Instead, as Ari helps me up embankments and supports my slippery descent over landslides, my fingers make a memory of the flexes in his grasp, the gentle squeeze under his knuckles, and the softness where my thumb rests beside his wrist, tracing his skin. Any doubts I had before, about being here with him, disappear as my hand absorbs the impressions his fingertips make along my little finger, which savours the sensation like it knows the touch will end soon and doesn't want it to. Relishing the dry warmth between our joined palms, I don't want the sensation to end either.

When we reach the end of the gorge, Ari springs ahead, releasing my hand. It quickly cools from the loss of contact, making me feel exposed and vulnerable. Not how I like to be. I rub my hands together until the feeling goes away.

Meanwhile Ari veers to the left of the cliff face, squeezes behind a large boulder sitting in its corner and disappears from view. I step towards the boulder. There's no trace of him.

"Come on." His voice echoes from somewhere.

I peer around the boulder's slimy curves but can't see where he's gone.

"Come on!" he says again.

I hold onto the boulder for balance, squeeze past the fungi mucous covering its surface and lean around it. "Where are you?" The boulder seems to be concealing a small cave entrance, no bigger than the boulder itself, but it's full of stacked rocks. It looks as though there's been a landslide inside the mountain. Since the stack blocks me from going further, I can't understand where Ari's gone.

His voice resonates again. "Becky!"

"Where are you?"

"Here." His voice is close as if he's standing next to me. I squint up into the foot-wide gap between the top of the stack and the cave's upper lip. There's nothing but a thin slice of blackness. Until Ari lowers his right boot onto the top of the rockslide and dangles down his hand. Further inside the cave, his darkened face beams at me. "Put your left foot on that rock, your right foot here. I will pull you."

"Up this?"

"I will not let you fall. And if you do, it's not that far to the ground. Come on, I will be careful of your leg. Whatever you've done to it, it looks painful."

I find the rock he wants me to use, put my left foot on it, then assess the second rock and reach up, inhaling slowly and focussing on the reassurance I'll feel when our hands reconnect. They do, I do, and I find myself gliding up into the dark.

"Let your eyes adjust," he says, steadying me at the top of the stack.

I look down. Only a brief gleam of daylight pushes up from the cave entrance. My shoes are barely visible. Giddy, I feel Ari's grip and close my eyes so they can adjust and I can regain my balance. When I open them again, the cave's ceiling stretches up into the mountain, shadowy but clearer, and a rough plain of boulders spreads before me.

"Come," Ari says. "We go this way."

He tugs at my hand and I let him guide me across the landslide. He glides over the rocks as if he's traced their contours a thousand times before barefoot and blindfolded. Water trickles in the distance, growing louder with each step until a definite splashing and gurgling resounds around the cave's dank walls. We begin to deviate, heading to one side of the cave. For a while the trickling noise is muffled. Then, as we manoeuvre down a channel of large boulders, the falling water sounds heavier and the cave brightens.

Soon, I can see each slippery step I'm taking and the air fills with the scent of freshly cut grass after a spring shower. I search for any sign that Mark might have passed through here. There's none. Instead, clambering around a final rock pile, I'm dazzled by a slim shaft of sunlight cutting through a tiny gap in the cave roof. A thin stream of heavy water plummets through the opening, deafening me. The waterfall slices through the rocky landslide on which we stand, and drums onto the cave floor somewhere beneath us. Sunlight reflects off each falling droplet, making the spray sparkle like a shower of diamonds. It's like molten silver being poured into a dark pit of pebbles.

"Stay here," Ari whispers, stroking my hand before releasing it. Bouncing over some nearby boulders, he's soon at the waterfall's base. He takes out his flask, empties it, and holds it under the flow's crushing fall. Once full he brings the spray-wet flask back to me. "Try it."

The flask feels like it's been plucked from a freezer. I take a tentative sip. It is smooth water, soft and weightless, yet crisp in temperature. I take a convinced gulp. "It's good."

"Straight from the glacier. Pure. Fresh."

I take another sip then pass the flask back. "This place is incredible."

"You don't have to say that."

"I mean it." I gaze up at the waterfall and around the cave's glistening green walls. Maybe Mark did come here. "It's magical." Wondrous.

Ari takes a deep swig, then wipes his mouth with the back of his sleeve and clears his throat. "Becky." He pauses, looking down at his feet. "This is a very special place for me. I never show it to anyone. I never even tell anyone about it. If anyone else knows it's here, I have never seen or heard them."

"Oh. Really?"

"Really. This," he stares at the waterfall, "is why I come to this side of the river. Fact," he smirks, "the moss on these walls is three thousand years old. Fact: I know how much your brother meant to you, and what it's like to lose someone, so I have shared this place with you. Okay?"

"Okay."

"Now you see where I hike and why, you can trust me."

"Okay." And, in that moment, I do. Looking into his hazel-brown eyes, noting the sincerity in his face, sensing all our conversations to date have been true—I trust him. I also like him. He's...cute—in a hiking blond Icelander kind of way.

I also don't like my liking. I know I'm not the only girl in the world to be hurt from a relationship. Mark's been telling me it's the only way you learn to appreciate a good thing when it does come along. Still, I'm not ready. I'm not.

So I expect to complain when Ari's arm finds its way around my waist, prompting me to rest my head on his shoulder. But when I feel his cheek against the top of my hair, I close my eyes and a part of me loosens, despite my not being sure if it should. The waterfall's magical cascade drums in my ears and I re-taste its liquid splendour in my mouth. I feel the slight pressure of Ari's head on mine and relish the closeness. I need to get to the police. I also need this. I need someone's touch, Ari's touch. My eyes well. Reaching for Ari's flask, I blink the tears back. "Thank you," I mumble, not meaning the drink.

He looks sideways at me. "Control is not everything, Becky."

"I know." And I wish someone would show me how to let go. I've been this way for too long already. I want to run in the rain again, throw Frisbees under the Norfolk Pines at Manly, and stuff myself full of jellybeans. I want to confide in someone, and Ari seems the type to listen, to care about doing so. Still, you can't know someone well enough after a couple of days. He could be a self-centred cheat like Riley.

Of course he could also be the opposite.

"Shall I show you where I found your brother?" Ari says after a while.

I nod, inhaling slowly.

"This way. Come." He takes my hand and leads me beyond the waterfall to a small hollow in the cave wall. Moss dangles from its ceiling but there's a glow of light behind it. Instead of a boulder, Ari explains, a curtain of mosses hides this entrance to his cave. He ducks under its low ceiling, pushes the plants aside for me, and we emerge onto the mountainside. Beneath us is a well-worn track that leads down onto the silt bank beside the glacier, as well as back up and over the mountain. I could probably jump onto it, if it weren't for my leg.

"I will lower you down," Ari says, leaping down then gesturing for me to sit on the edge of the hollow. "It's okay."

It will have to be. There's no other way of getting down. So once he's ready I perch on the rim, dangle my legs over and reach for his shoulders. This time Ari's grip is like a vice, though his movements are still gentle. I float down onto the track like a cautious elf emerging from hiding.

I brush myself down while he surveys the sky with disappointment. Sheets of murky white cloud smudge across it, smothering the sun.

He climbs a little further up the track. "Stay here. I will look at the weather and come back." He clambers towards a higher ridge.

I wait a minute, then follow. Higher up I'll be able to get a better view of the valley and the boulder where Mark was found. So I take my time, climbing sideways, holding onto rocks either side of me, and leaning all my weight onto my good thigh.

When I reach Ari, he's crouching with his back against the ridge wall, fingering a stem of grass while scrutinising the sky. From the ridge, we can see over the entire glacier. There's nothing to see in any direction but rocks, silt and ice. It's a beautiful national park, as everyone keeps telling me. No government presence.

"It sure is cloudy." My voice startles Ari but he recovers and makes room. I crouch down beside him.

"It means no auroras," he says. "No point staying until it is dark."

"Nice view though." I gaze out at the translucent white beauty of the ice and, full of marvel once more, wonder if Mark might have risked the river after all—if it meant seeing this. Ari could be right about others not knowing about his cave, but this ridge is right beside the track... What if someone showed Mark a photo and offered to take him? "It's amazing here."

"Be careful when you look at it," Ari warns.

"What do you mean?" I gaze at the cloud-filled sky. It's the same colour as the glacier, white with glimmers and hints of pale blue. If I squint it's impossible to distinguish any horizon between them. What seems like white ice swirls could also be cloud puffs, what appear to be waves of curling cloud could also be snow piles. Both stretch before me like thick blankets wrapping everything in sight.

"Whatever you do," Ari adds, smirking, "do not stand up."

His roguish grin urges me to do the opposite, so I pull myself up and assess the vast monotone expanse before me. It's at once both close enough for me to touch and infinite in depth. My head spins in the crisp Arctic air. From nowhere, a distant contour in the snow rushes towards me like a spacecraft speeding through hyperspace. It stops a few metres away, pulses, then rotates into the shape of something familiar before reversing to its original position. My eyes sting, euphorically dizzy with the illusion, and I topple to one side.

"Whoa!" Ari jumps up to steady me. "Did you see it?"

I nod. My heart quickening, I feel for the back of the ridge and grip a bunch of rubbery long stemmed grasses. Mark could easily have fallen to his death from here.

"The *fata morgana*," Ari says, helping me back onto the track. "It's a mirage, affects your eyes after you climb very fast."

"Oh." I reel at the lightness still spinning in my head.

"But já, the clouds are here to stay and it might rain. Sorry."

"I'll see them another time." I offer a smile but he doesn't see it— he's still assessing the white layers hiding the sky. "Really, it's fine.

I have to get back to Höfkállur anyway. And didn't you say that the Skepnasá is fiercer when everything melts? If there's no sun there'll be less heat, so less melting? It will be safer in the river?"

He rubs the stubble on his chin with a thumb and nods. "The water probably won't even reach the roof this time."

"Excellent."

Satisfied, we begin our descent. By the time we reach the triangular silt bank at the bottom of the track he's back to his usual cheery self. "Maybe you will want to come again tomorrow night, if the weather is better? The auroras are best here."

"So Anna said." And I did promise to see the auroras before I left Iceland.

I also know that—irrespective of why Mark might have come here—something is supposed to happen tomorrow in Höfkállur, and I may be at the police station all day. I still need to go, if only to talk everything through.

"When will you know if the weather's better?" I say anyway, to be polite.

"Er, maybe this time tomorrow. We can decide then. Do you see the glacier, and the lake?" He points, waits for me to nod. "You walk along the lake there, and when you reach the river, it is the third boulder you will find. I'll meet you when I finish if you want."

"Finish? Finish what? Where are you going?"

"To fix the window. It will need time to set, okay? Be careful," he warns, "the banks are made of silt. Underneath us here is rock," he stamps, "but over there it is volcanic dust floating on water. This is the reason for the two-metre rule. Do not step on something that is not there. Keep two metres between you and the water."

I nod, unsure why I'm frowning.

"You'll be fine, tough-girl." He lifts my face to his. "If you need me, go to the glacier and wave. I'll see you from there."

I look at how the bank angles around to the glacier. "Okay," I say, recognising the shoreline from the autopsy report photographs. If this really is where Mark died, I should probably do this alone anyway— goodbyes are private things. I also don't know how crazy things might get for me once I'm closer to the water. This is where all the voices have been telling me to go. The irascible yet familiar roar of the river echoes off the mountain face behind us and confirms I'm in the right place.

So, as Ari climbs back up the track, I hobble towards the glacier.

Chapter 16

After a few steps I glance back, expecting to see Ari climbing or hoisting himself into the hollow entrance of his concealed cave. He's already gone. Given how easily he scales heights, I'm not surprised.

The triangular plain ahead of me is as dismal as it appeared from the other side of the Skepnasá. Between the river, the glacier, its lake, and the mountain trapping them all in, there's nothing but an expanse of dark pebbles. A thick strip of brown sand and the odd grass stalk sprinkle the shoreline closer to the glacier. A crowd of boulders litter the riverbank itself, as they did in Ari's photographs. That's it.

Still I scan the ground before each step, snapping photos with my phone as I head towards the glacier. Now I'm alone I relax my thigh, until I'm practically dragging my injured leg behind me. The drag disturbs silt underfoot and a dusty dryness tickles my nose. It reminds me of walking on outback trails back home, where storms of blush dirt billows out from behind passing utes, covering everything with a thin film of earth. Here there's no billowing, yet everything's topped with similarly fine grains, including the blocks of azure-white ice floating house-high atop the lake's mirrored surface.

As I near the glacier, droplets drip and splash from melting ice with more and more prominence, growing louder until they fall with such piercing clarity they sound like a dozen taps tinkling into a dozen empty metal buckets inside a vacant warehouse.

Then, from nowhere, someone whispers my name. The voice is close, the breath warm.

I spin around. "Hello?"

I scan the plain. No one's there.

Slowly I turn back to the lake, glimmering, dripping, beckoning. My thoughts go to Mark and I move closer. Water is my sanctuary.

I'm a different person around water. I wish I could touch its crisp flat surface, taste its chilled fresh water, without the risk of falling in. Mark died here, so touching the water could reconnect us somehow, one last time…and I want that so much.

A gust of wind moans through the peaks behind me. I spin around again.

"Mark?"

The silence sends a shiver down my spine. I'm imagining things. Thank goodness I'm alone with this. I need to be alone with this.

The lake's glacial depths glint as occasional sunbeams peek through the cloud cover to strike through the water. Again I long to touch its reflective skin. Of course I'm not stupid—I'm not going anywhere near that edge. Amid the silt, however, I notice a shallow pool of water, and it too beckons. I can't see the harm, so hobble over and crouch beside it—no easy feat when trying not to rip the Leukostrips on my thigh— and carefully, gently I reach forward.

At first my fingertips feel wetness, then pain. They retract as though scorched by hot embers. The water is freezing and the shock of it unbalances me. Nothing but ice could survive in there.

I huff my fingertips back to life and continue on to the glacier. The air grows misty from the constant dripping of melting ice, moist enough for tiny pale rainbows to thread their arches through those occasional rays of sun. Immediately below the glacier a chunk of ice bobs, having recently fallen as a long vertical shard from the glacier's otherwise silt-dusted face. Left exposed behind is a clean, deep cross-section of lines that swirl horizontally in aquamarine and white layers. They look as fine and clear as the pink lines of flavour in a tub of raspberry-ripple ice-cream. I study the meandering lines. Like the rings of a tree or the soil-layers of a cliff, each winter's frozen snowfall probably tells some element of the glacier's story, its different hues bearing witness to the past. Did they witness what happened to Mark? Is that what all the dripping and gushing is trying to tell me?

No, no one can tell me that, it seems.

I glance over my shoulder and can at least see Ari's right: from this angle both the narrow ravine and the Eroder's back window are easily visible. Ari is injecting the glass with some substance in a syringe. I shiver, remembering the river, then realise there's an unkind temperature radiating from the glacier too. I wander closer to the exposed lines.

Centuries ago, snowflakes of a specific tinge once fell onto this glacier, where they froze and were compacted by later snowfalls to create the lines now before me. Soon, those lines will melt into the colourful droplets constantly dripping into the lake, then evaporate into the sky to fall down again as snow. Everything in the world really is cyclic: water, oxygen, nitrogen, life…energy. Irrespective of what scientists have or haven't proved, spiritual survival must be, in all likelihood, a simple matter of logic. Where else would the electrical energy in our brains go when we die?

I cock my head and think of Mark, of his cycle. If our consciousness truly is part of the Earth's energy cycle, it's entirely possible that Mark's energy has become another form of energy now: a form I cannot see or hear, but can sense. It's also entirely possible then that his energy could be here, at the glacier with me now, and that neither Anna nor I are going crazy.

Fact: until we know the answers, anything is possible. Myth, history, and religion might have obscured the scientifically-true extent of mankind's continuity from our current understanding, but Anna and Mark could be correct in believing the *Heimspeki* will help us finally understand our place in the world, and agree on it.

Fact: we are all part of the order of things, a part of nature's various cycles. What goes around comes around. Agreement would be a start.

I reach up and let my hand glide over a silty wet surface of the glacier's face, feeling its bumpiness melt beneath my touch. It's beautiful, though it feels like my skin will stick if I let my fingers linger in any one place.

We should value, Ólaf said earlier, *every second of life, every cell in our bodies…*

I don't want to lose a fingertip so keep them moving.

"Got to live life as best we can while we're here, don't we Mark?" I say aloud, remembering more of Ólaf's advice. "We could be gone tomorrow. Could have happened to me today in the river." No matter what I do from here, I should take more care. It's what Mark would want.

A cool breeze curls around my shoulders, giving me goose bumps. The ice towering above continues to radiate a frosty glow—my jacket isn't enough, I need gloves. I glance at the Eroder again. Ari's out of sight. So I snap a photograph of the glacier then stroll towards the Skepnasá, tucking my hands under my armpits. The cloud cover has thickened, filling in the pale blue holes where sunlight once peeked through. The lake isn't glimmering anymore either. I quicken my pace and cut across the plain to the river's slush-battled banks, and the boulder where Mark was found.

Now that I'm here, it's clear no one could ever fence off this river. The idea is ridiculous. Still, why did Mark come here when he should have phoned me? Ari's cave is wondrous. The glacier is amazing. But my brother could have seen them any other time. His missing head trauma was a report error. Folk in Höfkállur don't like lawyers. Some activist doesn't want me condemning their new legal system. Still, there has to be more to this.

In search of answers I drag myself forward, pass the first and second boulders, until I reach the third. There I stop to take more photographs. This is where Mark's body grew cold, his beauty stolen like the cloud-hidden sun. I listen to the deafening reverberation of the river, the same as the haunting waters in my head, and wait. Yes, I've heard this sound before.

"So this is where you are." I pocket my phone and zip it inside. "Why did you come here, Mark? Why didn't you simply finish your research and come home? I was so looking forward to seeing you. I hate to think of you here by yourself."

My throat sticks.

"I miss you so much already. I want you home. I want a hug, an email, anything. I'll even listen to you witter on about your stupid energy theories. You certainly picked a corker this time. Even got me thinking about this one."

I move closer to the boulder. If the riverbank can support its weight, it can support mine. Its skin is velvety with weathering, and when I lean closer I hear Mark whispering my name. I shut my eyes to listen, feel the heat radiating out from my head as he speaks.

"Becky," he says. "Be careful. You're not safe."

"But you told me to come here," I say.

He doesn't reply so I open my eyes. The river is catapulting itself so violently along its course that focussing on any one spot makes me dizzy. Am I encountering the *fata morgana* again? My head reels, the world tilts. I feel the ground moving underfoot, a heaviness on my shoulders. It feels like a hand.

"Mark?"

The rapids snarl as I say his name.

"Mark!"

Rotten branches and glacial debris scrape the upstream riverbank with a thunderous moan that grows louder and louder, until I realise it wasn't there before. The silt beneath me is crumbling like quicksand, the water before me surging. I'm too close, too close. I go to step back but my legs tremble with the moving ground. My gash wrenches as if gaping from its seam. My thigh doesn't have enough strength to support me on flat ground, let alone on stirring silt. I've taken a wrong step, I'm standing on nothing but volcanic dust and I'm going to fall.

I turn to look for Mark one last time, but the action makes me lose my balance and, as I drop sideways into the churning water, I scream at what I see.

There is no ghost behind me.

Chapter 17

The hand gripping my shoulder is as real as the breath in my lungs and the thunderous crack ringing in my ears. I follow Ari's panicked eyes towards the glacier, and realise the rolling moan I heard was a second chunk of ice breaking off the glacier. Now a torrent of water is raging over the banks as a gargantuan ice block sweeps down the Skepnasá towards us.

"No, no—Becky!" Ari gasps, teetering with me. He thrusts his spare arm back to tilt us away from the river. Water floods the bank mere metres away. His desperate eyes lock with mine, his teeth gritted like nothing will stop him from fighting gravity—but it's too late. The bank is already crumbling and, with my arms flailing, our angle is irrecoverable. He should let me go, save himself. He doesn't. A bubbling cauldron of dark water and ice devours the silt beneath us, and we collapse into the river.

"Don't fight the current," Ari yells as we fall. "Trust me, no control, just go with it! I know how to—"

I hit the water fast. A freezing wet slush caves over me, slapping me all over with a vicious cold. Liquid frost blasts into my ears and constricts my skin. My eyes widen with the instinctive horror of where I am. My arms and legs jerk into action against the freeze but all I am is under water, rocketing along its course. I kick and thrash against any sludge gleaming with the promise of sky, of air. My chest pounds as my body fights the asphyxia. I can't breathe.

I can't breathe.

My lungs heat. I don't know what to do. This current has a mind of its own. It's nothing like being in the ocean. It's nothing like swimming in warm waves, even those as tall as skyscrapers that sometimes force me to gulp air and water as I kick for the shore. This is much faster and there's no knowing which way is up. My fingers and face feel like they're coated in ice. I don't know what to do. I don't know what to do.

Then a surge from somewhere beneath propels me upwards. I see clouds! Peaks! I'm going to make it!

I push up until my mouth breaches the surface. I gasp, suck oxygen down. But no, this isn't an escape. It's a tease. Too soon a merciless cold yanks me back under and I'm moving fast again. The current is more determined now, slamming me forward with the speed of a skydive, pinning my arms behind me and beating my head with cubes of frost. Undercurrents roar like jackhammers. I need to get to the surface.

The current has other plans.

With a cackle, it aims me at a boulder lodged in the riverbank ahead. I arch my back away but it's no good—I slam into it face-first, my nose smashing into my skull. Cherry-bright blood bursts into the water. Soaring pain blazes through my head. I want to scream with the agony. I reach for my face but the current wrestles against my squirming and lines me up again, gurgling frenzied laughter through the roaring deluge. I squint ahead to see what's so funny. There's another boulder.

Don't fight the current.

I re-hear Ari's words, but my brain yells at me to fight, to swim away from the boulder.

No control, just go with it.

There are bubbles up ahead too. The current is sucking water through some fissure in the boulder. I have to get away, above. I have to swim.

Don't fight.

The voice isn't Ari's now, it's Mark's. I hear him as clearly as the pounding in my chest. Still, logic tells me to swim for the surface.

Fact: that is where the air is.

Trust me, no control…

The voice is Ari's: the voice is Mark's. Mark wanted me to trust my gut more, and my gut is telling me to trust Ari.

So I close my eyes and let the current take me. This is going to hurt…

I smash into the boulder. My shoulder bone explodes with the pain. My legs and hips disappear into the vortex whirling through the boulder while my chest jams between the rock's slimy husk, splintering ribs and wedging me in the crack. I struggle to free myself, picturing the bruises on my brother's chest. Agony stabs my sides. I yank my body around, try to wriggle free. The same death can't come to us both. It can't.

It's also no use. I'm stuck.

This is it. Ari was wrong.

I'm entombed under an impenetrable arctic mire, at the mercy of a depraved current, and my parents are never going to forgive me. I should have swum for the surface.

Regret strengthens my resolve and I heave against the current again. Nothing happens until panic buries me in its uncontrollable terror. There I rip and thrash like a newborn tornado, not thinking, just wild and irrepressible.

No, this isn't the way. Not my way. Emotions cloud clear thought.

I close my eyes, remember the Sannlitró-Völva, monks meditating, and concentrate on pooling the electrical energy lashing about my brain into a blue pearl of calm. My panic becomes focus and, in that moment, I know exactly what I have to do. This isn't about living anymore. If I want to see Mark again, in whatever energy form he's in now, I need to think about my own energy and tip it towards being positive in the majority. Then, when I die, we'll join together. I'd give anything to reconnect with him one last time. This is my chance. I find it and take it.

Just in time.

A stony weight thuds into my face to send a whole new realm of hurt down my spine, and the pain sends me over the edge. I have only seconds left.

So, as my last bubbles of oxygen escape, I think about Mark, I think about my life, what joys I've had, how precious they were, and make my peace with the world.

Chapter 18

Silence pushes against my skull like a hangover. It would have been nice to have company here in the darkness. But nothing reaches for my consciousness and nothing is ever going to reach for it. Mark is still wrong about that. There is only a black void tempting me to abandon my senses, to float free from care in its thick soup of absence. Perhaps it is different for those who die in other ways. But I doubt it.

Becky!

I can't tell where the muffled sound is coming from because I didn't put it there. It was quiet before. I wish it would be again.

Becky!

The voice sounds like Ari's. Is he here too? The blackness starts spinning. I wait for the giddy half-dead world of my slumbering psyche to settle.

It doesn't.

The voice doesn't speak again either.

Something jerks me instead. My mouth fills with liquid. My body shakes. The physicality of it jars me. A flame of hurt sears up my spine as it bangs against a metal edge. The hard surface beneath me vibrates with movement. Bruises throb. Slashes sting. Why must I feel them again? The inky black shroud dimming my senses is comforting. I don't want it to fall away. Sinking deeper into the weightless black void seems a much better idea. I urge it to drag me down again into a noiseless fog, a yearning buoyancy, an absence of time…

Here, it is peaceful. Here, the constant roaring of ice water in my ears has fallen silent. Here, I want to stay.

I look up at the ceiling of the Eroder. Then everything goes white.

Chapter 19

I can't tell if my disconnection from reality has been for seconds, minutes or hours before the muffled sounds return and become recognisable. I'm in a car, I feel its movement. I'm shivering, deathly cold. I'm also definitely in a car, not the river.

My head throbs like I'm hungover and my body aches like it's been contorted to fit inside a cramped space for hours. I drift closer to reality, then silence soon closes in once more.

Open your eyes, I tell myself.

It will hurt to be awake but I need to get back. The dark peace is nice. But there are still things I need to do, things outside of this darkness. In my black vision the outline of things have white edging. Are my eyes open?

The tang of damp rock infiltrates my nostrils. I breathe deeper and the tang turns into a sharp cold that pricks the insides of my tender nose, confirming I'm still in Iceland. I strain to hear more. I need to hear sounds, decipher and cling to them until they pull me up, out of the blackness.

But the dark persists, even when the rumbling movements rocking my body end with a jerk.

A rattling noise. A jarring against that metallic edge again. An agonising pain sears across my spine. The hurt wrenches away my strength, though I strive to stay awake, to stay here. If I pass out again, something bad will happen. The weightless black void covets me once more.

There, I dream of Sydney. I'm sitting on the sofa in my old unit, a bottle of paracetamol in my hand. There are a hundred tablets in the bottle. I empty them onto the sofa and there they sit. They stare up at me, crying, weeping projections of my solitude. Tears cascade down their sides. They sweat tears. Yet they feel so dry as I swallow each one down my tired aching throat, itself worn from crying. Each one absorbs a little more of the moisture lining my tubes, until a powdery dryness sticks to the arch of my mouth. Their sickening chalky sediment snags my tonsils, flavouring my saliva while they await a sip of water to carry them into my stomach. It makes me feel sick. Even my breath starts to irritate the moment. The air tastes like it's filled with the faint dust that breezes up into sunbeams from old books, or the fine fragments of dirt that bluster up from sweeping pavements free of leaves. I want to retch. Somewhere between my rib cage and my stomach I'm swelling too, ballooning full of dust. I need to rid my mouth of the tablets' grainy residue.

So I sip more water—only the water mixes with leftover particles to form a cloudy solution, the tang of which lingers on my teeth long after I swallow, aggravating my thirst. I stop drinking and get back to swallowing as many tablets as I can.

Slowly, they disappear from the sofa, one by one. They scour their way into my stomach, which churns at the thought of even one more finding its way inside. In the end, I only manage about eighty. If I take any more I'll be sick, and expel from my body the very things I'm determined not to reject—the tickets to my freedom, my path to eternal relief.

So I tip the remaining tablets back into their bottle, and wait.

The waiting makes me nervous and at first I think the reason for my shaking is fear. But a little fear isn't going to stop me. I have nothing left. No Riley. No career. I'm a pathetic waste of space that needs putting out of its misery.

So when my body starts to shake vigorously, I do nothing except lie down. Determined to see it through, I shrink away from the world in search of serenity. I find it with surprising ease and it feels nice, quiet. My body breathes, my hands move when I move them, but I'm not there.

Time passes and I see myself from above. I'm quivering all over in a deadly sweat now. It's my body dying, me dying. Still I'm not afraid, only curious. What will happen after I'm gone? What will happen to me, my body; what will happen to my family? Is Mark right about the light?

Wait, a phone's ringing—my phone. Is that Mark phoning because I'm not answering the doorbell?

Becky!

Yes, he's popped by to say hello, on the off-chance I'm in. He's on the other side of the front door. I can hear my phone ringing and so can he. He knows I'm in here now, not answering. He's been knocking for a while. He's worried.

Becky?

At least, I think the voice is Mark's. He sounds panicked now. He's kicking at the door. A massive thud makes me shoot back inside my body. Then I feel my brother's arms around me, shaking, slapping. There's a siren. It's not serene anymore; it's noisy and I want the noise to stop. Mark is crying, begging me to live. I don't want him to be sad. And all this noise is giving me a headache.

Hands lift me until I'm rocking inside a vehicle again. The siren is louder now. Its wail pinches at my heart and there's a sudden high-pitched tone: Mark screaming. I want to tell him it's okay, he doesn't need to scream—I'm going to make it. If only the noise could cease and my headache would stop, maybe we could go for a dive together? It's peaceful down there in the water.

Meet me there.

White flashes across my eyes until I'm dreaming of a river, its freezing cold bleak sediment swirling around me. I'm drowning in it. But Mark is there too. His beautifully unharmed face lights up on seeing me, his brown eyes sparkle, his lips widen into a warm smile that reminds me of birthday wishes. We hug and sink to the bottom. The swirling stops.

"Mark, I'm here." I tell him. "Why did you want me to come?"

He frowns. "I didn't. I told you specifically not to."

"You said 'let's go, to the glacier' on more than one occasion."

"No, I said *don't* go to the glacier, it isn't safe." He frowns.

"*Don't* go? Oh, I didn't hear that."

"I was trying to trigger the electrical energy in your brain so you'd have certain thoughts—I wanted to make sure you were alright. Perhaps I haven't quite got the hang of it yet." His frown lifts. "I should tell you—this is wonderful. Make sure you always wonder. It's the answer to everything. I love you."

"I love you too. But why isn't the glacier safe? I can't see what else the government can do, this is nature. What was so important about my reading your autopsy report?"

He looks at me, cocking his head to one side. "Because I was murdered."

I rub my forehead. It's burning hot like a fever. "Murdered?"

"You know I was."

"Yes."

Juddering to life, I thrash at the water like an electric eel marooned in a trawler net. I'm certain I'm awake, yet I'm still in water.

"Becky! It's okay, it's okay."

The air stings as I open my eyes. Soaring pains blaze across my body. Tiny white dots sparkle in my vision yet I'm in warm, bubbling water. Steam wafts up from its milky surface. Undisturbed, it tickles the water's skin like the flames of a small fire. It smells like the shower I had this morning, eggy and oppressive. The comparison brings reality closer: Ari is here, swishing through the water towards me. Vapour twists around him before evaporating into the light air. We are lower than the ground around us and sheltered by a low wall of black tiles. Beyond that is a dimming lilac sky.

"What? Where...?"

He puts an arm around me. "Calm down."

Different sections of my body scream at his touch. My thigh, my nose, my shoulder, my ribcage... Breathing hurts swellings I can't see. But the breath itself...oh, sweet breath. Dry and clean. I fill my lungs, expanding my chest and sucking magnificent air into every bronchiole and every alveolus. It feels exquisite, like sun drying freshly laundered flapping clothes, heavenly like glistening saltwater on equator-warming skin, and dry like the first beach day of a Sydney spring. I fill my lungs again and again. Until I notice the expression on Ari's face. He is preoccupied, anxiously searching the twilight around us.

"Where are we?"

"A natural spring," he answers quickly, "near the glacier."

"What happened?"

"You saved our lives."

"I did? How?"

"No control. You didn't fight the current." He caresses my shoulder with a thumb as he explains. "When I was a child, I threw everything I could into the Skepnasá—wood, leaves, rocks. It always ended up in the hole of that boulder. I knew the current would take us there. You blocked the gap. I climbed up you onto the boulder, then I pulled you up."

"You used me as a step?"

"Yes. Thank you, for trusting me."

"I...okay." I rub my temples, disorientated still. "How did we get here?"

"The boulder with the hole is near to where we parked the Eroder. You were heavy, especially asleep. You wouldn't stop shivering so I brought you here. It's geothermal."

I push myself upright, wince as pain stabs at me. We're in a natural pool of geothermal water, one of several dotted among the lava rock. Wooden walkways connect each pool to a small white building and there's steam everywhere. From over a mound of rock, I hear voices and splashing, though the pools around us are empty.

"There's a swimming pool over there." Ari gestures over the mound, then continues his surveillance. "We're the only ones in the hot pots."

"What's wrong?"

"Apart from that you are almost dead?"

He looks at me with such intensity his words don't resonate straight away. When they strike home, they clang with such fortitude inside my head the noise drowns out any other thoughts.

I almost died.

Again.

"Um," I mutter, looking down at the dense rippling water between us. My bottom lip quivers. Liquid detonates in my eyes. I squeeze them shut to stop tears falling. My parents almost lost both their children, in the same week, in the same place. I've let them down.

"Sorry," he whispers, moving closer. "I should not say that." He puts his arm around me, says nothing while I calm myself. "Becky."

"Yeah?" I mumble, rubbing at my eyes. I forget about my nose and hit its bruising. "Ow."

"Let me look." He lifts my face and studies me like I'm an exquisite painting. "Is your nose...does this hurt?" He feels for the arch of my nose.

"Ow! Yes!" It's agony.

"At least the bleeding has stopped. And your shoulder?"

I roll them both to test for pain. They aren't as bad as my nose.

"This one was dislocated." He points to my left shoulder. "I put it back before you woke up. Where else do you hurt?"

My thigh throbs under the warm water, as do my ribs. I search my ribcage until I find two points of excruciating pain mid-way down my right side. "I think I've broken a rib." I know I have. "Or two."

"Don't move. When you are warm enough, we will go to the hospital. I have some paracetamol in the car. You can take them."

"I'll be fine."

"They will help."

I almost laugh at how wrong he is. "No, really. It's fine. I can't take paracetamol anymore." Confusion nips his face but I don't want to get into that right now. "Long story. Are you hurt?" He must be.

"Nei. When I fell into the water I put my feet first, so they hit anything, not my head." The intensity of his look increases. "I am worried about you. I don't know how to say it, but this has made me..." he searches my eyes as if looking for the right words.

A red flush comes to my checks. Nervous, I press my lips together, sensing what might come next.

Sure enough, without another word, Ari leans forward and kisses me. The timing might be all wrong but I don't care—the gentle pressure of his lips against mine is tender and slow, soft and simmering. I close my eyes and let myself sink into him. The moment quickly thaws from surprise into understanding. Ari cares about me, and life is precious.

When the kiss ends, we open our eyes and something passes between us—something deep, primal and...instinctive. I can't remember ever feeling a connection like this through a single kiss. I gaze into his eyes and press my lips together to relive the heat of his mouth. Ari's smile is slow to arrive but he's soon grinning. Bashful, I drop my eyes to the warm circles of creamy water bubbling around us. There, a soft smile spreads over my lips too and, as the massaging waters jump up and down, a spasm of hunger tingles through me. I rest my head on Ari's waiting arm, stretch out my aching limbs and flex my gradually warming fingers. Steam caresses my face with its soft wisps, the hot pot's natural bubbling plays with the ends of my damp-darkened hair, fanning the strands back and forth over my shoulders, and I'm tempted to forget myself, plunge into the water and pull Ari with me. So close to death, life feels like an exquisite opportunity.

I look up at him.

He's returned to searching the lava rock and hot pots.

"What's wrong?" I ask him again.

"When you are warm, we will go." His tone is more serious now.

"Why do you keep looking around?"

"I...I'm not sure."

"Not sure about what?"

"When I pulled you out of the river, I thought I saw someone walking from the glacier, down the mountain behind the camping grounds. They had a, a..." He makes the chopping motion for an axe.

I cup water into my hands and splash it over my face, careful of my nose. The water cascades down my neck and shoulders. It gives me a moment to think.

Why is Ari concerned about someone walking away from the glacier carrying an axe? Ah...

"The ice, it wasn't an accident?" I mumble, remembering what Mark confirmed in my dream. "Both blocks? The ice that hit the Eroder *and* the ice that pushed us into the river?"

Ari shrugs. "The person I saw drove away in a grey four-wheel drive. And, I'm sorry Becky, but I know him, even though it is not possible for it to be him."

"What do you mean?"

"He is never at Jötunnsjökull and today he was sick."

"Sick?" My heart skips a beat. "Who did you see?"

"Jón."

Chapter 20

As I hobble along a walkway towards the little white changing room near our pool, anger flares instead of the fear I should have.

Jón just tried to kill us.

Ari wants to call someone for advice, either his father or Ólaf. He hopes there's a reasonable explanation for Jón's actions. I just want to plant a fist in Jón's face. I'm not a violent person. I've never been in a physical fight, even close to one. Yet if I were to see Jón now I'd charge him with the power of a rhino, smash his own nose deep into his head, knee him, then sidekick his ribs as he doubled over. Would I boot-kick him once he was on the floor? Hell yes! I'm ready for it. How dare he even think he could get away with this!

Fact: he almost did.

My towel tight around me, I peer over the lava rock mound. Another larger white building sits beside a rectangular swimming pool. While I was climbing out of the water, Ari ran to this building to fetch us towels and a first aid kit. A family of four now stands at the pool's deep end, getting ready to jump. Thankfully they're too far away to see the mess my face must be; they probably don't even know we're here. Ari said he parked the Eroder close to the hot pots so he could carry me straight into one. He's promised to turn its heater on as soon as he's dry, though says to take my time with my wounds. He must have injuries too, but didn't take anything from the first aid kit in my hands.

I'm about to let the changing room door swing shut when, over my shoulder, I see him standing in his wet clothes, watching the family. His shirt's so wet I can see his torso muscles underneath, but he isn't shivering. He's looking over the geothermal springs, warmed by the drifting steam. I follow his gaze. The father is holding hands with his two young sons as they wait to jump into the deep. The mother stands in the warm azure water shouting out their countdown. As the father glances from one son to the other, unadulterated pride seeps into his expression. They jump through the steamy air and plummet into the milky surface. Swirls of white froth gurgle out from where they disappear.

Ari waits until they surface, then continues into the male changing room. I wonder what he saw that I didn't—although my hand already knows. It's fallen to my abdomen to cradle the ache tugging at me again.

Shivering, I let the door go. I don't have time to linger on some medical prediction that might not come true, from a doctor who only saw what he wanted to see after a single appointment.

Still, as I peel off my wet clothes before the mirror, and my eyes evaluate my battered body, they can't resist assessing the wobble around my middle that refuses to disappear. Rebelling against me, it bulges defiantly with the fat it's storing until the famine it perceives changes to abundance.

From behind, I may very well look like a skeleton moving under a transparent pink coat, as the doctor described when showing me in his mirror last month. But from my front it's the opposite. Sighing, I consider doing some star jumps. Of course when I go to lift my arms and wince at the pain in my ribs, I laugh at the stupidity of the idea. This is not the time to be doing anything about the fat creeping into my thighs and onto my hips from that baguette at lunchtime. This is the time for treating wounds, then getting Jón taken into custody somehow.

The first bruise I uncover is a dark purple cloud on the right side of my abdomen. I'm pretty sure I can't do anything about broken ribs. Still, I've seen people wrap bandages around them in movies, so copy what I've seen.

Next I look at my left shoulder, find the ruby streaks that mark some post-dislocation tenderness, then realise I have nothing to treat that either.

My nose is a bulbous mess of burgundy and sapphire with a black split across its bridge, which might be bigger if not for my icy exposure. I find a thin adhesive dressing and cover the black split, pushing it together as best as I can.

Amazingly, the Leukostrips on my thigh still hold the gash together, though a trail of fresh crimson blood drips from it. I clean and dry it, find a large adhesive dressing to protect it.

Once I've checked for other injuries, I unfold the second towel to wrap it around me, only to find it's a bathrobe. When I leave the changing room, I find Ari wearing one as well. Pacing beside his car, steam swirling around each step, he's scratching at his stalk-stubbled jaw with a vigour that hints at the disorder in his mind.

When he sees me though, he rushes to help me reach the car. As I move, my ribs pinch like cramps and my limbs shake like they've run a marathon. I thrust them forward with what little coordination I can manage and, as soon as I'm in the Eroder, check my dressings aren't leaking. They're not.

"I will call my father first." Ari says, leaning into the back seat to search his pack for his phone. "He will need to know. He has known Jón a long time. They used to, er, help each other back in Reykjavík."

"Help each other how exactly?" Ari squirms but doesn't answer. "Ari, tell me. How did they used to help each other?"

"Security guards can, um, hear a lot of talk outside a courthouse, between lawyers and clients. When Dad was Höfkállur's Police Commissioner, and his more serious cases were sent down to Reykjavík, Jón was on security there. For the right price, he would…"

"Share what information he overheard?"

"Yeah." Ari hooks his phone to an earpiece. "Dad thought it okay because he was putting criminals away. After the discoveries, when he realised what the *Heimspeki* meant, he felt bad for using Jón. That's why he became a counsellor, got Jón a job with Höfkállur MUR. And he, Jón," Ari harrumphs bitterly, "made a deal with me. He was to tell me if he had any problems and I would not judge him. So much for that." He shoves the Eroder's gearstick into reverse and swings away from the pools.

As his front tyres hit the main road, he activates his phone. Before he can dial out, a digital tune hums in the silence. He tilts his phone to see its caller-id. "Director Úlfar," he says, surprised. His thumb is already moving to answer it.

"Don't answer!"

It's too late, his thumb has already depressed the phone's green answer button. "Halló?"

Listening through his earpiece, he doesn't speak for a few minutes. Then he asks questions in Icelandic and agrees to something before hanging up.

"We are to go to the morgue," Ari tells me. "Director Úlfar tried to call you first, but your phone isn't working."

"It's rather wet." It was in my pocket when I fell in the river, and its metallic weight still in my clothes when I undressed. Hopefully all the photos I took will be safely stored on my backup cloud. "Why does he want us to go to the morgue? I was planning on going straight to the police."

"Doctor Emil is there, waiting to speak with you about your brother."

"Doctor Emil? I thought he was away from Höfkállur until next week."

"Nei," he shakes his head. "Who told you that?"

"His assistant, Gunnar somebody."

"When?"

"He left a message on my phone last night. Why?"

"Gunnar Eyjólfsson," Ari changes gear and speeds up, "is missing. Doctor Emil tried to speak to him today but no one knows where he is. This afternoon they found your contact details on his phone. They also found emails between him and some group called Velja. It means 'to choose'. Director Úlfar says he's looking into it. He left a message on Gunnar's phone asking him to go to the Litrúm-Hús as soon as he got his message. He hasn't shown up yet."

"You think he's our activist? Is he working with Jón?"

Ari pauses in thought as we exit onto the highway. "I don't know."

"Ólaf said Jón was in a case yesterday. Do you know whether he was in it all day, or just the morning?"

"Actually, Jón has been having migraines for a few days now, coming in and out of work when he can. I think he only worked yesterday in the afternoon."

"Ólaf said he was there all day."

Ari shrugs. "I can check. Data from the scan booths go to Personnel too. There will be a record of his absence at the Litrúm-Hús."

"Can you check the scan booths for someone else too? Anna said Mark was at the Litrúm-Hús last Friday. He never went back to *The Himinn*. Your records might show whether he left the Litrúm-Hús with anyone or by himself."

"I can check after the morgue." Ari grips the steering wheel and eases up the acceleration.

The thinning grey road disappears fast. Few cars interrupt our speed. It brings me a degree of comfort and we settle into an urgent silence that has us on high alert, especially when a car of a certain colour rushes towards us from Höfkállur: a grey four-wheel drive. It couldn't be Gunnar or Jón of course, and, sure enough, the car passes us. I turn to watch as it continues on its way, then it skids to a stop, jerks into a turn, and shoots back towards us.

"Ari, that's a—"

"I see it."

I survey the road up and down. "No black sedan following us this afternoon?"

"No need if you're with me."

"Do you think it could be—"

"Jón? I wouldn't rule anything out."

The car flies towards us like an out-of-control freight train. It must be Jón. His erratic swerving revs closer and closer. All Ari can do is speed up. He slams his foot onto the accelerator, pinning me to my seat. Every muscle in my body urges our speed to outmatch Jón's. Trapped in my seat, I grit my teeth. There can be only one reason Jón has come back from Höfkállur—to finish a job he now knows is outstanding.

Chapter 21

We manage to stay ahead of Jón until there's a bend in the road, and a yellow and red sign telling us it's a sharp one. Ari flicks his eyes between the rear vision mirror and the road ahead, assessing Jón's speed and our distance to the curve. We're close. In fact, if Ari doesn't brake soon, we'll lose control. I gnaw at the insides of my cheek. It's not until our tyres actually meet the bend that he finally hits the brakes.

Tyres screech and Ari turns into the skid. He doesn't lose control. We straighten out and he speeds up again.

Behind us, the grey four-wheel drive swerves like it's being driven by a crazed lunatic: Jón takes the bend on its inside lane, gains on us then starts honking and flicking his headlights off and on, off and on. He lowers his window and waves frantically at us. Flowing white hair whips against the side of his car and I swear Jón is wearing a wig. Oh…

"It's not Jón," I realise. "Slow down, it's Anna!"

"Are you sure?"

"Pull over!"

Anna sees us brake and attempts to pull in behind us. But she doesn't brake hard enough and, when she reaches the road's gravelly verge, her tyres slue across sharp rocks at the edge of the lava field, searching for grip. Rubber scrunches against the rocks and there's an almighty pop as a tyre bursts. Panicking, Anna depresses her accelerator by mistake and spins the steering wheel in the wrong direction, skidding across the highway. She slams through the line of fluorescent yellow poles on the opposite roadside and rams into a boulder. Then all is still.

Ari leaps from the Eroder and runs to her. If a car were to come around the bend right now, it would nip the boot of Anna's car, sending it spinning again.

I spring my door and hobble to where Ari is pulling Anna out. "Anna! Are you okay?"

She sends me a look to say she is, yet struggles to put any weight on her right foot. We sit her by the roadside and check her over. Her neck is tender from whiplash. Her right ankle is either broken or severely sprained. She can't move her left wrist and blood trickles onto her black bustle dress from a cut hidden beneath her reddening, matted hair.

"What were you thinking?" I ask gently. "Why are you here—is everything okay at home?"

Shaken and embarrassed, she shrugs in response but doesn't look either of us in the eye. She also doesn't notice my injuries. "I...I need a moment."

Ari assesses her cut, then her car. "It can't stay here," he says, meaning its angle across the road. "It's a danger to other drivers. I'll pull it over there." He sets about detaching the Eroder's winch and hauling it over to Anna's car.

I sit beside her. "What are you doing here, Anna?"

"It was getting late. I was worried."

Worry is one thing. Driving like a lunatic to a remote glacier is another. "So you thought you'd come and find us?"

"I had to do something. You know me, I couldn't wait at home."

"Why not?" What did she think might happen to us? "If we were having a good time, we'd have been much later than this."

"But, after Mark..."

"What about him?"

"I, um..." Her struggle to explain reeks of guilt.

"Anna, why didn't you tell me Mark was helping you research corruption at the Litrúm-Hús?"

"Ólaf told you?"

"Yes."

"Oh." She searches my eyes for a way out, deflates when I don't offer her one. "I didn't want to tell you until I was sure you were ready to do something about it." She bows her head again. "But you are right of course. I should have told you. I know what you're going through, that's all—how confusing this stage is. You need time to adjust."

"Adjust to what?"

"I'm sorry, Becky!" She thrusts the words at me like her entire soul depends on them. "I didn't know they'd go this far."

"Anna, I think you need to tell me everything. Start with why you're really here."

"I was worried. That's the absolute truth."

"Anna, I know you can't lift me." I ignore her innocent, confused expression. "You said you helped me to bed last night. You couldn't have, you're not strong enough. I know it was Jón. I heard him." I smelt him. "Why did you lie?"

Again Anna's eyes dip to the ground.

"You already know what happened to Ari and me at the Skepnasá, don't you? That's why you're here. You know Jón tried to kill us, and you—"

"What?" Anna's voice quivers. "No. What are you saying? He couldn't have." Looking up, she notices my nose for the first time. Backing away to get a better focus, her expression turns to disbelief. "What happened?"

"I told you. Jón tried to kill us."

"It's not possible."

"It is possible. It happened. How do you think I got this?" I point to my nose. "Did Jón hurt Mark too?" I shake my head as I ask the question.

"No!" Anna insists. "Jón came home after work last Friday, stayed with me at *The Himinn* all weekend. He couldn't have gone to Jötunnsjökull and back. But his..." She bites her lip, looks over at Ari. He's attaching the Eroder's winch to her rear bumper. She wants to say something but can't find the words before my patience runs out.

"Anna, unless you tell me what's going on, Ari and I are going to the police to have Jón arrested, or whatever the hell they call it now, for attempted murder."

"No! You can't!"

"And if we accuse him of Mark's murder too, your alibi won't save him, not when there's eye-witness testimony from Ari and me against him."

"You don't understand, Jón would never have hurt Mark—he wants to be Iceland's next MUR Director! He's promised his mother a big house in Reykjavík. That's why he accepted the job up here—he's been saving up for years. His brother's this highflying accountant, his mother idolises him. Jón's determined to prove himself to her. If she found out he was under examination for murder, he...he'd..."

"He'd what? Try to kill us again?"

"No, you've got it wrong. He didn't kill Mark. And if you accuse him of attempted murder you may as well shoot him in the head. Yes, he does things he shouldn't sometimes, to get the money he needs to impress his mother, but he's a good man. Becky, listen, you've got to believe me. He's in trouble, that's all. We have to help him."

"Sure, we'll help him, and anyone else in trouble, as soon as you tell me why you're here."

"I can't let anyone else get hurt, Becky."

"Who would do the hurting?"

She gazes at my face, then tuts and looks away. "You're alive, Ari's alive, your parents are waiting for you. You should just take Mark home and forget about it—it's nothing."

"If it's nothing, then tell me. And make it quick—Ari's almost finished."

In fact, he's reversing the Eroder to align it with the winch. As the slack in the cable tightens, Anna straightens.

"Okay," she lowers her voice to a whisper, "so...Jón couldn't have killed Mark because he was with me. But someone else could have driven to Jötunnsjökull and back last weekend."

"And why would they have done that?"

Anna takes a breath then speaks fast, as if the words are too hot to keep in her mouth any longer. "I think my research got Mark killed. I think someone drove to Jötunnsjökull and killed your brother because he found proof."

"Proof of what, the corruption? Is there an activist or isn't there?"

Anna reaches to touch my hand. "Becky, listen, this is important... you can't tell anyone, do you understand? No one. No matter what."

"Okay," I agree, though I suspect I don't mean it.

"I don't know who exactly is doing what," she whispers, "but Jón is always speaking with them on the phone. He never says their name out loud, but they talk a lot about something that happened before Jón came to Höfkállur, so it has to be someone who knew him from Reykjavík. He calls them 'Chief'." She eyes Ari again, then looks me up and down. "Why are you both in bathrobes?"

I raise my eyebrows. She's only just noticed? I explain the last few hours to her and, as I do, her expression fixes on pained regret. I feel nothing for her except disappointment. She should have told me about Mark and the Litrúm-Hús.

"Okay, Anna." I say after telling her about Jón and the ice, "what I need you to do now is tell me about your research, everything you've been doing, everything you know. Go."

Anna pauses, closes her eyes, then starts explaining her theories to me. They reflect almost exactly what Ólaf's already told me about Pàll, his hit and run, Anna's argument with him, how Jón must be keeping the driver's identity a secret, and about the battlelights again.

After a while she opens her eyes but rather than look at me, she watches her car as she speaks. Metal scrapes against rock in high-pitched squeals as Ari drags her car off the boulder. The noise is piercing, yet I sense Ari listening to Anna through his open window. I don't point this out to her—I want Ari to overhear, because then he can tell her that she's nuts, and that I'm nuts too. I don't want my brother to have died because of some crazy widow's research into corruption in a far away country—one he actually loved very much.

At the same time, Anna's explanations begin to sound all too feasible. She has such a way with words. So, taking a deep breath, I force myself to listen to the reality she's painting—a world I didn't know existed: a world where lives can be stolen and never returned, where my brother might have made a fatal mistake, and where I might have made one too. What if she's not crazy?

Sat on the roadside with the weight of her words pressing on me, my head slumps forward. How can any of this be actually real?

Becky, says a voice, *are you okay?*

Chapter 22

L it only by the faint-blue of dusk, surrounded by a head-high lava field, I watch Ari towing Anna's car away from the bend, I hear Anna talking about her research, and I know this moment deserves my utmost attention. At the same time, I'm barely able to comprehend where I am. Everything feels so abstract from life, from the continuous toil of breathing and swallowing and blinking.

Becky, are you okay?

My head grows so heavy I struggle to keep it upright.

The next minute it's weightless, like the top of my scalp has wedded one of the few stars twinkling faintly in the navy sky closer to Höfkállur. I open my eyes wide, try to take in more oxygen. I have to listen to Anna.

"Becky, love, are you okay?" Anna asks.

"I'm fine," my mouth lies. I'm slurring. I swallow and try again. "Just a little lightheaded. Go on."

"I said, have you ever wondered why people scheduled for examination in Höfkállur bother to plead not-guilty? Why, when they know we use the Sannlitró-Völva and it will find them out?"

Anna waits but I can't articulate an answer. I haven't been listening close enough. My head and nose are pounding in sync.

"Maybe they believe," she supposes for me, "they can outwit the machine? Or…maybe they really are innocent?"

"Go on." While I rest my brain.

"Jón's always very busy before and after these not-guilty cases, so I began to wonder. Yes, he wants a big career. He's also not the type to work harder than he needs to ensure the course of justice runs smooth. So what's he doing? Maybe it has something to do with his phone calls with his 'Chief'?"

I nod to assure her I'm listening.

She puts her arm around me, then continues. "I started looking into things and found all the offenders causing Jón this extra work were wealthy. Not only that, but they were all sent to the Reformation Cooperative for minor offences and, according to local government records, they all owned investment properties. I kept checking, looking for connections. Then one of the offenders' investment properties was sold while they were still in the Cooperative."

"Now," she clears her throat, "under our new system, if an offender continues to deny their guilt after two years in the Cooperative, the MUR reserves the right to seize assets to fund their extended counselling. However, this particular property was sold *a month* after the offender arrived at the Cooperative. So I entered my details into a real estate website to get alerts when any of the other offenders' properties were sold, and found a pattern: not-guilty plea, plus wealthy offender, equals property sold one month later. Don't you see? Jón and his Chief are selling these properties early and pocketing the sale money!"

"I'm guessing you don't have any proof?" Otherwise she would have made an anonymous tip-off before now.

"I've been trying. I have a diary of Jón's work patterns, when offenders were sent to the Cooperative and the dates their properties were sold. But how can I show it to anyone at the Litrúm-Hús? I might end up confiding in Jón's Chief, whoever that is." Her gaze fixes on Ari. "Ólaf said it wasn't enough proof anyway. He thinks we need evidence to negate *any* possibility the properties were sold under 'administrative error', prematurely or otherwise. We need proof that someone is tampering with the Sannlitró-Völva on purpose. Then, before we hand over our proof, we need to be certain we're handing it to the right person. Otherwise we'll never find out how high up this goes."

"So how do you intend to do all that?"

"Ólaf and I thought up a plan, though we've been having trouble implementing it—there are only so many times I can watch examinations without raising Jón or his Chief's suspicions. Then Mark came along."

"And he said he'd help?" Of course he did.

"He was going to record the next not-guilty examination—someone called Sigmar—on his phone."

"Which is was why he was at the Litrúm-Hús last Friday?" I ask, feeling more earthed now. "Was Mark's postscript about this in any way, the one he was adding to his thesis?"

"His postscript?"

"Yes. Did he talk to you about it?"

"Of course. And yes, in a way his postscript was connected, though from a philosophical perspective—you know Mark. But now his phone and laptop are missing, and I still need a recording. Just one, Becky! Then Pàll can rest."

"What has any of this got to do with Pàll? Did he lose any property?"

"No."

"Does he have anything to do with anyone losing property? Does his death?"

"Not that I know of. But his visits are most strong before and after the not-guilty cases. He obviously wants me to stop them."

"You can't know that's what he wants." Because there's no way I can be certain of Mark's messages, if that's what they are.

"You forget, Becky. I've been seeing Pàll's energy for a year and a half. I know what he means now."

"Why does it even matter to Pàll?"

"The *Heimspeki* could save so much fighting, Becky, it could bring peace to the world. It's already brought peace to Pàll and I, knowing we'll be together in the end. Imagine how much peace it could bring others. Something so beautiful can't go into the world on the back of a flawed technology. And who knows what Jón's Chief has planned for the Sannlitró-Völva? If they've been getting away with all this here, they could get away with it anywhere—in any country where the machine is integrated into the legal system. Remember all the countries Director Úlfar is negotiating with at the moment? There'd be no limit who they could or couldn't find guilty—they could accuse anyone, *anyone*, of committing a crime, anywhere...or have them set free. I need a recording. I need proof the Sannlitró-Völva is flawed. At least...I thought I needed it. Now I'm not so sure. Pàll wouldn't want anyone else getting hurt. I don't either."

"But isn't that why you wanted me to familiarise myself with the Litrúm-Hús?"

She rubs my shoulder rather than answer. "You've got to understand, once Ólaf and I have a recording, all we need to do is wait until that particular offender's property is sold, then we can drive straight to the Cooperative, re-examine them with equipment we know isn't contaminated, and it'll all be over. The two recordings will show different results and implicate Jón, who'll then *have* to name his 'Chief' to the authorities to save his career. He'll be the hero."

"What if he refuses?"

"Then we'd submit him for an examination. Our evidence would be enough for a submission rather than an invitation."

"What's the difference?"

"If you're 'invited' you're given notice, a night to think about it, you have access to your phone, email, social media. Jón and his Chief would just leave the country. But if there's solid evidence…"

"They're formally accused," Ari interrupts, appearing by my side. "No invitations, no phone, no email. Then the first question you'd ask Jón is who he's working with at the Litrúm-Hús. It was a good plan."

Anna doesn't reply, just watches Ari crouch before her. As he takes her damaged ankle in his hand she braces herself, as if fearing he's going to snap it.

"Anna," he says, finishing his inspection, "if Jón wants his career so much, why did he try to kill us today?"

She speaks her reply slowly. "I don't believe he did. I can't."

"Anna," I lean forward until she looks into my eyes, "Ari saw him."

"Did *you* see him?" she asks me.

I tut.

"Even if he was there," she adds, "he might only have been there because someone made him."

Ari rests his hand on her ankle, and peers into her eyes. "Do you really think anyone could make Jón do something he didn't want to do?"

She doesn't answer.

In my memory, I hear Anna complaining about Jón not helping her with Pàll. "He's been stubborn enough over Pàll." I remind her.

"Pàll?" Ari asks.

As I tell him about Anna's late husband, Ari's eyes dart from side to side as if processing the information.

"Pàll who, exactly?" he asks after I've finished.

I look to Anna.

"Pàll Hinriksson," she mumbles.

"That was two years ago?"

Anna nods.

"When Jón arrived?"

"No. Jón didn't move here until six months after Pàll died."

"Huh-huh." Ari says, deep in thought.

"What are you going to do?" Anna asks.

He studies her, then jumps to his feet, grabs her hands and pulls her to standing. "First we'll go to the morgue so Doctor Emil can look at you both. I need to know you aren't hurt more than it looks. Then we'll hear what Director Úlfar has to say about Mark, and why he's in

Höfkállur. Then, we'll submit Jón for an examination, tonight."

"How?" Anna moves her head to get a better look at him. "I don't have a recording yet."

"I have the authority to submit Litrúm-Hús personnel for immediate preliminary examinations if I have 'just cause'. All I need is your evidence, Anna, to justify the examination." He puts an arm around her and pulls her towards the Eroder.

Her car is now sitting beyond Ari's, within the boundary of the highway's hard shoulder but far enough from the bend to be easily seen. A couple of triangles forewarn approaching vehicles.

"But," I say, hobbling after them, "if Jón's desperate enough to kill us," I ignore Anna's glare, "why would he let you examine him? He wouldn't, not without a fight. I don't want you getting hurt either."

Ari thinks for a moment. "Director Úlfar's in Höfkállur," he says, closing Anna's door, "we'll ask him to perform the examination, say it's about security, that we all have to answer some questions."

I'm climbing into the Eroder but Ari's words make me stop midway.

Perform the examination.

I hover in the doorway, pain stabbing my ribs like a hot poker. But more painful is the realisation that's hitting me. It doesn't come from logic, from answered questions, or any particular fact. Instead, everything I've learnt since arriving in Iceland, along with everything that's been marinating in my subconscious for last few years, has finally coalesced.

Oh shit!

I know who Jón's Chief is, without a doubt. The answer strikes with such clarity I cannot breath. The Skepnasá River almost killed me; it also left me a consolation prize: instincts are not obsolete impulses, inferior compulsions no rational person needs; gut feelings are not illogical nonsense. They're here to help, and I'm listening now—thanks to Ari and that river. Call it a hunch, a feeling, an inkling, intuition... Yes, I've even met people like Jón's Chief before, in Jersey—people who hid their motives, people secretive about their purpose and underhanded. Sometimes what people say isn't what they mean or even want. That's why facts and evidence don't always reveal the truth. I need to look elsewhere.

"Director Úlfar," Ari continues, thinking out loud, "will not say anything to Jón about today, he will tell him he needs help examining an aggressive offender about a security breach. Jón won't know that offender is him until he's already in the Dómstólls, being examined."

I wait for Ari to notice my reaction but he doesn't. He continues to the driver's seat, leaving me with the increasing sound of roaring water in my ears, and a warmth spreading over my head.

I'm right, aren't I, Mark?

A wave roars towards a cliff and smashes over its rocky base.

Anna's theories, Jón's supposed coercion, Mark's 'accident' — there's only one person who could be responsible for it all, one person with the power, the access, the resources. It's the only answer.

For once, my gut is leading the way.

I close my eyes, incredulous it hasn't dawned on me before, and wonder what else my subconscious might have figured out that I have missed.

Chapter 23

The corridors of Höfkállur Hospital illuminate in sections as sensor-lights perceive our approach and flicker into action. While Anna limps along, supported by Ari, I hobble and feel like I'm negotiating a slippery precipice. On one side is a limitless chasm of doubt over what I've realised. On the other is the steep mountain face I have to climb to convince everyone my answer is sound. I've spent the entire drive back to Höfkállur reviewing and updating my notes on what everyone's been telling me. Ari lent me his phone so I could access my online notes. Muddled together, facts can be as indistinguishable as the disconnected pieces of a puzzle. With a little organisation, the picture usually becomes clear. Now I'm convinced—I've made a critical error. We all have. Some people simply can't help themselves. Mark said it himself.

Those occasional few...

Some people can never have enough, believing they're more entitled to it than others. Sometimes it's the people with too much power already—power corrupts. Sometimes it's the people who want to protect their careers or reputations—self-preservation can force people to take extreme measures. Sometimes it's the people who crave financial reprieve—money brings out the worst in people. Sometimes it's all these things yet none of them. Sometimes it's a secret that, really, everyone knows but doesn't want to confront because difficult truths can be hideous to face, raw and bare. Deep down, we know they're there. But sometimes we'd rather be whores to normalcy than expose ourselves to its ugliness. So we ignore it.

Yes, since coming to Iceland, I've been favouring certain facts, ignoring others. I didn't want to see them for what they could be. I couldn't bear to acknowledge many things outright. But Ari is right, new facts—such as Mark helping Anna, Ólaf having the litagjöf, Ari seeing Jón at the glacier, and Gunnar's absence—have made me think differently about old facts. Facts can often be unreliable when dealing with people. In such cases, it *can* be more logical to trust your gut, listen to your instincts, go with a hunch, faith in your subconscious reasoning...

Mark wanted me to trust my gut more, and my gut is telling me that ignorance is no longer a choice. People can get away with murder, literally and figuratively, if they know how to intimidate— either directly with words or actions, or indirectly by relying on unchallenged reputations to cover tracks or create illusions people would rather believe because they're beautiful and easy. But I know from experience that easy is not self-satisfying. Easy can allow weeds to sprout through the soil of your everyday living and grow where you least expect them. Until, one day, you wake to find yourself a nervous wreck wishing you'd faced the ugliness of truth—however raw or bare—rather than let yourself become infested with other people's lies. I am not worthless and never have been. I am not crazy and never will be. Riley was a cheater and I know now how to spot them.

My choice is made. It was made for me years ago when I was a young woman working with bullies, and decades ago when I was a little girl with new glasses. It was made for me when Mark died in pursuit of some truth he sensed but never saw—Anna's truth. She wants closure. I can give it to her. I don't need the police anymore; there's only a question of timing to resolve. I have no evidence, no facts, no proof—and not everyone can be swayed without them, not everyone will happily trust another person's gut feelings. I know I wouldn't. So I need to wait for a moment that will convince everyone of the truth I now know, a moment when no one will shrink from a truth they don't want to face. Including me.

Ari slams his shoulder against the door of the morgue with a satisfying thud. I too feel like pounding inanimate objects, but my nose and ribs are so tender that when I clear my throat the hurt pierces through what pain-repression adrenalin has granted. I need to rest. Rest, though, will have to wait.

Two figures hover over my brother's body. If I were alone, I'd run to his fleshy pale shell and hold it close. But not here; not now. I ignore the sadness twanging my chest and look anywhere else. The burly frame of Doctor Emil is bent, studying Mark's head injury through a magnifier. Dressed in medical scrubs, he looks less like a Norse warrior now. Yet when he clears his throat, his husky reverberation echoes into the corridor and, as he straightens to scratch at his blond beard, his stout solidity fills the room.

Standing beside him, dwarfed and chubby by comparison, Director Úlfar listens intently to the doctor's mutterings while re-tucking his shirt into a well-rounded waistband. When he notices our arrival, he beckons us inside. Avoiding eye contact with me, he specifically seeks out Ari, smoothing flat his bouncy brown hair as he does.

This is not the right moment to play my cards. So I keep my poker face and watch.

Immersed in his work, Doctor Emil acknowledges our presence not with a greeting or gesture, but by launching into his report on my brother's re-examination. "So, Mark Dales, a 26-year-old white male presen—"

Ari interrupts. "Excuse me, Doctor Emil...I must speak with Director Úlfar, immediately," he adds, "in private. Can you wait some minutes?"

Emil nods and indicates a corner of the room.

All too eager, Director Úlfar waddles into it with Ari, eyeing him up and down as he did the receptionist at Reykjavík's Central Travel Depot. The two of them whisper about Jón and make hushed phone calls. All the while, Director Úlfar takes every opportunity to rest a hand on Ari's forearm or shoulder, and I realise what he meant on the phone yesterday when he said Ari was *very* nice. He meant he has a crush on him.

Doctor Emil lifts his head magnifier, scratches his beard and goes to put some instruments away. He notices the cut on Anna's head and my bulbous nose. "What has happened to you?" he asks, shuffling around the room to examine us. Anna explains something in Icelandic. When he fetches what he needs, she sends me a look to reassure me she's only told him what he needs to know.

The ensuing minutes of prodding and probing seem like hours. How many times do I need to wince and agree to the pain he's measuring before he concludes what I already know? I've broken my nose and several ribs.

With huge hairy hands that make me question how he can be so graceful with his care, he reapplies bandages and sutures my thigh with fresh Leukostrips. Then it's Anna's turn. I hear him mutter the word 'x-ray' but Anna shakes her head and points to my watch. She has more pressing matters to attend to. We both do.

When Ari and Director Úlfar turn, Director Úlfar's lips are taut, the lines on his forehead deep in furrows. His expression could denote anxiety, embarrassment, possibly anger; the one emotion it does not denote is surprise. He knew this was coming. "Jón is at the Litrúm-Hús," he tells me, still without making eye contact. "I have called ahead to authorise his examination, to be performed personally. Ari has also called ahead."

"Why is Jón at the Litrúm-Hús when he called in sick today?"

"He waits there for Gunnar, and me."

I check my watch. "It's past 9pm."

"I was at the Cooperative today..."

"He met with *Sigmar*," Ari interrupts, emphasising the name. Sigmar's examination was the one Mark tried to record last Friday. "Director Úlfar knows about Jón already."

"Nei. I knew about someone. I did not know it was Jón." Director Úlfar huffs and finally makes eye contact, his expression heavy at having to share this with me. "One of the Skyggður we employed to review procedure, Haraldur, was noticing certain trends, so we started watching the Cooperative." He pauses. "Last night Haraldur went to meet their newest offender, only to find it was an old friend of his, Sigmar Thorsteinson. Haraldur knows Sigmar from school and knows how very bad he was at maths, and technology. So how did Sigmar misappropriate funds from a college bursary account in Sauðákrókur? Naturally Haraldur realised he couldn't have, even though the Sannlitró-Völva found him guilty, so he said I needed to come to Höfkállur straight away. Haraldur and Sigmar are on their way from the Cooperative as we speak. We're meeting as soon as they get here, at the Litrúm-Hús, to identify Jón as the MUR officer who arranged Sigmar's examination. We were going to proceed from there."

"Someone's also watching Jón," Ari adds.

"So Jón already knows we're onto him?" I ask.

Director Úlfar shakes his head as if the very idea is nonsense. "He thinks he's there to wait for Gunnar. He doesn't know he's the one being watched."

I nod as if that's okay then. But it's too coincidental, that Director Úlfar is here taking action now, tonight, on the same day I almost drowned. And why is Doctor Emil examining my brother's body when Gunnar already admitted his mistake? "Um, Doctor Emil, what prompted you to re-examine my brother today?"

Doctor Emil frowns, as if the answer is obvious. "Because of what you said to Director Úlfar."

"Why though, after Gunnar admitted his mistake?" Blank looks. "He left a message on my phone, apologising for forgetting to include

Mark's head injury in his report."

"So," Director Úlfar tuts at me, "this is why you didn't send me a photograph of your brother's head? I was expecting it."

"There was little point after Gunnar explained his mistake. He said he'd spoken to you about it." I look to Doctor Emil for an explanation. He shakes his head. "I never spoke to Gunnar."

I go to pull out my phone and show them Gunnar's message, but my hand slides down the towelling of my pocketless robe. No clothes; no phone. "He said you received my message and were going to take measures to ensure he never made a mistake like that again."

Doctor Emil crosses his arms. "I didn't get a message from either of you."

"After you called me," Director Úlfar says, pleased with himself, "I followed up, asked Emil for his revised report. He didn't know what I was talking about, so I told him what you told me."

I frown. "I definitely left a message on your phone. It said 'welcome to the message bank of Doctor Emil'."

"This is why I don't trust VoIP," Anna says, appearing by my side with two sets of light blue medical scrubs. She eyes my bathrobe. "If people can hack into banks, they can hack into computerised messaging services. Here, for you and Ari."

I take a pair and pass a set to Ari. "But why bother deleting my message to Doctor Emil when I'd already spoken to Director Úlfar?"

"You used the morgue's analogue phone to speak to Director Úlfar." Anna reminds me. "They can't monitor those, they're not VoIP. They mustn't have known about your call."

Doctor Emil comes over to us, drying his hands as he walks. Director Úlfar asks him something in Icelandic. He shakes his head in reply. "Gunnar is a good assistant. I've never known him to make a mistake like this." He turns to face me. "I am sorry, Miss Dales, I didn't have time to check Gunnar's report before you arrived yesterday. If I had, maybe this would not have happened."

"Is that why you were reluctant to give it to me, because you hadn't checked it?"

He nods. "I do not understand how Gunnar missed something this important."

"Unless," says Anna, "he missed it on purpose."

I pick up on Doctor Emil's use of words. "Why is Mark's head injury *important*? Does it alter Mark's cause of death?"

"Considerably." Doctor Emil moves towards Mark's body. "If you look at the injury its shape is angular and, if you look here," he uses tweezers to lift a flap of Mark's blood-stained scalp, "a metallic fragment is imbedded in the wound."

Anna looks to where he's pointing but I take his word for it. Glasses wouldn't sit properly on my nose right now, and I don't want another dizzy spell disrupting my concentration.

"I no longer believe the cause of death," Doctor Emil continues, "was asphyxia due to drowning. Also, the body was found in the Skepnasá River on the afternoon of Sunday twenty-eighth of August but, according to my calculations, death occurred in the morning of Friday twenty-sixth of August. Gunnar got that wrong too."

"In the morning?" I look at Anna. She's staring at Doctor Emil as if he's slapped her around the face with a wet fish. "Where was Jón," I ask her, "and Gunnar, last Friday morning?"

She doesn't reply, just continues staring at Doctor Emil as if she'll find an answer in his face. I don't expect her to know about Gunnar, but she said Jón couldn't have travelled to Jötunnsjökull and back because he was with her last Friday night and then all weekend. What about Friday morning, where was he then?

A moment of acceptance sweeps across the room.

"Okay," Director Úlfar says, commandeering everyone's attention, "it is enough. We will go to the Litrúm-Hús now. This will be sorted quickly and quietly, tonight. Please, everyone..." He moves to the door and holds it open.

Ari immediately joins Director Úlfar at the door. Anna follows, using the stainless steel counter to hobble around the room. I'm the last to move. I'm still watching Doctor Emil. He covers Mark with a white sheet and slides the body tray back inside its drawer. As it clicks into place, I watch the tiny light above Mark's drawer turn back on, rejoining the other two lights flickering on the mortuary cabinet. Mark is sleeping again.

With a sigh I move towards the door. I'm about to pass Director Úlfar when I turn and recount the tiny drawer lights. There are three.

Three?

"Doctor Emil, has anyone died since yesterday?"

"Not that I know."

"Only two drawers were occupied when I was here last night."

Doctor Emil scratches his beard. He pulls at the drawer next to Mark's, looks at the toe tag, closes it, then peers at the temperature gauge on the drawer directly above it. "Hm, this one's not set correctly." He tugs it open.

The instant the drawer opens, a rancid tang fills the room. There's no toe tag on the body inside, no toe to even tie a tag onto, just a pair of shoes at the end of trousered legs. Doctor Emil yanks the tray fully out, recognises the bloodied face atop the fully clothed body and reels back against the mortuary slab.

I cover my nose and mouth. "Who is it?" I stutter.

Ari moves around Anna to get a better look at the skinny pale blond splattered with blood. "Gunnar," he mumbles.

The mortuary cabinets purr in the silence that follows. There's a gun in Gunnar's right hand. It's obvious from the gaping wound on his head what he's done. His blood has dried in the dark cavity of the drawer into a deep burgundy that sits in large globular splatters over the tray and stains his skin. He must have pulled himself into the drawer before squeezing the trigger.

I feel a swell of sympathy and pity. Gunnar is one of the unlucky ones. No one was here to help him. No one came to save him. He was all alone.

A memory swallows my heart.

But Doctor Emil has already recovered from the shock and is leaning over Gunnar's body, pressing the sleeve of his white lab coat over his nose. I follow his stare. He's looking at the expression fixed on Gunnar's face, whose eyes and mouth are wider than I would have expected for someone in the depths of despair. Then the doctor is on his hands and knees, looking under the tray to examine its rollers. I bend my head to see what's interesting him.

"There's blood all over the front rollers," he says.

I'm about to point out that there's blood all over the inside of the drawer, and that he just pulled the body out over the blood, when he begins an analysis I don't want to interrupt.

"Blood would have dripped under the tray, run under the rollers and dried," he says. "But, if the tray was stationary, how did blood get onto the tops of the rollers at the front? There's no blood on the tray by his legs and blood can't drip upwards." He looks at Director Úlfar. "The tray must have been rolled out while the blood was still fresh, then rolled back in."

"Someone knows he's here," Anna murmurs.

"Nei." Doctor Emil shakes his head. "You don't understand. Gunnar was a good assistant. We were friends. Friends enough to know he was left-handed."

I look at the gun. It's in Gunnar's right hand.

"Why is this important?" Ari says, cringing as he realises the answer.

Doctor Emil closes his assistant's eyes before answering, then closes his own before speaking. "Gunnar did not pull that trigger."

Chapter 24

Everyone stares at the gun in Gunnar's blood-splattered hand, but my attention is drawn to Ari, who leans closer than the others to examine it. Director Úlfar mirrors his action and they exchange a knowing look.

"What?" I want to know. "What is it? Ari?"

"The gun," Ari says, "I've seen it before."

Anna clears her throat and faces me, rolling her eyes. "It's a double action nine millimetre semiautomatic—MUR standard issue." She makes eye contact with Ari. "That doesn't make it Jón's."

"Somebody was in there with him," Doctor Emil moves his eyes between Ari and Anna, "pulling the trigger. They had to push themselves back out before closing Gunnar inside."

"Ari," says Director Úlfar, touching his forearm, "take Anna home and pick up her evidence. Doctor Emil, please examine Gunnar quickly. I want a report in the next half hour. I will go to the Litrúm-Hús, download Jón's Litrúm Maps, and," he points to Anna, Ari and I, "meet you three in the Dómstólls."

I remember what Ari told me about the Litrúm Maps scanning a person's state of mind for certain results. "What are you expecting Jón's Litrúm Maps to show? He wouldn't have been so stupid as to leave them lying around, surely?"

"Precisely." Director Úlfar moves to hold the door open for everyone except Doctor Emil. "I do not expect to find any. I expect him to have deleted them. This I will use to question him."

"Do not question him alone, Director," Ari says.

"It's okay," Director Úlfar taps his side as the four of us leave the morgue, "I have my gun."

The thought makes me shudder.

Once we're in the corridor, Ari insists on helping Anna hobble up the stairs and across the car park. On the way, Director Úlfar signals for us to be quiet while he makes a call, muttering in hushed Icelandic to someone who answers succinctly to three questions. After he hangs up, Anna tells me he was speaking to the man sent to watch Jón, who's confirmed that Jón is still inside the Litrúm-Hús.

Director Úlfar then re-dials, speaking loudly and jovially in Icelandic. I hear the names 'Jón' and 'Gunnar'. Again Anna translates the call. That was Jón. He's confirmed Gunnar still hasn't showed up at the Litrúm-Hús. Director Úlfar has asked Jón to wait there until he arrives, in about fifteen minutes.

Hell—in fifteen minutes Jón is going to get the shock of his life. He thinks Ari and I are dead.

Director Úlfar runs a fingertip over his eyebrows, waves farewell and breaks off to go to his own car. It would be better for us to stay together until we're at the Litrúm-Hús, but Director Úlfar also has a gun with him and I don't want it anywhere near me. Yet.

So Ari drives us to *The Himinn* and within minutes we're parked in Anna's driveway. Anna tells him where to find her evidence and gives him the password for her computer. He'll be quicker on his feet than either of us.

"It's in the folder called 'grænt nótt'," she tells him.

Ari darts into the house with his daypack and a USB drive from his glove box. We see his shadow yanking open the flip-down keyboard of Anna's hallway laptop. Moments later, he's scaling the staircase like a monkey up a tree. Anna has a shoebox of evidence in her wardrobe.

"Maybe I should help him," Anna opens her door, winces as she puts weight on her ankle.

I reach over my seat and rest my hand on her shoulder. "Ari will find it. If he can't, he'll shout down for help."

Anna nods and sits back. The hum of the Eroder's expectant engine fills the silence.

"Don't be nervous," I say, although it's a ridiculous request. She's been building up to this moment for years. In fact, I doubt she's even heard me, her eyes are so fixed on *The Himinn*. She's desperate to go inside. She's worried about her evidence. Her hands rest on her lap, gripped into fists.

I bite my bottom lip, unsure how to reassure her. I can barely think how to reassure myself. Until we saw Gunnar's corpse my theories were still just that, theories. Now they've become something else. They've become real.

I take a deep breath, detect a faint fragrance in the air and identify it as cinnamon, dancing in a baking aroma that drifts towards us from a neighbouring house. The detail helps ground me and that's where I am when Anna speaks, low and firm.

"Do you know what, Becky," she says without shifting her gaze, "I think you should stay here, at *The Himinn*. There's no need for you to be at the Litrúm-Hús tonight."

"No way. I'm coming."

"It could be dangerous."

"I didn't come to Höfkállur to play it safe." Not that I came expecting danger.

"I don't want anyone else getting hurt. Jón is my business now."

"And Mark is mine."

"You don't need to be there."

"Need?" I lean into her peripheral vision. "Anna, there's a man at that Litrúm-Hús who can tell me how and why my brother died last Friday morning. I'm going." I send her a look of determination. She goes to argue but I get in first. "Besides, do you really want to be sitting there alone when Jón starts saying awful things to you?" I close a hand around one of hers. "Because you must know he will. You're about to betray him."

"For his own good," she says like she's trying to convince herself. "He'll understand, eventually. What he's doing now, stealing all that money, it's no good for his energy."

"Not to mention murdering Gunnar." Possibly Mark too.

"That's not proven yet."

"Either way, he's still going to make you cry."

She shrugs, weary, and speaks with a sigh. "Putting on a show is second nature for me now. If I need someone, Ólaf will be there."

"I'm counting on that." Ari would only ever call Ólaf to help with an examination this significant.

"I'd still rather you were safe. Mark wouldn't want me putting his sister in unnecessary danger."

"He'd also want me to be there for you. I was hoping we'd stay in touch after this is over." As I say the words, I realise how true they are. I've already forgiven Anna for not telling me about the corruption, or Jón. She was only doing what she thought was best. She still is. "There's so much you haven't told me about Mark yet, about his postscript and what he was researching. He said Höfkállur had the best coffee in the world too, some little shop by the harbour? I was hoping you'd take me there and tell me everything. We could go tomorrow morning?"

She brings a hand on top of mine, squeezing it as if it's a lifeline thrown amidst stormy seas. "I'd like that. You still shouldn't come tonight."

"Nothing will happen to us, Anna, not as long as Ari's there. And he will be."

She stifles a laugh.

"What?" I ask.

She returns her gaze to *The Himinn* as a shadow descends the stairs and jogs out the front door. "I don't doubt you once made an excellent lawyer, Becky. You…you're very determined. Too determined for your own good sometimes."

"Yes," I smile to myself as I face front again, "some people call it stubborn."

Ari slams himself into the driver's seat. He's changed into some spare clothes he must have had in his daypack. "Okay?" He shows Anna a shoebox.

"Yes," she tells him, "that's everything."

"Gott, we have to go. Director Úlfar phoned me. Jón is asking to go home already. Becky, do you want some clothes?"

"It's okay." I pat my set of scrubs. "I'll change into these on the way."

Ari shifts the Eroder's gears into reverse, turns and accelerates. As we drive, I feel my own gears shifting too. This is it. We have the evidence we need. We have Jón. All we need now is the Sannlitró-Völva. Even the pinching of my ribs and the tenderness in my limbs as I slide my thin blue scrub pants under my robe and pull the top over my head doesn't bother me as much as it should. All I want is to get there now.

I go over my notes in my mind, thinking how best to get the information I want from Jón once he's in front of the machine, and how best to achieve the moment I need. I think about the responses he's likely to give to certain prompters, and about the responses he's not likely to want to give too. I wish I had some concrete evidence of my own, to back up my theory and settle my unease, but I don't and I hate feeling so out of control.

Control is not everything, Ari said earlier.

It didn't help me in the river.

Still, I need to do something.

"Ari, can I borrow your phone again?" Writing down questions will at least help me plan. Ari slings me his phone and I jam what I can into my notes app. I've barely had time to get down the essentials when Anna leans to peer over my shoulder.

"What are you writing?" She stares at my file, though its individual words will be indecipherable from where she's sitting. Thankfully.

"Notes on what I've learnt about the *Heimspeki* over the last forty-eight hours. I want to actually understand Mark's thesis when I read it. So I've been writing down what everyone's said to me since coming to Iceland, where things conflict. Facts. Theories. That sort of thing."

"You've made notes on what everyone's said?"

"Everyone."

Ari glances at me as we pull into the Litrúm-Hús car park. "I am in there?"

"I did say everyone. In the interests of figuring out who Jón's partner might be, of course."

Ari raises an eyebrow.

"Who's at the top of your list?" Anna wants to know.

"Um," I pretend to review my notes, "Director Úlfar."

Ari throws me a look of disbelief as he parks the car and switches off the engine. "Director Úlfar, as in the Press Secretary and Director of the MUR, who we just left at the morgue?"

"The very one."

A look of stunned sympathy washes over Ari's face. His expression is nothing compared to the look he'll have later, when I tell him what I know.

"Why not him?" I ask. "He's been overly-attentive, tried to persuade me not to come up to Höfkállur. He's power-hungry, has enough influence to make anything happen. He's guarded about every word he says—yet why should he need to if everyone's living by their hearts, so to speak?"

"He doesn't even work here," Ari points out. "And he's got more than enough money."

"He could be planning a retirement in Hawaii for all we know." I eye Anna as I make my next statement. "And it's always the ones you least expect. No one should be beyond suspicion. Plus," I turn back to Ari, who's popping open his door, "he wanted me to stay away from Höfkállur, and now he's suddenly here on the day someone tries to kill me. Can you pass me my bag please?"

Shaking his head, Ari passes my bag over, helps Anna and I down from the Eroder, then asks for his phone. "I need to tell Director Úlfar we're here," he says with an impatient snap.

It doesn't matter whether Ari believes me or not right now, so I don't argue and simply pass the phone over.

He cradles it in his shoulder to make his call, helping Anna inside at the same time. It takes her forever to hobble up the Litrúm-Hús steps, but once we're inside Ari's voice echoes through the dark empty corridors with such clarity I worry Jón will get wind of the surprise heading his way.

I smell the air, checking for a sour post-cigarette odour—the odour I smelt last night when I fell asleep in the pink leather armchair.

But as we walk towards the Dómstólls, only silent corridors flank our progress and only shadows close in behind us.

Chapter 25

As soon as we enter the Dómstóll, Ólaf sees Anna and his face fills with dismay. From the sag in his heavy cheeks, he clearly can't imagine a worse place for her to be. He rubs a hand over the short grey hair at the back of his head, brings it to rest on his bald patch, then tuts at her and glares at me.

I shrug at him, then look around the Dómstóll. Director Úlfar is nowhere to be seen. It's then I realise stealth should have been the least of my concerns. If Jón didn't suspect that Ari and I were still alive when Director Úlfar told him to remain at the Litrúm-Hús, his partner would have helped him figure that out by now. Of course they know what's about to happen. My presence, or Ari's, won't be a surprise for anybody. All I can hope is they don't realise: I know who they are.

We walk across beige carpet to where Ólaf has returned to adjusting the plasma membrane of the Sannlitró-Völva on its trolley, fingertips gripping the embossed *Heimspeki* symbols.

When the trolley wobbles, Ari rushes forward to help, only to face a tired hand waving at him to sit.

"I've got it." Ólaf says, his mouth twitching. "I do this all the time without you, you know."

Anna limps towards her cousin, supporting herself on the backs of pinewood benches. "Is there anything we can do to help, Ólaf?"

"Go home." He holds out some cords.

She reaches for them.

"Don't be silly, Anna." I take the cords from her. "He's passing them to me. Sit and rest your ankle. She's hurt her ankle," I tell Ólaf, hoping he won't want to waste time asking why.

Thankfully, he's too busy to do anything other than dip his chin. "Takk, Becky. Wind them up and put them under the trolley. Ari, seeing as you're here too, plug this extension into the socket over there. Anna, my dear, go home."

"If you want to help," I tell Anna, winding a cord around my forearm, "turn your phone to translation for me."

Anna takes a seat at the back of the room and fiddles with her phone.

Once Ari's plugged in the machine, he asks Ólaf. "Anything else?"

"Nei. Unless you can persuade my cousin to—go—home."

Ari smiles at Ólaf's persistence until there's movement in the corridor. He peeks out the doorway. "Sorry, Ólaf. Too late. They're here."

I abandon the cords and hurry to connect my earpiece to Anna's phone.

She's nervous, seesawing to straighten the gathered creases of her black bustle dress and drawing her rust-red ballet shoes under her. As the smoked glass doors swing to attention, we exchange a glance that scorns the wisdom of our presence here tonight. It makes me hope all the more that I know what I'm doing.

Seconds later, Jón strides into the Dómstóll, freezing the room into silence. Director Úlfar is at his heel, waddling like a penguin against Jón's bearlike height, panting as he attempts to keep up. Neither man notices Anna and I shrinking at the back of the room.

Jón doesn't even react when he sees Ari. He merely runs a hand through his shiny shoulder-length hair and brings his other hand around to tie it into a sleek black ponytail. "Right, let's get on with this, Ari," he mutters, massaging the weathered bronze skin of his forehead. Anna's phone translates everything. "It's late, I'm sick and want to get home. What's this security breach all about?"

"Take a seat, Jón," Ólaf says, his eyes locked on the controls before him, "this won't take long." He scrunches up his nose to reposition his glasses.

"Where's the offender?" Jón turns to check behind him, sees us for the first time. His annoyed expression lifts into astonishment, then concern. He's a good actor. "Anna sweetheart, what are you doing here?"

"I had to do this Jón, please understand. I'm so sorry. It's for your own good."

"Understand what? Do what?" Jón moves towards us, squinting as if spying an arctic fox hidden amid snow dunes.

I squint back at him. This is the man who killed my brother.

He ignores me and focuses on Anna. "Sweetheart," he coos, his intense eyes, which yesterday shone with a charm that reminded me of Mark, narrowing into slits. "What have you done?"

Anna grabs my hand as he closes the gap. I feel only calmness. Right now all I need do is sit back and let events unfold naturally.

"Take a seat Jón." Ólaf's unusually stentorian tone commandeers Jón's attention. "But not there," he adds, reaching around the back of his head and settling on the nape of his neck where a certain crenation of flesh protrudes. "Behind the Sannlitró-Völva please."

Jón turns, chafing the thin black hair of his goatee. "Is someone going to tell me what's going on?"

"I will." Director Úlfar glides close. "First I'll take that." He pinches Jón's gun from his holster only to dangle the piece of metal before him like a soiled nappy. "Now sit." He bats the air with his empty hand, gesturing towards the Sannlitró-Völva.

"I'll take that for you, Director." Ólaf relieves Director Úlfar of the shiny weapon with the stealth of a submarine.

As he does, Anna releases her grip on my hand.

"Almáttugur," Jón swears under his breath, folding his arms. Anna's phone just catches it: *God almighty.* "What the fuck's going on?"

"It's a matter of national security of course." Director Úlfar smirks, nervous. "What else would require *my* presence?" He taps his chest.

"Jón," Ari explains, his voice confident in his natural tongue, "we've evidence that proves you're selling the properties of innocent offenders while they're in the Reformation Cooperative and taking the money. We don't need to get into details tonight; Reykjavík will do that later. For now we only want to know who you're working with here at the Litrúm-Hús, so please take a seat and behave."

Jón blinks and waits for someone to contradict Ari. No one does. "Are you telling me there's no offender waiting downstairs?"

"Take a seat Jón." Ólaf's head is awry with impatience. "Let's get things moving."

Jón scans the room. "And you all know what you're doing?" He waits until he's received a nod or two in reply before moving. "All of you? Anna? Ari? Ólaf?"

"Ólaf?" Director Úlfar's eyes flash from Ari to Ólaf and back again. "Are you Ólaf Stefánson? When Ari said he'd phoned his best technician for this, I should have known he meant you."

Ólaf stretches over the Sannlitró-Völva to shake the director's hand. "It's been a long time."

Director Úlfar hesitates before taking it. "Not since you developed the scan booths, I think. Amazing work, truly amazing."

"Thank you." Ólaf glances at me, buttoning up the immaculate navy suit he still wears from this morning. "You always seem to do a review when I'm out of town."

"Do I? How funny. Well, I'm glad Ari picked you for this. Ari, I just remembered something. The people I arranged to meet here tonight don't know where we are. I need to go find them. Remember what I told you about them?"

Ari nods. He means Sigmar and Haraldur.

"You stay here and get things started. There's also a matter of," he clears his throat, "that thing I'm waiting for from Doctor Emil and I seem to have left my phone in Jón's office. Excuse me, will you everyone?" Smiling thinly, he teeters on his heels and shrinks out the door faster than a slinky on an escalator.

Looking at Ari's face, I expect to see an expression that reflects the oddness of Director Úlfar's sudden departure. Couldn't someone simply call Haraldur and Sigmar? But Ari's too busy looking through Anna's evidence to realise.

Luckily, Anna isn't. "Ari," her words are urgent, "someone should go with Director Úlfar, to make sure he returns. Someone fast on their feet." She stares at him until he realises she means him.

But she can't possibly mean him. I told her at *The Himinn* that nothing would happen to us as long as Ari was with us.

Ari sees the surprise on my face and misinterprets it.

He mumbles something to Ólaf, points at what I assume is the safety lock on Jón's gun and moves towards the door. "If," he says to Ólaf, gesturing at Jón, "if he so much as breathes in the wrong direction, shoot. If he goes near them," he motions towards us, "shoot. If he comes at you, shoot. Okay?"

Ólaf wrinkles his nose to reposition his glasses. "You can trust me, Ari."

Jón whips around at Ólaf's statement, and stares at Ari and Ólaf as if to ask them what the hell they're doing. I agree. Ari shouldn't leave. I need to stop him. I also can't blurt out my theory yet. No one will believe me. Ari should stay here.

"Ari," I call to him as he reaches the door, "can't you phone Director Úlfar?" *Phone.* My online notes application is still open on Ari's phone. "Actually, you still have my file open on your phone. Have a look at it before you go, will you? Just the first page, make sure I haven't *missed* something." It's the only way I can think to let him know what I know. Events are not unfolding the way I want anymore so it's time I played a card.

"What document's that, Ari?" Ólaf shuffles through the shoebox on the flip-up table of his workstation. "Isn't all of Anna's evidence here?"

"Ari," I call out. He's already opening the door. "Have a look now, please, before you go?"

"I'll read it on the way," he throws over his shoulder. "Ólaf, you're in charge. Start with the basics. I want to be here for the rest. And remember," he snaps with a venom that hints at the betrayal he's feeling, "shoot him, if you need to."

Then the door is swinging shut and I'm gnawing at the insides of my cheek again.

Shit.

This isn't what I planned.

Chapter 26

Ólaf taps two final buttons on the Sannlitró-Völva controls, then leans back in his seat to count how many seconds it takes the machine to charge. The whole time I struggle to decide what to do. My instincts urge me to go after Ari and confront him with the truth. Yet going after him will leave Anna alone with Ólaf and Jón. And now Ólaf has a gun.

Ólaf has thought this through better than I could ever have anticipated. He probably wouldn't let me hobble after Ari now even if I tried. He'd know the only reason I'd chase after Ari is if I were scared of being alone with Ólaf and Jón—and the only reason I'd be scared of that, is if I knew Ólaf was Jón's partner.

And I do.

He's the only senior Sannlitró-Völva technician the Litrúm-Hús has ever seen. He developed the scan pods, has access to Litrúm Maps and is a highly trained software developer. He handles the results of every examination, requests not-guilty cases from Reykjavík, and is the only one who 'performs' not-guilty examinations because he's the best at what he does. I don't know what's motivating him, but he's at the top of my list because everything about him tells me to put him there, and today I'm trusting my gut. He's the only one with the opportunity, the technology, the intelligence, evident acting skills...

And now we're alone with him.

And he has a gun.

He catches me looking at it. His eyes blur. He can see right through me. Seconds later, he knows that I know. He presses his lips together as his eyes refocus, resigning himself to whatever Plan B he's plotted. He rests the gun on the machine's controls but says nothing to me, letting his silence menace instead.

Jón's outline appears on the Sannlitró-Völva's screen.

"Okay." Ólaf begins, cool and calm. "So, for the record, are you Jón Ásmundsson?"

"What are you doing?" Jón hisses. "That thing's recording!"

I press my earpiece in deeper. If I tell Anna now, will she believe me? No. I still have no reason for why Ólaf would partner with Jón. Until I can guess that, no one will believe me. He's good old Ólaf, the one Anna and Ari would never suspect.

Is it money, power, self-preservation?

Is it a secret no one knows or wants to face?

There's something buried deep in him—I recognise it because I have something buried deep in me. People like us can recognise each other. But Anna will never see it unless I can guide her there.

"We're recording only the basics for now," says Ólaf, "like Ari said. Trust me, Jón, I know what I'm doing."

"This isn't what we agreed," Jón adds a qualifier, "with Ari."

"Ari and Director Úlfar have gone to fetch witnesses. I didn't realise there were any witnesses, so it's better this way."

"Witnesses change nothing."

"You're wrong. Now for the record are you, Jón Ásmundsson who works at Höfkállur Litrúm-Hús, guilty of appropriating property from innocent offenders in the Reformation Cooperative? And did you do this by faking examination results, then telling offenders they could only equalise their energy and one day leave the Cooperative, by giving to charity—your charity?"

Anna frowns a little, but Ólaf's sudden excess of knowledge about Jón's bribery doesn't make her twig.

"Okay, Ólaf. You've made your point." Jón grins, though his face is as unfunny as a clown in a horror movie. "Now turn it off!"

"Pastel blue with gold indicates a truth. Takk Jón. Now," Ólaf says quickly, "did you throw the body of Mark Dales in the Skepnasá River? And did you today try to kill Rebecca Dales and Ari Halldórsson? And did you kill Gunnar Eyjólfsson?"

"You bastard!"

"Pastel blue with gold. All true. Takk Jón. And you've killed before this too, haven't you?"

"Reset that thing or I'll…"

Ólaf picks up the gun and aims it at Jón's head. His arm is as solid as a marble statue. He glances at the screen, scrunching up his nose to reposition his glasses. "Pastel blue with gold. Gott. Now shall we expand a little on that last truth, about what happened before, or shall we leave it there for today?" He pauses, smirking.

Jón rolls his head from side to side, boring a warning into Ólaf.

Ólaf shrugs, moves a finger to tap a command into the machine. "I think we'll leave it."

"No Ólaf," Anna calls out, stopping him, "you haven't asked him about his partner!"

"She's right." Jón unbuttons his ruffle-necked shirt until his chest is free of restrictive tailoring. He leans back in his seat and flicks his ponytail. "If I've been working with someone, I should tell her who it is."

"Navy blue with electric blue," Ólaf reads the colours on the screen, "indicates you're about to lie."

"Of course it does. Because you're controlling what it indicates."

I taste blood in my mouth. I'm gnawing on my cheek too hard. Ari needs to hurry back. This is not going to end well.

"I'm not controlling it," Ólaf waggles his head in innocent amusement, "but someone must have been controlling it for you to send innocent offenders to the Cooperative all this time. Who is it Jón? Is it someone here at the Litrúm-Hús tonight?"

"Oh, this is perfect." Jón throws his hands up. "Now you start the script."

"Pastel blue with gold. Is it Director Úlfar?"

"Let me see now, what was I supposed to say? Ah yes," he switches to a tone so insincere it has its own rhythm, "you know I'd never work with someone like Director Úlfar, people would get the wrong idea."

"Electric blue. Not Director Úlfar then. Is it Ari?"

Anna edges forward, grips onto the hardwood rim of the bench.

A surge of dread swells in my stomach, making me nauseous.

"Sure. Why not Ari? Quick, quick, everyone! The golden boy has been found out, you'd better run after him. There probably aren't any security guards on duty for the next ten minutes, conveniently—for him!" He resumes his usual voice. "How fucking ridiculous."

"Pastel blue with gold," Ólaf mutters with such practised dismay even I want to believe him. "He...he's telling the truth. Ari is Jón's partner! But that's not possible." He squints at the Sannlitró-Völva's screen. "It can't be."

"What a performance!" Jón stares at Ólaf with such fake adoration it looks like he's going to start clapping in sarcasm.

This time, Ólaf taps a command into the machine without hesitation. It powers down.

Slowly Anna stands, her eyes focused on a void of air before her, her lips tight, her breathing shallow.

"Sit down, Anna," I whisper into her ear. "It's not Ari. It's a trick."

"I'm afraid the Sannlitró-Völva cannot be tricked, my dear," Ólaf says.

He heard me?

"Unless," Jón pauses for emphasis, "you want it to trick an old schoolmate who made it good," he raises his eyebrows at Ólaf, "so good you couldn't resist taking it all away from him the second you had the chance, to show that bastard he should never have called you 'Freak' in the playground."

"That's enough, Jón." Ólaf unlocks the gun's safety.

"Why, Freak? Don't you think they'd like to know how it all started, how your mates at school used to call you Dustman because of *that* bastard? You hated him for what he did, even though that's what you are of course—a freak!"

"I'm warning you, Jón."

"The doctors knew it. Your wife knew it. That's why she left you." He laughs. "It wasn't because of the years you spent specialising so you could prove your schoolmates wrong. It wasn't because you worked too hard, all those long hours. No. It was because you're a freak. A short—balding—Freak!"

"Shut up!" Ólaf yells.

"Was the look on his face worth it, Ólaf, when you sent him off to the Cooperative? I'm guessing it was, because that's why you got me to help more often, wasn't it?" Jón laughs. "Every time you noticed some rich prick's energy was more navy than it should have been, you attacked their guilt like a shark smelling blood. Freak!"

Ólaf shudders. "Shut up. No one laughs at me anymore."

I can feel the blood rushing to my cheeks as I turn to Anna. This is it. This is what Ólaf has kept buried inside him. I swallow to relax the tightening in my throat. "Anna," I whisper, though I know now there's little point given the room's apparent acoustics, "I think Jón's telling the truth. Ólaf is his partner."

Anna shakes her head as if pitying my ignorance.

"Think about it, Anna, what does he do for a living?"

"Becky," she closes her eyes and whispers in English, "I know you don't want it to be Ari. But do you really think Ólaf would be so stupid as to perform this examination himself if he were in any way involved? Nei. You said it yourself, it's always the one you least expect. Who do you least expect, Becky?"

"Anna, you're not thinking this through."

"Neither are you! How do you think Ari rescued Mark's body if the silt at that boulder was so fragile you fell in yourself? And he said he saw Jón at the glacier earlier, but did *you* see Jón? Did you even see Ari fall in?" She resumes an audible volume. "I'm sorry, Ólaf. I think Becky's having trouble believing it's Ari...for obvious reasons."

Ólaf nods his head. "It's okay. She doesn't know me well enough to trust me."

"Anna," I pull her closer, "Ólaf told me Mark went to Jötunnsjökull because of a girl. You know as well as I do Mark would never have been interested in any girl, and he certainly wouldn't have gone hiking to impress one. Why would Ólaf make something like that up unless it was to distract me?"

"Maybe he was trying to help," she says, more as a statement than a question. "He remembered wrong, that's all."

"I understand, Anna, I really do." I keep my tone placatory. "He's your cousin, Ari's close friend. It's illogical someone like that would hurt—"

"That's enough, Becky," she urges softly, "you've got it wrong. Ólaf is the most honourable, respectable man I know, and I've known him all my life. You remember my family came to Höfkállur every year? We came to see my father's family—Ólaf's parents. I played with Ólaf when we were kids. He's been helping me. Don't embarrass him because you can't admit it's Ari."

"Why don't we call Ari?" Jón leans forward. "He'll tell us where he is and we can tell him to hurry back," he raises his voice, "because Ólaf is my partner and he has a gun on me!"

"Why are you saying all this, Jón?" Ólaf lowers the gun. "Is it so Ari can escape with the money? Did you plan this together?"

"Escape? Oh no," Anna struggles to her feet. "Ólaf, stay here and guard Jón." She hobbles towards the door.

"Anna, sweetheart, don't leave." Jón retrieves his phone from a pocket. "We can call Ari."

"Put the phone down, Jón." Ólaf raises the gun again, pushes his glasses up his nose with his spare hand. "We all know Ari won't pick up. You're delaying us so he can escape with the money and share it with you later."

"He mustn't escape!" Anna mutters.

"Anna!" I plead, heading after her. "Wait! This is exactly what he—" I bang my thigh as I slide out of the bench. "Argh!" Anna's phone clangs to the floor. Blood drips down my thigh. The Leukostrips have snapped. But Anna's already loping into the corridor. So I scurry after her, clinging onto bench backs and doorframes as I go. My leg smarts with each footstep but I have to reach her. "Wait!"

She doesn't. As I enter the corridor, she's limping away from the Dómstóll as fast as she can.

"Wait Anna! You're wrong. It's not Ari! We need to get back inside before—"

It's too late. The paralysing sound of a single gunshot explodes through the air. Stunned, we survey each other for an explanation. There is only one.

We throw ourselves back down the corridor, spiralling into the Dómstóll to hear the shot still tolling around the room.

Chapter 27

My eyes flash to the blood-spitting entity at my feet. Anna collapses to kneel beside it.

"Jón," she whispers, easing his head into her lap, "what happened?"

"He tried to escape!" Ólaf says in English, waggling his head. He drops Jón's gun onto the machine's controls, one hand on its grip. "I've never used a gun before. I was aiming for his leg." He peers over the machine to inspect the perfect cherry circle he's inflicted on Jón's torso. "Reykjavík still needs to examine him. Can he talk?"

Jón coughs a colony of ruby droplets into the air as he tries to speak. His bronzed face is lined with agony as he struggles to communicate.

"Shh, Jón, shh," Anna murmurs. "Don't even try, love. Save your strength."

Jón shakes his head, determined. He's going to say something but I won't understand him because my earpiece has disconnected from Anna's phone.

Shit.

I search under the benches for her phone, then realise I could also use it to call for help. It's near where we were sitting. I inch towards it while Ólaf talks.

"He threatened me," he says. "He said he and Ari killed Mark because he threatened to expose them, and now they would to do the same to me. He...he went for the gun."

I look at Jón. He's fallen right in front of the Sannlitró-Völva. There's blood over the back of the examination chair. A round splatter sits at chest height. Jón was in the chair when Ólaf shot him, in cold blood.

I pretend to slump onto the bench, then shuffle my foot sideways until it finds the phone. As I scrape it towards me, Ólaf hears and snatches up the gun. I throw myself to the floor, grab the phone and start dialling.

"You really want to do that, Ms Dales?"

I glance up.

He's changed his aim to Anna, not that she's noticed. She's intent on stroking Jón's hair to discourage him from speaking, fanning the sleek black strands of his ponytail over her lap, stroking the fine sides of his goatee. "Not a word, Becky." Ólaf warns me, his mouth twitching. "Move in front of the Sannlitró-Völva now please. You shouldn't have come back." He sounds disappointed. "Now I have no choice. I thought you'd have realised that. Anna," he continues in Icelandic, "Jón keyrði Mark…"

I reconnect my earpiece, only catch the last two of Ólaf's words.

"…Friday morning."

"Doctor Emil said the same thing," replies Anna. "But I can't believe it."

"It's true. Now Becky," Ólaf says to me. "Move over there please, next to your brother's killer."

I step over to the examination chair, squinting again at the man in Anna's lap—if only looks could kill. Blood oozes from his chest, making my stomach flip and a burning bile creep up to snag my tonsils. Even so, I take only satisfaction from the sight. He deserves everything hell might bring.

"But," Ólaf grins as he continues, "here's something Doctor Emil wouldn't have been able to tell you, Anna, about Pàll." Jón shakes his head so vigorously he splutters on the blood filling his throat. Droplets speckle his goatee. "There in your lap is also the driver who killed your husband."

"Don't be ridiculous, Ólaf." Anna glances at me. "Jón wasn't even living here when Pàll died. We met shortly after he arrived, months after Pàll, I remember." She looks to Jón for confirmation, switches into Icelandic. "You moved here how long after Pàll died?"

His arm trembling, Jón reaches up to hold Anna's hand, keeps his eyes locked on hers. "It…was…dark." He pushes the words out with such force his body judders with each syllable. "He came…from nowhere. Didn't…see…ice…"

"Who told you this sweetheart?" Anna whispers.

"I'm telling you." Jón pants, exhausted.

"Jón." Anna gulps as if trying to swallow the realisation swelling inside her. "What did you do? You'd only just arrived. 'Only just' means days, not months, right?" Then it clicks. Her lips quiver. "That's why you wouldn't help me? Not because of resources or because you were protecting someone, but because it was you? You?"

He creases his eyes to avoid witnessing her disillusionment.

"For all these years it's been all I needed to know," her tone becomes wistful, "and it was you?"

"I wanted..." His mouth opens to say more but he doesn't have the strength. His eyes roll back and his head tilts to one side.

"I...I've dreamt of this moment. What I would say, what I would do." Anna stares into space, then turns back to notice Jón's lack of response. "Jón...Jón!" She paws at his shoulders, then throws herself across his torso. "He's still breathing. Ólaf, call an ambulance! Quick!"

"Sorry it had to come to this, my dear," Ólaf says, not looking up from the machine. He's busy programming it.

"I don't understand. Call an ambulance!" She looks at me, notices the phone in my hand. "Becky, ambulance!" When I don't move, she pounces at the phone.

"Anna, stop!" Ólaf yells.

Finally Anna sees the gun pointing at her and freezes. "Ólaf?"

"Go and stand next to her," he narrows his eyes at me, "by the examination chair. Now please!" He watches her step towards me, tilting his head back and gazing at her with a lust he needn't hide anymore. "I was trying so hard. Of course as soon as Ari called me tonight I knew—I knew this would happen." He refastens his grip on the gun. "Why couldn't you forget about Pàll and move on? Things could have been so different between us..."

When Anna reaches me she seeks out my hand. "But...you're my cousin...you've been helping me."

Ólaf shudders as if banishing some irritation. "Anna, my dear, the only good thing about helping you was that it kept you close. You told me every property you found. I knew where you kept your diary, how long I had left to make Jón responsible for it all and be on my way. You served a purpose."

"You're lying." I goad him to bide time. "You're her cousin. You care about her and what she's gone throu—"

"Oh don't get me started on the poor widow. What about me? My wife left me, took my son with her to Norway, and now they're living with her bastard lover."

"She married that bastard, Ólaf." Anna searches his eyes. "Years ago."

"So time heals all wounds, does it?"

"Does money?" I ask him.

"I think you'll find I have a scientific obligation to keep myself cheery, keep my energy as positive as I can after all my years of suffering. A beach house in Canada will help. National gratitude for my unrecognised gifts will help too. My plan, originally, was for you to go with me, Anna, to Canada. That's not possible now of course." He glances at the Sannlitró-Völva controls. "The trauma from today will probably force me to retire early, next week I think. Now if you don't mind I should go before the others return." Keeping the gun steady, he uses his spare hand to tap further commands into the machine.

"But," I say, trying to think of something to keep him here longer, "that wasn't your only plan, was it? You planned for something much bigger." He used the words 'national gratitude'. "You wanted the whole country to be thankful."

He waves the gun in the air. "Of course! I'm sorry Anna but Jón was always going to have to die. If it makes you feel any better it was for a good cause: Iceland doesn't need another philosophy to get fanatical about, no country does. People deserve to know the *Heimspeki's* inherent flaws. No matter what life after death promises, some people will always believe they're entitled to take what others have—circumstances simply make it the right thing for them to do! Nothing should encourage that way of thinking, don't you agree?"

"So you didn't want the Sannlitró-Völva to be sold to other countries? I thought you were helping promote it?"

"The Sannlitró-Völva is different to the *Heimspeki*, my dear. Once people see the machine in action, of course everyone will want one. Unlike philosophy, criminal detection and deterrents do actually work. They'll need a good technician, though, one with the litagjöf who can ensure the machine functions properly, without interference."

"And you'll be the one for the job?"

"As I am here today."

"There I was thinking Jón was the mastermind."

"Him? Ha! When he came up here, all he cared about was impressing his mama. He ran over Pàll his first week here. I saw his energy change straight away. It was an accident, that's true, but he couldn't stuff up his big break now could he? So I helped him keep his secrets, as long as he did what I told him. Ah, now you cry."

Tears cascade down Anna's cheeks.

"Gott." Ólaf says, seeing her. "That's how I've felt every night for the last ten years. You know, Anna, I went to Jötunnsjökull when she left me, but no love glowed to me! I lost everything, same as you. No one came to make it better."

"And you think this will help?" I ask. "What about your energy? A beach house in Canada can't make up for killing people!"

230

"Well, some people in this world have to be more negative than positive, Becky, otherwise surely there'd be an imbalance of energy?" He smirks as if he believes no such thing, then bends forward to open the glass case of the Sannlitró-Völva's generator. Prying it off at the hinges, he slams it across the floor. It doesn't shatter but it does glide out of reach. "Okay, gott. All ready. You've got ten seconds. As you know, Becky, that's how long it takes this thing to charge, and that's how long it'll take me to reach the door. Now don't move. Though, it would look more like an accident if you did." Pressing the last onscreen button, he dashes for the door.

We're out of time.

"Still think beauty makes you untouchable, my dear?" he says to Anna, pulling the door behind him.

Chapter 28

Ólaf keeps the gun on Anna and I, closes the Dómstóll's reinforced glass door, pulls his yellow keycard from his pocket and locks the door pad. He waits until the Sannlitró-Völva's generator sparks into life, then mouths 'bless' and strides away, tucking the gun into his belt and pushing up his glasses. Anna and I are speechless. The machine's power source is about to be unleashed and there's nothing we can do.

The top doors.

I grab Anna's arm to pull her towards the administrators' exit at the back of the room, but she yanks me to the ground. As I collide with the floor, a flash of searing light blazes past me to bite a galvanic black hole in the wall behind us. It's already too late to reach the top doors. We're trapped.

"Quick!" I shout over the crackle of electricity building. "Over there!"

We crawl towards a table as a second electric spindle flashes across the room. We dive behind the examination chair, though it won't give much cover, there are too many slats—so many that we can see Ólaf hurrying away.

"No!" Anna yells, so lost in her cousin's escape she stands.

"Keep down, Anna!" I pull her down. The smell of scorched wood darkens the air and there's no telling when the next zap of electricity will come.

But then something happens to Ólaf that distracts me too. He stops a metre before the Dómstóll's glass windows meet the wall, and the smug expression on his face drains as fast as storm water down a gutter. His mouth twitches as he talks with someone. He gesticulates emphatically and points towards us with a look of panic on his face. As he moves back, the person he's addressing eases into view.

Ari.

His body rigid, Ari takes one look inside the Dómstóll, sees us behind the chair, then lunges at the gun threaded through Ólaf's waistband. Ólaf is too slow to react and Ari aims the gun at him before Ólaf even realises his lies haven't worked. Ari pulls his phone from his pocket and shoves its display in Ólaf's face. He's read my notes. He waves the gun at the door, shouting until Ólaf retrieves his keycard from his pocket.

Before they reach the door, however, there's a high-pitched hum and a snap. A flame of electricity zaps towards the glass window. Ari jumps as it makes contact with the glass. As the electricity recoils, his expression changes into one of inspiration. He aims at the window, pulls the trigger.

Nothing happens. The glass is bulletproof.

He pushes Ólaf at the door as the electric hum of the machine builds again. Ólaf bends to slide his keycard through the door pad, but when Ari steps towards the glass to get a better view of us, Ólaf kicks the gun from Ari's hand and throws himself on top him. Ari buckles under the surprise of Ólaf's charge.

"We've got to get out of here!" Anna screams, watching them grapple on the ground.

More and more zaps punch out from the machine. Burnt wood and scorched paint smoulder like wounds around the room. I can't see a way out.

"He mustn't get away!" Anna screeches, looking around. She spots something on the wall. "Can you reach that socket?" She points at where the Sannlitró-Völva's extension cord is plugged in. The socket is on the other side of the machine and, with wild zips of electricity now flashing steadily around the room, it's impossible to reach.

I shake my head. "I'm sorry!" I yell over the throb of energy. I wish I could, but I can't. I've failed her.

Anna's eyes dart around the room, searching for alternatives.

Outside, Ólaf scrambles to his feet and kicks Ari in the face. Ari's head hits the floor with a whack, dazing him. There's nothing I can do for him either. Ólaf leans against the glass window, prepares to stamp a foot in Ari's throat. Ari manages to grab Ólaf's shoe as it slams down, slowing its crushing force. Still, Ólaf's clearly winning.

"No, no, no." Anna's voice trembles with desperation as Ari paws at Ólaf's leg. "He mustn't get away!" Her eyes fill with a wildness that settles on the Sannlitró-Völva. "Stay here," she commands, flying towards the machine with complete disregard for the two thousand volt impulses thrashing around the room.

I grab at her clothing but she's too quick, she's already flinging herself towards the machine's extension cord. She snatches it up and is about to yank it from the wall when a jagged ray of golden electricity twists after her like a lightning fork in slow motion.

The hissing viper thrusts its spindly finger of destruction into her for what seems an eternity.

When it recoils, Anna falls limp, the cord in her electrified grasp. It's enough. The weight of her body yanks the cord from the wall and fells the zapping octopus to a deadly hum.

Chapter 29

The stink of scorched skin poisons the air. A soft hum smoulders in my ears. The visual scar of a tentacled monster flames yellow-white radiance across my eyes. But outside the Dómstóll, Ari is still struggling to breathe under the crushing weight of Ólaf's shoe. I leap over bodies, furniture, wires, anything in my path until I'm tugging at the door. It's still locked.

"Ari!" I scream.

Ólaf glances up. Our eyes meet. Ari uses the distraction to twist his body and pull Ólaf's leg with him, sending him crashing to the floor.

Seconds later Ari is standing, panting and coughing. He stabilises himself and waits for Ólaf to rise. As soon as he does, Ari crowns his left cheekbone with a jab from the right, lifts his chin with a left fist.

Ólaf stumbles, eyes glazed, his bulbous cheeks red and sore. Ari doesn't wait for him to recover. He thrusts an elbow under Ólaf's ribs and, as Ólaf gasps for breath, Ari drives a punch through his nose. He finishes by swinging his fist down onto Ólaf's jaw, splitting open his bottom lip.

"Ari!" I rattle the door.

He finds Ólaf's keycard on the floor and unlocks the door. Behind him I see Ólaf. Dazed and bleeding but still alert, he's crawling towards the gun.

"Behind you!" I yell, pointing.

Ari hears my muffled warning but the door gives way before he understands what I'm saying. By then I'm already throwing myself into the corridor, spiralling towards the gun. I crash onto my side, shriek in agony as my ribs bear the brunt of my fall.

But in my hand is Jón's gun and Ólaf is too late. "Stop!" I tell him, my heart thumping. "Stay right there."

"Why? You won't kill me." Ólaf sits up, cradling the nape of his neck. "I did you a favour. I shot the man who killed your brother."

"Jón would never have touched my brother without your telling him to."

Ólaf cocks his head. "You want to know what happened? You want to know what your brother said to Jón when we accused him of stealing Sannlitró-Völva technology? We thought he'd be intimidated, pack up and leave." He snorts at the memory, hauls himself to his feet. "Nei. Your brother told Jón he was a Neanderthal!"

My jaw clenches. I don't want to hear these details, not from Ólaf. At the same time, I'm mesmerised. It's why I'm here.

"Now," Ólaf continues, sensing my interest, "Jón prides himself on controlling his temper. He knows power is nothing unless it can be harnessed. But this, from someone like *Mark*. It was too much. So he hit your brother, who fell, hit the desk, didn't wake up. Game over." He steps towards me.

"Stay there!" I yell.

"It was very inconvenient," he continues. "I had to disengage the emergency exit alarms," he moves closer again, "squeeze him into Jón's car. Ari hadn't sorted out the security guards yet, otherwise it would have been a lot harder, I suppose." He takes another step.

I back away, tightening my grip on Jón's gun. Words like "inconvenient", "squeeze" and "game" repeat in my mind, making me want to pull the trigger. Alone the words mean nothing. Together they are everything. They treated Mark like an object, disposed of him like rubbish.

I play with the trigger.

Becky! a voice yells in my head, swishing around my skull in the loudest gush of water I've heard. My head feels like it's on fire. I try to shake away the sound. It only yells louder. *Watch—him—die!*

I close my eyes. I promised myself to value life, to never again treat it with disrespect. Not mine, not anyone's, no matter what. I can't kill Ólaf. I can't kill anyone. Yet...these *are* unusual circumstances.

"Becky," I jump as Ari puts his hand around the gun, "I'll watch him. See how badly Anna and Jón are hurt."

I grip the gun tighter, then realise how much my hand is trembling. I release the gun and, for a moment, forget what I'm supposed to be doing. Ari has taken the gun; he's taken away my temptation. Would I have killed Ólaf? Maybe. I don't know.

It's only when Director Úlfar slams through the Dómstóll's top entrance that I jump out of my trance.

"Go check on Anna," Ari reminds me.

"Anna," I mumble, throwing myself back into the Dómstóll. I fall at the head of my friend. She's cold and unmoving. One hand rests on her abdomen. The dress encasing her is crisp, burnt onto her fried black skin. "Anna?" I roll her into the recovery position. I don't know what else to do.

Someone fumbles with the generator's cover.

Two men arrive and check on Jón. One of them identifies Jón, the other says he can still feel a pulse. I must have dropped Anna's phone somewhere nearby as I can clearly understand their Icelandic. I just can't grasp the implications of what they're saying: Ólaf and Jón are both alive, whereas Anna...

I place two fingers on her neck, check her pulse by pressing to feel her jugular. The movement must trigger something in her because, as my fingers push against her skin, her eyes shoot open, making me reel back with fright. "Anna!" I gasp.

A silent petrified expression calls out from her eyes as she speaks three terrifying words to me. They sound as though they're cutting her lungs with a knife. "Watch me die." Her word mirrors those I heard in the corridor.

"What? No!" I yell. "You have to live! You haven't told me about Mark yet. We're going for a coffee tomorrow!"

She turns her gaze to the ceiling and closes her eyes. A smile almost makes it to her lips before trembling away and, as the tension in her neck muscles weaken, her expression relaxes into a limpness that can only mean one thing.

"Anna. Oh, Anna." My eyes settle on a single curl of her bouncy white hair, until an unexpected hand on my shoulder makes me jump.

Ari hovers over us, blood dripping from a cut on his bruised cheek. "An ambulance is coming," he says, "Jón bleeds a lot but he will be okay. The Sannlitró-Völva did not get him."

I nod, thinking about Anna's words.

Watch — me — die.

Behind us, someone slots the Sannlitró-Völva's glass case back into place with a rattle. It sounds like ice clattering over pebbles in some dark lonely river. It makes me wonder. Did the voice in the corridor say to watch 'him' die or 'her' die? Mark said his message weren't getting through to me right. Did he mean to refer to Anna? Rehearing the voice in my head, my eyes go to the machine. "Ari, do you know how to work the Sannlitró-Völva?"

"A little, why?"

"Turn it on."

239

"I don't think…"

"Quick!" I throw myself sideways and reach for the machine's plug. "We need to be quick." There's no time to explain. I can't even explain it to myself. "Trust me."

Ari stands, unmoving, until I drag Anna's body closer to the examination chair. Then he seems to understand and goes to the machine's controls. As the generator charges, he mumbles something about being sorry for not reading my notes earlier, that he should have known Ólaf was the only one with the expertise, the opportunity, the determination…

Overhearing him, Director Úlfar apologies for leaving. "When I heard Ólaf's name, I recognised it," he explains. "Haraldur had a list of administrators involved in not-guilty examinations—I went to check if Ólaf Stefánson was on it. He was of course. I thought he was."

I don't hear the beginning of Ari's reply, only the end when he promises to track down the money, the innocent offenders, rectify everything—starting with Sigmar Thorsteinson.

Someone thanks him, and that's when I look at the two men with Jón. One of them is the boy with shaggy hair from outside the Dómstóll yesterday: Sigmar.

"The machine's ready," Ari says eventually.

I heave Anna into the chair.

"Fljótt, Becky!" Ari shouts at me before I can finish. "Quick, look, look!"

My legs feel like dried cement but I stagger over to the machine's screen.

A pulsating glow is hovering around Anna's rapidly cooling body.

"It has deep brown, yellow and gold," Ari says. "All positive."

I gaze at Anna, the screen, then Anna again.

Director Úlfar joins us, sidling as close to Ari as he can. "What is it?"

To the naked eye there's nothing around Anna. Through the Sannlitró-Völva, however, there's a golden-brown glow—a glow that intensifies…and moves.

Slowly, it travels along the contours of Anna's body, brightening as it gathers around her shoulders and head. Reaching upwards, it twinkles and curls into an oval pinnacle above her temples. It pauses, then swells into a circular ball of light. There's no sound but, an instant later, it implodes into a brilliant white light that drifts up towards the ceiling. There it floats, waiting.

"What's happening?" I ask.

Ari shrugs.

Director Úlfar shakes his head, unknowing. "Are you recording, Ari?"

"Já," he mumbles.

Sensing something, I look for the two other men and Ólaf. They've already gone.

Director Úlfar whispers an explanation. "Jón's bleeding is stable, so they took Ólaf to the cells."

Still the white ball of light floats and waits.

"What's that?" Ari points to the left hand side of the Sannlitró-Völva's screen.

A separate ball of white light appears from nowhere and glides across the screen, speeding up the closer it gets to Anna's light ball. For a split second, it looks like the two are going to collide. Instead the lights spin around each other, so fast that, in their downward spirals, it's impossible to distinguish between them.

By the time their spiralling slows, the two balls have fused into one, throbbing brighter together.

"You were right, Anna," I murmur to myself. "The light in Ísland can play tricks."

The light throbs twice more before sparkling into nothing.

I watch the screen for a few moments, not sure what I've just seen. A part of me waits for clarification, but none comes. Eventually I realise only my gut will offer an explanation.

"What was that?" Ari asks.

"Pàll." I murmur. "Together until the end." I inhale deeply, thinking about Pàll and Anna, but the air is so flavoured with singed flesh I stop mid-breath. "They're gone." I say after a while.

Director Úlfar doesn't comment on my use of the plural. "Or we can no longer see her through the Sannlitró-Völva. Það er long leið frá Ísland til himnaríkis: it is a long road from Ísland to heaven."

We pause in thought until footsteps pound outside the Dómstóll, hammering towards us like storming soldiers. We turn towards the noise and wait for the doors to be thrust open. Two paramedics rush in with a stretcher and medical case. They start towards Anna, but Ari redirects them to Jón. As the medics busy themselves reigniting Jón's fading pulse, Director Úlfar removes his jacket and creeps respectfully towards Anna. I don't know why, but there's something about the way he looks in my direction that bothers me.

Chapter 30

It's close to midnight when Ari drops me off at *The Himinn*. I want him to stay but he needs to get back to the Litrúm-Hús. He has to secure arrangements for Ólaf and Jón, and he wants me to sleep. It's easier said than done with a body as broken as mine, as pumped full of adrenalin, with thoughts layering upon thoughts.

I lie in bed and try to switch off, but each time I close my eyes I see Anna's light on the Sannlitró-Völva. It was so white it reminded me of the nothing I once saw on the ceiling of that ambulance, the vacant void I saw for three minutes. It looked like a white slate of nothing. Perhaps it wasn't nothing? Have Mark and Anna been right all along?

I roll over to get comfortable. I could wonder and suppose to my heart's content but there'll be no knowing tonight. So I fight against my thoughts until they drift into fictions that assure me I'm dreaming, that I'm finally asleep.

When I wake it's to the distant sniping of a lawnmower and the clanging of metal tools on a driveway. The sounds plant in me a seed of hope that I might be waking to an ordinary day, to a life the same as it always was. Then memories return and I know I'm in a new reality now—a reality where people really can die this frequently in a matter of days.

Unable to put it off any longer, I call my parents from the bed. They can tell from my mumbled greeting I have bad news for them. I don't know how to explain, so try telling them that Mark was a hero, that he died trying to save innocent people. After all, it's true.

Still, I hate that someone laid their scabby hands on my brother, *my* brother, and ended his beautiful life. The injustice of it is so hard to bear I again wish I'd evened out the score last night: put Ólaf out of his misery, then marched straight back into the Dómstóll and put Jón out of his.

243

But Ari stopped me, and now Mark's murderers live.

As Mum and Dad cry and whimper on the phone, they only strengthen my regret.

For a while, we simply share our devastation. The words don't sound real, so we state and restate them in different ways until abstract concepts such as death and murder develop form and become solid enough to one day, maybe, absorb. For me the conversation passes in a blur, dreamlike until practicalities like repatriation and coffins force me to pay attention. They ask about my returning to Sydney. They want me home. Dad says there's a Jet Cruiser from Reykjavík to Sydney every night via London, and he wants me on the first one.

"What about Anna?" I say. I want to go to her funeral. Ideally, I'd like to stay until Ólaf and Jón's trial.

Mum's cries reignite and Dad reminds me that I haven't been home since I left for London. I have to think about them too.

So in the pause that follows I imagine the hugs they'll give me when I see them again and my throat tightens. "How about I promise to do my best? I'll send you a text later with my arrival time. I love you," I tell them.

"We love you too," they say, "come home."

After we say goodbye, I sit in bed for a while. My stomach doesn't claw at me this morning, probably thanks to yesterday's baguette, and my wooziness is minimal. Still, I feel sick, trying to process everything that's happened. Is this all there is to Mark and Iceland? Have I crossed everything off my list, connected everything I need to connect before going home?

My eyes settle on a section of carpet and I study the shadowy furrows in its lush cream pile while I wait for the nausea to pass. In the corner of my eye I see pink, but can't bear to look at the leather armchairs. In fact, I need to get out of here.

I drag myself into the ensuite and try to clear my mind with a shower.

Once I've finished, a notification on my phone tells me Ari has called. I phone him still wrapped in my towel. "When are you coming?" I ask.

"I'm not. Doctor Emil says you must stay in bed today and rest."

"I want to come to the Litrúm-Hús, make my statement while everything's fresh."

"Reykjavík wants to take your statement direct. Ólaf and Jón are being transported there tomorrow. Today you must rest but I thought I'd take Mark in the Eroder tomorrow for her, if his air tray fits in the back, then you can ride with us?"

I like how Ari refers to Mark and him as 'us'. "But why does Mark need to go to Reykjavík? He's not evidence, is he?"

"No!" Ari reassures me. "I am taking him to the airport for you."

"What about Anna's funeral? I want to go." Mark would want me to.

"Her funeral won't be for weeks, Becky. I need to search for her will, contact relatives in Canada. You need to go home. Take Mark. Be with your family. If you want, I'll go to Anna's funeral for you."

"What if no one else goes?"

"She won't care, Becky. She's in heaven now."

Heaven. The word reminds me of something, something to do with heaven and hell. Something Anna said…

"The auroras!" I remember. "I promised Anna I wouldn't leave Iceland without seeing the auroras." I tell him about the lookout she mentioned, east of town, and about her belief in the battlelights.

"So," Ari decides, "if you rest today I will take you to the lookout tonight. You do not need to stay for a funeral in a strange room that Anna might never have seen. I will pick you up at seven o'clock. Okay?"

"Okay."

"Gott," he says with a sigh. He sounds tired.

"What about you? Are you okay?"

"I…" He clears his throat. "I regret a lot. With Ólaf."

"You weren't to know."

"You did."

"Not because of anything obvious." And someday I'll have to figure that out. I made notes and used logic to join the dots. I also trusted my instincts, subconscious reasonings and gut feelings that told me to look for a man with something hidden, a secret relished with delusions like a cheater's rationale. I listened to the watery ghost of my brother too. If I think about it, every culture on Earth believes in ghosts in some shape or form. I never did, until now. Still… "I should have said something sooner."

"Nei, I should have listened when you tried to tell me. If I had, Anna might still be alive."

"I could say the same. Nothing went to plan—no one did what they were supposed to do."

"Because you can't control people, Becky."

Mark used to say the same.

You can't control people with notes or lists.

"We're lucky you realised at all," Ari continues. "Without your notes I wouldn't have come back to the Dómstóll when I did—you might have died also. Or Ólaf might have killed Jón and the truth with him. We might still be listening to Ólaf, believing every word, and he'd be supervising every Sannlitró-Völva in the world. Fact is: you did everything you could, you worked out who Ólaf was without even knowing him. That was my job. I should have known it was him."

"Don't be so hard on yourself, Ari." It's not his fault. "Ólaf lied to you for years. He lied to everyone. I was simply an outsider looking at things with a fresh eye. You did your best. We all did our best," I tell him; I tell myself. "That's all we ever can do."

"Já," he says, sighing again. "You're right of course."

I am. So is he. So are Mum and Dad. I need to go home.

So after we hang up, I text Mum and Dad to tell them Mark and I will be flying home tomorrow night. They text back, pleased. I am too. It will take Reykjavík months to prepare for the trial. Whereas I have family to be with, and a thesis to publish. I want Mark to be awarded his doctorate posthumously.

My only problem now is that it won't take me long to pack yet there are hours to stretch out before seven o'clock. I start organising myself anyway, taking my time. I wander downstairs, make a coffee, pick at yesterday's breakfast leftovers Anna put in the fridge. When I go back upstairs to finish packing, I realise I kept no count of what I ate. Usually I'd panic, go back over everything and overestimate the calories. Today I'm too exhausted for panic, and it seems almost insulting to worry over something as trivial today. So I reassure myself that, as long as I'm sensible for the rest of the day, I won't get fat. Not if I'm sensible.

An hour or so later the doorbell rings.

For a moment I'm tricked into believing time has vanished like a post-eruption geyser sucking at surface water—because of course it must be Ari at the door. But when I check the sky outside light blue gleams above the guesthouse; the sun shines white highlights through its crispness. It's the middle of the day.

I go downstairs, and open Anna's front door to a man I really don't want to see.

"Góðan dag, Miss Dales."

"Director Úlfar. What can I do for you?"

"I have come to check you're okay, of course." He grins but I don't like it. I especially don't like how he doesn't wait for me to answer; just walks straight into Anna's kitchen. After clicking on the kettle, he perches on a stool, interlaces his fingers and leans forward on the kitchen island. His creaseless white sash strains over his thickened middle. "I also want to tell you what I have decided to do."

"About what?" I grab two mugs and sit opposite him. "Couldn't you have just called?"

He chuckles, ignoring my comment. "You remember I told you Höfkállur is an experiment, já? It is not finished."

"Even though the Tourist Board advertises it as perfect."

He pulls a tedious expression. "Every country in the world promises its tourists perfection. But we do not name Höfkállur in our films, I checked. And after we learn from these minor teething problems, I want..."

"*Minor* teething problems?"

"Já. It probably doesn't feel that way to you right now, but all new movements experience difficulties like this, until they become a systematic part of society. Think about the violence that accompanied women's rights, equal rights, gay rights, race riots... The important thing is to keep reviewing procedures until the implementation of the *Heimspeki* is perfect."

"Will any amount of reviewing help? Some people will never be able to help themselves." And I hate that Ólaf agrees with me in that.

"You are right." He gets up, places his hand on the kettle, then stops. "Some people will always think they have more to gain from acting negatively, which is why Höfkállur will re-commission a small police force." His fingers drum the kettle's handle. "I will provide them with LitróGuns to detect lies. That will act as a better deterrent. And we need more security. All of this will begin today."

It's the way he says today that makes me catch my breath. Today is Friday.

"I will," Director Úlfar continues, "do everything in my power to ensure the world only sees the potential of the Sannlitró-Völva. Ordinary lie-detector machines are not reliable—they record negative results whether you lie, or your heart rate increases because you're angry or nervous, or because you're excited. The Sannlitró-Völva is more." His voice rises slightly. "We must not allow the sceptics to win—they never understand until they see it," his eyes bore into me as if I'm the exact type of sceptic, "but they must! All those hundreds of years of war over what God's word actually is, ha! God is us and we are God. It's time for the nonsense to end. God is now, not thousands of years ago, and his words were always ours, *are* ours, all of ours. The Sannlitró-Völva proves that. You agree, já?"

I don't know what he wants to hear. "It proves our actions and our energy are…very closely linked," I concede. "But, as you said yourself, there are still problems to iron out. You wouldn't want the *Heimspeki* to go into the world on the back of a flawed technology," I quote Anna, "would you?"

"Nei." He places the boiled kettle between us on the kitchen island. "I…we have an obligation to ensure its message is delivered in the best possible light." He locks eyes with me. "So what do you say?"

Water bubbling in the kettle sounds like the Skepnasá. I listen, but no message accompanies the sound. "What do I say about what?"

He raises his eyebrows. "About being a press ambassador for the Sannlitró-Völva."

"A press ambassador?"

"Já," he says as if his meaning is obvious, "like I said in Reykjavík."

"You never said in Reykjavík."

"I did. I said I wanted your help. Despite what's happened, will you still consider it? We want to share the Sannlitró-Völva overseas. We have press ambassadors already for America, Canada, Brazil, France and Germany. You are Australian, and you work for Britain's leading legal journal, so you could help with both countries?"

"You never said 'press ambassador'."

"Of course I did. We spoke about how you work for *Dictum*, remember? Every lawyer and legal decision-maker in the UK reads that journal."

So this is why he's been giving me such special attention, why he's been acting so strangely?

He notices my scowl. "What's wrong?"

I shake my head, trying to remember everything he said in Reykjavík. "I, um…what's so special about today?"

"Today?"

"Yes, you said you wanted me back in Reykjavík by Friday?"

"Oh, oh, the Sannlitró-Völva's patents were granted today. Yay!" He claps himself. "We were going to have a press conference to celebrate. Of course when Haraldur called the other night I had to cancel it."

"Why didn't you just tell me it was for a press conference?"

He laughs. "The opposition period did not lapse until today, and you are a member of the press—we couldn't risk any leaks inspiring last-minute opposition." He scans the cupboards behind me. "Do you know where Anna keeps her coffee? Instant is okay, takk."

I fetch the coffee, some spoons and milk from the fridge while I think. Something still isn't adding up. "But if you wanted me to be a press ambassador, why have me followed?"

"I didn't want an international enquiry! Especially at the moment. A brother and sister injured in the same week in the same place—it would not have looked good."

"But you're the director of the MUR. Don't you have an assistant who could have talked to me about all this?"

"I, er, get a slight commission for any overseas sales of the Sannlitró-Völva—it's no secret," he adds, heaping coffee into our mugs. "And sharing our technology will benefit the world too...so it's win-win." He pours in the hot water and milk, then explains his proposal in more detail. As he talks, he begins to sound more like Mark than I care to admit. He's as passionate about the country's new energy theories, as hopeful for the future and for an end to the violence caused by religious differences. His words remind me I still don't know what Mark's postscript was about.

"Director Úlfar," I ask, "you mentioned God earlier, and people passionate about their religions. There seem to be plenty of people passionate about the *Heimspeki*, devoted to it even—almost like it's a new religion in itself?"

"Nei, of course it is not! It does not require you to 'sign-up' before you can enter heaven like other religions. There are no specific beliefs or codes you must follow. People do not even have to believe in it! It is science, a scientific equation, whether you believe in it or not, whether you use it to improve your life or not. It is simply what happens."

His answer gets me thinking. "That's what people always think." Over time, mankind has used laws, philosophies, religions, and now science in their quest to improve human nature. We've been certain about our theories and impressed them on each other. Yet, because mankind cannot change its inherent nature, each one of those systems has failed. "It never works."

In isolation.

Mark wanted to put an end to the fighting, as does Director Úlfar. Also like Director Úlfar, Mark wanted to unite everyone under the banner of science. But if Ólaf's actions and arguments are anything to go by science won't succeed because there will always be those with an innate materialism so strong it blinds them to the consequences of indulging their greed, either that or a belief so embedded in their subconscious it blinds them to their ignorance, or a passion so powerful it blinds them to their own corruption. Such people will always do as they wish, with or without organised religion, law, military, science, or spirituality.

In his thesis notes, Mark said he'd found the answer.

'Energy. The numinous,' he wrote. 'It's both, together. I told you anything was possible! We need both. We need to be various.'

Various—that was his revelation.

"No single system will ever unite mankind," I mutter as Director Úlfar stirs his coffee.

Human beings are so various, we need a variety of belief systems to make society work. The answer is inclusivity.

I take a deep breath, certain now I know what Mark's postscript was about, and why he believed it more important than the thesis itself—he no longer wanted the demise of organised religion. Sure, he wanted to reason with those overly righteous, who doesn't? Sure, he saw the benefit in asking the world to believe in something scientifically grounded, rather than based on myth or legend. It would show evolutionary progress. But, after living in a pro-science community that based its laws, policing, politics and culture on that science, he must have realised his naivety in thinking our species would continue to thrive by maintaining only its pro-science beliefs. Science will never change mankind's psychology, I doubt anything ever will. But, for argument's sake, should we even want it to change—over a few generations, or at all?

Whether it's science, deities, spirits, visions of utopia, red hats or blue hats, whenever there's only one belief system in a community, that community inevitably becomes fanatical about it. So maintaining a variety of belief systems is the only answer. Different people's brains respond to the same stimuli differently—some more emotionally, some more practically. With a variety of belief systems in place, there's at least a greater possibility that one of those systems will strike a chord with the people who just can't help themselves, and make them strive for self-control. It's our variety that makes us successful as a species.

Watching Director Úlfar sip his coffee, I can almost hear Mark's realisation in my head.

"I should tell you," he said when I was unconscious under the Skepnasá with him, "this is wonderful. Make sure you always wonder..."

That's it too!

He wanted me to wonder, he wanted everyone to wonder. He said he wrote a whole section in this thesis about the importance of the numinous experience for mankind. He said in his notes that, whether it's sensible for us to do so or not, there's a part of us—an innate, natural part—that longs for every numinous experience we can find, a part that needs to wonder at the world, to not have all the answers, a part that yearns for unknown possibilities. It's why our brains have often interpreted events creatively, rather than through rational explanation. Over time, science will probably expose all of mankind's myths and theories, including the numinous experience.

But should we want it to?

My life, for one, has fizzled dimmer since I came to believe nothing waits for me after I die. I didn't share that experience with Mark because I didn't want his to fizzle dimmer too.

Yes, I can see it now—the crux of his postscript. We need science, critical thinking, rationality and reason too. We also need wonderment—mystery and numina. Science and spirituality. Yin and yang.

Energy. The numinous. It's both, together.

Like two sides of the same brain.

I want to think more about it but, as Director Úlfar puts the milk away, he drops his next bombshell. "Oh, and I need you to come to the morgue with me, after we finish these." He lifts up his mug. "Paperwork. And, while we're at the hospital," he winces, "Jón asks to see you. I think it is good idea also," he adds.

I stop stirring my coffee. The abrupt cessation of my spoon tink-tinking hangs in the air like the resonance of a burst balloon. The last time I saw Jón he was close to death, bloodied and unmoving. That's how I'd prefer to remember him. He shouldn't even have enough breath to make such a request.

In the uncomfortable silence that follows, Director Úlfar shifts in his seat. As he moves, there's a glint at his waistband. He has his gun with him. It taunts me. Yes, I once made a promise to myself, to value life. But that was when I lived in a different reality. Promises can be broken.

"Okay," I say, not caring anymore why Jón might want to see me. "We'll go after our coffee."

Chapter 31

Jón is awake when Director Úlfar leads me past an armed guard into his hospital room. Although dressed in a white hospital gown and attached to machines, Mark's murderer is far from death. He springs to life when he sees me, grabbing his phone from a side table with the speed of an arctic hunter sensing ice cracking beneath him. He switches on its Word2Word translator and directs its speaker at me.

"You can wait outside, Director." The translator makes Jón's voice sound staccato, grating, as it did that first time I heard it on the Austurleid SBS.

"I'd prefer he stay." I tell them both, noting Director Úlfar's location. He's on my left. He keeps his gun on his right-hand side. If I were to walk in front of him, my left hand would connect with the gun.

"Thank you for seeing me," Jón says.

That's okay, Jón, I want to say, *thanks for helping me kill you.*

"I wanted to tell you," he continues when I don't reply, "in case I don't see you again: Ólaf lied about your brother."

"What about him?" I close the door.

Jón clears his throat to speak but a wet cough interrupts him.

I edge closer to Director Úlfar and get ready to make my move. I'm going to do this. I'm going to grab the gun, aim it at the bastard and pull the trigger. Bang! Blood everywhere! Pay back.

So I do.

In one swift move I pull the gun from Director Úlfar's belt and point it at Jón's head. "What about my brother?"

Still coughing, Jón can't answer straight away. He shakes a palm at me. His eyes plead for me to wait until he's regained control. His bronze Inuit skin pales as he fights for breath, his mobility limited by the intravenous drip in his hand and the bandages around his torso. He's no picture of health after all. He is suffering, as he deserves to suffer. I allow myself to enjoy his pain.

"Okay, Jón?" Director Úlfar passes him some water, eyeing me on the way, assessing his gun as if making his own plans. "Take your time."

Jón takes a sip, clears his throat again. This time, there's no coughing. "It was an accident," he says, his voice strained from exertion.

"An accident?" I laugh.

"Your brother fell against that desk. I didn't hit him."

"Ha!"

"It's...I thought you'd want you to know."

"Especially now, right?" The metal of the gun feels powerful in my hand.

"I thought it would help you feel better about your brother."

"How nice."

He shrugs. "You cannot live in Höfkállur and not come to believe in the *Heimspeki* at least a little."

"So that's what this is really about, the *Heimspeki*? He's kidding, right?" I ask Director Úlfar. "He wants me to feel better about my brother's death?"

Director Úlfar pulls a seat towards me. "And himself."

"Oh, no way! You want me to listen so he can clear his conscience and be all positive again?" My raised eyebrows elicit only looks of confirmation from them both. "No!" Let his guilt torment him! "Mark was a genius and you stole him from me. He wouldn't have said boo to a goose, hurt a fly, wish ill on his enemies—not that he had any. Yet now he's dead. So it's my turn to steal something from you!" I unlock what I assume is the gun's safety.

"She's right," Jón says, holding up his hand to dissuade Director Úlfar from interfering. "Let her do it. Tell them I attacked her or something. I might not have hit her brother, but it was my fault he stumbled backwards. I thought I was doing the right thing. It didn't work."

I'm amazed by his lies. "How...how could you possibly think you were doing the right thing?"

"I was trying to scare him away. I was going to turn Ólaf in, get my promotion, prove my mother wrong." He harrumphs as if impressing his mother were an impossibility. "That's all I wanted." He stifles another cough. "Being aggressive can calm people down, calm situations down. It can dissolve friction. I was born like this," he gestures at his physique, "to a mother who thought me good for only one thing—violence. She was wrong. Anna taught me this."

Anna. I tighten my grip on the trigger at the sound of her name. Jón didn't kill her. She's still dead because of what he did.

Ignoring me, Jón smiles at some memory, his weathered skin creases with the grin. "When I met her, she needed my help. She ended up helping me. She had such focus." He fills his lungs until they quiver with the strain. "I was trying to get your brother out of Ólaf's way." He looks into my eyes. They're intense again, shining with charm like Mark's. "Ólaf's crazy. I wanted to get you out of his way too, that's why I threatened you on the Austurleid. If you'd both stayed away, I could have turned Ólaf in as I planned. No one would have got hurt."

I don't buy it. "You tried to kill Ari and me."

"You weren't supposed to fall in."

"We didn't *fall* in. We were swept in!"

He lowers his eyes. "Ólaf assured me you wouldn't be. He said a couple of small ice blocks would scare you into believing the Skepnasá was dangerous, then you'd go home believing Mark fell in by accident." He looks up at me again. "I'm sorry. I'm not from here and I believed him. When you survived the first block, I didn't think the second would be any different."

"Why not simply tell someone what Ólaf was doing? I'm sure there are entire bureaux for dealing with this kind of thing!" I glance at Director Úlfar, both for confirmation and to check he's not creeping up on me. Director Úlfar looks at the gun, at me, then the gun again.

"You're right," Jón says. "But Ólaf threatened to tell Anna that I hit Pàll. It would have been the end of us."

"She would have found out eventually."

"Yes, but from me, in my own time, and once I'd put Ólaf away. Anna wanted the *Heimspeki* to change the world. I didn't understand at first, I didn't care what Ólaf wanted me to do at examinations. But, watching his litagjöf, I started to care, about many things. As long as Ólaf was that machine's senior technician, the *Heimspeki* had no chance at changing anything."

"And Gunnar? I suppose he was an accident too?"

Jón shakes his head. "Ólaf hit him over the head. He was already dead when I put him in the morgue. Shooting him merely disguised the wound."

Director Úlfar steps forward. "Doctor Emil confirmed this last night."

Jón shrugs. "Ólaf created a scan booth record showing Gunnar entering the Litrúm-Hús with guilty intentions, then leaving with my gun. All I had to do was say I left my spare gun and silencer in the bottom drawer of my desk."

"And of course shoot Gunnar in the head!" I scoff, readjusting my grip on the gun. It's starting to get heavy. "What about Gunnar's parents? If it wasn't for Doctor Emil, they would have thought their son committed suicide."

"I was biding my time. I would have told them. I needed to placate Ólaf a little longer, that's all. I would have liked to apologise to Gunnar's parents, as well as Ari. I let him down. Of course that can't happen now." He glances at the gun in my hand.

"Anything else you want to get off your chest?"

"Nothing. I'm ready. Do it."

I sneer at his permission, test the trigger, and picture a bullet smashing through his face. I imagine Mark standing by my side, smirking too. This is what he wanted, revenge for his murder.

Except the Mark I imagine frowns in disappointment.

"You're going to hell!" I tell Jón, hoping to please my brother. "Like you deserve!"

"But," Mark whispers to me in a watery gush, twanging my brain's synapses with his energy, "you would have put him there. Life is too precious a gift to throw away. No matter what, remember? Even a life lead as miserably as his…or yours."

My smirk fades. My head pounds as it warms.

"Oh, and eat more, will you?" Mark adds. "Please. You're killing yourself all over again." Then he fizzles away.

I wait a moment to see if he's going to reappear.

When he doesn't I take a deep breath, then relock the gun's safety. Begrudgingly, I hand the gun back to Director Úlfar, twisting my ribs in the wrong place as I do so. "Ow." I double over, gripping at the hurt to make it stop.

Director Úlfar eases me into the seat, presses a green call button on the wall. "You need an x-ray," he says.

I nod and see this moment for what it is. This is it now. All there is to Mark and Iceland.

"Sorry, Becky." Jón says.

I glare at him in silence. I might not want to kill him anymore, but I still hate his guts.

Chapter 32

As Ari enters the coordinates for the lookout into the Eroder's computer, he tells me about our destination, a range of hills five kilometres east of town. His enthusiasm for what we're about to see is as infectious as ever and I'm glad the sky is a crisp navy, with high pressure and no clouds. He tells me this means the air outside will be bitter to the bone, but that it's also archetypal aurora-viewing weather. I actually don't care about the cold. It only matters that he rang Anna's doorbell at 6.56pm and not a second later.

Soon after leaving Höfkállur, we ascend into the range. Thick white steam billows out from random hillside crevices, quickly disappearing into vapour. Their steady roar suggests origins deep in the centre of the earth and act as a reminder of the land's volatility. Anything could happen here. Everything already has. Dark and foreboding, the rolling landscapes mirror my heart.

Ari drives around a series of hills, each plastered with huge slabs of charcoal rock. Every time I think the next hill will be our last, another appears behind it.

Eventually the road converges with a signposted dirt track that ascends with such a steep gradient Ari has to use the Eroder's rubber spikes to stay on it. We climb up and up until, mere metres from the hill's summit, the track levels and opens into a clearing littered with rock debris. We park beside a number of cars, then Ari helps me onto a path that leaves one side the clearing to curve around the edge of the hill. It narrows into a foot-pass so slim it prevents us from walking side-by-side and I have to hold onto the hillside to hobble instead. It's fine until we encounter a huge slither of rock propped against the side of the pass, blocking half of it.

"It's okay," Ari tells me, stepping around it. "It's always here."

He holds out his hand and, with it, I ease my way around the slab, then look down and notice how high up we are. The road leading back to Höfkállur looks like a piece of string draped over the hills. One false step or quake in the ground, and I'd fall to my death.

"Don't look down," Ari says. He tugs my hand forward. "Not yet."

So I follow him around the path to the lookout and, as we clear the pass, I see what he means. A massive ledge of mossy grass stretches out towards a breathtakingly expansive yet darkening view over the lava fields south of Höfkállur. At the back of the ledge a sloping wall of rock sprawls up to the hill's summit. At its far side, a waterfall cascades over six or seven different rock formations, distributing its trickle from side to side until it reaches the outer rim of the ledge, where it falls to the hill's base as fine spray.

I listen for an echo of water inside my head. There is none.

Mark?

Ari spreads a picnic blanket, some distance away from the other aurora-seekers, and we sit in silence for a while, leaning against each other as the sun sets like a fiery red bomb crashing into enemy territory. An arm appears around my shoulders and I snuggle into Ari's chest. The peaceful sound of his breathing brings peace to my thoughts, except for the most persistent.

Mark.

In the comfortable quiet, I still can't believe I'll never see my brother again. Pressure builds behind my eyes as I remember the last time I was snuggled this close to a man and close to tears...

Why did I ever let Riley inside my head? I came so close to losing myself. I probably did for a time.

Never again.

"Life isn't about avoiding the tears, Bex." Mark told me after they resuscitated me in the ambulance. "It's about the joy you find in between them." He held me this close. I could hear his breathing too.

As I wonder why I'm remembering this now, the dim light descends into the bleakness of night, and the lava fields disappear into the stomach of a hungry blackness. Above us, trillions of tiny twinkling white dots remind me of holidays my family used to take up the New South Wales coast when I was a child, to Foster, and further north to Coffs Harbour. The transparency, its vastness, makes me homesick for Sydney. It is indeed time to endure that long flight home, watch movies back-to-back and stretch sitting-sore legs at the back of the plane.

It's time to sit in my parents' home, serenaded by a whirr of cicadas so constant you have to tell yourself to notice. It's time to see Sydney's big southern moon dazzle the harbour and peek in through the venetian blinds of my old bedroom until farewelled at dawn by hoot-hollering kookaburras. It's time to take Mark home, be with my family, reconnect. At some point I'm going to have to figure out how to balance trusting my instincts against the security of facts and how to live for the life that might come after death. But first I need the world to stop spinning, just long enough so I can get off and fall into the arms of those I love.

"Come here." Ari pulls me closer. "You're shivering."

His hands rub me with the vigour of a paramedic. Then he stops, taking a breath so deep I look at the sky. It's twinkling, yet still and black. Confused, I turn to see Ari's eyes dipped to the grass at his feet.

"This is probably the wrong time for confessions," he lets go of his breath, "but you've hit me harder than anyone and didn't even take a swing. You are the strongest woman I know, Becky, adventurous and brave. Don't say anything. I know this is the wrong time. But, before you leave tomorrow, you have to know: I like you a lot."

I feel the corners of my mouth rise. "It's not the wrong time at all." I relax into the hardness of his chest. This is a starry night, an enchanted evening—just like Mark said it would be. "Do you dive?" I ask him.

"I'm happy to learn."

He'd be good at it too. "In that case, I'll be coming back to Iceland very soon."

"I will miss you until you do."

"No, you won't," I tease. "A couple of days, max."

"Longer."

"You might find someone you like more, I'd never know."

"I never cheat on women." Ari grins until the bruises Ólaf gave him make him wince. "Life is stressful enough as it is—why complicate it more?"

"If only every man saw it that way."

He shrugs. "Do you need every man to see it that way, or just one?"

"Mark used to say the same thing."

He grins again, softer this time. "That's the first time you've spoken about your brother without sadness in your voice."

It was always going to be a long journey. "I've been cheated—"

"It will not help to think that way for long. I know, with Mum. You will celebrate what your brother did, já, and not dwell on what he didn't?"

"I will try."

He squeezes me tight. When he lets go, I breathe in the spicy aroma of his aftershave. It's a classic scent, one that I can't help but liken to the cologne gentlemen in black and white films might once have worn.

You were right Mark, you were right.

As we settle again into a relaxed embrace, a feeling of unrivalled intimacy burgeons between us, a feeling that makes me want to believe we were meant to find each other in that Höfkállur bus depot, in that Litrúm-Hús Dómstóll, inside that mountain, and on this blanket high above the lava plains. I should have come to Iceland sooner. Holding each other here, the tenderness of the moment feels invincible, and the rest of the world simply slips away.

So it's only when we hear distant murmurings of people gasping 'oh' and 'ah' that we look up into the star-lit sky.

Above us, a long curtain of glowing green light is waving through the night sky, a thin red trim at its base. It glitters so bright it makes the surrounding stars seem dull. It moves with such delicacy it's like fine green fairy dust glittering through the sky, only atmosphere resisting its fall, as water resists drifting sands with its rippling currents. The fluorescent red trim at its base stretches towards the black lava plains beneath us, which reflect its warm glow, while its green extremities reach up seemingly infinite in height.

The sight takes my breath away and, for a long time, I hardly speak. I do not want to disturb what the night has come to be: perfect.

Instead, a soft crackling accompanies the sparkling lights as they dance, like the fizzle of a firework's whirling explosions. Alternate sections of the wispy curtain glow the strongest, until it looks like there's a stream of power throbbing along its width. The colours hum with electricity and, after a while, I feel a warm glow in my face, as if I'm staring into a bonfire. The warmth tingles in my cheeks and throbs under my hair with a now familiar feeling that makes my smile broaden. Turning to Ari, I notice he has the same contented beam. There's a soft gleam all about him. Yet, when he senses my gaze upon him and turns to me, I realise the gleam is not just around him—it's around us both.

An image comes to my mind of Mark. He's smiling, warm and dry. No water. No roaring noises. He hasn't been stolen from the world—his visit this time has simply been cut short.

Before I know it, the gleam around us begins to dull and the warmth I felt dissipates. The top of my head grows cold, as if my hair is freezing into stiff clumps. The moisture in my battered nose, and in my rib-bruised lungs, becomes hypersensitive to the chilly air. Ari and I edge even closer together, wrapping our limbs around each other to rekindle what heat we can.

Then, sensing something pulling at my attention, something instinctive, I break my gaze with Ari to look up. A gleaming ball of translucent white-hot light is floating up from between us like a cloud. It has a warm sparkle that reminds me of the white ball I saw yesterday in the Dómstólls. It can only be one thing.

"Mark?" I whisper, my hand going to my chest. I'm filled with numinous wonder.

Ari follows my gaze but as soon as his eyes meet the sky, the whiteness shoots towards the aurora, disappearing into it like a shy animal escaping into undergrowth. All Ari sees is the sudden intensity that flickers along the aurora's fluorescent green lights. Before returning to its previous steadiness, the aurora's undulating glow shines sunbright for a few moments, leaving Ari wide-eyed and open-mouthed.

"This is the most magnificent aurora I have ever seen," he tells me.

"It's beautiful." More beautiful than I'd hoped, and everything I dreamt it could be. "I feel like I'm as close to heaven as anyone alive." And I feel a haze that's kept me prisoner for years dissolve into clarity.

What if I do want children, one day?

Ari and I lie down together and, as our breathing slows into a peaceful rhythm of awe, it feels like we've known each other all our lives. It's the most romantic feeling I've ever felt and I half-suspect the light in Iceland might be playing a trick on me when I see another larger white ball shoot across the sky from Höfkállur into the auroras.

"Did you see that!?" Ari asks, not needing an answer.

We both know it's not the shooting star other aurora-seekers on the hillside will assume it to be: it's two lost souls finally entering heaven together.

Anything is possible.

My eyes dry from staring, I blink to refresh them, squeezing them tight.

A tear trickles down the side of my cheek.

This time, I don't stop it.